ON ANGEL MOUNTAIN

Part One
of the
Angel Mountain Saga

Brian John

Greencroft Books
2018

First Impression 2001
Reprinted 2002, 2003, 2005, 2007, 2009, 2010, 2013, 2015
Tenth impression 2018

Published by
Greencroft Books
Trefelin, Cilgwyn, Newport,
Pembrokeshire SA42 0QN
Tel 01239-820470. Fax 01239-821245
Email: greencroft4@mac.com
www.brianjohn.co.uk

ISBN 978-0-905559-80-3

Typeset by the author in Palatino 10 pt on Apple iMac computer
Cover design: Martin and Alison John
Printed and bound in Great Britain by Cambrian Printers Ltd,
Llanbadarn Road, Aberystwyth SY23 3TN

CONTENTS

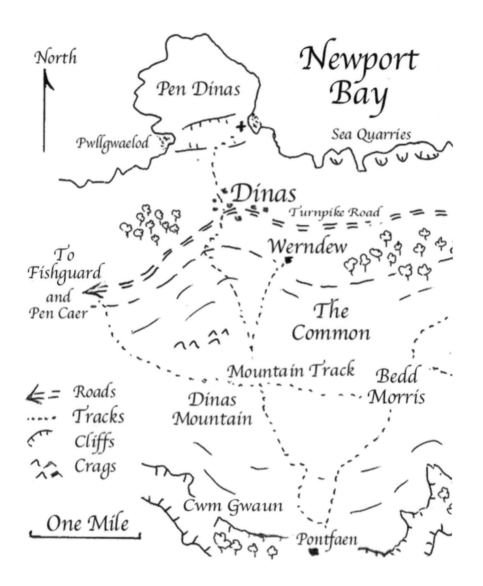

North

Pen Dinas

Pwllgwaelod

Newport Bay

Sea Quarries

Dinas

Turnpike Road

Werndew

To Fishguard and Pen Caer

The Common

Mountain Track

Bedd Morris

Dinas Mountain

Roads
Tracks
Cliffs
Crags

Cwm Gwaun

One Mile

Pontfaen

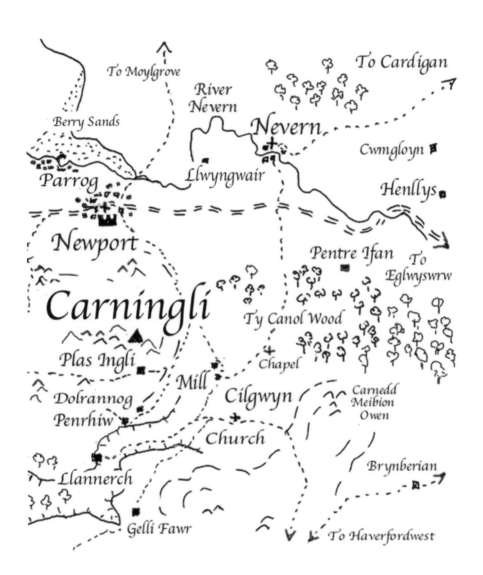

To Moylgrove
River Nevern
Berry Sands
Parrog
Llwyngwair
Nevern
To Cardigan
Cwmgloyn
Henllys
Newport
Pentre Ifan
To Eglwyswrw
Carningli
Ty Canol Wood
Plas Ingli
Chapel
Dolrannog
Mill
Cilgwyn
Carnedd Meibion Owen
Penrhiw
Church
Llannerch
Brynberian
Gelli Fawr
To Haverfordwest

To Inger
and the other inhabitants
of Angel Mountain

KEY CHARACTERS IN THE STORY

The Morgan family of Plas Ingli

Grandpa Isaac Morgan, born 1740, married in Jan 1758, died 1820 (two
    children, William born 1758 and Betty born 1760).
Grandma Jane born 1742, married 1758, died 1821.
William (David's father) born Dec 1758, married 1776, died in fire in
    April 1794.
Bethan (David's mother) born 1760, married 1776, died in fire 1794.
Griffith (David's brother) born 1776, lost at sea 1795.
**David born 10 June 1777. Married Martha Howell on 21 Aug 1796. Died
    12 Feb 1805, aged 27.**
Thomas (small brother) born 1781, died in fire 1794.
George (small brother) born 1785, died in fire 1794.
Rose (small sister) born 1790, died in fire 1794.
Aunt Betty born 1760, resident in Solva.

The Howell family of Brawdy

George Howell (Martha's father) born 1745, married 1765, died 1817.
Betsi (Martha's mother), born 1748, married 1765, died 1841.
Sioned and Sion (twins born 1767, died in infancy 1768).
Morys (elder brother) born 1770, Baptist minister, married Nansi 1797.
Elen, oldest sister, born 1773, studied music in Bristol.
Catrin, sister born 1776, moved to Castlebythe as tutor 1797.
**Martha born 12 May 1778 at Brawdy. Married to David on 21 August
    1796. Started diary 23 Aug 1796. Died 27 Feb 1855, aged 76.**

Plas Ingli staff

Bessie Gruffydd, born 1776. Maid. Started at the Plas in 1795, after the
    fire. Family lived in Nevern.
Billy Ifans, born 1763. Cow man / carter / handyman / shepherd.
    Started at the Plas 1777, when he was 14.
Shemi Jenkins, born 1782. Gardener and farm labourer after Moses'
    downfall in 1797. From Blaenwaun, oldest son of Daniel Jenkins.

Hettie Jones, born 1770. Dairymaid. Husband Daniel is a fisherman. Four children. Started at the Plas 1795, after fire.

Moses Lloyd, born 1773. Labourer and gardener. One of the Lloyd family of Cwmgloyn. Came to the Plas in 1793.

Blodwen Owen, born 1750. Housekeeper/cook (widowed -- four children: Bethan, Sian, Dafydd and Will). Started at the Plas 1765.

Other Key Characters

Ifan Beynon of Berry Hill. Clerk to the Justices of Newport and Nevern.

Eleanor (Ellie) Bowen, born 1776, oldest daughter of the Squire of Llwyngwair. Martha's friend.

John Bowen, Squire of Llwyngwair. Senior JP, father to Ellie. Son William was in charge of the Newport Division of the Fishguard Fencibles in 1797.

John Campbell, Lord Cawdor of Stackpole. The most powerful member of the gentry in Pembrokeshire. In charge of the forces drawn up to oppose the French invader in 1797.

George Griffiths and wife Mair. Tenant farmers at Dolrannog Isaf. Son Gethin and his wife Liza help on the farm.

Joseph Harries of Werndew, known as "the wizard", b. 1761, d. 1826.

George Howell, Squire of Henllys. Wife Megan. One son (John) and one daughter (Mary). (Unrelated to the Howells of Brawdy)

Will Ifans and wife Daisy. Tenant farmers at Dolrannog Uchaf.

Mary Jane Laugharne, born 1775. Daughter of Squire John Laugharne of Pontfaen. Martha's best friend.

George Lewis (Lewis Legal). Family lawyer from Fishguard.

William Probert (Will Final Testament). Lawyer from Newport.

Benjamin Rice, Squire of Pentre Ifan. Wife Maria. One son, Joseph, b. 1776.

Thomas Tucker, tenant farmer at Penrhiw. Wife Mary, three children.

Alban Watkins, Squire of Llannerch. Wife Myfanwy. Two daughters, Rose and Daisy, born 1780 and 1781.

Caradoc Williams and wife Bethan. Tenant farmers at Gelli. Daughter Sian is Martha's friend.

John Wilson, cooper, from Newport, occasional constable.

1. The Box in the Attic

Some day, if Martha Morgan is to be believed, the white bones of Moses Lloyd will be found by chance, among the boulders near the summit of the bluestone mountain we call Carningli. There never was a proper grave, and it is ironic that the flesh of such a man should have rotted into the core of a mountain said to be populated by angels.

Down below, on the flank of the little mountain, and about two miles from Newport in Pembrokeshire, there is another skeleton, all that remains of a substantial dwelling house called Plas Ingli. It is set in the midst of a maze of stone walls and enclosures. Above the ruin there are a few stony fields with erratic shapes, now covered with gorse and heather, created by the earliest farmers, tended by a hundred and twenty generations over three thousand years, and extending up to the limit of the mountain's scree slope. Below, there are larger and more modern fields, acid and waterlogged, extending down to a minor road that leads to three farms. The Plas (as it was and is called by the locals) is connected to this road by a rutted track, still just about negotiable, with wide grassy verges.

The ruin lies above the 600 foot contour, higher up than a house should be, surrounded by a broken stone wall that can no longer resist the tide of bracken, bramble and willow scrub surging in from the old fields. Within the curtilage there are the remains of other stone buildings including a barn, a cowshed, a stable, and a coach house, ranged around an elongated farmyard. Smaller structures once sheltered chickens, hounds, pigs and geese. On the northern and western flanks of the inhabited area there was once a windbreak of oak, rowan and ash trees; they are now all dead or dying, having lost the will to resist the unceasing assault of salty wind and acid rain. Only one tree remains alive in the old orchard.

The sea is only a couple of miles away, on the other side of Carningli, but it is not visible from the Plas. If you sit in the weed-covered yard when a northerly gale is roaring onto the coast, you can smell the salt spray, and you will have sheltering gulls for company. If you climb the mountain path on a May morning you can sit on the warm blue rocks of the summit and watch the quiet sea a thousand feet below. You can see the hazy outlines of the Wicklow Hills of Ireland far away on the western horizon, and the summits of Snowdonia to the north. You can hear the exuberant

The Box in the Attic

harmonies of a choir of skylarks ranged across the arch of the blue sky. You can see buzzards and ravens riding the wind and wheatears going about their business among the boulders. You can stride out over the technicolour moorland of gorse, heather, spiky bullrush and brittle grass and stumble across Celtic enclosures and fortifications. And if you close your eyes and tune in to the history of this place, you can hear the banshee winds from the west that have scarred the souls of those who once lived here; or smell the terror induced by six-month winters; or feel the dumbing and deadening effects of little warmth and no light; or taste the famine that has more than once insinuated its way across this vulnerable land. And you may even see the ghosts of Martha Morgan Plas Ingli, Joseph Harries Werndew, and George Howell Henllys drifting through the bracken.

In this prominent position the Plas was built to be seen, rather than to see. The locals say that in its heyday it was whitewashed, and that it could be seen against its mountain backdrop from more than thirty miles away. This was a sign of considerable status. When it had eyes to see, the big house looked south-east into the deep wooded amphitheatre of Cwm Clydach. To the east, it could see Tycanol Wood and the skyline rocks of Carnedd Meibion Owen, and to the south-west the deep gash of Cwm Gwaun winding its way to the sea at Fishguard. With the eyes in the back of its head it could see the mountain -- crags and boulders to the north and open moorland to the west.

The big house was abandoned little more than thirty years ago, but the windows have all been smashed by small boys and the roof timbers are rotting now that opportunists have started to remove their burden of prime Caernarfon slates. The buildings are made of dressed Carningli stone, so hard that it melts tungsten steel drills, and highly prized as a facing stone. So the site is now a quarry as well as a playground, and soon there will be hardly anything left of it. The local children stay clear of the place once the afternoon light begins to fade, for they have picked up the local tradition that the Plas is haunted. They say that this is where Billy Evans hanged himself, but they have got it wrong, for that happened in 1980 at Dolaeron, about half a mile down the track. The ghosts that live here at the Plas are very much older.

This story is not really about Plas Ingli, but this is where the key players in the drama lived and loved and died. The strange tale related by

The Box in the Attic

Martha Morgan in this book was lost two hundred years ago, and has only recently come to light. The process was triggered off by an incident during the rebuilding of the Plas roof in 1955. The old slates had all been stripped off. Two local workmen, perched up in the precarious remains of the attic, were levering away the rotten rafters from the wall-plate. One of them noticed something metallic glinting in the sun, tucked tight into the narrow angle between joists and rafters. It was all but buried beneath the sawdust and chaff that had been used by the early inhabitants of the house as loft insulation. It turned out to be a locked metal box. There was no trace of a key. It had the initials "MM" painted elaborately on the lid. It was larger than a cash box and smaller than a trunk, and it was inordinately heavy.

As the men pulled the box out into the daylight they were surprised to hear a woman's voice. They could not work out where the voice was coming from, but it was close at hand, clear and rich, and it was speaking Welsh. They both heard the words "Peace is mine, but those in mortal sin must make their peace with God." They both felt a frisson of consternation since there were no Welsh-speaking women in the neighbourhood at the time, but they felt no real fear. The moment passed, and in anticipation of some great discovery they concentrated on the box rather than on the voice.

The men let the metal box down on their pulley and then carried it to the then owner of the house, Mr Jacob Phillips, who was living during the building work with his wife Judith and small son Ben in a caravan in the yard. Naturally enough the workmen and the members of the family all assumed that the box contained some lost treasure. Now, in a state of high excitement, they forced it open only to find that it contained no jewels, family heirlooms or banknotes. But it was packed full of books and papers which had survived in remarkably good condition.

Having set aside his natural disappointment at the failure to find a treasure that would pay for the re-roofing of the house, Jacob spent several productive evenings looking through the contents of the metal box. He found that almost all of the documents were written in Welsh, by the same strong, fluent hand. But none of them was signed, and Jacob could not find a signature anywhere. There were four volumes of diaries, beautifully bound in leather and purchased -- at considerable cost, no doubt -- as blank record books from various bookbinders in Haverfordwest and Fishguard. Each one covered several months and each entry was dated. The earliest was 23rd August 1796, and the latest was just over one year

The Box in the Attic

later. But the sequence of recorded events was by no means continuous, and late in 1796 almost two months passed without any entries. Two pages had been torn out of the back of the last of the diaries.

There were some little sketch-books containing amateurish drawings of leaves and flowers, and rapidly-executed watercolour paintings of local scenes, some of them spoiled when the artist had been caught out in the rain. There were some sheets of musical manuscript paper with snatches of tunes written onto them, crossed out and re-written. In one bundle, tied with ribbon, there were about ten pages of neat hand-written Welsh poetry, probably laboriously copied from books. Jacob thought that two of the poems might have been hymns, for the name "Charles Wesley" was written beneath them. There were various newspaper cuttings and posters relating to the great events of the day -- the 1797 invasion at Fishguard, the adventures of Napoleon Bonaparte, corn riots in England, and the reports of speeches made by William Wilberforce. There were some pages of a pamphlet written by Thomas Paine. The collector must have been a person with liberal, if not subversive, instincts. But there was no will, and the box contained none of the items found in family papers of the day, such as invoices and receipts, account books, deeds and legal documents, or items relating to animal husbandry or the farming year. There was one bundle of letters, which Jacob at first assumed to be love letters, but he changed his mind when he discovered that they were written in a number of different hands, some of them on small scraps of paper, written by folks who were only just getting to grips with the art of hand-writing. All of them contained the name "Moses Lloyd", and all were dated 1797. Some of them were signed or initialled by the writers, but their names could not easily be made out.

The most intriguing item in the box was an envelope tucked into the pages of one of the diaries. It had "Confession" written in English on the front, and it was sealed with wax. Embossed on the wax were the initials "MM". With trembling fingers, aware that he was breaking into the most intimate part of someone's life, Jacob broke the seal and opened the envelope. He found within a small piece of paper with a hand-written message on it. The writing was clearly that of the author of the diary, and like the diary it was in Welsh. The only words which Jacob could recognize were "Moses Lloyd Cwmgloyn".

The Box in the Attic

Jacob, with the agreement of his wife, now came to the view that the volumes and loose papers constituted some sort of personal history or testament, probably written by a woman. She had had a considerable interest in current affairs and liberal politics, and Jacob concluded from her music, poetry and artistic efforts that she must have been moderately well educated. This would be expected of any resident of Plas Ingli, since the house had for at least three hundred years been the seat of one of the minor gentry families of north Pembrokeshire. There was no clue to the date of her death, but who was this person whose initials were "MM"? Frustrated by the fact that neither he nor his wife spoke or read Welsh, Jacob made some inquiries as to the past occupants of the house, but none of the locals could remember who had lived there prior to 1900, and the building society had the deeds to the house locked away in Halifax. Jacob could have obtained copies, but he never got round to it.

Since Plas Ingli was being smashed to pieces and rebuilt in 1955, Jacob had limited time available for his literary sleuthing, and he soon tired of the task. His wife wanted the house finished, since the caravan cramped her style. He made some notes, put these on top of the books and papers in the box, and closed the battered lid. Then he forgot about the mysterious lady of the Plas, for he had other things to concern him. For a start, it blew a gale and stripped off the builders' tarpaulins, and then it rained for three weeks and saturated every cranny of the roofless house. Work eventually resumed, but then the builders walked off the job on several occasions, complaining that the house was haunted. They said that in one particular upstairs room looking eastward towards Ty Canol Wood they had tried on several occasions to take up the old floorboards and to remove the decayed window-frame, but had been frightened out of their wits each time by a sudden chill in the air and by the sound of a woman's voice. The two men who had found the box said it was the voice that they had heard previously, low and clear. On two occasions their electric tools had inexplicably cut out on them. Then the Council's Building Inspector put his foot through a rotten floorboard in the same room and broke his ankle, thereby creating a very complicated insurance tangle.

After a host of problems and delays the house was brought up to a modern standard and opened by the Phillips family as a guest house. But they could not make a go of it, and word spread that the house was doomed, or haunted, or both. Most of the old estate had long since been sold off, and there was no tenancy money coming in. Jacob and Judith sold all of their remaining 230 acres of rough grazing land, and their lower fields, in an effort to clear their debts, but in 1960 they were forced by the building society and the bank to sell up, and they moved to Fishguard. After that three other families owned the house, each one driven by some fanciful money-making scheme and each one forced to retreat in disarray. The last owner failed to find a buyer, and suddenly disappeared. The gentlemen of the local "committee" (five elderly farmers who meet down on the Cilgwyn road every morning to discuss sheep prices, the weather and the state of the world) claim that they went off to darkest Spain to grow cannabis, but that story is not universally accepted.

By 1966 the Plas had been left to its fate, and in 1998 nobody had any idea who owned the ruins. Probably the deeds, for what they were worth, were held by one of the banks in Fishguard or Cardigan or by one of the building societies. The fragmentary memories of both the house and its eighteenth-century inhabitants appeared to have been scattered downwind.

ΩΩΩΩΩΩΩΩΩΩ

2. The Key to the Treasure

Two years ago I had a visit from Ben Phillips, the son of Jacob who had opened up the mysterious metal box in 1955. He told me that his father had recently died in Fishguard, and that he had rediscovered the box on going through his things. He had remembered the excitement of the original opening ceremony, although he had been only seven years old at the time. Now he had opened it up again and had set in train some investigations of his own. He was still inclined to his father's view that the writer of all the documents was a woman. Could I help? He knew of my interest in local history and folk beliefs, and assumed that I might have some leads. I was intrigued by the story that he told, and agreed to help him along the detective trail. First, we checked in the County Library and the County Records Office for information on Plas Ingli, only to come away empty-handed and with the helpful advice that family papers might be found in the archives of the National Library of Wales in Aberystwyth.

A trip to Aberystwyth appeared to be necessary, but before heading north into foreign territory we decided to check out the local graveyards. There were six or seven to choose from, but I reckoned that since our mysterious friend from Plas Ingli probably belonged to a family with social pretensions she was not likely to be buried in either of the graveyards belonging to Caersalem or Jabes Baptist Chapels. Rather, she might be found in one of the parish churchyards, either in Newport or Nevern. But there was another small churchyard in the parish of Cilgwyn, hidden in a copse of heavy yew trees and no doubt visible in the old days from the upstairs windows of Plas Ingli. I knew that the churchyard was a sad and neglected place, but it was worth investigating. According to the weather man an October gale was on the way in, but Ben and I agreed to meet at the churchyard next morning, wearing waterproofs and wellington boots and carrying slashers and billhooks.

It was a miserable grey day with the wind gathering speed and with spots of rain splattering the crumbling west end of the little church. The building itself is a simple Victorian structure in a poor state of repair, with cracks in the walls and holes in the roof. It is now abandoned, but until a year ago a few services were held here each year, for reasons of sentiment

The Key to the Treasure

rather than anything else, attended by a handful of local people of all denominations. Ben and I speculated that the church would soon be in ruins, the last of a long line of sacred buildings on the site. There must have been something here as far back as 1485, for tradition has it that Henry Tudor camped nearby and worshipped in Cilgwyn Church on his way to Bosworth Field.

The grass had not been cut for years, and had now been largely displaced by brambles, thistles, docks and foxgloves. We were surprised to find one or two recent graves with marble headstones close to the entrance gate. A thickening jungle of bramble and laurel and fallen yew branches confronted us, and as we hacked our way through it we frightened a fox which had been resting in the undergrowth. We noted with satisfaction that the deeper we penetrated, the older were the headstones. Dafydd William Edwards of Trefach, died 1912, aged 24. Harold Jenkins of Penybont, 1859-1899 and his beloved wife Hettie, 1865-1903. Eliza Griffiths of Dolrannog Isaf, 1844, taken to the bosom of the Lord aged three weeks and two days. John Owen of Gelli Fawr, died 1830, aged 20. Some of those lost souls among the brambles would have been local squires or tenant farmers; others would have been teachers or merchants or lawyers; and those who belonged to the "lower orders" of society had lived short and probably miserable lives. We discovered that there had been many deaths in the 1830s and 1840s, which had been the time of the Irish Potato Famine and the Rebecca Riots. Many of the headstones were inscribed in English, which was the preferred language of the gentry after 1800, although we knew that almost all of the headstones of equivalent age in the Baptist graveyards were inscribed in Welsh.

Then, round at the back of the church and in the middle of a tangle of laurel branches, as if protected by the thigh-thick tentacles of some monstrous marine creature, we spotted the crumbling top of a stone wall some ten feet high. We slashed our way forward and were relieved to find that the brambles eventually gave way, having been starved of light by the thick evergreen foliage of the laurels. We squeezed through small gaps in the heavy recumbent branches and pushed aside layer after layer of flat smooth leaves. Then we found ourselves at the entrance of a walled enclosure measuring about fifteen feet by ten. At one time an iron gate must have served to protect the privacy of this little sanctuary, for the rusting brackets were still fixed in the stonework. The walls, made of dressed bluestone, were in a reasonable state of repair, given that they supported the branches of the collapsing laurel trees which were now, in the rising gale, grinding back and forth ominously. We entered the enclosure as the rain arrived in earnest, but we were afforded some shelter by a green leafy laurel roof. This haven of calm proved to be the family enclosure or mausoleum of the Morgan family of Plas Ingli.

They must have paid a lot for it, and since it was the only enclosure in the graveyard it spoke volumes for their status in the local community. The ground was covered with moss and leaf mould which had accumulated over many decades. Had we excavated a little we would, no doubt, have found the slate lids to a number of graves. The internal walls were hung with strings and loops of ivy, and when we pulled these away we counted that there were at least eighteen members of the Morgan family buried or commemorated here. Some were immortalized in memorial tablets fixed to the walls, and others in headstones at ground level. Most of the slabs were made of local slate inscribed with spidery and shallow-cut lettering, and the oldest ones had weathered so badly beneath a crusting of lichen that the writing was virtually indecipherable. We could at least see that all of those from the eighteenth century were written in Welsh. After scraping away moss and lichen we could make out some dates and names. Ezekiel Morgan of Plas Ingli, died December 1745, aged 59 years, and his wife Sara, died February 1753, aged 64 years. Jenkin Morgan, Gent, died 1781, aged 71 years, and his blessed wife Elizabeth Ann, died 1783, aged 76. William John Morgan, Gent, of Plas Ingli, his wife Bethan and three others, presumably his children Thomas, George and Rose, all died on 7th of April 1794. (We wondered what appalling tragedy could have overtaken all the members of this family on the same day. How and where had they died?) Griffith Morgan, lost at sea 1795, aged only 19.

After the year 1800 all the inscriptions were in English and easier for us to interpret. Another Sara Morgan, taken by the Lord 1830, aged 25. Dewi Morgan, drowned at sea 1820, aged 16. And then, to our great joy, the following words on a slate plaque near the entrance:

To the beloved memory of
David John Morgan, Gent
died 12th of February 1805
Aged 27 yrs

The Key to the Treasure

and his beloved wife
Martha
Mistress of Plas Ingli
released from her shackles 27th of February 1855
Aged 76 yrs
having suffered long with blessed fortitude.
May they rest together in peace
in the bosom of the Lord.

We had found our author. Ben and I read the inscription in silence with increasing incredulity, as the wind battered the yew trees and as the rain filtered through the laurel canopy over our heads and reformed itself into a cascade of heavy droplets. Now we were starting to get seriously wet in spite of our waterproofs, and we retreated back to my house. In the warmth of my kitchen we were able to discuss things further.

David Morgan was only 27 years old when he died, leaving behind a young widow. She had written her diary when she was only eighteen or nineteen years old, possibly before the couple had married. Because her diary entries had stopped in 1797, we had assumed that she had died in or shortly after that year -- but it was now apparent that Martha Morgan had survived her husband by fully fifty years, had continued to live as a widow at Plas Ingli, had been accorded the rare title of "Mistress" of the estate, and had at last died at the advanced age of 76. What was her maiden name, and where had she come from? Her death was the last recorded of all the Morgan family, so when she died Plas Ingli must have gone to a family with another name. There were no children mentioned on the memorial tablet, but could Sara and Dewi have been the offspring of David and Martha? There could have been other children too, but if they had been girls who married their names would most probably be inscribed on other headstones, possibly in other churchyards miles away from Cilgwyn. And what were the tribulations that Martha suffered for so long with "blessed fortitude"? Whatever they were, those tribulations must have been widely known in the community, and her fortitude widely admired. Finally, since English was clearly the first language used by the major landowners of the area, why were Martha's papers almost entirely written in Welsh, a language despised by most of her peers? Did she use Welsh because it was the language of her heart and soul, or did she use it in case her papers were ever discovered by others who might be shocked by their contents? And what was the relationship with Moses Lloyd of Cwmgloyn?

With so many questions still unanswered we went back to the churchyard in the afternoon when the rain had blown its way towards England. Armed this time with notebooks and pencils, we faithfully recorded all of the legible wording and the precise dates of death on all of the Morgan family memorial stones. Then we went our separate ways to undertake further research. Ben went up to Aberystwyth the following week on a fruitless expedition, and came back convinced that any of the Plas Ingli papers that still existed must have been incorporated into the documents relating to some larger estate, following either a property purchase or a marriage. However, he did find some references to Plas Ingli in some old topographical books, and discovered that in the mid-eighteenth century it had an annual income of around £800, derived mostly from the rents paid by four tenant farmers and various tenant cottagers. The estate at that time extended to some 600 acres, and qualified the Morgan family to be counted among the lesser gentry. Probably the head of the family would have been involved in local politics and the administration of justice.

I started to research the old electoral registers and the parish records of births, marriages and deaths, and found a few bits of information that carried us forward in our quest for Mrs Morgan. In the records I found the dates of birth and marriage details for several members of the family, but strangely there was no record anywhere of the marriage of David and Martha Morgan.

I also started to ponder on the significance of Martha's confession and of the single name contained within it. I did some research on the Lloyds of Cwmgloyn and found that they once owned a substantial estate not far from Nevern. Their family papers, in immaculate order, were stored in the County Records Office. There was a birth record for one Moses Edward Lloyd on 13th March 1774, but no record of a marriage or death. Could he have moved away from the area? More intriguingly, in view of his frequent mentions in the bundle of letters, could he even have been Martha's lover?

Ben and I now decided that our speculations about the contents of the box were leading us in ever-decreasing circles, and it was clear that we needed a Welsh speaker in order to make further progress. I offered to organize a translation. I was convinced that the papers were interesting and possibly important, but I was already beginning to get attached to Martha and I did not want the material to be dissected by some translation agency or by some Welsh social history graduate intent upon the production of a doctorate thesis. Anyway, there were more than 500 pages of hand-written script, and cost was a consideration. Also, my instinct was that the text was written in a code or local dialect which might make it largely inaccessible even to a fluent Welsh speaker.

I took one volume of the diary and a few other papers at random, and popped in to see Tony Evans at the local bookshop. I knew that he was fluent in Welsh, but that he had learnt the language not as a child but as a young man. I was interested to see what he would make of Martha's Welsh. For a few minutes he scanned the pages of the diary and then said "Good God! This is the strangest Welsh I have ever seen. Where on earth did you get it? The structure is not only archaic, but there are many words I've never seen before. I think some of it is in a sort of private code. All I can think is that this was written either by somebody from North Wales, or by somebody fluent in the old Dimetian dialect that was used in parts of North Pembrokeshire in the seventeenth and eighteenth centuries. It's more likely the latter, since the differences between southern and northern Welsh are mostly differences of pronunciation, not vocabulary. You wouldn't pick up these subtleties in a written text. I can't help you much, but you must talk to Abraham Jenkins on the Cilgwyn Road."

"You mean Abraham Jenkins Waun Isaf? From what I can see, he spends most of his time leaning on the gate watching passing vehicles and chatting to Billy Howells, Tom Brithdir and Bob Thomas Blaenwaun. He seems quite content contemplating the passing of the seasons, reading the weather signs and complaining about the way the local area is being taken over by hippies and travellers."

"Appearances can be deceptive, my friend, as I learnt when I lived next door to him some years back. Abraham was brought up in Cwm Gwaun before he won a scholarship to Oxford. He never took it up because of the war, but he was a brilliant poet and won the bardic chair at the Wrexham National Eisteddfod in 1938. He was a conscientious objector and spent part of the war in jail. Later on he was given the bardic name "Ingli", which he thought a bit over the top since it translates as "angels" from old Welsh. Then he inherited the cottage and a few acres under Carningli, gave up poetry and academic pursuits, and concentrated on looking after a hundred sheep and five cows. He sold the cows when the milk quotas came in, and the sheep more or less look after themselves. You never know your luck. He might have the time and the inclination to help you. Go and see him."

So that evening I knocked on Abraham's door. He opened up cautiously and was clearly surprised to see me. He does not get many visitors, and my only previous contacts with him had been through the exchange of pleasantries about the weather down on the Cilgwyn Road. He invited me in and inquired as to the contents of the heavy metal box I was carrying. When I left several hours later the moon was sliding down towards Mynydd Melyn, and I had a deal. He was fascinated to hear that the box had come from the old Morgan family of Plas Ingli, for he had heard some strange things about them when he was a child. He would not elaborate. "Leave it with me," he said. "The sheep are running with the rams at the moment, and there's not much to do in the garden. I'll get back in touch before Christmas."

Christmas came and went. Eight months later he stopped me as I was driving up to town and said "Call in this evening, if you have a mind to." I did as I was told, and Abraham presented me with the translation. It was meticulously written in English, on more than a ream of A4 paper. Without saying a word he wrapped it up in brown paper and tied it with binder twine. He looked tired. Then he said "The forgiven sins of Martha Morgan."

"Pardon?"

"Strange things have happened on the slopes of this mountain over the centuries," he said, "but none stranger than the story told by this brave and troubled young woman. It is written in a sort of Dimetian dialect that has entirely died out, but which was once common around Solva and Croesgoch. Her diary confirms that she came from that area. I had the devil of a job sorting out her vocabulary and phraseology, but at last I cracked the code, and the task became easier and easier as the months went by. I tried at first to render it in naive English, using the Welsh structure of sentences where possible. She was a young woman with only a limited vocabulary but a good way with words. She was to my mind highly intelligent, and her ideas and her writing style developed during her twelve months of diary writing. Take my translation away, young man. Do with it what you will. I don't want payment, for I have just spent the most rewarding eight months of my life in the company of the indestructible Mistress of Plas Ingli."

There were a thousand questions I wanted to ask him, but he anticipated my impatience and said "Don't ask me anything. The answers to all your questions are in the manuscript. Read it for yourself, if you can cope with the combination of my handwriting and Martha Morgan's way with words." And with that he pushed the tin box and the brown paper parcel into my arms with a twinkle in his eye. He showed me the door while I spluttered a few words of inadequate thanks.

"By the way," he shouted after me, "I have also translated the bundle of letters and Martha's confession. The confession was written in Dimetian Welsh, but the letters were written in the normal form of the language used in these parts. Very interesting indeed. I have tagged these items onto the end of the diary narrative. Good night!" And he closed the door.

I have spent a further twelve months sorting out the narrative, editing out superfluous material, getting the family tree and the sequence of events straight in my mind, and trying to get Martha's diary into a form fit for publishing. When Ben Phillips and I first embarked upon the task of entering into the small world of Mrs Morgan Plas Ingli, we had not the faintest idea what manifestations of good and evil we would discover within.

ΩΩΩΩΩΩΩΩΩΩΩ

MARTHA MORGAN'S STORY

EXTRACTS FROM THE PAGES OF HER DIARY FOR 1796-1797, TRANSLATED
FROM THE DIMETIAN WELSH DIALECT BY ABRAHAM JENKINS

3. Going and Coming

23rd August 1796

This is my farewell. I am a stranger at Plas Ingli, and those who belong here will be better off without me. ,

Before I left home, I read in an old book that before you take your own life you must write a long and beautiful letter saying goodbye, for those who are left behind to read with tears in their eyes. Perhaps this is it, but I have no fine sheet of vellum to write on, and I have stolen a book of blank pages from Grandfather Isaac's desk instead. He will surely not mind me writing a few words on page one before I go to meet my Maker. I know no moving poems, and I have not done this before, so I know not how to start.

What is to become of me if I stay alive? My short life, sweet as it has been, can lead nowhere, give nothing to others, lighten no dark places. Waves of sickness are passing over me each day, and I am hardly able to eat. My body, which I loved two short months ago, is now an object of self-loathing. I am but eighteen, with child, and shut away here in a big dark house among strangers. This is a lonely, dismal place, and I hate it. The house is habitable, but all around it there are half-built structures and piles of timber and stone. The heat presses down upon me so heavily that I can hardly breathe. I cannot even see the sea from here, or smell the salt spray. Above me looms a cruel mountain covered in tumbling rocks, where you can slip into a deep crevice and shout and scream, and never be found again. Perhaps, tomorrow, that is where I will go, and perhaps I will throw myself into the depths and simply disappear. David and Grandpa and the servants will be out in the fields helping with the Dolrannog harvest, and Grandma will be in the dairy. Nobody will notice me slipping away. They will search and search, but they will never find my body.

Going and Coming

Or maybe I will go over the mountain tomorrow to visit the wizard. I have made some inquiries, and it seems that he lives along the summit track and then down on the flank of Dinas Mountain, at a place called Werndew. They say he has magic potions and mixtures for all manner of ailments, and I am sure he will give me something that will let me and my child slip away without pain. Then I will cause no trouble to anybody any more, and David can make a fresh start with a new wife who deserves his love. He is but nineteen himself, and in time he will settle into his rightful place among the better class of people in this miserable area.

I think I am writing this for David. Dear David! Leaving you is my main regret, for I love you with all my troubled heart, and I know that you love me. You have stood by me through these terrible weeks when many, indeed most, would have left me to my fate. And you have never blamed me for my weakness. You and your dear grandparents have moved many stones from my path, and have made me welcome here at the Plas, but I feel that there are still a million boulders rolling down from the mountain to crush me. My own parents have planned and schemed from the day that I told them of my disgrace, but probably for their own sakes rather than mine. A scandal would hurt them far more than me, since genteel families have their reputations to think of. How I hate all their lies and deceptions! The horrid departure from Brawdy, the endless journey along the road to Carmarthen in a covered carriage in the heat of high summer, with me so poorly with the morning sickness that I thought I would die. Then the strange and secret marriage, with you and Grandpa and Grandma and my parents by my side, and my beloved Morys bending church rules and falsifying documents. Then the farewells to my nearest and dearest, and another endless journey through the dust and the heat back to the Plas. And all for what?

That was all two days ago. Now here I am with a new name, no longer a child but a married woman. Security, warmth and comfort are replaced by uncertainty and even terror. If I stay, will I ever see my friends again, and will I ever enjoy the gay balls and parties in Haverfordwest and Tenby that my sisters Elen and Catrin have enjoyed? I think not. Freedom and frivolity are things of the past, and I see ahead of me nothing but drudgery and responsibility, the twin penances for an old matron with a lined countenance, soiled hands and bent shoulders. I know not who I am, or what I am doing here, and it is best after all this misery to end it all.

Going and Coming

Nobody understands what is going on in my head or my heart, and I feel as if I am being spun about and battered to death in a butter churn.

I know, dearest David, that you have already had more tragedy in your short life than any man should be asked to bear. But you are young. And you are strong -- you have already shown that. And you, as Master of Plas Ingli, have Grandpa Isaac and Grandma Jane by your side, and they will guide you gently into a new life. Leaving does make me sad because I know that I am loved by brother Morys and my two sisters, and my good friends in Solva and St Davids. But my parents do not know me at all -- they say they love me and will do anything for me, but they are far too old to understand the turmoil in my heart.

Will you all miss me when I am gone? I suppose you will, but time will heal, and my memory will fade as the autumn turns to winter. When the rime is on the trees I will be with my Maker, smiling on you from my place in the sun. I am a burden to too many kind folk, and my passing will be seen, all in good time, as a pure and noble thing. I will sacrifice myself for the greater good.

Now I am weeping, and I am making smudges on the paper as I write. I have no wish to spoil Grandfather's expensive book, so I will stop now. Tonight I will lie with you, David, and try to give you my love, but I will be brave and you will not see my tears. Tomorrow, I will be gone, but a soft memory in the minds of others. Farewell.

ΩΩΩΩΩΩΩΩΩΩ

24th August 179

My mother always said that you should never take too seriously the wild threats of an eighteen-year-old, and I am glad to say that she was, and is, quite correct. I am still in the land of the living, and I have come to think better of my foolish and morbid plans. My little note written twenty-four hours ago seems, with hindsight, to have been ill-advised, and I have now taken counsel from someone wiser and older than I; and he has given me new courage to fight against whatever adversity may come my way. Those things which appeared to me to be unbearable burdens may indeed be

Going and Coming

blessings, and I must be grateful that I have more beauty in my life than many other women who may have fallen from grace.

It happened like this. After the completion of my farewell note I rejoined dear David, Grandma and Grandpa in the dining room, where they sensed my distress, calmed my nerves and talked long into the night of the good times to come, and the wonderful things we would do together at the Plas. They were so kind and loving, and so genuine in their concern for me, a young and foolish newcomer in their midst, that I began to feel it would be a betrayal of their trust should I walk away into the darkness of everlasting night. Then David took me to bed, and gently removed my night-gown. We lay together in the darkness, enjoying the warm velvet of the August night. I still felt too sick and tired for loving, and like a good kind gentleman he did not force himself upon me. But he caressed every inch of my body with his hands and his lips, and this I loved too, in spite of my precarious state of health. Then he wept because he loved me so much! What a strange and beautiful thing for a man who is normally so cool and composed! He said that he had nobody in the world but me and that he could not live a moment without me, and I felt my resolve weakening even more. To tell the truth, there is much pleasure to be had in the act of loving, and I would certainly miss it if I were to go off to Heaven ahead of time. Indeed, I have my doubts as to the merits of Heaven anyway, since it is surely populated by the sanctimonious and miserable people of Horeb, Caersalem, Jabes, and Tabernacle, sitting in rows of hard wooden pews up among the clouds.

By the morning my dark resolve had, to some degree, returned, and my head was spinning with both morning sickness and conflicting loyalties. On top of this, I was worried about keeping my disgrace a secret from the staff. So far I do not look as if I am with child, but a sudden marriage always causes suspicion, and I am sure Bessie and Mrs Owen suspect that a child is on the way. As we broke our fast I tried to remain cheerful, but once David and Grandpa had kissed me and set off for Dolrannog, I broke down and wept. After Bessie had cleared away the dishes, Grandmother Jane gently suggested that my erratic state of mind was all quite normal for a woman who was with child, and since I was not able to keep down my food either she suggested that I should return to bed until I felt better. This I did, and by midday I was feeling so much stronger that I told Grandma I would take a brisk walk upon the open mountain.

Going and Coming

The furze was flaming gold and the heather deepest purple, and as I climbed up among the rocks I could see the men and women hard at work with their scythes and hay rakes down in the Dolrannog Isaf barley field. I disturbed an ancient raven, which complained bitterly and flapped off to find a new perch. I came upon a bottomless crevice between two huge boulders of bluestone, and I thought for a moment that I should cast myself into its depths. But then I thought better of it, since the sun was warm upon my back and the swallows were playing in the sky, and I could see below me the wide blue acres of Cardigan Bay. To go to one's maker on such a day would surely be a sacrilege.

So I turned westwards along the mountain ridge, still with my mind racing and unsure of what to do, and I determined to follow the route that would lead me to the wizard. I crossed one road and at last came to another, and turned down towards Dinas. I was in a sort of trance as I walked, and it came into my mind that maybe I should ask the wizard to help me to lose the baby instead of taking my own life. Which of these two would be the lesser sin? I have heard that there are herbal potions that will take a baby away, and that Molly John of Roch was helped last year with such a thing by a witch from Middle Mill.

At last, having twice asked the way, I came to the wizard's cottage. It was made of clom and rough thatch, and there were fragrant roses climbing up its walls. There was a little garden of herbs by the front door. With my mind in a turmoil I knocked timidly. There was nobody within, but I heard a call from the back of the house, and went round to find another garden there, full of flowers and herbs the like of which I had never seen before. A tall man, maybe aged about thirty-five, emerged from behind a row of yellow beans. I was greatly taken aback, since I thought that all wizards were old and grey and shrivelled, but this man looked far healthier than I. He was slim, and held himself well, and he had a sallow complexion and piercing blue eyes. "Good day to you, madam," he said, with a broad smile upon his face. "May I introduce myself? I am Joseph Harries of Werndew, sometimes referred to by the locals as "Doctor Harries". And to whom do I owe the pleasure of this visit?"

I gave him my name and told him where I came from. Then he said "Ah yes, the Plas. A most beautiful place. Bad business about the fire, a very bad business indeed. But now it is risen from the ashes, and the good times will come again. I assume you are here to ask me for some help. But

Going and Coming

I must tell you at the outset that I have had no formal training at a school of medicine. I have, however, studied for some years at Oxford, and have trained for more years than I care to remember under various wise men whose like the world will never see again. So what can I do for you on this fine summer's day?" I was lost for words, and so confused by his cheerfulness that I started to cry. The kind gentleman took me by the hand and motioned me to sit on a bench in the shade beneath a great beech tree.

He coaxed from me the purpose of my visit, and I told him my whole sorry story. I confided that in my unhappiness I had thought of taking my own life, and I asked him whether there was some potion he could give me to assist me in my task. Whether he sensed that my will was wavering I know not; but I little expected his fierce reaction. He leapt to his feet and berated me without a break for several minutes. I was so taken aback and petrified with fear that I do not recall his exact words; but he said that it was an outrage to all the values of civilization that such a pretty one as I, with a loving husband and family, and so much to live for, should ever contemplate such a thing. He asked in a loud voice whether I had a roof over my head, and a warm bed to sleep in, and food in my belly, and golden guineas in the cash box, and a caring family to run to my aid should they be needed. I replied, somewhat crestfallen, that indeed I had. And then he asked whether I had, that very day, felt the sun upon my back and the west wind upon my cheeks, and heard the skylarks above, and seen the buzzard soar among the white clouds, and smelt the strange sweet heady scent of the flowering furze. I replied, with a flush in my cheek, that indeed I had. And then, as tears began once more to trickle down my nose, he sat beside me and again took me by the hand.

"My dear sweet friend," he said quietly. "You are very young, and you find that life is very complicated just now. You may think that your life is at an end. But it is not. The world is too full of beauty for you to even think for a moment of leaving it. Your presence multiplies that beauty a thousand-fold for those who know you. You are surrounded by love, and you have good people at your side. You deserve them. And they deserve you, for you will grow strong as an oak, even if a little gnarled. You will live through turbulent times. You will bring children into the world, and you and they will share great joy. It is your destiny to bring happiness to many, and your sufferings during a long life will give strength to others."

Going and Coming

I thought this very strange. And then he said an even stranger thing: "Your destiny and mine are bound together in some way I do not understand. But our paths will cross many times, and we will give comfort to each other."

Then he fell silent, and as I wiped away my tears he said "Go now, my sweet friend, back to your loving husband and family, so that you may love and be loved. I will not harm a single hair of your body, and although it is in my power I will do nothing to help you harm yourself. And, since I know that you have thought about this and had it in mind to ask, I will do nothing to harm your baby. For a new mother to give birth to a firstborn child is the most beautiful thing in this world, and those who say that an innocent baby can bring shame upon the mother are hard and evil people who have no love in their hearts and no respect for the beauties of creation. I am not a man of church or chapel, but I know my God, and he has no truck with those who preach the gospels of hate and who heap strange and contrived sins upon the backs of the innocent."

I could see that he was getting agitated, and I put my hand upon his arm to calm him down and to indicate that I needed no more sermonizing. He stopped and smiled, and our eyes met. I was somewhat confused by all his theology, but I got his message, and realized that indeed I had more reason than many poor souls to look forward to life with hope in my heart. I got up and thanked him, and offered to pay for his consultation, but he shook his head and said "Perhaps I have helped you now, but you have also helped me to clarify my thoughts, and you will help me again. No money will ever pass between us."

And he showed me round to the front of his house and sent me on my way home with a broad smile and a cheery wave. I walked back over the mountain with a lighter heart and with a great liking for the wizard, for he had talked to me as an equal -- unlike so many others who persist in referring to me as "dear child". In my estimation, if I am old enough to have a baby, I am old enough to be reckoned an adult.

So here I am, alive and kicking, with the heir to the Morgan estate in my womb, with another friend to help me along the way. I have a deep feeling within me that Dr Harries, a man twice my age, will prove to be a good ally and a faithful counsellor as the years roll by. With so many friends and so much love around me, I begin to like this place. Maybe I will stay after all.

Going and Coming

28th August 1796

The high summer heat-wave goes on, and every day there are hazes and mirages over Tycanol and Carnedd Meibion Owen. Most of the woodland birds are now quiet, but there are so many bees and other insects at work that the very air seems to be alive with sound. I spend as much time as I can in the cool of the dairy with Grandma Jane, where we use the icy water piped down from Ffynnon Brynach for washing all the milking things. How David and Grandpa and the other men can carry on working in this heat is quite beyond me. The gallons of rough cider which they drink must have some magical property unknown to science. The harvest has now moved on to Trefach, on the other side of Cwm Gwaun, and there must be thirty men working with their scythes and stacking in the top field of oats. Everybody says that the harvest is very big this year. The hedgerow blackberry harvest is also substantial, much to the delight of the poor labourers and their families.

As I write, it is past noon and the heat is at its fiercest. I have been given a little room upstairs, in the south-east corner of the house and next to the master bedroom which I share with David. It is, I believe, called a dressing room, but I do not care to dress myself in it, and instead I have put into it a small table rescued from the fire together with some books and other personal things brought over from Brawdy. It is a light and airy room with a big window, and it looks out over Cilgwyn and the cwm and away to the purple hills of Presely on the far horizon. I feel happy here, as cosy as a sparrow chick in its downy nest, hidden away in the depths of a blackthorn bush. I prefer a room that looks towards the pearly dawn, which is often subtle and gentle in Pembrokeshire, and full of hope and promise. Much, much better than the guest bedroom on the west side, facing the brash purples and reds of the dismal sunset.

I have taken over Grandpa's big book with the blank pages. With a sheepish look on my face, I admitted to him that I had taken it the other day from his desk, and asked him if I might use it for jotting down some poetry or observations on country life. "Keep it, my dear Martha," he said. "I am delighted that you are now well enough to continue your studies, and to take an interest in what is going on around you." He may look forbidding with his piercing eyes, high forehead and wispy grey hair, but he is a generous and sensitive man, and I am already very fond of him. Little does he know what I wrote on the first two pages of his precious leather-bound book! One part of me feels that I should tear those pages out and burn them, but another part feels that my "farewell to the world" was but a part of growing up, and that in years to come I will look back at it with some amusement. Anyway, I think I enjoy my little scribbling sessions, which help me to understand myself, and also give me a time of solitude each day. This seems to be turning into a sort of diary, but it is not intended as such. Maybe I will abandon it when the baby arrives, since I daresay I will then be too tired for any writing activity other than the occasional letter home to dear mother and father. I am now almost three months gone.

David and Grandpa Isaac have been having some fun at my expense, just as my old tutor Mr Hopkins used to do, teasing me about my "improper" Dimetian Welsh! This is the Welsh I know best, but I know that even the younger people in the Solva district are not now so fluent in it as their parents used to be. In fact, most of them have entirely abandoned the language. Father taught me to use it because he was a scholar of linguistics in his younger days, and thought it important that it should be kept alive as the most precious jewel of our culture. Perhaps, when he and his generation have died out, I will be the only person speaking and writing Dimetian Welsh! My own private language!

ΩΩΩΩΩΩΩΩΩΩΩ

4th September 1796

For the last couple of days it has been too wet for the men to work on the corn harvest, or for the women to pick blackberries. So all of the locals have been up on the mountain, collecting long green spiky rushes from a particular boggy place near Carn Llwyd. I went along to help, although I was probably more of a hindrance. It was dirty work, with some of the older men splashing about in the mud, selecting the longest and greenest rushes, cutting them carefully close to the ground, and then throwing them to their helpers for tying into soggy bundles. The bundles were then carried down to the farms and cottages on horsedrawn sledges. Over the coming weeks they will be dried and partly stripped, and then dipped in melted tallow after *Calan Gaeaf* to make rushlights.

Now I have been at Plas Ingli for more than two weeks. I am getting to know David and his grandparents better, and the servants as well, and they all seem to be good people. For a house with twenty-two rooms surrounded by a large country estate there are very few servants, with only four living in and one travelling up from Parrog each day. There are also a number of labourers living in tied cottages on the estate, and work is sometimes given to their wives and children and to occasional travelling harvesters and vagrants.

The house is really run by Grandma Jane, Mrs Owen the housekeeper, and Bessie the maid. Grandma is a short, wiry woman without an ounce of spare flesh on her, and with thick hair as white as snow. She is still in her mid-fifties, and she tells me that she was married at sixteen. She only had two children, Betty who now lives in Solva, and William who was David's father. She seems to have an endless supply of energy, but she is a woman of few words, and a casual observer might think that she is unintelligent or uninterested in the affairs of the world. But the casual observer would be wrong, for she knows exactly what is going on in the house, out on the estate, and further afield. She is very close to David, and indeed has acted as his mother since the fire. From my very limited observations thus far, she is very intuitive and astute, and keeps Grandpa and David on the straight and narrow path with little hints like "Would it not be better if...?" or "Have you thought of the consequences of doing this?" whenever there is some important matter under review. I find her intimidating to a degree, and it is not at all easy to see inside her head or her heart, but I respect her greatly, and I am sure I will grow to love her.

Mrs Owen is a large and jovial woman, widowed but probably younger than she looks, who has been with the family since she was a girl. She has four children, but they are all old enough to be in service in Newport and on surrounding farms. She is a source of wonder to me, since she acts as cook as well as keeping the house in order, and she is just as likely to be found milking the cows or making butter in the dairy as she is to be found in Newport doing the weekly shopping. She and Grandma Jane may be servant and mistress, but they are as close as a pair of well-worn boots, and I find her a great support, since she loves to cluck around me like a mother hen with a single chick to look after. She probably knows I am with child, but she hates tittle-tattle, and I am sure she will not say anything to anybody outside this house.

Bessie has come into service here since the fire, and is from Nevern. I like her a good deal. She is a couple of years older than I, and very vivacious, and because of her good looks she is already beginning to attract the attentions of assorted farm lads from the neighbourhood. Dai Darjeeling, the tea-man who comes over from Fishguard once a month, is apparently dizzy with love for her, and she receives with good grace the romantic verses which he delivers to her in little brown envelopes. But she is a hard worker, and Mrs Owen keeps her in order. I enjoy talking to her, and she and I will assuredly become good friends.

Then there is Billy Ifans the carter. He does not spend much time with horses and carts, since there are hardly any left after the fire, but he is also a plough-man, shepherd and cow-man, who helps on the estate with whatever is needed. Billy has been here for at least twenty years, and is in his mid-thirties. He is a rough and happy-go-lucky sort of a fellow, as honest as they come, who probably drinks away all his wages down at New England or at the Rising Sun. But that is his privilege, as a bachelor with no responsibilities. Shoni Hallelujah tried to save him once, but apparently got short shrift from Billy, who said he quite enjoyed being slightly sinful now and then. Currently he lives in the house, but he says he would be just as happy sleeping in the hayloft above the cattle in the temporary cowshed.

Hettie Jones comes up from Newport every day to help in the dairy and with the chickens and geese. She is a busy little woman with a huge enthusiasm for life. She is married with four children and lives with her family in a cottage down on the Parrog, at the mouth of the estuary. Her old mother lives with the family, and she takes charge if Hettie stays at the Plas overnight, which she sometimes does if the weather is inclement or if she works late. She says the people who live by the sea are very tribal and independent; she is fiercely loyal to her little fishing and boatbuilding community, and she cannot bear it if you refer to her as a Newport person, even though the town centre is less than half a mile up the road. She was born on the Parrog, and says she has fifty percent of salt in her blood. Her husband is a fisherman, and she sometimes brings up baskets of mackerel, pollack or herring when the shoals are in the bay. By all accounts she also brings up the essential news of the town, the telling of which will no doubt brighten up the kitchen on cold and windy days once autumn sets in.

The only one of the servants about whom I am uncertain is Moses Lloyd, who looks after the garden and the orchard as well as working with the animals. With him, I suspect that what you see is not necessarily what you get. He is only a little older than David, maybe twenty-one years old. He is extremely good-looking, and burnished and fit from working in the open air. He has dark hair, an olive complexion, and piercing brown eyes which he uses to good effect. He clearly enjoys the fact that women are greatly attracted to him. I must admit that the other day, when I noticed that his eyes were fixed upon me, I felt a flutter in my heart and a flush upon my cheek. Although he is tall and well built, he is strangely uncoordinated when he moves, and to my mind this gives him a certain boyish charm.

I am still mystified as to how the Plas is run, but I am trying to learn more. David is actually Master of the estate, but Grandpa (who is only 56 years old) should really be in charge. When I asked him the other day about this strange state of affairs, he said that because of some complicated matters relating to marriage settlements and debts, the lawyer from Fishguard, one Lewis Legal, had arranged for ownership of the estate to be transferred from him to his son William. When he died in the fire Griffith had inherited it, and when Griffith was lost at sea it passed intact to David although he is still strictly under-age. All very peculiar.

The other members of the local gentry are amazed that the Plas runs with so few staff, that Grandpa Isaac and David spend their days in the fields with the men, and that Grandma Jane spends every day with her sleeves rolled up. Some of the gentlemen farmers are impatient that the Morgan family has slipped out of the local social scene, and is absent from the summer balls and from the meets of the local hunt. But they know about the fire, and I think it is common knowledge that a wooden box with all the Morgan family treasure went up in the flames. So far as I can see, the bulk of the family's income comes from the rent paid by the three tenant farmers at Gelli, Dolrannog Isaf and Dolrannog Uchaf, but they always seem to have problems in paying on time. In the old days there was rent from a farm called Penrhiw as well, but that was sold by Grandpa's father Jenkin to pay off a large debt. After the fire Grandpa had to sell most of the black cattle herd, most of the horses and all of the hunting hounds in order to start the rebuilding of the house, and he has taken various loans from merchants and landowners in the area. Grandma is very worried about the conditions attached to some of these loans, but she will not elaborate further. And I know that my own father has just made a substantial payment to the estate from his own fortune, following a long meeting with Grandpa and David in Fishguard last week. Perhaps this is what they call a "marriage settlement", and perhaps it gives me some rights in the estate.

I know that the staff have been very loyal, and the three who were here before the fire have agreed to stay on at lower wages, with the promise that when things improve they will be amply recompensed. Mrs Owen tells me she and Billy each have to survive on six sovereigns a year, Hettie on five, and Bessie and Moses on four. I wonder how they can manage it. But indeed there are many worse estates to work on. I am coming to realize that this is a beautiful place, well located between mountain top and valley bottom, and with land that responds to wise husbandry. Now that the house is rebuilt, the staff have warm dry rooms to live in, and they share the good food of the family, including wheat bread on the Sabbath, beef and pork, fruit from the orchard, and plenty of eggs, milk and butter. The cottagers and the poor people in town have to survive on oat cakes, porridge, herrings, potatoes, white cheese and buttermilk, and seem often to be on the edge of famine. The three surviving members of the Morgan clan (I hesitate to include myself in their number until I am somewhat more established) are sweet, kind people who speak on the level to their staff, share daily labour with them, and will certainly defend them with might and main should any misfortune come upon them. It is almost as if the fire has burnt its way into their souls, and has forged some iron link that holds them together.

Together, I am sure we will rebuild this estate in some style. Within a year the outbuildings will be ready, and the farm will then be exceedingly well appointed. It will surely be a model for others to admire, and I feel a growing aspiration to be a benign and elegant Mistress. I think I am turning into an optimist.

ΩΩΩΩΩΩΩΩΩΩΩ

4. Incidents

6th September 1796

I have to report that I am increasingly intrigued by our servant Moses Lloyd. I have been keeping a little eye on him while -- of course -- not making my interest too apparent. For a start, I have observed that he does not know much about cows, sheep, vegetables or apple trees. He appears to know even less about building work, and clearly has little taste for the mixing of mortar or the moving of stone. I perceive that he does not greatly enjoy work of any sort, and also suspect that he thinks it beneath his station. I am not quite sure where he comes from, but Mrs Owen says he is one of the Lloyds of Cwmgloyn, with whom the Morganses of Plas Ingli had a feud earlier in the century. That would seem to me a pretty good reason for keeping him off the place.

Bessie, who knows all the local scandal, thinks that after wasting his father's money at Eton and Oxford, Moses got into some serious trouble three or four years ago, and that David's father William took him on as a gesture of good-will, hoping to heal some ancient festering wound. He speaks with a strange sort of affectation possibly picked up when he moved in high society. Grandma Jane does not trust him and neither does Bessie, but I hesitate to think ill of him myself. He is certainly more interesting than your average farm servant, and in everyday conversation he is witty and even erudite. Let us hope that he has learnt something from the mistakes of his youth.

The men appear to have no problem with him. Grandpa Isaac seems satisfied with the work that he does, and David treats him as a sort of replacement for brother Griffith. The two are very close indeed; they spend much time in manly conversation, and I suspect that David admires the understanding that Moses has of the wicked ways of London and Oxford in particular and the world in general. As a good wife, I must do my best to respect their friendship.

ΩΩΩΩΩΩΩΩΩΩΩ

Incidents

8th September 1796

I have not yet written about the fire. David and his grandparents hardly ever talk about it, and I am still not sure of all the details, but I have pieced together some sort of history of the tragedy from Mrs Owen and the other workers and tenants on the estate. It has left terrible scars on David's mind, for he has twice woken up in a panic in the middle of the night, and I have had to console him and tell him that all is well. All is certainly not well, and indeed I know not what demons of guilt and fear dwell within my dear husband's breast.

I was reminded of this matter because today the weather broke, and Grandpa Isaac and David decided that they should burn the last of the charred timbers of the old house. After two years or more, they were dry as a black thorn-bush in a desert. They have been standing for all this time in a jagged and ugly pile at the bottom of the yard, having been left there during the demolition of the ruined house. They wanted to burn them early in the summer, but dared not, for fear that sparks would set the common on fire. Billy and the other men lit the fire in the rain, and the blackened joists and rafters and purlins are now reduced to a pile of ash; but David could not watch.

The old house was, they say, very grand but old-fashioned, with small rooms and winding corridors and two narrow staircases. In the month of the fire the Morgan family of seven people were all living in the house, together with Mrs Owen and three other servants downstairs at the back. David and his older brother Griffith were sleeping downstairs at the time, together with Grandpa Isaac and Grandma Jane. Father and mother and the three younger children were sleeping upstairs.

It happened in the month of April, shortly after Easter. Mrs Owen told me they had all gone to bed early, for it was a windy night with heavy cloud, and the rushlights and candles kept on guttering and dripping with all the draughts. It was an easterly wind, the sort of wind hated by everybody in these parts because it is dry and cold and cuts through everything. She suspects that one of the older boys -- possibly David, although I have not pressed him on this point -- left a candle burning at the top of the stairs, having been to the upstairs office to fetch a book to read in bed. At any rate, she heard some shuffling and some footsteps on the stairs

Incidents

after she had settled down for the night.

In the blackness of the early hours they were all asleep when Mrs Owen was wakened by the dogs barking in the kennel and by Moses banging on her door. At once she smelt smoke, and when she got up to investigate she was horrified to find that the centre of the house, around the main stair well, was well alight. Moses was already dressed, but she rushed out wearing only her night-gown and shawl. Together they woke up the old people, and David and his brother, and they at once discovered that they could not get up the stairs because of the flames. The back staircase was also filled with black smoke and was impassable. They shouted and screamed warnings to those who were trapped upstairs, but there was no response. Frantically they started to carry pails of water in from the pond, but their pathetic efforts had no effect on the flames. There was at that time no pipe carrying water down from the mountain spring. The upper storey of the house was now full of smoke, and as the windows began to break the east wind was fanning the flames and turning the house into a fiery furnace. Still the would-be rescuers did not hear a sound from Master and Mistress Morgan or the small children. Perhaps they died peacefully from the effects of the smoke rather than from the terror of the flames -- let us hope so for their sakes, God rest their souls.

By now the smoke could be smelt at Dolrannog and the flames coming through the roof were visible against the skyline from down in the cwm. David and Griffith and the others worked like demented souls in Hell, for they knew that there were five members of their family still upstairs. I am so horrified that I feel a tightening in my stomach as I try to imagine the situation more than two years after the event. Then the stairwell collapsed in a ball of fire, and they could still not get up the back stairs because of the swirling smoke. Both David and Griffith tried to crawl up the steps with wet sheets and blankets wrapped around them, but they could not breathe, and Grandpa had to rescue both of them before they threw away their own lives. One of the servants, named Eli Mathias, took a ladder, climbed up and entered an upstairs window to try and rescue Master and Mistress Morgan, but he was engulfed by a great tongue of fire and smoke, and was terribly burnt before he could be dragged clear by Grandpa. Then the neighbours from Dolrannog, Penrhiw and Blaenwaun started to arrive, and they made a sort of chain to carry water from the pond to the house, using pails, barrels, milk-churns and anything else they could find. Thomas

Incidents

Tucker Penrhiw took the long ladder to try and reach the window of the children's room, but it was so full of smoke that he dared not go inside. He shouted and shouted their names, Thomas, George and Rose, but all he heard in response was the fearsome roar of the flames.

In the end, by all accounts, with the east wind encouraging the flames to even greater destruction, the house became such an inferno that nothing further could be done. The flames spread to the thatched roof of the barn, and that too was destroyed. Then the stable and cowshed caught fire, and four horses and twelve cows were killed. The neighbours, and those who escaped from the flames, had to stand well back and watch, in their grief and horror, as the flames completed their gruesome work, illuminating the darkest hour before dawn. David and Griffith, and the grandparents and servants, all in a state of deep shock and utter exhaustion, were taken in by the neighbours from Dolrannog and Penrhiw. Doctor Havard from Newport turned up while it was still dark, and treated the two boys who could hardly breathe on account of the smoke they had inhaled; but he could do little for poor Eli Mathias, who died from the burns to his face and upper body.

It was two days before the house cooled down enough for anybody to go inside and investigate. Most of the roof timbers and the upstairs floor timbers had gone, and only a few pieces of furniture from downstairs had been rescued. They never found the bodies of David's parents, or his brothers, or his little sister Rose who was only four years old. But they were in there somewhere, their ashes mixed horribly into the smouldering piles of debris that now covered the ground floor of the old house.

This was the most dreadful event that anybody can remember in Cilgwyn or Cwm Gwaun. Six people dead on one fateful night. I have not asked for too many details of the funerals, but brave Eli was buried at Brynberian, and there was a very grand funeral service for the Morgan family at Cilgwyn Church attended by people from as far away as Fishguard and Eglwyswrw, for they were held in great affection by both rich and poor. I know that a memorial plaque was put on the wall of the family enclosure in the churchyard, for I walked down and looked at it the other day. But I know not what is in the hallowed ground, for there could hardly have been anything to bury.

Incidents

12th September 1796

Today it has been raining and blowing from the south-west, and the inclement weather is holding up the completion of the carting and rick building. This morning, as we were sorting out papers in the office, the conversation turned to Moses. He has been looking at me in a way that I find uncomfortable, and I think he suspects that I am with child. On mentioning this to David, he swore that he has not told him or even hinted at my condition.

He then said that he is thinking of training Moses up to be a Secretary or Steward for the estate. I was surprised at this, since we can hardly afford to pay him a poor labourer's wage, let alone the wage of a professional man. In expressing my concern, I reminded David that Moses did not exactly have a high reputation for hard work. I also said that at least some of the female members of our household were very circumspect in their dealings with him, for reasons I did not fully understand. "I know, I know," said David. "Moses has had a chequered past, but I think he has settled down. We all know he does not like labouring work, but he is after all a member of an old gentry family, and may do better using his brain instead of his hands. He is good with figures, writes and reads well, and has an excellent command of both Welsh and English. He even speaks French better than I do"

"Has he asked you to appoint him as steward?" I intervened.

"Well, not exactly," replied David, flushing slightly. "But we have talked at length about the options that we might have for the future good management of the estate."

At this I could feel my temperature rising. "My dear David," I said, "Should you really be discussing this sort of thing with a servant? This is no time to rearrange estate responsibilities. I know next to nothing about matters of high finance, but should not any spare money in the chest under the bed be used for repaying debts, completing the building work and buying new stock? Grandpa says that at the very least we need a breeding mare, a couple of good draught horses, a young bull, twenty head of cattle, and fifty sheep if we are to start on the process of restoring the estate to what it was before the fire. Besides, we have a new baby on the way, and money will be needed for cots and garments and other baby things to replace those that were lost."

"Yes, yes, I know all of that," said David, with his temperature also rising. "But we must plan far ahead. That is what good administration is all about."

I could sense an argument coming on, but I was in no mood for it, so I put my arms around him and said in my best wifely voice "I know, dearest, that you want to make wise decisions, and show Grandpa, Grandma, and the rest of us that there is a firm hand on the plough. But I beg you to do nothing hasty until you have talked things through properly with your grandparents. Will you promise, for my sake and that of our baby, not to give Moses any hint of what is in your mind?"

David thought for a moment and then said "Oh, very well. There is not actually any hurry over this, and we do of course have other things to think about." He smiled and gave me a long embrace. And then, with the rain having blown over, he went off to supervise some stone clearing work in one of the top fields.

In writing about this little conversation, I feel a tightening in my breast. While I have no reason to dislike Moses, I fear that he has been exploiting his friendship and putting pressure on David. I hope I may be wrong. But I am resolved to keep a careful eye on this particular manservant over the next few days.

ΩΩΩΩΩΩΩΩΩΩΩ

18th September 1796

A stiff breeze has been drying out the land after the recent spell of rainy weather, and Grandpa, having read the weather signs, says that a late heat wave is on the way. If he is right, the last of the barley harvest will be safely carted within a few days.

Today I must report on further observations on the behaviour of our friend Moses Lloyd. After breakfast I decided on a walk down the lane to Dolrannog Isaf to see if I could borrow some knitting yarn from old Mair Griffiths. I had not gone very far when I was nearly startled out of my wits by a head which popped up from behind a stone wall.

Incidents

"Good morning, Mistress Martha," said the head. "I trust that you are well on this fine bracing day?"

"Oh my goodness!" I exclaimed. "Moses, you almost frightened me out of my wits! Yes, thank you, I am very well indeed. I thought you were working in the garden today? What on earth are you doing here?"

"Oh, just repairing this stone wall. Part of it collapsed during the heavy rain the other day," he explained. Then his face broke into a broad grin and he added "Somebody has to keep this place in good order!"

"I am sure we are all very grateful for your efforts in that regard," I said, noticing that the stone wall looked perfectly sound. "But don't let me delay you any further." And I nodded, signalling an end to the conversation, and walked on.

But the conversation did not end there, for Moses sprang over the wall and stood in front of me. "Mistress, I urge you to be careful," he said, looking me straight in the eye. "The harvest has just finished, and there are still many itinerant labourers in the area, not all of whom are honest. Would you allow me to escort you so as to ensure your safety?"

I was greatly surprised by this suggestion, for he spoke more like a gentleman than a servant. But after a moment's thought I replied "Thank you, Moses, for your consideration, but I must decline your kind offer. It would not be appropriate for us to walk together. Nor is it necessary, for I assure you that I do not feel at all threatened by itinerant harvesters, and am quite capable of looking after myself. And now, if you will be kind enough to get on with your activities for the day, I will get on with mine."

"As you wish, Mistress," he replied, moving to one side and bowing deeply. "Good day to you." And with that he vaulted back over the wall and made a great show of heaving heavy stones about while I continued on my way to Dolrannog. As I walked I saw not a sign of an honest itinerant harvester, let alone a dishonest one.

Earlier this evening, when Bessie was helping me in the bedroom, I mentioned this strange episode to her. "You just watch out for him, Mistress," said she, wagging her finger at me. "He is up to no good, that's for sure. Servants do not offer to escort their masters and mistresses, married or unmarried, on country walks." On giving the matter further thought, I am convinced that David has said something -- or perhaps not said something -- to Moses, and that our esteemed manservant has come to the view that I am standing in the way of his advancement.

Incidents

19th September 1796

This morning I took my water-colour paints and brushes, and some stiff sheets of paper, and went up to Ffynnon Brynach. There I sat on a rock by the gushing spring for a couple of happy hours, doing my best to portray the mellow beauty of the landscape in its late summer clothing. On my return, purely by chance, I happened upon Billy as he worked on a wagon wheel in the barn, ready for the last of the harvest carting. After a cheerful exchange of greetings and pleasantries about the weather, I said "I trust that the recent wind and rain have not caused too many problems on the estate. I gather that one of the stone walls at the side of the lane collapsed and had to be repaired."

"Well, yes and no," said Billy cheerfully. "A few stones did fall off one of the walls, probably dislodged by one of the sheep. But that wasn't down by the lane -- that was on the wall up on the mountain, not far from Ffynnon Brynach. I mended it myself in just a few minutes."

ΩΩΩΩΩΩΩΩΩΩ

20th September 1796

It is now almost one month since David and I were married, and I am moved to record something of the strange circumstances surrounding our wedding. Maybe, in years to come, I will read these secret words again and find some comfort in them, since there was surely more love in the air than I realized at the time.

It all started when David and his elder brother Griffith moved to Solva to stay with their Aunt Betty after the fire. They were both in a most agitated and nervous state, and both had breathing problems because of the smoke they had inhaled. Gradually they recovered, and since Aunt Betty knew our family she brought the boys over to Brawdy on a number of occasions to see us. She thought, quite rightly, that the boys needed some young company, and we all got on well together. Morys, my older brother, was 24 at the time and training for the ministry at Lampeter, so the Morgan boys did not see a lot of him. My older sister Elen was away in

Incidents

Bristol studying music and living with Great Aunt Lizzie. My other sister Catrin, two years older than me, immediately got on well with Griffith. And I became quite besotted with David although I was only sixteen years old at the time. He was tall and strong, with fair hair and blue eyes, and although he bragged a lot and pretended to be older than he was, I thought him more gentle and sensitive than any other boy I had met. He told me later that his heart was mine from the moment he first met me at Brawdy.

We four enjoyed a happy two months together in the early summer, spending as much time as our parents and tutors would allow walking on the wide sands of Newgale and on the cliffs towards Solva, exploring caves and mysterious clefts in the rock face, and cooking up gulls eggs on driftwood fires on remote pebble beaches. The months of May and June were dry and warm, and I still have clear pictures in my mind of sheer cliff faces of brown and grey rock, clifftops awash with sheets of blue spring squill, pink thrift, white sea campion and yellow kidney vetch, and of great rafts of puffins and guillemots bobbing about on the sea in the lee of the headland of Dinas Fawr. There were seals patrolling the beaches and coves, and gulls and terns wheeling and screeching overhead. Griffith and David could hardly believe the clifftop colours or the abundance of bird life which Catrin and I took for granted, for they had never been to this coast before. For hours on end we four simply sat and looked out over the glittering waters of St Brides Bay, inventing strange tales about the mysterious islands of Skomer and Grassholm far away on the horizon, and speculating on the exotic cargoes being carried in and out of Porthclais and Solva by flocks of little ships with white sails.

At last David and Griffith had to go back to Plas Ingli to help with the rebuilding work, and for Catrin and myself life returned to normal. Lessons in Welsh with my father, in English and history with the pompous Mr Hopkins, in piano with the sweet Miss Evans, and in art and embroidery with my Aunt Lucy. Catrin and Griffith drifted apart, but David and I were so greatly taken with each other that we contrived to meet several times over the next eighteen months, at Portfield Fair in Haverfordwest, at Newgale Races, and at various gatherings of the north Pembrokeshire gentry. Gradually I learned more about him -- of his scrapes as a youngster, of his love of shooting and fishing, and of his time at Eton. He told me of his fascination with the strange game of *cnapan* which the young men play around Newport, and -- much to my embarrassment -- showed me the scars of battle on his legs and chest! Our mutual attraction became deeper and stronger, and was cemented further in May of this year by the tragedy surrounding his elder brother.

Griffith was never very keen on the country life, and never wanted to take on on the mantle of Master of Plas Ingli. He loved the sea and enjoyed nothing more than rowing and sailing small boats, and after many family arguments Grandpa Isaac finally allowed him to join the crew of the sloop "Sara Jane" trading out of the Parrog in Newport under Captain Watkins. On his very first voyage, returning from Bristol past Lundy Island, the ship almost sank in a fearsome storm, and Griffith was lost overboard. His body has never been found. David and his grandparents were distraught, for this was yet another tragedy less than two years after the fire that had killed the rest of the family.

On hearing of Griffith's death I convinced my parents that we should visit Plas Ingli to help David and his grandparents through this difficult time, and they agreed to this. They were a great support to Grandpa Isaac and Grandma Jane; they knew all about running a big estate, and with only three servants now left at the Plas they turned their hands to many of the tasks that needed to be done. David and I spent many hours together. Every day he was on the edge of some personal abyss, waiting for some message from Swansea, or Tenby, or Cornwall, to say that a body had been found washed up on some distant shore. He kept up a tough exterior, but in private he wept frequently, for he had now lost both his parents and all his sisters and brothers, and could face no more horror. Somehow I gained strength from the need to support him, and we walked every day on the mountain and talked endlessly about fate, and God, and justice, and atonement, and the meaning of life and death.

I suppose that my dear Mother and Father, and David's grandparents, knew what was going on, and sometimes they went to great lengths to ensure that we were not left alone together. But they probably approved of a match between us even though we were still very young, since the future of the Morgan family, and of Plas Ingli, now depended upon a "good" marriage, preferably sooner rather than later. On one occasion my mother took me to one side and said that she loved David almost as a son, and was very happy to see us together; but she warned me to be very careful in the midst of the high emotions surrounding Griffith's death. Of course I knew what she meant, but I feigned innocence. Then one June day, in Tycanol

Incidents

Wood, under a canopy of oak leaves and on a bed of moss, in a whirlwind of kisses and embraces my love and I were swept higher and higher away from the sadness of the real world to a bright and happy world of our own making. It was the first time that either of us had ever loved. Afterwards, on three other days before I returned to Brawdy, we loved again in the same place in the woods, with no guilt and no thought for the future. I knew in my heart that there would never be anybody I would love as I loved David. He swore on pain of death that he would love me always, and promised that we would be married as soon as he reached the age of twenty-one.

When I realized in the early part of August, having missed two bleeding times, that I was with child, I knew not what to do. I felt in my heart that David would stand by me, but I was also aware of the social pressures that weighed down upon my family and his -- the obsession with status, long pedigrees and "good marriages" that went with membership of the gentry. I have always been close to Catrin, and now I confided in her, and she held me in her arms and wept with me. I was so frightened! She said that we must tell Mother, and the sooner the better, so we called her in, and we three sat in the living room while I poured out my heart.

I expected some fierce admonition from my mother, but instead she embraced me and said, with tears in her eyes: "My dear Martha, there, but for the grace of God, went I. I know something of how you feel. Your father and I married for love, and not because our parents wished it. He was almost cut off from the family fortune because he refused to marry one of the horrid Stokes daughters of Cuffern. Ours was a passionate romance, and we loved four times before we were married. After thirty years or more, I still remember counting the days to every bleeding time, and the wave of relief that came over me when we safely came to the day of our respectable wedding."

Then Mother frowned deeply and said: "We must make plans. It is in nobody's interest that there should be a scandal. I must talk to your father." And off she went to a meeting of the War Council. After what seemed like a very long time, they both came back into the living room. Father embraced me, and I think there was a tear in his eye. He gave me no rebuke, but said "*Cariad*, we have all made mistakes. Your mother and I were very foolish before we were married, and now you and David have been foolish. Love makes fools of people, and arranged marriages have

46

something to be said for them. You should have resisted temptation, you know that, and we should have seen the danger signals in the way that you and David behaved towards each other on our last visit to the Plas. We should have ensured that you were never left without a chaperone. But what is done is done."

After a few moments of contemplation he took a deep breath and suddenly put all emotion to one side, in that strange way that men do. There was no further talk of duty, or love, or family, or security, or motherhood. He asked me, point blank, for the date on which David and I had loved for the first time. I blushed, and since there are certain dates that one does not forget, replied that it was on the fifteenth of June. "Almost two months have passed," he said, "and there is still time to save face. But you and David must marry immediately, even if there is no time to work out the details of a marriage settlement. I will send a message to Isaac and Jane at the Plas to inform them about this development, and ask them to talk to David."

Then he added, looking me straight in the eye: "Will he marry you?"

"Yes, yes, I am sure of it," I replied, in hope rather than expectation, since I know that young men do not lightly give up their frivolous pursuits in exchange for an early marriage.

"Good. There is no time to arrange either a great wedding or a little wedding here at Brawdy Church. The Rector is hardly ever here, and he is an idiot anyway. And there is no time for all the reading of the banns, or for the bidding, or for making the arrangements for a feast. I will write to your sister Elen in Bristol to inform her of what has happened, but she is too far away to attend the wedding. I will write to your brother Morys near Carmarthen and ask him if he will perform the marriage ceremony by license. He is discontented with the established church, but he knows the rules, and he will know the means by which he can exercise discretion in the matter of marriage ceremonial. We were all sad when he left Pembrokeshire, but his little church more than fifty miles away may now prove to be very useful to us. We will arrange to travel to Carmarthen and meet up with David and his grandparents there, in one week's time."

"George, this is all very well," intervened my mother, "but how on earth will we keep this away from our friends and neighbours, and, more to the point, away from our servants?"

Incidents

Father thought for a moment and said "You are right, Betsi. We must not involve anybody else -- least of all the servants -- in any of this. We will say nothing outside this room, and I will not use the servants for carrying messages either to the Plas or to Carmarthen. I will ride over to the Plas myself tomorrow and discuss things with Isaac and Jane. Over the coming week we will put it about that you are going to Llandovery at short notice to take up an appointment as tutor in the mansion house of a relative -- we will not be too specific about the details. You, my dear Martha, will say farewell to your friends and cousins around Solva and St Davids. Then we will travel to Carmarthen in the coach, and I will drive it myself. Ifan in the stables knows that I enjoy driving, and I will tell him that he is needed to help with the harvest. After the wedding you will travel with David and his grandparents directly to the Plas, and that will be your new home. In due course people will discover that that is where you are, but after twelve months or so have passed the truth will be easier to manage."

At this Catrin, who had been sitting quietly through all the plotting, said that the disappearance of a daughter from Brawdy might be less easy to explain than we might think; but this was as nothing compared to the problems to be faced at the Plas with the sudden appearance of a new wife for the 19-year-old heir to the estate.

Catrin always was too practical for comfort, and a shadow passed across Father's face. Then he smiled a sly smile and said "No, no. It may not be such a great problem after all. The servants and the locals have met Martha, and they probably know that she and David are intended for each other. They need not be too surprised by a quiet and sudden wedding far away from the Plas. They know that the estate is all but bankrupt after the fire, and that there is hardly enough money to pay the servants, let alone pay for a grand wedding. They also know that there is great pressure on David, as the last of the line, to marry early and thus ensure the family succession. All of us involved in the plot must insist that this is a good marriage rushed through because the future of the estate depends upon it. There will be wagging tongues, of course, and almost everybody will suspect that a child is on the way. But if the baby behaves itself and delivers itself on time, or perhaps a little late, in seven months from now, it will be just about on the right side of respectability. We can say that it has arrived two months prematurely -- unusual for a first child, but not unknown."

Incidents

Then Father took my hand and looked at me with great tenderness. "My dearest child," he said, "I can see no other course of action than that which I have described. If David and his grandparents agree, and if Morys will help us through a liberal interpretation of the rules of matrimony, we will all be involved in a frightful deceit. Both families will need the Lord's forgiveness, for there will be many lies and half-truths to be told over the coming weeks. But in my heart of hearts I cannot see what we are about to do as a sin, for nobody will be hurt, and many -- you, your child, and our two families -- will be protected. Can you accept this course of action?"

My mind was in a tangle, and there were so many subtleties and complications in what Father had proposed that I knew not what to think, or indeed where to start on the thinking process. But Catrin came to my rescue and said "Martha, my dearest sister, much as I love to have you here at Brawdy with me, you must now do as Father says. If you do not, you may end up here with a child born out of wedlock and no prospect of a good marriage. It would not be good for you or for the baby. It would involve a scandal which would certainly reach as far as the Plas, and this would harm both David and the good name of the Morgan family. In the tiny and pathetic world of the Pembrokeshire gentry he would become known as a philanderer, and what young lady with a good fortune would have him then? In any case, do you want him to marry anybody else? If you love him, and he loves you, then you must marry. Your baby will be surrounded by love, and that is the only thing that matters to a child. People may speculate about your baby being conceived out of wedlock, but that will pass, and you and David and your new family can share in the rebuilding of Plas Ingli with two good old people at hand to help you. You must do it!"

And so I agreed. And so it came to pass. Father travelled to the Plas next day and, much to the relief of the whole family, got the full agreement of David and his grandparents. A message went off to Elen in Bristol. Another went to Morys in Carmarthen with the mail coach, and a letter came back four days later to say that he would perform the marriage ceremony in private. We put the word about that I was leaving home to take up a teaching position. I said my farewells to my friends. And then, early in the morning, with father driving, and with Mother, Catrin and myself inside, and with trunks and boxes of my possessions on the roof, our coach set off along the road to Haverfordwest and thence to

Incidents

Carmarthen. It was already savagely hot, and I was exhausted and distressed because of all the play-acting that had been required of me over the previous week. The roads were dusty and full of pot-holes. I was also suffering from the morning sickness, and Father had to stop the horses several times so that I could be sick at the roadside. To make matters worse, he insisted, every time we passed through a town or village, that the blinds should be drawn in case any of his acquaintances should see who was within the coach. When we reached the village near Carmarthen where Morys had his living, I felt weak and dirty, but my dear brother was kindness itself, and I was able to wash and lie on his bed for an hour or so.

David and his grandparents soon arrived, having borrowed a coach and four from some kindly neighbours. He came up to the bedroom and we spent a little time together. I had feared that his love for me might be somehow diminished as a result of all that had happened, but he held me in his arms and told me that he was more than ever resolved in his love for me, now that his child was in my womb. We ate a simple supper together, during which Morys talked about the marriage vows and the meaning of love. Even though he is my brother, he probably felt it his duty to say certain appropriate things, but he must have known I was in too much of a daze to listen to anything. A man came and we had to swear some sort of oath and sign our names on a document. Then, when it was dark, we went down the road to a little bellcote church where Morys performed the marriage ceremony for David and myself, with my parents and Catrin on one side and with Grandpa Isaac and Grandma Jane on the other. We signed our names again, this time in a big book. There were no hymns, sermons, celebrations, gifts or feasts, but there were tears and warm and loving embraces. Then, exhausted, we all returned to the vicarage. Somehow, he found space for all of us to sleep, and in the heavy warmth of the summer's night we slept until the dawn.

Next morning, with the sky still cloudless and the heat-wave set to continue, we all said our farewells. The Howell coach set out along the road towards my old home at Brawdy. I sat in the borrowed Morgan coach, miserable and apprehensive even though David was by my side. He and Grandma Jane tried to cheer me up as we headed north on the road to Newcastle Emlyn, Newport and Plas Ingli, but I felt like a small frightened child anticipating some dreadful punishment.

Incidents

22nd September 1796

Grandpa Isaac has had a very lucky escape. Around mid-day, as he always does on a Friday, he set about the business of going into Newport to see various merchants and to enjoy a pint or two of ale with his friends. He fetched his favourite little pony from the paddock and led it into the yard. He tethered it next to the coach-house door, and then went inside to get the trap lined up, planning to harness the pony between the shafts.

Just as he was straining to move the trap into position a heavy oak rafter came crashing down, missing his head by inches. He was struck on the shoulder and fell to the ground, pinned underneath the rafter. He says that he almost lost consciousness, but after a few minutes he was able to clear his head and shout for help. Luckily Moses was in the garden, not far away, and he heard Grandpa's shouting. He rushed into the coach-house, saw what had happened, and was able to lift the beam just enough to take the weight off Grandpa. Then the two of them continued to yell at the tops of their voices. Hettie and Mrs Owen were in the dairy, and when they heard the commotion they rushed out into the yard. "Over here! In the coach-house!" yelled Moses, and they were soon on hand to haul Grandpa clear. Just in time, it appears, for a moment later Moses collapsed too, from the strain of holding up the beam.

Soon we were all milling around, and the two of them were carried to the kitchen. Moses was given a stiff drink of brandy and recovered quickly, and to his credit he was far more concerned about Grandpa Isaac than he was about himself. Mrs Owen thought that Grandpa had broken his shoulder, and so Billy was dispatched to Newport to fetch Havard Medical. The good doctor arrived at last, examined Grandpa, and pronounced that the shoulder was out of joint but not broken. He did some sort of manipulation to put the bones back in place again, causing Grandpa to yell and curse mightily. Grandma Jane was very embarrassed about the cursing in polite company, but greatly relieved when Doctor Havard said "Don't you worry, Mrs Morgan *bach*. He's only a youngster. His shoulder will swell up and get very bruised, and he will have a lot of pain for a couple of weeks. But he will have no ill effects, and he will be fine again by Hallowe'en. Give him some more brandy and put him to bed."

Incidents

So Grandpa is now tucked up nice and cosy, with ministering angels hovering around his bed. Moses is the hero of the hour, and is greatly enjoying it. Billy and David are getting the blame for the accident, for it was they who put a dozen heavy oak beams up in the roof of the coach-house to dry, intending them to be used as rafters for the new cow-shed on which they have started work. They pulled them up with the aid of a block and tackle, about a week ago, and they swear that all of them were resting securely on the cross-beams fixed to something called a wall-plate. At any rate, one of them must have been balanced very precariously, and it was Grandpa's ill luck to have been beneath it when it fell.

As I write, David, Moses and Billy are down in the coach-house again, pulling the fallen rafter back up into position and checking that all of the others are quite secure. I am still not sure what to make of Moses, but we should all be grateful that he has a good ear and a strong back, and has the knack of being in the right place at the right time.

ΩΩΩΩΩΩΩΩΩΩΩΩ

24th September 1796

Today it is the Sabbath, and a warm and mellow Sabbath at that, without a breath of wind and without a cloud in the sky. It is evening. With the sun still riding high and the skylarks singing as if it is still spring, the world seems unsure of which season it is in. But it is late summer, and the harvest is almost finished, and the quietness settled upon the landscape is like a holy benediction.

I feel strong, and the morning sickness is now much reduced, and this morning Grandma and David decided that it was time to introduce me to the parishioners who attend Cilgwyn Church. I did not object, for I wish to know them better too. And I thought it quite a pleasing idea to make an impression on our neighbours. I think I have a nice figure, and I still do not look as if I am with child. But my bosom is larger than it was, and people seem to like the look of me. Am I getting vain, now that I am Mistress of Plas Ingli?

So off we went in the morning sunshine, all dressed up in our Sabbath

Incidents

finery, in the light carriage. We left Grandpa behind, for he is still in pain and confined to the house after his accident. As we went down to Trefelin, across the ford and past the mill, people shouted their greetings and put the three of us in a good mood. The church is not in a good state of repair, and there is talk that it will need to be rebuilt if the money can be found from some rich benefactor. We put a posy of late summer flowers in the family tomb, and then went inside and sat through the service with good grace. It was not very entertaining, but I was aware that all eyes were focussed upon me rather than upon the Rector in the pulpit, so I did my best to look pious and to close my eyes in all the right places. The congregation was small and mostly made up of elderly people, but when we spoke to them afterwards they were very kind and welcoming. The squire and his family from Gelli Fawr were there, and also some of the other ancient well-bred families from Cwm Gwaun and Cilgwyn, all ensconced in their special seats. Some of the tenant farmers and labourers sat on benches at the back of the church. No doubt I will get to know all of them -- rich and poor -- as time goes on.

This afternoon, with the sun high and hot, everybody else at Plas Ingli wanted to sit and snooze under the trees in the orchard. But I felt so full of energy that I told them to watch out for falling apples and took my leave of them. I put on an old dress and some strong boots, dispensed with my bonnet, and walked up onto Carningli. I spent three wonderful hours all on my own scrambling among the blue rocks. Grandpa Isaac told me shortly after I arrived at the Plas that some very ancient tribes of Druids have lived on the mountain in the past, and that the rocky slopes are covered with fortifications, old fields and paddocks and places where they had their huts. He also told me that they kept away their enemies by rolling boulders down on them from the summit of the mountain. As I climbed higher and higher, I became in my own mind a learned antiquarian, and I found many of the things Grandpa had told me about, as fresh as if the primitive people had moved out only yesterday. I could hear the war-cries of the attackers, and the sounds of arrows and spears flying past, and the rumbles of boulders crashing down, and the screams of warriors close to death.

Then I got to the summit, and discovered to my amazement that it is not at all a fierce place but a place of great calm. The old raven and his mate were wheeling about on the rising currents of warm air. Here, high

53

above the rest of the landscape, I could see the whole of my little world basking in the sun, fast asleep. Grandpa has already taught me something of the local geography. To the north, Newport and the estuary and the quiet waters of Newport Bay between the headlands of Dinas and Morfa. To the east the Nevern Valley and the rich farmlands and open fields stretching away towards Eglwyswrw. To the south, the Plas, close enough for me to see David and his grandparents asleep in the orchard, and further away the dusty green woodlands of Cilgwyn and Cwm Gwaun. Further away still, the purple hill summits of Mynydd Presely. And to the west the treeless mountain ridge, glowing with purple heather and golden furze, stretching towards Fishguard.

Far away, maybe twenty miles towards the horizon, I could see the little hills of Carnllidi and Penbiri near St David's, and this gave me a lump in my throat, for I was reminded of picnics and other family expeditions to their summits with my family over ten years ago, when I was a small girl. Then my nostalgia was swept away in wonderment when I realized that I could see, far across the sea and shimmering in the September haze, distant mountain ranges to the west and the north. How excited I was to see these distant peaks! I felt like Captain Cook gazing at the snow-capped mountain summits of some new continent.

At last I shook myself out of my reverie and started to explore further among the craggy rocks of the mountain summit, which were smooth and warm in the sun and crusted with strange brittle plants coloured green and yellow and black and orange. I was still greatly taken with the calm and almost sacred feel of the place, and I decided that this mountain built of colonnades and crags of blue rock would be my church. And then I remembered David telling me once -- maybe on the first occasion that we met -- that the mountain close to the Plas was the place used by St Brynach to commune with the angels. He said that Carningli actually means "mount of angels", and that in the old days the scholars used to call the mountain Mons Angelorum. I have never seen an angel myself, and suspect that they may not even exist, but if they do exist this would certainly be a fine place to commune with them. David said that the old saint, who had his little church and band of disciples just down in the valley at Nevern, used to come up here to escape from the cares of the world and to fast and pray to God. I wondered to myself, in recalling all of this, whether tough old St Brynach ever had a little shelter or cave near the summit where he would shelter from the winter storms, and being suddenly fired with enthusiasm I set out upon a search.

For maybe an hour I explored every little nook and cranny on the west, north, and east faces of the mountain, scrambling among great banks of broken stone, boulders as big as houses, and crags of the hard blue mountain rock. Then I started to explore on the south side, where there are steep rock cliffs and huge banks of broken stone tumbling down hundreds of feet to the top fields belonging to the Plas.

Suddenly I found the cave. It was flanked by two pinnacles of rock close to a little wind-stunted rowan tree, and maybe two hundred yards from Brynach's Spring, which provides us with our piped water supply. Its entrance was blocked by two huge boulders that must have come crashing down from the summit during some horrid cataclysm, and to find it I had to squeeze through a very narrow slit hung with clumps of moss and damp grass. And then I was inside. It was cool and dark, but not too dark to see, for light was finding its way in through cracks in the rock and round the edges of the guardian boulders. Its sides were about six feet apart, and it extended about thirty feet into the mountain. It had a gravelly floor, but I plucked handfuls of moss from outside the entrance and made a cosy little bed against one smooth wall, and I sat there in the cool silence for I know not how long.

I was certain that this was Brynach's cave. Nobody but I knew about it, and I determined that I would share my secret with no-one -- not even David. This would be my secret place on my private mountain, to which I could retreat when I needed peace. Inside I felt that I could feel the pulse of the mountain in the living rock, and curled up on my bed of moss I felt as if I was in the comfortable darkness of a womb. The small baby in my own womb, at first the object of my fear and loathing, quietly became the object of a wonderful love. I began at last to feel like a mother.

ΩΩΩΩΩΩΩΩΩΩ

Editor's Note: There are no diary entries for the period 25th September to 24th November 1796.

5. Acceptance

25th November 1796

I have lost my baby. I have had to endure two months of purgatory, weeping until there were no more tears to flow upon my cheeks, my mind and my spirit trapped inside a black prison with no windows, no door, no light, and no escape.

At last I think a little brightness is beginning to filter in, and I feel almost ready to look outside. Today I feel quite calm. The great love I have been shown by David and his grandparents is surely having some healing effect, and I must be brave enough to admit that the grief I have suffered has also been felt by them. David has surely suffered most since he has lost his baby too, but in giving me strength he has not dared to show his own deepest feelings. For his sake, and my own, I must try to pull myself out of this dark place and back into the light. It is not easy, now that the winter darkness is upon us; but today there is a weak and watery sun low over Cwm Gwaun, warming my face as I look out through the window, and this gives me some comfort. Until now, I have not been able to face writing anything about the event in my private little book, but the wizard says that I should try since it will surely help me to rid my mind of a multitude of phantoms and demons.

It happened on the day after I climbed the mountain and found Brynach's cave. I woke early and spoke long with David about baby matters before we rose for breakfast. It was a calm misty morning with the sun burning its golden way through the haze over Carnedd Meibion Owen. Everybody but me had urgent tasks to perform. David, Grandpa and Moses decided to pick in as much of the apple crop as possible before the weather broke, and set off for the orchard with their wicker baskets. Billy went down to Gelli to inspect a young bull which Caradoc Williams wanted us to buy. Hettie walked over to Dolrannog Uchaf to help with the milking since Daisy Ifans was sick. Grandma Jane, Bessie and Mrs Owen walked off to the bottom fields, where the two ponies were grazing some weeks ago, to pick the mushrooms before the dew was off the grass. Before she left Grandma said "Just you take it easy today, Martha *bach*, and look

Acceptance

after the house for us. After all that mountaineering yesterday you probably need a bit of a rest." In retrospect, that was code, instead of saying "You are over three months gone now, and must be very careful not to over-exert yourself." But I felt so full of energy, especially since the morning sickness seemed to have passed, that I waved them off and got on with sorting out the world.

I tidied up our bedroom and my little dressing room, swept out the living room and ironed our linen table-cloths. I should have left all of this for Bessie, but I wanted something to do. Then I noticed that there were no logs piled up in the *simne fawr* in the kitchen, and thought I should carry some in from the log-shed. I could not find any wicker log-baskets, and remembered that they were all being used by the apple-pickers and the mushroom-pickers. Undeterred, I went down to the log-shed, made a pile of logs and picked it up, supporting it with my arms below and my chin on top. I walked gingerly towards the back door with my load, but I could not properly see where I was going, and as I entered the kitchen I felt a dagger of pain in my stomach and at the same time stubbed my foot against the edge of a slate floor slab.

After that my memories are very confused and hazy. I remember finding myself pitched forward on the kitchen floor with a pile of logs beneath me, and a terrible fierce pain in my stomach. I remember feeling dizzy, and I may have been sick, and I do not know how long I lay there. Then I became aware that my skirt was soaked in blood, and that there was blood on the floor and on the logs beneath me. I do not think I was fully aware of what had happened, but I remember thinking "I must not let them see the blood! I must not let them see the blood!", and this went round and round in my head as I got to my feet. Somehow I took off my shoes and threw cold water over them from the pail in the scullery. Then I think I made my way upstairs, and although I was doubled up with the unbearable pain I somehow managed to drag off my dress and my petticoats and to wash myself at the washstand.

I have nightmares still of the increasing sense of panic that overtook me as I rushed to put on clean clothes and made my way back down to the kitchen. I plunged my bloody clothes into a bucket of cold water. As if in a dream, with the pain still continuing, I took a stiff besom from the wall and washed the blood off the logs and stacked them at the side of the kitchen fire. Then -- I have but a slight recollection of this -- I must have taken several buckets of cold water from the tank outside the back door and washed down the black slate slabs of the kitchen floor, washing away all traces of the blood down the step and into the gully that runs across the yard. To do this I must have moved some of the benches and chairs that were in the room. In a trance I must then have put away the bucket and the besom before being overcome with waves of nausea.

Grandma told me yesterday, when we talked about the event for the first time, that when she returned with her basketful of mushrooms she found me slumped in a chair with my head resting on the table. She thought at first I was asleep, and seeing the wet kitchen floor she said "*Cariad*, I see you have washed the kitchen floor. That was very kind of you, but in your condition...." And she stopped as I looked up with a face paler than death, and realized at once what had happened.

Then I must have fainted, and as far as the next few days are concerned I have only a few poor recollections: more bleeding, anxious faces round my bed, tears, embraces, drifting in and out of sleep, more terrible pains in my stomach, and a body so drained of energy that I could hardly stand or lift a hand. David and his grandparents sat with me for several days and nights, and they tell me that Bessie and Mrs Owen were always on hand as ministering angels. I am told that Havard Medical came to see me more than once, and said that rest was the only healer. And he was right, for gradually I felt my strength returning.

There came another scene in the melodrama when I plunged into such a whirlpool of melancholy that I thought I should never fight back to the shore. I felt as I had on those early days following my arrival at the Plas, when I knew that the only solution to my misery was to take my own life. I stopped eating for some days, and it was only the endless pleading of my beloved David that brought me back to the conviction that there was perhaps something left for me in life. But how I hated my body! I felt unclean, and unworthy, and ugly, and old as the grey rocks of Tycanol. How could anybody be so stupid as to love me? I felt a deep anger at all of those around me for bringing me to the Plas and even for their concern and endless patience which brought my own inadequacy into sharp relief.

On some days I felt like a child, and I remember that I cried for my mother. They must have sent for her, and I know that she came, and cradled me in her arms as she had when I was very small. And on some days I felt like an old crone, weighed down with the sins of generations and condemned to a life of penance and pain.

And how I hated myself for my own stupidity! If only I had listened to Grandma Jane's quiet warning! If only I had not been so stupid as to try and carry logs, of all things, into the kitchen just at the most dangerous time in my child-bearing! I -- and nobody else -- had been responsible for the death of my own child. I had murdered my own baby. And then I had swept the poor mite into the gully with a bucket of cold water, to be mixed with cow shit and filth from the yard. How could I have done this? How could I? How could I? Would God ever forgive me? Would David ever forgive me? Would I ever forgive myself? Was the death of my child some dreadful punishment from God for the sin that David and I had committed out of wedlock? Why should the poor innocent child have been punished more than I, when it was I that had sinned? On and on it went in my head -- this endless nightmare cycle of pain and guilt and fear and recrimination. And on it goes, even now.......

I am sorry, but I cannot continue.

ΩΩΩΩΩΩΩΩΩΩΩ

30th November 1796

Gradually, I am coming out of my melancholic state of mind. The calm bright weather continues, and I find that the sun helps my mood. There is no wind, and the sky is clear, and the night frosts are bringing a sparkling freshness to the air. I even find a strange beauty in the white and russet and blue of the mountain, and I am intrigued to find that the images of dead bracken and cold rock do not now distress me. Although I could not finish my entry of some days ago, I think that the process of writing has helped me, as the wizard said it would. He is a very wise man, and I shall stop calling him a wizard, since wizards are involved with magic and mischief and I am sure he is involved in neither. He is kind, and caring, and knows far more about the healing of mind and body than most of the locals appreciate. He has the true calling of a doctor, and deserves that title far more than the untrained quacks who charge large sums of money for the disservices that they do to innocent sick folk all over Pembrokeshire.

I omitted to record on the foregoing pages that Dr Harries called at the house on the day after I lost my baby. I have hardly any recollection of his visit myself, but according to David he knocked on the front door in an agitated and distressed state, having had a powerful premonition, at the precise time of my fall, that something terrible had happened at the Plas. He knew that it involved me and my baby. According to David, he came up to my room with tears in his eyes and said to me "My dear Martha, your time has not come. You have much work still to do." And then he put both hands, one on top of the other, on my forehead, and kept them there, perfectly still, for several minutes. David, and Mrs Owen, who was in the bedroom at the time, both said that they could see the energy draining out of him. His hands trembled, and the colour faded from his cheeks.

Then, when David thought he was going to collapse, he took his hands away and bent and kissed me on the forehead. He said to David in a shaky voice "I have given all the healing that is in me. She will recover, but it will take time." Then he gave David a bottle of some herbal mixture, and told him that he must give me a spoonful of this each day until it was all gone. David promised to do this, and asked the doctor if he would pray for me. Apparently he said "Indeed I will, but not in the way that you pray, and not to your God. In the quietness of my own place of worship I will send all the healing that is within me to send." And then he went unsteadily down the stairs, took his leave, and rode back over the mountain towards Dinas on his white pony.

ΩΩΩΩΩΩΩΩΩΩ

2nd December 1796

I have felt strong enough and confident enough over the last few days to go out for several walks around the estate. I have also studied some music and done a little practice on my harp. I am not yet sufficiently recovered to climb the mountain, but David says I must be patient. Yesterday, with not much to do on the farming front apart from checking on the sheep and the

Acceptance

rams as they prematurely demonstrate the joys of spring in the frosty winter fields, David took me in the pony trap to see Dr Harries. Both of us needed to thank him for his concern and his assistance in the healing process. We had to go round the long way, since there is no proper road along the mountain ridge, but as we trotted through Newport I was greatly touched by the cheerful greetings of the townsfolk, and by their enquiries after my health, and by their good wishes for my early recovery. I suppose they simply know that I have been ill, for no word about the loss of my baby will have passed the lips of Doctor Havard, or Bessie, or Mrs Owen. They are all good friends of the family, and models of discretion.

When we arrived at the front door of the little cottage at Werndew, Joseph Harries was standing there to greet us, for he had heard the pony and trap coming up the track. He opened his arms wide, and gave us both a heartfelt embrace. I thought this was wonderful, but David was slightly taken aback, since not a lot of embracing goes on in the circles within which we are accustomed to move. "My dear friends!" he exclaimed. "How good to see you! Come in! Come in!"

I had not been inside his cottage before, and I was instantly captivated by it. There was a peat fire in the big open fireplace, and the warm air smelt of peat smoke, herbs and spices. It was obviously a place lived in by a bachelor with no servants, for there were piles of books everywhere, unwashed dishes on the table, clothes hanging from hooks along the walls, boots in the middle of the floor, bunches of dried herbs tied to the beams, and bottles and pots of strange liquids and ointments everywhere. It looked as if a winter storm had swept in through the front door and out through the back. Before I could stop myself I said "Doctor, it looks to me as if you need a wife!" and I discovered that the three of us were laughing together. It was the first time I had laughed since the day of my fall. The Doctor said "All in good time, my friend. But more importantly, for the moment, I observe that you are a great deal better."

David and I sat down while the doctor prepared a drink of hot punch for us, and then the three of us talked and talked as if we had known each other for years. I poured out my heart to him about my continuing feelings of guilt and unworthiness. I felt calm enough to speak without getting distressed, and this pleased me. The doctor listened intently but said little. Then David -- who does not normally find it easy to talk about his emotions -- described the course of my illness over the past two months, and his own distress. I was surprised to learn that he was far more aware than I of the tunnels of light and darkness through which I had passed. He also put into beautiful words his own torment about the loss of the baby -- his baby -- and his feelings of inadequacy in trying and failing over and again to pull me out of my melancholia. And as he spoke I realized for the first time that he also felt guilt and a host of other emotions, and had also picked up on the prevailing wisdom that our tragedy, like all tragedies, was a sort of divine revenge for sins committed.

At last the doctor said "My dear young people, you have suffered a great deal. But you have been learning the art of survival, albeit at a much more tender age than you or I would have liked. You will both be stronger and braver because of what has happened to you." And then he turned to me, and took my hand, and said "Martha, waves of melancholia have swept over you in the last three months, but they have failed to sweep you away. Do not forget that there have been good times as well as bad."

"I know, I know," I replied, tuning in to the images in his mind. "As I look back over these past weeks, I feel as if I have been caught up in the turbulent waters off Dinas Head, where two streams of the ocean meet and where there are great waves even when the weather is calm. Day after day, even with David at my side, I have been wide awake, but with my head bursting with nightmarish dreams."

"Now it is over," said the doctor. "From today you are out of the turmoil and into the haven. You two fine young people now need to make a new life for yourselves. I want to say several things to you. First of all, Martha, your baby did not die because of your fall. It was dead already, because of some problem within your body beyond our knowing." When I heard this my eyes must have opened wide in astonishment, and I must admit, for the first time in my life, to being quite lost for words. "I have helped many other young women who have lost their babies," he continued, "and the loss is seldom if ever to be laid at the door of the mother. So you must feel no guilt on that score. You would have lost the baby even if you had not carried logs into the kitchen, and even if you had not fallen."

The doctor was still not finished with his little speech. "Never, never accept that what has happened is a punishment," he said. "You have committed no sin, unless it is a sin to love and be loved. Maybe you have been innocent and foolish, but that is the way of youth. We have all done foolish things, and we must learn from them. Take counsel from each other before you ever consider taking counsel from anybody else. Trust each other always. Love the baby that you have lost, and grieve for your loss, but go on to make a new family, for that is your destiny. Your love for your children yet to be born will be the stronger and the surer for what has happened. And remember this -- you live in a cold and artificial world where etiquette and wealth count for more than a good head and a pure heart. In a strange and cruel way, fate has decreed that you will bear no child within a year of your marriage. Wagging tongues will be silenced, and doors will open for you that might otherwise have closed. Your contacts with your friends and family no longer need to be in secret; you can visit them, and they can visit you, in the full light of day. They will give you strength and confidence. You are Master and Mistress of Plas Ingli, young enough and strong enough to rebuild your estate and make it as successful as it was in the days of Grandpa Isaac's father and grandfather. You will never be very rich, but that does not matter. People will crave your friendship and your patronage, and you will both have it in your power to do much for those -- and there are many -- who are worse off than yourselves. Now go and get on with your lives."

And with that he smiled and showed us to the door, and we drove home with the wheels of our trap crunching through the early evening ice on the puddles of the Werndew track.

ΩΩΩΩΩΩΩΩΩΩΩ

6. Learning

5th December 1796

Now that I am up and about again, and have been able to share in mealtimes in the kitchen in the convivial company of family and servants, I am reminded of David's attempt, some months back, to promote the idea of Moses taking on greater responsibility in the affairs of the estate.

This has come into my mind because Moses has been extremely attentive of late, fixing his eyes upon me on a number of occasions, making a great show of opening doors for me, and frequently asking after my health. More than once has reminded me, with some subtlety, of his heroism in rescuing Grandpa Isaac from the fallen rafter in the coach-house. When I am within earshot he frequently asks the old man how his shoulder is getting on. Last Wednesday he went to great pains to show me the garden produce he is storing over the winter, and took pride in explaining how some new potato variety he has harvested will keep in perfect condition until next Easter. David has been preoccupied with work for the last fortnight, and may not have noticed any of this, but Bessie and Mrs Owen certainly have.

This morning, when Bessie was helping me with my hair, she said, quite out of the blue "Well now, thinking of Moses, there's kind and gentlemanly he is these days. He has taken quite a liking to you, Mistress *bach*, that's for sure."

I must have blushed, and Bessie must have noticed, for she could see my face in the mirror, but she continued to plait my hair as she waited for my response. "I am not sure that he likes me any more than anybody else," I said. "But it is always a pleasant thing to have a gentleman -- even if he is a servant -- asking after one's health and doing little things to help one on the road to recovery."

I expected Bessie to reply, but she did not, and after a long silence I blurted out "Grandpa and Grandma, and my husband, are so busy these days that they hardly have any time for me. David spends nearly all his time out on the estate and on the building work, and seems hardly to notice me. Surely I cannot object to just a little chivalrous attention in the circumstances."

"Mistress Martha!" exploded Bessie, with fire flashing in her eyes. "You must not speak of your family in such a way. You have been very ill, and you may not have been fully aware of the days and nights that they have spent at your bedside, praying for you, consoling you, and giving you whatever support it was in their power to give. They love you more than anything in the world, and don't you forget it."

I must have looked like a child caught in the act of stealing sweetmeats from the pantry, but Bessie would not let me be. "In the month of October, when we doubted whether you would come back to us, poor Master David was almost beside himself, and went for over a week without sleeping or eating. Did you not notice how thin and haggard he became? We thought we might lose the two of you. Grandma Jane had to read the Riot Act to him, and he had to be more or less force-fed by Mrs Owen before he started to come to his senses. Didn't you know any of this?"

"No, I am afraid not," I replied sheepishly. "But if they love me so much, why can they not give me a little more attention, as Moses does?"

"Mistress, do you want all of their attention, all of the time?"

"Well, I suppose that might be a little selfish of me."

"Indeed it would," said Bessie. "You must remember that the estate is still under-staffed, and while you have been ill all of us -- and especially Master David and his grandparents -- have been neglecting our farming and domestic duties. The Master now judges that you are well enough to spend some time in your own company, as you used to do, while he catches up with all the things he should have done over the last two months. And Moses, who could teach a dog fox a thing or two, simply sees a little opportunity and seeks to make the most of it."

I was shocked at this suggestion, and protested "Bessie, I cannot believe that. What on earth could Moses have to gain from flattering me or doing me little favours?"

"Mistress, I am only a little older than you, but maybe I have seen a little more of the world. I cannot say what his purpose might be. Moses might be intent upon getting into your head, or into your heart, or into your bed."

"Bessie, you cannot mean what you say!"

"Indeed I do, Mistress Martha. He was in my bed the other night. Luckily I was not there at the time, and when I went to bed and found him

Learning

between the sheets I pretty quickly cooled him down and sent him packing with a gallon of cold water over his head."

This removed my embarrassment at a stroke. I could restrain myself no longer, and collapsed into a fit of giggles, and soon the pair of us were in hysterics. After some minutes we managed to calm each other down, and I was able to continue our conversation. "Was that what all the pandemonium was about the other evening?" I asked, with tears in my eyes. "I heard it, and thought you had simply slipped while carrying a bowl of water into your room."

"That was it," said Bessie at last, having recovered the power of speech. Then she breathed hard, regained her composure, and said to me very quietly, face to face "Mistress Martha, please accept that I am gravely concerned. Moses Lloyd may simply be seeking, for some reason, to win your approval. Even if he does not get it, he may succeed in driving a wedge between you and David. Jealousy is a terrible emotion, and men can behave like idiots in matters of the heart."

Suddenly the image of a moorish nobleman leaped into my mind, and I recalled several weeks spent early in the year studying, with my tutor in Brawdy, the text of Master Shakespeare's "Othello". I felt as if a shaft of cold steel had been thrust into my heart, and the colour must have drained from my face, for Bessie said "Mistress, are you all right?" I thought I was going to faint, but I gripped her hand and held it hard for a while, and eventually recovered. Bessie, like the blessed friend that she is, knew that there was some turmoil in my breast, and said nothing more.

At last I said "Thank you for your concern, Bessie, and for your awareness of the ways of the heart. Some day I will explain to you the image which has come into my mind and which has so frightened me. But now I feel much better, and I should like to be alone. I will finish putting my hair up by myself." I gave her a smile. She smiled back, her eyes still enquiring as to my state of mind, curtseyed, and left the room.

On recalling our conversation, I am intrigued that Bessie should have spoken to me as a mistress might address a servant, and that she should then curtsey on leaving the room. More seriously, I am now resolved to place this Moses business before David, and to kill off, once and for all, any hopes which he may have of giving his sly friend greater involvement in the running of the estate.

Learning

7th December 1796

This morning I woke early, long before dawn, and lit the candles on the washstand near the bedroom window. David is a heavy sleeper, but I woke him too, and told him that I wished to share with him a number of matters concerning Moses Lloyd. He was more asleep than awake at first, but as I opened my heart to him he began to appreciate my fears. I told him everything -- the incident in the lane to Dolrannog, the lie about the collapsed stone wall, the little flirtations and attempts to win my approval, and the episode in Bessie's bedroom. I even admitted to a certain pleasure in Moses' company and in his witty conversation, in the hope of setting off some danger signals in David's mind.

My husband Othello has apparently been blissfully unaware of the subtleties of Iago's behaviour towards me. He finds it difficult to think ill of any man when he is wide awake, and even more difficult when he is half asleep, but I persisted with my entreaties, and went so far as to say that I believed Moses to be dangerous as well as devious. I said that I would allow nothing -- not even the friendship between one man and another -- to come between us, and I reminded him that every woman in the house was gravely concerned about his friendship with Moses. *"Cariad,"* I said, "Moses will manipulate you and insinuate his way into this estate. He knows that you trust him and value his friendship, and maybe he thinks that you actually need his advice. The danger is there for all to see. Don't you see it yourself?"

David thought for a long time. Then he said "I think you may be right, Martha. When I see everything in the cold light of morning I see that he has been pressing me a little too hard for changes in the manner of running the estate. I have refused to discuss such things with him since I made my promise to you some months ago, but his behaviour does suggest that he holds you responsible for my reticence. Perhaps he is in love with you. Perhaps he just craves friendship from any quarter, having had his share of rejection in life. But it would be prudent to assume, in the present circumstances, that he is intent upon winning your favour in pursuit of some larger objective."

"I wish I knew what that objective was," I said. "Moses Lloyd is too intelligent by half. I remember my mother saying once that intelligence is a dangerous thing in a servant. But intelligent people are not always prudent, and my instinct tells me that our beloved manservant will, if left to his own resources, bring trouble down upon his own head."

Just then Bessie knocked on the bedroom door and announced that the hot water was ready for our morning ablutions. We had to cut short our conversation, but by the time we went down to breakfast we had agreed on a common response to any attempts at familiarity by Moses Lloyd. I fear that in refusing to give Moses my approval I will make him angry and resentful. But I declare that I am not at all frightened of him. And with David, and Bessie, and the other servants to strengthen my resolve, I think I can cope.

ΩΩΩΩΩΩΩΩΩ

10th December 1796

My recovery continues. I have been strong enough of late to get out and about on the estate, having been too sick or too distressed to show myself in public in the months following my arrival. Now David and Grandpa Isaac have made a point of introducing me to the neighbours, and they seem for the most part to be sweet and kind people. It has been good to meet them, but as a consequence of my meetings I feel confusion and concern in my head and my heart. Out there, beneath the leaky thatched roofs of a thousand cottages and hovels, there is more hunger, poverty, and sickness than I could ever have imagined, and I know not how much these poor people can bear. I will write more of this, but not now since I have little time.

Of our three tenant farmers, I like Caradoc Williams Gelli the best. He is a huge man, rough and tough as a Cwm Gwaun oak tree, who earns the occasional golden guinea as a pugilist and who patronizes the Rising Sun more than his wife Bethan would like -- but she keeps a strict house, and their five children are always tidy and well behaved. Their oldest daughter Sian is plump and bubbly as the froth in a milking pail, and almost the same age as I, and although gentry and tenants are not supposed to mix I am sure we will become good friends. The two Dolrannog farms, a little way up the track from the Plas, are both farmed by elderly people. Will and Daisy Ifans at Dolrannog Uchaf are about as exciting as hermit crabs, coming out by day to work the land and look after their animals, but hardly ever (so far as I can see) setting foot beyond the hearth between the hours of dusk and dawn. They are people of few words, and when we called to see them we could hardly get a look in the eye, let alone a word out of them; but Grandpa says they are good neighbours who worked until they dropped during the fire and who gave great assistance during the rebuilding work.

George Griffiths Dolrannog Isaf must be eighty if he's a day, and his wife Mair must be almost as old, but they are as sprightly as Easter lambs. They keep their farm in good order, and try to pay their rent on time. In this, they are probably helped by their son Gethin, who also lives in the farmhouse with his wife Liza and three grown-up children. He seems, as my father used to say, to have "good contacts". He obtains various precious goods (including Portuguese wine, Dutch tobacco and best English silver cutlery) from mysterious sources, some of them in the south of the county. He sells these items to friends and neighbours and at Fishguard market, no doubt at a goodly profit. David says that he has occasionally attracted the attention of the constables and the excise men, but that he is far too smart for them.

I cannot understand how these tenant families manage to survive from one summer to the next. None of them has more than fifty acres off which to make a meagre living and pay the rent. The rents are not high by Pembrokeshire standards, averaging only about £70 per year, but in addition they each have to deliver to us six hens and thirty eggs at Christmas, thirty eggs at Shrovetide, and a goose at the feast of All Saints. Then they each have to cut turf for one day, cart turf for another day, and cart lime for two days for the Plas. I cannot see that it is possible for a family to buy food and clothing for less than £30 per year, so the poor farmers have to find at least £100 a year just in order to survive. But survive they do, even with the cost of living going up so much that there have been corn riots in Haverfordwest and Cardigan. Sometimes the wives and daughters earn money from spinning and knitting, or from taking labouring jobs on other estates. Caradoc Williams says he sometimes works in the sea quarries near Parrog to earn extra cash whenever things are quiet on the farm.

Learning

Grandpa tells me that our tenants are quite well looked after, for although they have to repair gates and fences, keep the farm buildings in a sound state, and practice good husbandry, they do not have to maintain their farm tracks, and they get hospitality and extra paid work from the estate. They are helping just now on our building projects. Much of the food that they contribute is fed back to them at feasting times! Grandpa also says that the rents have not gone up for many years, and that he and David's father were always very flexible when it came to rent collecting, often accepting labour or animals instead of cash. Our estate is unusual in that we collect the rents ourselves rather than using the services of a local lawyer or agent. David thinks we should put up the rents and be harder in collecting them in view of the poor finances of the estate itself; but everybody knows that there is a lot of resentment against the landowners just now, and my instinct tells me that we must be very careful.

Bessie is calling me for Sunday supper, and I must put down my pen. I will continue when I can.

ΩΩΩΩΩΩΩΩΩ

14th December 1796

For the last week I have been driven by my conscience to write about the conditions of the poor. From what I hear, the peasants are even worse off than the tenants of whom I have already written. There seem to be a great number of them on the estate, with little clom cottages at Yet-y-rhos, Blaenwaun, Brynaeron and Plain Dealings, and more down in the woods of Pentre Ifan, Cilgwyn and Cwm Gwaun. Most of the men work as labourers on our estate or on one of the others, earning about fourpence a day. They are supposed to pay rent out of this, but I thank God that the Morgan family has no great reputation for collecting rent from the cottagers. Children are given work on stone picking, bird scaring and gathering in the harvest. The poor families get barley bread, buttermilk and potatoes from the estate, and they also get beer and extra food at sowing time and harvest time. They are allowed to glean the cornfields after the harvest. If there is a good herring catch, they get a barrel of salted herrings each. If there is an

Learning

illness in one of the cottagers' families, the estate usually pays the fees charged by Havard Medical or one of the travelling doctors. David says our estate workers are very well off, for they are paid an annual wage, whereas many of the workers on other estates are paid by the month or season, leaving them close to starvation with no money coming in through the winter part of the year.

Even if we treat our workers well by normal standards, I was horrified when David took me down to meet Huws Plain Dealings and his family. It was the first time I had been into a poor labourer's home. Their cottage measures no more than twenty feet by ten, with no scullery at the back and with only one door and three small windows. There are no internal walls, but two flimsy partitions that can be moved around. The walls are made of clom and the roof of leaky thatch. There is a miserable peat fire in the hearth but no chimney, and I suppose the smoke simply filters out through the thatch. The floor is made of hard-packed mud, with a few slate slabs laid here and there so as to avoid turning the whole place into a mud-bath. Among the movable furniture are three flimsy chairs, a stool, a tin chest, a settle and a couple of wooden shelves. There are two small cupboard-beds along one wall, but this does not seem to be enough for a family of six, and I suppose the children sleep in shifts, or with the parents, or on the floor. There is absolutely no privacy. The cottage is cold, damp, draughty and smoky, and at this time of year it is dark too, with the only light coming from the dull glow of the fire and from a pair of spluttering rushlights. Outside there is a small cottage garden used for growing potatoes and turnips, a pigsty used for the Christmas porker, and a little patch of land knee-deep in mud and occupied by a bony cow and half a dozen chickens.

When we visited, Tomos Huws was out working, but Myfanwy and the children were very welcoming and offered us a glass of buttermilk which we declined with thanks. We talked a little of the weather, and they kindly enquired after my health. They had some salt herring cooking in a big iron pot on the hearth, but I noticed that there was no bacon or ham hanging in the roof as one might expect at this time of year. I asked Myfanwy about this, and she replied with tears in her eyes that they had raised a fine porker in good time for *Calan Gaeaf,* but had been forced to sell the whole carcass to cover their debts to the merchants in Newport who were threatening to force them into paupery at the Petty Sessions. The poor things, dressed in tattered clothes, covered with grime and coughing and spluttering from assorted ailments, clearly had not a penny's worth of Christmas to look forward to, and I could not for the life of me understand their apparent good cheer under the weight of such cruel fate. David said he would try to do something to help them, and I began to understand the meaning of poverty. So we took our leave. Myfanwy and the children thanked us profusely for our visit, with much servile curtseying and nodding of heads and dropping of eyes. If one had happened upon the scene by chance, one might have thought that they were responding to a visit from the Queen of Sheba, or were thanking us for a delivery of manna from Heaven, and this made me feel very uncomfortable. My face flushed, and I hope our hosts did not notice.

When we were walking back up to the Plas, I could restrain myself no longer. "My goodness, what a terrible situation those poor people are in!" I said. "We, who have so much, must do something for them at once!"

"My dear Martha, I told them that I will try," replied David. "But you must realize that their situation is not unusual. You have led a very protected and privileged life so far, but I must tell you that there are many hundreds of families who are much worse off than the people at Plain Dealings. At least they have a roof over their heads and food in their bellies."

"So are they supposed to feel eternally grateful for those particular small mercies?"

David chose not to answer my question, but pressed on with his explanation. "There are other families living rough in the woods, surviving on poaching and stealing turnips and potatoes from fields belonging to us and the other gentlemen of the area. Some of those who are caught are transported to the penal colonies. Some poor devil poaching in Pengelli Woods a fortnight ago lost a leg in a man-trap and is due -- if he survives -- to appear before the next Quarter Sessions, where he may well be sentenced to be hanged."

"What, hanged for poaching a few rabbits or pheasants?"

"Why yes. We landowners are the ones who suffer from poaching and the loss of crops, and we also serve as Justices at the Sessions."

"Very convenient, if you happen to be a landowner."

"Martha! Your cynicism ill becomes you. Grandpa Isaac is a Justice of the Peace, although he has had neither the time nor the inclination to attend the Sessions since the fire. Maybe I will be asked to join the bench when I am older. I must say I can see why severe penalties are needed to deter paupers and vagrants from law-breaking. The local constables are worse than useless, and hardly anybody gets caught, but an example must be made of those who come before the magistrates if society is not to collapse around us as it has in France."

"David!" I exclaimed in horror. "You sound like some crusty old hanging judge who is too old to see that the world is changing around him. You are only a little older than I, and if you cannot recognize the effects of starvation and poverty when they stare you in the face, God help you! If you had no money in your pocket, and a sick wife and starving children in your home, would you not go out and risk life and limb to save them?"

"Well, maybe I would....."

"I know that I, as a feeble woman, would steal or kill to give them food. Maybe you men have other priorities -- power, privilege, and the rule of law -- above compassion, humility, and duty towards those whom you love."

I was quite surprised to hear myself speaking thus indignantly, for this was the closest I had been to a quarrel with David. I was probably getting red in the face. David was even more surprised than I at this turn of events, and for a moment he looked as if he might respond angrily. But he controlled his anger, took me by the arm and said "Martha, I hear what you say. But we cannot suddenly relieve all the poor people of this area of their poverty, and neither can we afford to sink into a great trough of despond caused by guilt. We did not cause the poverty which we see around us. We cannot interfere in situations controlled by other squires and gentlemen. Don't you see that?"

I acknowledged reluctantly that I could.

"It is in our power as good landlords and generous employers to do something to relieve the ills that exist on our own estate, but we are only just surviving as it is. Should we give away all the food and money that we have? And what would happen then? The creditors who are already banging on our door would force us into bankruptcy, and the estate would pass to a red-fanged wolf like Laugharne Pengelli Fawr or Price Plas Llanychaer. Is that what you want?"

"No, no, dearest David, you know that I want the best for the estate and for our family."

Learning

"These matters are very complicated indeed, and Grandpa Isaac has tried many times to explain them to me," said David. "I don't pretend to understand all the twists and turns of the argument. But it seems to me that we have a destiny to run the estate as good and progressive landlords and to look after those on our land who are poor and ignorant. If we are hard and cruel our tenants will hate us, and theft, insubordination and even riots will be the result. But if we are too generous, the word will get around and we will find a flood of paupers and vagrants moving onto our land and throwing themselves upon our mercy. Besides, Grandpa says we must constantly watch out for the powerful men who run everything in this area."

"Why should our generosity, or lack of it, be of concern to them?"

"Because, *Cariad*, people talk. Poor people talk in the inns and at the markets. Haven't you heard the gossip that Hettie carries up the hill with her from Newport? People of our class talk at the card table, at the races and at their cosy social gatherings. We get on well with most people, but we do have enemies, some of whom pretend to be our friends. There is already some talk in town about the fact that we do not collect rent from our poorest labourers and that we are far too generous with the allowances of food which we give to our servants. When this sort of thing becomes common knowledge, it reflects badly on those who squeeze their tenants dry and who use the law quite mercilessly to silence even the slightest whimpers of distress from their labourers."

"Isn't the law supposed to protect the weak?"

"In theory, yes. In practice, no," said David. "Look at the way that Price of Plas Llanychaer treats his people. He increases rents, evicts tenants, and cuts back on the food he gives to his servants and labourers all the time. He has enclosed a hundred acres of common that his tenants used to depend on for grazing their animals and cutting their peat. He has probably created twenty paupers and has, to the best of my knowledge, caused four local men to be transported to the colonies for minor misdemeanours. Three others have gone to the gallows. Landowners like him fear bankruptcy almost as much as they fear social unrest, and even though they are wolves they are small fleabitten creatures. There are bigger wolves like Philipps of Picton Castle or Campbell of Stackpole waiting in the dark forest, and they will destroy the smaller members of the pack just as soon as they show weakness."

Learning

"Well, maybe we should try to stay out of the forest."

"Impossible. We live in a cruel world populated on one side by arrogant and power-hungry men whose pretensions are as big as their egos, and on the other side by poor men who are trapped by circumstance and who are on the edge of rebellion. Grandpa Isaac sees and hears many things that are hidden from us, and he says that we must employ great caution in our dealings with the rich and the poor, at least until the estate is free of debt."

"Oh dear," I sighed. "This is all so complicated. Of course I see the sense in what you say. I just hope that as the years go by you and I will be able to do something, here on these stony acres beneath the mountain, to improve the lot of those we have in our care."

So we arrived home as the black clouds of dusk were rolling in from the west, thoughtful and a little wiser, but far from enlightened.

ΩΩΩΩΩΩΩΩΩΩ

18th December 1796

David has said nothing to me, but yesterday I noticed Mrs Owen slipping off down the track towards Cilgwyn, trying for all she was worth to become invisible. This was not easy for her, since she is built like a galleon under full sail and since she had a large bundle clasped to her ample bosom. She returned half an hour later carrying only her bosom. I also noticed that two plucked and dressed fat hens have disappeared from the pantry, together with four loaves of wheat bread, a flagon of fresh milk, and a quantity of butter and cheese. I have not pressed the good woman on the reason for her expedition, but I am sure that she has been on a mission of mercy to Myfanwy Huws Plain Dealings. I also have no doubt that her visit was made on David's instructions. What a good man I have for a husband! However hard his words may be, he has a heart of purest gold, and with every day that passes my love for him broadens and deepens.

I must report that since David and I made our agreement some ten days ago to resist the blandishments of Moses Lloyd, the atmosphere

75

surrounding our manservant has become distinctly chilly. David and he talk every day, but there is a new air of formality in their relationship, and I am sure that this is down to David's refusal to stray either into the domain of small talk or into matters of estate strategy. I have also made a point of avoiding contact with Moses, and this has been made easier by the rising tempo of Christmas preparations.

Last Friday there was a sudden change in Moses' mood, and I realized, with a mixture of relief and apprehension, that he had come to terms with the failure of his programme of insinuation into our family affairs. He now looks at me in a way that I cannot properly describe. I wish I had a little more experience in reading men's eyes. His voice, already surprisingly high for a big man, seems to have gone up a note or two, maybe because of a tension in his throat. Suddenly, he speaks to me with a sneer, as if I have become a non-person, or as if I was in some other place -- "And how is Mistress Morgan today?" or "I trust that Mistress Morgan slept last night," or "I hear that Mistress Morgan plans to go to Newport tomorrow." *Ach y fi!*

As a result of this change of mood, Moses has been transformed, in my mind at least, from an interesting reprobate into an arrogant and somehow pathetic creature. I have now told David that I will never, never allow him into our part of the house, for any reason. I cannot abide the thought of him digging about in the office, or in the library or, for that matter, in any other room. Grandma commented yesterday on Moses' change of mood, and she is clearly worried. Her instinct tells her we should dismiss the wretched fellow sooner rather than later, but Grandpa Isaac is unmoved. He does not say much, but I think he still intends to keep him on out of respect for William's judgment, and does not want to go against that judgment now that William is dead. However, I am now Mistress of Plas Ingli, and I am not bound by sentiment. If I have a fancy to do so, I will simply dismiss Moses Lloyd from our service.

ΩΩΩΩΩΩΩΩΩΩΩ

7. Festivities

28th December 1796

David and Grandpa are talking about sheep, the way men do. I have an evening to myself, and so much to write about.

I begin to feel like one of the locals, having just enjoyed my first Christmas at the Plas. It has been raining and blowing since mid-December; white Christmases are very rare here although the older folks say that Yuletide snow could be guaranteed when they were young. I am not sure what to make of all this singing, feasting, drinking, and praying. It has all been very strange, with religion one moment and merriment the next. But if Jesus was at all human, he must surely have had a sense of humour, even if the Gospels are not exactly packed with jokes. So I do not hold with those Nonconformists who say that all merriment leads to debauchery and fornication. Without investigating too closely what goes on among the servants and labourers in the barn late at night, I would say that most of our Christmas has been innocent and wonderful, helping to bring all of us on the estate closer together.

Some of the things that happen here at the Christmas season are rare or non-existent in the Brawdy and St David's area. For a start, Christmas continues at the Plas for three weeks, with only the most essential tasks going on in the fields and around the farm buildings. This is probably because the weather is so miserable that people have learnt to leave the land alone until the colder weather of January sets in, followed by the lighter evenings of February. In my home parish of Brawdy, on the west coast, the midwinter weather is a little drier, a little warmer and a little brighter, so farm work is still possible around Christmas and the New Year. Then we have the *Plygain*, which has faded away at Brawdy, and *Hen Galan*, which the Bishop of St David's will have nothing to do with, and many other little traditions which I have never observed before, maybe because in my childhood I have not been looking.

Christmas really began for me almost a fortnight before Christmas Day, when the kitchen was transformed into a sort of military base. The men were banished and had to skulk about in the dining room and living room, which they did not enjoy since the kitchen is by far the warmest room in the house. However, they were allowed in for the preparations relating to the cider and the ale, and they were all involved in the butchering of the ox and the cleaning of potatoes and turnips.

As a relative newcomer to all this Christmas business I had to submit to the orders of Mrs Owen and Grandma Jane, and indeed I was much lower down the pecking order than Bessie and Hettie, whose skills in cooking and preparing feasts far exceed my own. But how I loved the warmth, the comradeship, the gossip, the steam, the glorious kitchen smells of spices and fruit and baking bread, the clanking of pots and saucepans, the laughter, and the growing piles of prepared food put away into the cold scullery! Mrs Owen and Grandma are miracle workers, for they know how to make everything from sausages to puddings, from treacle toffee to pickles, from punch to fruit cake, without ever looking at a book or a recipe. As one cooking day followed another, they knew exactly how much of everything would be needed, and would say things like "There will be thirty people eating this one, so we'd better add another pound of suet and another teaspoon of salt." They would rush about from one steaming pot to another, using a well-licked finger for testing purposes and saying things like "This is still too runny. Martha *bach*, put in another half-pound of currants, another pound of breadcrumbs, and another pinch of rosemary, if you please."

It seemed to me that the fortnight in the kitchen was the perfect prelude to Christmas, even though I spent most of the time wearing old clothes and ragged aprons, with my hair tied up in a bun, and with my bare arms plunged into sausage mixtures, bread dough, or hot soapy water. It was a novelty for me but also a therapy, for in the quick banter, belly laughs and fits of giggles around the kitchen table the last traces of the misery that had afflicted me for so much of my time at the Plas were blown away. I learnt much about myself as the days passed, and I also grew to love the good women whose friendship and support I will certainly need over the coming years. We also shared some convivial time with Mistress Williams Gelli, Mistress Ifans Dolrannog Uchaf and Mistress Griffiths Dolrannog Isaf, who turned up at various times bearing plucked chickens and eggs as required by their tenancy agreements.

The fact that everything was ready by breakfast time on Christmas Eve came as a great surprise to me, but the others were perfectly nonchalant about everything, and when the men arrived with the plough the kitchen was spotless and we were all on duty dressed in our Christmas finery. The arrival of the plough was new to me, and it seems to be a tradition peculiar to this area, but it has a beautiful symbolism that appeals to me. Midway through the morning there was a knock on the back door, and it was my duty as mistress of the Plas to open it. Outside stood David, Grandpa Isaac, Moses and Billy, with three or four of the labourers from the estate, carrying a spotlessly clean plough.

"Mistress Martha," said Billy as the chief worker on the estate, "may we beg your indulgence and ask you to look after our plough until such time as we need it again?"

"It will be my pleasure," I replied (having previously been instructed by Grandma Jane). "Please come inside and I will see what I can do." Then, according to tradition, I looked under the kitchen table and found that there was ample storage space available. "Why, I do believe that this space is just perfect! By all means place it here, and I will guard it with my life until the ploughing time arrives."

With due ceremony the men then took off their boots and entered the kitchen with the plough, and placed it beneath the heavy oak table as gently as if they were putting a sleeping baby into its cot. Then everybody burst out into applause and laughter, and there was much back-slapping and embracing to signify that the year's work was over and that the holiday had begun. David and Grandpa fetched out the shiny brass pans of warm ale which had been simmering before the fire, and this was served to all and sundry. But before touching the ale each of the men anointed the plough with a few drops from their mugs, and Grandpa explained that this was to signify that the plough, although now put away, was not forgotten, and that it would in due course be brought out again to turn the green turf of the lower fields. He said that similar ceremonies were going on at the two Dolrannogs, Gelli, Berry Hill and all the other farms of the area at precisely the same time. After a discreet interval, we ladies left the kitchen to the tender mercies of the men, who got on with the two serious matters of consuming Christmas ale and passing on the farming news.

During the afternoon Moses asked David if he could go and spend Christmas and New Year with friends, and David gladly consented to this, since the plough is now under the table and no work is needed in the orchard or garden. In any case, there would be one less mouth to feed, and as far as I was concerned a few days without his dark and surly presence would be good for everybody. I saw him go, wrapped up well and walking none too steadily down the track towards Newport, having consumed a considerable quantity of warm ale. I wondered where he was going, and what mischief he might get up to. When I mentioned to Bessie that Moses would be away for a few days, she sighed, and smiled, and said "Thank God for one small mercy! Fancies himself, that one, and no mistake! Finds it very hard to take no for an answer. I can sleep a bit easier in my bed, and more joy he will have in the taverns of Newport than in the servants rooms of the Plas." And she gave me a big wink.

On Christmas Eve we did not get much sleep, for we had to set off for the *Plygain* service in the parish church at four in the morning. Billy stayed at home, for he is not much interested in matters religious, but the rest of us wrapped up well and set off to walk the two miles into town, carrying our candle lanterns and with spare supplies of candles in the deep pockets of our coats. There was not much of a moon, and the stars were hidden behind a heavy black blanket of cloud, but mercifully there was no wind to affect our candles, and as we walked we could see little lights glittering everywhere down in the cwm and on the hillsides, all moving silently towards the town. The effect was quite magical, and for a moment I felt that I was walking in the heavens, looking down on the Milky Way. David and the others must have been similarly entranced, for we all walked in silence, drinking in the beauty of the moment. Soon we joined the Cilgwyn Road and the happy band of pilgrims heading towards town from Gelli Fawr and Trefach and Tregynon and Cwm Gwaun. The glittering groups and their shadows merged and the silence gave way to greetings and back-slappings, and for the rest of the way to Newport the old roadway glowed and hummed with conversation and good cheer. Every other roadway into town was no doubt similarly transformed as people left behind their poverty and their problems for a little while, to celebrate the birth of their Lord.

As we dropped down Greystones Hill in the company of the Jenkins clan of Brithdir, Penybont and Blaenwaun, we heard the noise and we saw the light. The whole town was in festive mood, and there must have been two thousand people on the streets. The Christmas ale had clearly been flowing freely for some hours, and many of the young people were none too steady on their feet as they wandered about in little processions of their own, singing sacred and profane verses, organizing piggy-back races and other silly contests, and even playing torchlight football. David and I were tempted to join in, but it would not have been seemly for people with our standing in society. Everybody carried a candle-stick or a candle lantern, and Mrs Owen said *"Duw Duw*, there's well Cynog Candle-maker must be doing, what with all these people having *Plygain* candles from him at a ha'penny each! They do say he has a secret recipe to stop them from blowing out, and that he is off to London after *Hen Galan* to make his fortune. I wonder if he would have an old widow woman like me?" And she rolled about with laughter, having had more than a few sips from her gin bottle as we walked down from the Plas.

We wandered round the town, marvelling at the way in which the crowds and the candle-light had transformed the dim streets and dingy buildings into a magical and flickering backdrop suited to some ancient mystery play. We met and chatted to all manner of folk, including both Church people and Nonconformists. This particularly pleased Grandma Jane, and she explained that although there was much animosity between the Baptists, Presbyterians, Methodists and the members of the established Church, this was the one occasion during the year when all came together under one roof and sang in harmony. Soon my head was spinning with the multitude of well-meaning introductions to which I was being subjected. "Good morning, Master and Mistress Williams," Grandpa would say, "and a very merry Christmas to you! Let me introduce our beloved Martha, David's new wife, who has brought great joy to all of us at the Plas." And I would smile sweetly, and Master Williams would bow, and Mistress Williams would curtsey, and we would exchange a few pleasantries, and then Grandpa would spot Master and Mistress Jones Siop Fach, and he would shout "A very good day to you, Master and Mistress Jones ...." And so on and so on.

It was a relief when suddenly, on the dot of five-thirty, a great shout went up from the town youngsters and a crowd of them rushed off to the Rectory waving flaming torches of dripping tar high over their heads. I asked David what was going on, and he said that they had gone to escort the Rector to the Church and to protect him from evil spirits on his hazardous journey. Soon he emerged, and as he walked to the church the sounds of revelry died away and all conversation ceased. The only sounds we could hear were the footsteps of the Rector and his youthful escort on the gravel street and the spluttering and spitting of the torches. Then, as the Rector entered the church, we found ourselves swept along in a silent glowing tide of townsfolk and countryfolk in his wake.

In the moment before David and I passed through the churchyard gate I glanced back along the shadowy street and was greatly surprised when my eyes met those of Moses Lloyd. He was heavily muffled, and he stood with another man at the entrance to a narrow passageway between two cottages. Immediately he realized that I had seen and recognized him he melted into the pitch blackness. Then the moment was past. I am sure that David had not seen him, and I said nothing.

In the midst of the throng, the Plas Ingli contingent shuffled through the porch and into the church. We joined the happy multitude which filled every corner of the building -- nave, pews, aisles, altar steps, side chapels and even the normally dark recesses behind the organ. Others were left outside for lack of space and for fear of fire, since everyone was mindful of the risks involved in carrying five or six hundred candles within a confined space. Darkness was now quite banished from the church, and as I looked about me I could see more candles gleaming on window ledges and in recesses, and a drapery of holly and ivy on the organ and pulpit and even on the altar. I could also see what a sad state the place was in, with holes in the roof, crumbling masonry on the walls, and broken windows; but nobody seemed to mind, and soon all the members of the congregation were concentrating upon the ancient service, eyes wide and mouths agape, sallow angel faces lit by the flickering of their candle flames.

The service was a long one, with an abbreviated Morning Service followed by duets and trios, Bible readings, prayers, solos and choruses. Not a single note of music was played on the organ or any other musical instrument, and although I must admit to falling asleep once or twice during the proceedings, I was fascinated to hear many unusual carols being sung with great gusto and with very peculiar harmonies. Later on, Grandpa told me that these carols were set to traditional metres and tunes, and that while some were very old others had been composed recently by local poets and musicians. There was no sermon, and as the hours passed I found that my thoughts turned time and again not to the mysteries of the nativity but to the dark and foreboding presence of Moses Lloyd outside the church. Why was he lurking in a black passageway while every other able-bodied person in the town was inside the church? I played about with various theories by way of explanation, but felt uneasy with all of them. On the other hand, I knew that an answer would not be long in coming.

The service droned on. But as soon as the Rector spotted the first light of dawn through the eastern window he gave a special Christmas blessing and brought the *Plygain* to an end. The bells started to peal, and we all filed out of the church, with the stumps of our candles still alight, to make our weary ways home. For those of us who lived at the Plas, it was uphill all the way, and we were all exhausted when at last we arrived. We collapsed into our beds, hoping to catch just a couple of hours of sleep before the business of Christmas proper began.

ΩΩΩΩΩΩΩΩΩΩ

29th December 1796

Last night I was too tired to write more, but today the house is quiet and I can continue to write of our beautiful Christmas Day. Following the *Plygain* service, it seemed that my head had no sooner hit my goose-down pillow than Bessie was drawing back the curtains on a drizzly Christmas morning and chirping "Good morning, Master David and Mistress Martha! A very merry Christmas to you! Ten o'clock it is, and not very nice outside, but you'd better get up since the tenants will be arriving for Christmas breakfast in half an hour. Hot water is in the jug, Mistress, and your blue woollen dress is put out in your dressing room." And with that she trotted off jauntily down the stairs, humming some private tune. I made a mental note that I should remind Bessie to be less cheerful in future, and rolled out of bed feeling a hundred years old. David said he planned to stay in bed all day, but I would have none of it, and pulled off all the bedclothes while giving him a little sermon on the duties required of him. Some men need a firm hand to guide them.

When we got downstairs, probably looking like ghosts, we found that Mrs Owen was achieving miracles in the matter of breakfast, having clearly suffered no after-effects from the carolling and gin-drinking of the early hours. Many of the tenants and their families had already arrived, and Grandpa and Grandma were already installed in their high-backed chairs on either side of the *simnai fawr*, tucking in to their oatcakes and hot milk. We were soon brought back to our senses by all the commotion, and were caught up in the conviviality of the occasion, and indeed it was good to see so many familiar and unfamiliar faces from the estate tucking in around the kitchen table or perched on whatever benches and stools they could find. The poor labourers and their families were particularly pleased to get a square meal into their stomachs, and I noticed with pleasure that Tomos and Myfanwy Huws and their four children were there in the thick of things. They all consumed prodigious quantities of oatcakes and hot milk, ale and cider, toasted wheat bread and cheese, cold meats, mince pie and currant cake. The children particularly loved Mrs Owen's treacle toffee, for which she has a reputation extending, so I believe, beyond Eglwyswrw. And the adults rounded off their breakfasts with cups of Darjeeling tea, the precious brown leaves having been obtained from Gethin Dolrannog Isaf, who in turn got them (so he says) from a man whom he met purely by chance on the road to Tenby.

In the midst of the tempest of laughter and fragments of conversations which swept past me as I did my duty as the good hostess, I picked up a few words here and there about some mysterious thefts from empty cottages in Newport while the *Plygain* service had been in progress. According to the gossip, three old widow women had had their houses broken into, and one of them had had all her savings stolen from under her bed. In my mind's eye I immediately saw the shadowy figure of Moses Lloyd drifting through dark and silent streets. I had no opportunity to press for further information from these bearers of bad tidings, nor indeed did I wish to interrogate them, for they had happier things to talk about. Then they were gone, together with their friends and families, replete and serene, into the greyness of the December afternoon. They all promised to see us all again later in the day for the serious business of eating the Christmas dinner.

Most of the adults from the estate decided that a midday nap was needed, while the young men and girls went off to Dolrannog Isaf to play Christmas Day football, and the small children ran off cheering to the woods near Cilgwyn Mill to catch squirrels. As they scampered off down the hill, I asked Mrs Owen what they would do with the squirrels when they caught them. "Why, skin them and grill them over a wood fire they will, of course!" she replied. "But so far as I know, no Christmas Day squirrel has ever been caught around here. Daft as they come, the children are, when it comes to the matter of hunting. Shouting and screaming they will be, and making so much noise that the squirrels will surely hear them coming when they are half a mile away. According to the rules, they must be knocking a squirrel out of its tree by throwing sticks and stones at it. They will probably throw sticks and stones galore and use up lots of energy, but they won't see a single squirrel. Some of the children will fall in the river, and they will all get covered in mud, but they will have great fun. And they will all be back again this evening, starving and ready for their share of the Christmas goose." David and I felt quite exhausted after hearing about all this frenetic activity, and although we were just the right age to have joined in the football game at Dolrannog Isaf, we decided, like all good and respectable citizens, that a Christmas afternoon nap was the preferred option.

We slept until four, and at dusk the revellers were all back again. As the tenants and their families arrived, bright and shiny in their Christmas best, David and I had to greet them at the front door, which was opened for tenants and labourers only on formal occasions. Since all of our guests had to be seated for this meal, many of them brought their own stools and chairs with them. As they arrived, they were each given a mug of hot punch, and soon the house was full to overflowing. There must have been fifty or sixty excited people crammed into the kitchen and dining room, and it is no wonder that Grandma Jane and Mrs Owen reckon that the minimum needs of the kitchen have to be met through the slaughter of one ox, one pig and three geese, in addition to a mountain of potatoes, turnips and cabbages and enough cider and ale to fill the Gelli millpond. The places were all laid out beautifully around the kitchen table and the dining room table, and every other table we could lay our hands on. I wondered where on earth Mrs Owen had managed to find so many place settings, and she told me later that they had been begged and borrowed, but not actually stolen, from almost every house in the district. Bessie had decorated the rooms tastefully with holly and ivy, and she had even managed to find a sprig or two of mistletoe, which is a very rare plant in this neighbourhood.

For a few moments I stood by the fireplace listening to the buzz of conversation and the waves of laughter and savouring the wonderful smells coming from the black iron cooking pots in the fire, over the fire and near the fire. And I thought how lucky I was to be a part of this warm extended family, some good and some not so good, some Church and some Chapel, some friends and some rivals, some well off and others grindingly poor -- but all tied by the bonds of hard work and mutual dependence, and now brought together in a spirit of love to celebrate the birth of Jesus. I do not know why, but I felt tears welling up and I had to fight hard to control my emotions. I hope nobody noticed.

Mrs Owen passed the signal from the hearth that all was ready for the feast. I wiped my eyes and swallowed hard. Then I went over and squeezed David's hand. He was more than a little nervous, for this Christmas dinner was his first formal occasion as Master of the Plas, and indeed the first time that the rebuilt house had been used to entertain those who lived and worked on the estate. He stood next to me on a stool in the doorway between the kitchen and the dining room, where everybody could see him. He must have had all sorts of emotions draining through his body, but when he spoke I was so proud of him.

"Dear friends," he said, "I am as nervous as a small child taking its first steps and letting go of the kitchen table for the first time. But I want to welcome you all here to the Plas for our first Christmas together since I became master of the estate. You all know the terrible circumstances which have conspired to thrust this responsibility upon me, at an age when I thought I should be doing the things all young men do before settling down. But here I am, for better or for worse, and this is the first chance I have had to thank you for all that you did during and after the fire, and then for your loyalty and sacrifice in the aftermath, while we have tried to build the Plas once again as a place we can all be proud of."

His voice cracked at this point, and his eyes dropped, and I thought he would not be able to continue. Instinctively, I put my hand into his. There was not a sound from any of those who listened. Then he breathed deeply and, after what seemed a very long time, continued.

"Now we must try to forget the past. We all have difficulties at the present, due to the high price of corn and other matters beyond our control. But we will come through these difficulties, and the estate will once again be a model for others to follow. Grandpa Isaac and Grandma Jane are still here to guide me, and I thank them from the bottom of my heart for their love and for the lessons they teach me every day." Then David turned to me with a little smile, and realized that we were holding hands. He gathered me up with his eyes, and continued: "And you may just have noticed that I have found a beautiful new wife." The tension was now broken, and everybody laughed and looked at me, and I am ashamed to say I blushed the colour of claret. David laughed too, and said: "She is even younger than I. It has not been easy for her to settle in to the Plas, and many of you will know that she has not been well. But I thank God that she is fully recovered. Already she has won over the hearts of all who have met her, and I will lean upon her a great deal in the years to come. The decisions that we make here will be made together, and we ask, dear friends, for your patience and your support. I have said enough -- far more than I thought myself capable of! And now I ask you to raise your glasses in a toast to Plas Ingli and those who belong on its green acres. Enjoy our hospitality. And a merry Christmas to you all!"

With the cheers of all those present ringing in his ears, David stepped down from his stool, shook many friendly hands, and came back to embrace me. He gave me a long and public kiss on the lips, as if to demonstrate his love to all those watching, and of course I did not object. When he did this our guests were initially shocked into silence, for public displays of affection are not at all acceptable in polite company, but then they all laughed and shouted their approval. Then we all sat down at our appointed places, with the tenant farmers and their families joining us in the dining room and the labourers and their families around the big oak table and the other tables set up in the kitchen.

We all enjoyed the same fare -- beef and goose roasted on the spit, boiled ham, potatoes, turnips and cabbage, rich gravy, mincemeat pie, puddings, wheat breads and cheeses, stewed apples and pears covered with cream, and plates full of treacle toffee and other sweetmeats whose recipes were known only to Mrs Owen. All of this was washed down with plentiful supplies of spiced ale and cider, served warm. We all helped with the serving and the washing up, since all the guests knew that servants were in short supply at the Plas. There were choruses and solos and duets, and four or five of the youngsters got out their tin whistles and fiddles and gave us a few folk tunes. Bessie and Billy knew the steps and led the dancing. Much to our surprise, Will Ifans Dolrannog Uchaf recited a long and slightly rude poem, and his neighbour George told some funny stories. As fatigue began to take its toll, Grandma Jane got out her precious harp and played for us some beautiful wistful Welsh airs, which were listened to in rapt silence.

At last various mothers and tired small children took their leave, and as the evening wore on numbers were further reduced as courting couples disappeared into the darkness. Then the elderly couples set off with their lanterns, and a warm peace descended on the household. I have faint memories of cider and laughter, and people asleep around the kitchen table, and being carried up to bed by David. And so my first Christmas at the Plas came to its lovely end as I drifted into warm oblivion in the arms of my husband.

ΩΩΩΩΩΩΩΩΩΩΩ

30th December 1796

May God forgive me, for I have married an idiot. I don't know whether he is more idiotic than other men, but he certainly seems to have a very strange sense of duty, and he is showing an alarming tendency to get involved in situations that he would be wise to keep out of.

Hettie, who has been coming and going over the last few days because she has her husband and children to think of in their cottage on the Parrog, turned up after breakfast with the news that Moses had been arrested by the constables for drunk and disorderly behaviour in the Black Lion in Newport. David was greatly surprised, and said it was his understanding that he had gone off to his relatives or friends for Christmas. I said nothing, but it was no news to me that he had been in Newport all the time, spending most of his wages -- and maybe other peoples' money as well -- on a drinking spree in the company of assorted rogues.

Last night, said Hettie, he was so drunk that the landlord refused to let him have any more ale, upon which he ran amok, throwing chairs and tables around, smashing mugs, abusing the locals as "miserable bastards and slobbering swine", and threatening with a knife those who tried to restrain him. Someone had grabbed the knife, and he had been beaten up by a gang of fishermen from Parrog. Hettie reported that he was in the lock-up in a gruesome state, and that the constables intended to charge him just as soon as he was sober enough to understand what was going on. She thought he would quite likely end up at the Quarter Sessions, charged with assault and causing an affray, and would then be shipped off to the colonies to cool off. "Good riddance," she said, spitting into the fire. "He'll probably be in Haverfordwest Gaol by tonight, and we'll never see him again."

I was horrified by David's reaction, for he said "Oh my God! What a fool! I must go and see if I can help!" And with that he flung a cloak over his shoulders, ran outside to the stable, saddled the grey pony, and galloped off down the lane to Newport looking like King Henry the Fifth about to save the nation.

Two hours later he returned, with a dejected and filthy Moses sitting behind him on the horse and hanging onto his shoulders. Grandpa Isaac and Mrs Owen helped him off the horse, and as pity gradually replaced loathing we were all sucked into the rescue operation. He was covered in blood, vomit and mud, and Grandpa and David had to carry him into his room and undress him. When he was stripped naked and stretched out on the bed, Grandma and Mrs Owen took over. We decanted hot water from the kitchen cauldron and filled a large basin for them, leaving the wretch to their tender mercies. "Huh!" said Mrs Owen, "He won't like being washed like a baby by two fierce old women, but exactly the same as all other babies he is, under the clothes, except for a bit more hair here and there."

As we waited outside his room we heard coughs and moans and muttered oaths as they washed him, bathed his wounds, and applied bandages and assorted healing ointments. Finally they got him into his night-gown and covered him with blankets. During the whole operation he uttered not a word of regret or thanks, but they were not surprised since he was clearly in great pain and in a deep state of shock. Then they left him to sleep.

Closing the door as they left the room, Grandma announced: "Nothing broken. He'll survive, for he's young and fit. Beautiful he is not, for he's got two black eyes, a swollen lip and two missing front teeth, as well as bruises and cuts all over his body. Those boys from the Parrog know how to use the boot. I hope he learns a lesson from all this, for he won't be in much of a state to enjoy New Year."

Afterwards, as we all attended an inquest for the living around the kitchen table, David told us what he had done on his rescue mission. He had gone first of all to the Black Lion, to find it looking like the aftermath of the Battle of Agincourt. There had been broken chairs and tables everywhere, with smashed mugs and bottles all over the floor, in the middle of pools of spilt ale and cider. Brynmor, the landlord, had been sitting dejectedly in the middle of the mess, making no attempt to clear up; and he had explained that he was waiting for Squire Bowen of Llwyngwair to arrive so that he could see the damage for himself. As the leading Justice of the Peace in the Newport area, this would, he thought, help the great man when it came to remanding Moses to appear at the Quarter Sessions. It had been clear that the landlord was intent on pressing charges. However, David had managed to convince him that this was not a sensible option since he would most likely never get a penny in recompense for the damaged furniture and mugs. Moses, he had explained, was probably now penniless, having spent all his wages on ale. "Much better," he had said, "if you accept this five shillings from me here and now and buy replacements. I will make you this generous offer on condition that you do not press charges and that you immediately clear up the mess before the Squire gets here." After a little thought Brynmor had agreed to this, and David had paid him the money and left him to his cleaning up operations.

Then he had gone down to the lock-up on Long Street, where a constable was guarding the dangerous prisoner. "Luckily I recognized the constable," said David. "It was Benjamin Mathias, the cobbler from East Street, who was just coming to the end of his term of duty. He never really liked being a petty constable anyway, and wanted to get back to full-time cobbling as soon as possible. Father helped him out once when he was short of cash. He was sitting in the outside room, looking thoroughly miserable, having had hardly any sleep himself, what with Moses moaning and groaning all night behind bars, just a few feet away. I told Benjamin that Brynmor Black Lion was not going to press charges, and that it would cause a great deal of trouble if he persisted with a charge of riotous behaviour, or common assault, or causing an affray, or criminal damage, or whatever. At first he was reluctant to see the sense of this, but I reminded him that a case at the Quarter Sessions could cause him great difficulty in view of Moses' family connections, and in view of the fact that none of his assailants had been arrested. He began to waver. Finally a silver shilling did the trick, and he released Moses into my tender care and promised to forget the whole sorry business."

Festivities

"So now you feel like the Good Samaritan," I said indignantly, "having rescued a foolish and arrogant servant from spending the rest of his life in the penal colonies! In my humble estimation, twenty years of hard labour in New South Wales would do him a lot of good."

"I understand your sentiments, Martha," replied David, "but things are not quite that simple. For a start, he is my servant, and I have a duty to look after him if I can. Second, I look on him as a friend. And finally, when Father first took Moses on, he made a promise to Squire Lloyd Cwmgloyn that we would do everything in our power to keep Moses out of trouble and to make him a worthy son of the family."

"Huh!" said Grandma Jane, not impressed. "To be a worthy son of the Lloyd family all he has to do is behave like a viper, sliding about in the long grass and burying his fangs into anybody who gets in his way. And now we are six shillings worse off than we were before."

"Don't you worry, Grandma. Those six shillings will come off Moses' wages. I don't know what other debts he may have, but with a wage of four pounds a year he will not get a penny from me until four or five weeks have passed. I hope this episode will teach him a lesson, and make him into a better and more loyal worker."

"Do you really think Moses will thank you for rescuing him?" I asked, with my eyes blazing. "As well as being lazy, he is arrogant, and we all know that he hates working on the land, getting wet and dirty. He thinks he demeans himself every time he turns a sod in the garden. Can't you see that? And this drunken thug is the selfsame man who had ambitions to become our steward on the estate!"

"Well," replied David, looking crestfallen, "I must admit that he has gone down in my estimation and has now condemned himself to remain at a lowly level in the natural order of things. But if I was in his unfortunate position I am sure I would be grateful for a kindly act on the part of my employer."

At this, Grandma Jane intervened, taking my side and responding to the behaviour and facial expressions of Bessie, Mrs Owen and Billy who were sitting round the table with us. "My dear David," she said quietly, "No matter what miserable condition he now finds himself in, Moses is a member of the gentry. Isaac and I know the minds of the local squires and their families, both good and bad. The Lloyds have done us no favours over the years. When he recovers, young Moses may be initially grateful

91

for being rescued from the convict hulks and the penal colonies. But soon, I fancy, his thanks will turn to hatred. No rich man enjoys falling low and depending upon the generosity of others. No proud man -- and Moses is an exceedingly proud man -- enjoys being indebted to those whom he sees as inferiors. We gave him a job when nobody else would look at him, and now he is even more in our debt. And let us not forget that his famous good looks are now somewhat diminished by the loss of two front teeth. The ladies will see him in future not so much as a Don Juan but as a buffoon. Great seducer turned into figure of fun, banned from the Black Lion and a laughing stock in all the other local inns and houses of ill repute. You mark my words -- Moses will hate us for what has happened, even though his problems are all of his own making. We must watch him with the eye of an eagle from now on."

Not even Grandpa Isaac, who has been in all respects a good friend to Moses, had any reason to dispute any of this, and indeed he nodded in agreement. So I said "Why don't we dismiss him now and send him packing, back to Cwmgloyn?"

"That will not be quite as easy as it sounds, " said Grandpa, "for he has already been disinherited and sent packing from there by his father. If we send him out of here he will end up on the street as a pauper or a vagrant. In any case he is too badly injured to go anywhere just now. It seems to me that a little Christian charity is required of all of us at the moment, whatever the risks may be."

He was of course quite right. So Moses was given a reprieve, and will probably be confined to his bed for the next week or two. We will get on with the festive season, and change his bandages and feed him on porridge and milk when we find the time. But poor David! Nobody has much sympathy for what he did, although it was done for the best of reasons and with a kind heart. Maybe I would have done the same myself if I had been a man, and Master of the Plas. But I must say, on balance, that he has been impetuous and very naive, and he has shown a lamentable lack of the common sense which we women take for granted in ourselves.

ΩΩΩΩΩΩΩΩΩΩ

Festivities

2nd January 1797

Moses is still in bed, his face puffed up like a patchwork pin-cushion, and too morose to say a civil word to anybody, but he is out of sight and mostly out of mind. I have almost forgiven David for his failings in understanding human nature, and we have been caught up in the happy eccentricities of New Year.

I think I love New Year more than Christmas, for it reminds me that whatever our veneer of polite manners and good breeding may be, we live very close to the edge of civilization. Some of the things that go on would be more in place in some fearsome jungle inhabited by a tribe of ape-men, and I cannot understand why our raw and primitive rituals are so condemned by our Nonconformist friends at Hebron, Tabernacle and Bethesda, for they send shivers of excitement down my spine and yet seem to be entirely harmless.

It all started at midnight on New Years Eve, with the old kitchen clock chiming in the New Year. In order to ensure good luck for the coming year we all had to go through a strange "first footing" ceremony which I was at a loss to understand. Then we all wished each other a Happy New Year, and consumed a few too many mugs of hot punch, and went to bed with sore heads.

At four o'clock in the morning we were awoken by a wild commotion downstairs as Mrs Owen let in all the small boys from the estate who were the bearers of the New Year Water. This was fresh spring water, newly collected from the holy spring of St Brynach up on the mountain, and now carried in a pottery vessel decked with sprigs of holly and other evergreens. The boys sang a New Year carol which I had not heard before, and proceeded to rush around the house opening all the doors and sprinkling those who were in bed with a few drops of the New Year Water. Even Moses was thus anointed, though I gather that he was not amused. It would not have been seemly to get up, and indeed tradition dictates that good luck can only be assured if one is sprinkled in one's bed. In exchange for this service the small boys were given a few pennies, and off they went at a run, yelling like a tribe of savages, to their next destination at Dolrannog Isaf.

We were all up late, and after a good breakfast we exchanged our littl⸍

gifts. They were not very substantial, for we are all aware that the estate is on a financial knife-edge, with spending money for luxuries in short supply. But I gave David a little painting of Carningli which I have managed to complete secretly over the last few weeks when he has been out in the fields, and he gave me a very delicate lace shawl, which I think one of the most beautiful pieces of handicraft I have ever seen. I gave him a long and loving kiss of thanks and scolded him on the basis that it must have cost a great deal, but he just smiled an enigmatic smile and shrugged his shoulders, rejoicing in my pleasure.

Then the youngsters started to arrive in little groups, girls and boys this time, to collect their *calennig*. This had to be completed before noon. Each little group would knock on the front door, with a leader carrying an orange (if the group came from a tenant farmer's family) or an apple (in the case of labourers' children) decorated garishly with ears of corn, sprigs of evergreens and herbs, raisins and acorns. The children would sing a New Year carol, translated as

"I rose early and walked, as fast as I could, to ask for *calennig*.
If you feel it in your heart,
Give a penny or two.
A happy New Year for a penny!
A happy New Year for a penny!"

Then they would stick out their hands for their rewards, and having been rewarded, rush off giggling and shouting to the next farm on their itinerary.

After noon David and I set off into town with the pony and trap to fulfill another New Year obligation, namely the repayment of debts. We were trying to rid ourselves of the loans taken from various local businessmen for the rebuilding of the Plas, and now we visited two of the wealthiest merchants in Newport, Benjamin Watkins and Shoni James, to pay something over fifty pounds back to each of them. We were well received by the gentlemen and their families, and enjoyed their New Year ... for a little while. They were happy to see their money returned, ...d David explained to me as we trotted slowly ...that there were now only three more loans to be ...hot summer had brought a good barley crop, and ...some degree from high corn prices. We had sold ...ristmas at six shillings a bushel but had refused to join the "ring" of wealthy landowners and merchants who had held onto their crops and forced the market price up to eight shillings a bushel. "If we had joined the ring and sold at the high price," explained David, "we could have paid off some of our other creditors as well. But the price of commercial greed would have been great ill-will on the part of the poor people, who have been forced to the verge of starvation by the very men whose hospitality we have just enjoyed down in the town."

"But don't we still have a barn three-quarters full of the barley harvest?" I asked.

"Indeed we do," replied David. "We will thresh it over the coming weeks and sell it at a fair price directly to those who need it most."

I sat silently on the way home, realizing that running our estate is an extremely complicated matter, with many conflicting needs to be met -- the need to behave honestly and charitably as a matter of principle, the need to "keep in" with the other landowners of the area, the need to maintain a good commercial reputation in case loans are ever required, the need to look after the servants and labourers, and the need to buy and sell fairly so as not to create social unrest. I reminded myself of some of the things that David had said to me before, and I realized that he was trying hard to be a good Master of the Plas, building on the reputation for fairness and generosity built up by his father and grandfather. In this matter, I understood a little better why he had behaved as he had in the affair involving Moses and the Black Lion, and I loved him a little more. I squeezed his arm and gave him a smile as we passed New England and headed up the track to the Plas.

ΩΩΩΩΩΩΩΩΩΩ

8th January 1797

Twelfth Night has come and gone, and I must record that the occasion was enlivened by a visit from the carriers of the Wren House. This was something familiar to me from my years at Brawdy, but certain details of the Cilgwyn tradition seemed to me to be quite charming. It all started with a knock on the front door shortly after dark, and when I opened up I found four of the young men from the cwm standing there and groaning as if weighed down by some mighty load. Their load consisted of a little funny house which looked like a doll's house, about twelve inches long and eight inches high, covered with ribbons and strips of rags. It even had a small door with a latch, and windows made of cow-horn at each end. It was held up in the air by four poles, with each pole attached to one corner of the house. Upon being invited in, they crossed the threshold, making a great play of the huge weight they were bearing, and then launched into a long and complicated song, sung as a sort of chant, about shooting the cutty wren with bows and arrows and guns and cannons, carrying her home by means of a big ox-cart, cutting her up with hatchets and meat cleavers and cooking her in brass pans and cauldrons. Then they went on to say that they had come to sell her for a shilling, and to spend it on good ale. And the song concluded with a verse about the cutty wren flying away -- notwithstanding her sad demise -- to return "along the old meadow paths" in the year to come.

When the men had finished their song, they were greeted with warm applause, and David, as Master of the Plas, invited them into the kitchen to be rewarded with their shilling and a few mugs of ale. Having first anointed the plough under the table (as all male guests to the kitchen are required to do), they drank with gusto, for carrying a cutty wren about is thirsty work. Once I had ascertained that the cutty wren in the house was still alive and unharmed, we spent a happy evening chatting about old customs and folk beliefs, and the bearers left at last having promised to release their prisoner back into the wild. When they had gone, Grandma told us that we were highly honoured. Ours was the only house visited this year, on the basis that David and I were the only couple in the neighbourhood to have married within the last twelve months. The visit was, she said, a sign of goodwill from the community, and was part of a very ancient fertility ceremony designed to bring good luck and many children into our household. Again, we went to bed that night feeling that we were surrounded by love.

However, the after-glow of Christmas and New Year has been dimmed by a number of social calls from neighbours and acquaintances, not all of whom wish us well, and by reciprocal visits which we ourselves have had to make. I do not greatly enjoy responding to the call of duty, and

Festivities

I sometimes wonder how well suited I am to the business of being Mistress of the Plas.

The "paying of respects" is a very tiresome thing, although David assures me that it is one of the penalties of moving in respectable circles. In advance of each visit messages fly back and forth, and I am intrigued by the manner in which visitors invite themselves to pay visits. Very little discretion appears to be left to the poor host when a visit is signalled, and indeed he might greatly prefer to sit by the fire reading a good book than to entertain dull people from some distant mansion to food and drink.

Grandma Jane informs me that it would be extremely ill-mannered to deter an intended visitor, since the paying of respects is a recognition of social status. For example, she says that a gentleman visited by a squire -- or, even better, by two squires in a social season -- is immediately lifted in the esteem of his neighbours. If you are lucky, she says, a visiting family will come in the morning, and will be happy with a cup of tea and some sweetmeats. If you are unlucky, they may arrive in time for dinner, with coaches full of sons and daughters, aunts and uncles, and with coachmen and other servants also to be fed. If you are even more unlucky, the whole army may stay for a fortnight. All of this enforced entertaining can be a very great drain on the resources of an estate, especially if it occurs around Christmas and New Year. "However, there are minor compensations built into the system," says Grandma. "First, every social visit has to be reciprocated, so every family that overstays its welcome, or arrives at an inconvenient time, will expect us, in due course, to descend on it and enjoy our revenge. Second, for every five offerings of hospitality at the Plas, we obtain five equivalent meals at somebody else's expense. And third, thank the Lord for our remoteness. The Plas is not an easy place to get to, and most of the bigger squires spend the winter social season in London or in Haverfordwest. Then in the summer they go to Tenby. So long as they stay well clear of us, we will probably survive!"

So, ever mindful of our responsibilities in the social sphere, since Christmas we have paid our respects to our three tenants, to the Rice Family at Pentre Ifan, to the Laugharnes at Pengelli Fawr, to the Beynons at Berry Hill, and to John Ladd who is the mayor of Newport. We have also received, with as good grace as we could muster, the Howell family of Henllys, the Edwardses of Llwyngoras, and the Prossers of Frongoch. Some of these are kind and honest people who have no other intention than to develop social intercourse and to relieve the boredom of their daily lives through a few hours spent in convivial circumstances. There are debts and credits, both financial and social, involved here and there. Other families with whom we have come face to face have other matters in mind, and sometimes beneath the thick warm layers of conversation I have discerned frost and even frozen ground. Some, like the Howells and the Rices, I perceive to be our enemies, and Grandma does not disabuse me of this opinion, saying only that hospitality and civility cannot harm difficult relationships and can possibly do some good. She says that wives who get on well can sometimes prevent warfare between their embittered husbands, and indeed I see her point.

In addition to all these exhausting social occasions, we have had to put up with visits from various notables from Newport whose pretensions are considerably greater than their talents. Oh dear -- that last remark appears, even to myself, to be arrogant and intolerant, but perhaps the making of it explains why I have felt for some days the need for a bonnet of wide sky over my head and a shawl of silence around me. After an excess of polite conversation, smiles and curtseys, and rushing hither and thither, and after putting up with delicate interrogations and arrows nicely flighted so as to graze me rather than to do me great harm, the mountain is calling.

ΩΩΩΩΩΩΩΩΩ

10th January 1797

After some days of high wind, this morning dawned bright and clear, with a gentle breeze from the south. I enquired of David whether he would like to come for a walk on the mountain, but he said it was a good day for shooting woodcock, and that he planned to go down into the Dolrannog Woods with Billy in order to find us some supper. I told him I would take a walk up to the crags by myself, and he said "Excellent, *Cariad*! The fresh air will do you good after all the recent social events. But be careful -- the winter rocks are always very slippery."

I climbed up the old cart track leading towards Carn Edward and Dinas Mountain, and then swung to the right near the western end of the crags. As I came up to the tumbledown walls of the old hill fort the wide sweep of Cardigan Bay came into view. There was a strong swell running, and the bay was dotted with white sails. I wondered where they were coming from and where they were going to, these trading vessels carrying herrings, flannels, barley and wheat, salt mutton and beef, wine, spices and fruit, and a multitude of other essentials and luxuries. It was too hazy to see Ireland and North Wales, but I enjoyed a little reverie about the peoples of those distant parts, their languages and their ways of life. In spite of the southerly wind it was too cold to linger, and I climbed right up to the summit whence I could look down on Newport and the estuary.

As I climbed, the wind carried the sound of shots from the woods where David and Billy were hunting. On the highest crag of the mountain there were no angels in residence, but the sense of peace was as real as ever, and I thought that perhaps the word "angel" is just another word for peace, or tranquillity, or serenity, or even harmony. Perhaps when you meet an angel there is nothing to see at all, but simply something to feel. I sat on a bluestone boulder with my back against a north-facing slab of rock and sheltered from the breeze, gazing out over the grey winter expanse of the ocean, and I realized why old St Brynach had come here often. He had come to find space and peace, to pray, to contemplate, to cleanse his soul, to escape from the mad whirl of people, and talk, and food and drink, and the social imperatives of seeing and being seen. Up here, how vain and empty the social life of the Morgan family of Plas Ingli seemed!

I started to shiver, and in the sure knowledge that there was nobody near enough to monitor my movements, I decided to pay another visit to my secret cave. I scrambled down onto the south-facing flank of the mountain, jumping from one giant boulder to another and praying that I would not slip or otherwise lose my footing. Some of the rock outcrops and boulders are so large that any observer at the Plas or one of the other farms would have had but fleeting glimpses of me as I traversed the mountain side, and if I had fallen I would certainly have come to rest in some fearsome crevice with broken limbs and a broken head, probably impossible for any search party to find. But I had no sense of fear, and soon I came to the little rowan tree and the guardian boulders, and I squeezed between them into the cave. It was just as I had remembered it -- warm and dry, and sheltered from the wind. I sat myself down onto my bed of moss, and remembered that my last visit had been on the day before I lost my baby. Images from that time came flooding back into my mind, but I was by no means distressed, and found that I could meet them with equanimity. Other things also drifted into my mind, and I found that the negative thoughts about silly neighbours and stupid servants and social responsibilities gave way to more positive thoughts in which my beloved David, my family and friends, and the warm joys of the Christmas season featured prominently. I felt my busy mind calming and my heart opening, and I confess that I must -- without realizing it -- have been caught up in something that might be described as prayer or contemplation.

I know not how long I sat in my cave, but suddenly I realized that I was hungry and that the light was beginning to fail. Cloud was piling up from the south-west, and the wind was rising. I knew that rain was on the way. I scrambled to my feet and made my way cautiously across the banks of broken rock towards Ffynnon Brynach, where I took a drink and anointed my forehead with a splash of the sacred water. I laughed at myself when I realized that I had invented a little ritual, but I thought it quite a pleasant one and determined to maintain it on future visits. Then I followed the water pipe down to the Plas, and arrived to find some feathering of woodcock in progress in the kitchen.

"We were beginning to get worried about you," said David. "Where have you been?"

"Oh, just up on the mountain," I replied.

ΩΩΩΩΩΩΩΩΩΩ

15th January 1797

The holiday season has now gone on for three weeks, and at last the plough has been taken from under the kitchen table. I have tired of the holiday, not so much because there has been nothing to do, but because there have been too many people and too many celebrations in this house. The happy Christmas and New Year events which I have already described have made, I am sure, a lasting impression on me, and I will do all in my power, as Mistress of the Plas, to see that they continue in the years ahead. And my visit to the mountain last week brought a lovely moment of calm.

Festivities

Another cause of great happiness was the invitation which we received to the big house at Pontfaen to celebrate *Hen Galan,* the Old New Year. Since they changed the calendar about fifty years ago, I gather that there has been great confusion in this area since many people are refusing to cooperate with the new order of things. In Cwm Gwaun, in particular, some families still insist on celebrating Christmas on 6th January, which is the day following Twelfth Night for the rest of us. Then they celebrate New Year on 13th January and have their Twelfth Night on the fifth night after that! They claim that this is all a matter of great principle, but Bessie says that the message about the new calendar has not yet reached the remoter parts of the cwm. My own theory is that the people in the cwm are smarter than most people think, and that the apparent confusion simply gives them the opportunity to celebrate all the happiest occasions of the festive season twice over.

At any rate, David and I, and Grandpa Isaac and Grandma Jane, were all invited, and this was taken as a great compliment, for not many people from Cilgwyn or Newport are invited into the cwm for *Hen Galan* since it is normally strictly a family event. We think the invitation may have something to do with the fact that all four of us use Welsh as our first language -- which is more than can be said of most of the gentlemen, squires and their families in north Pembrokeshire. Also, Grandpa is of the view that following the fire, and then Griffith's loss at sea, the Laugharnes of Pontfaen have followed the rules of good behaviour by not seeking to draw us into occasions of frivolity and good cheer too quickly. Our wedding, although conducted under very strange circumstances, is of course now common knowledge among all the local gentry families, and is taken as a sign that the family has -- at last -- come out of mourning and is thinking positively about the future.

So off we went on a starlit frosty evening with the carriage somewhat heavily loaded. We were well wrapped up in our heavy cloaks and mufflers, and we bore some simple gifts for our hosts. The journey took us well over an hour, and we were cheered at last to see the bright candle-lit windows of the big house on the side of the valley at Pontfaen.

We half expected to see some huge party in full swing, but there were only a few other coaches and traps in the driveway, and Grandpa explained that Hen Galan was not a wild extravaganza but an occasion for convivial celebration with family and friends. We were warmly greeted by Squire

Festivities

Laugharne and his wife and daughters, and were formally introduced to a little group of maybe fifteen other people. No children were seen, but they were heard with a vengeance as they had their own fun and games upstairs. The reception room was gaily decked out with holly and ivy, and hundreds of candles had been lit for the occasion. There was a traditional yule log, now almost burnt end to end, spitting sparks and roaring away in the fireplace.

The household was run on much more formal lines than our own, and I was impressed to see that three servants were hard at work serving drinks and food, but the atmosphere was none the less pleasant for all that, and we had a perfectly agreeable evening seeing in the Old New Year. We had musical entertainment from two of the squire's daughters on the pianoforte, solos and duets from other ladies, and a sprightly rendition on the violin from Master Higgon of Tredafydd, who is the squire's cousin. David noticed a harp in the corner of the room and pressed me into playing it; this I did, although I was somewhat out of practice, and although the tuning took longer than the performance. The assembled company were delighted, since most people nowadays learn to play the pianoforte. The squire's old uncle George gave us an over-long monologue about the excesses of the French Revolution, which I thought not to be in the best of taste. But mostly we drank good wine, ate well from an excellent table, and passed the time in intelligent and good-humoured conversation.

Naturally enough, as the new arrival at the Plas, I was the centre of attention, and a certain Mistress Vaughan and the other ladies in our little circle did their best -- in the politest possible fashion -- to delve into the circumstances surrounding the quiet and distant marriage between David and myself back in August. They got nowhere, for I am now well practiced, like the rest of the family, in explaining that David and I fell in love and wished to marry quickly, and that we agreed to a quiet wedding conducted by my brother so that the scarce resources of the estate could be conserved for the repayment of loans. None of my listeners needed to be told about the devastating effect of the fire, nor did they need reminding that both big and little weddings in this area have been known to bring apparently wealthy families to the verge of bankruptcy. I noticed many surreptitious glances at my bosom and my stomach, both from the gentlemen and the ladies. I have a nice bosom and a flat stomach, and I deliberately wore my prettiest low-cut dress for *Hen Galan*. I am flattered to think that the glances from the gentlemen were born of a simple desire to enjoy what they saw; but the ladies were looking carefully to see whether I was with child, and I took a certain perverse pleasure in demonstrating to them that I was not.

I liked Mistress Laugharne and Mistress Higgon and their daughters a good deal, and we got on splendidly, talking of music and poetry and other artistic pursuits, and I felt that they were genuinely interested in me and David and wished us well at the Plas.

I particularly liked the openness and charm of Mary Jane, the oldest of the Laugharne girls, who is very beautiful and cultured but who does not flaunt her accomplishments in any way. She has an observant eye and a sharp and earthy sense of humour. She is also very intuitive, and directed conversation onto other things whenever she observed that I was getting a little flustered -- for example, when pressed for details of my family background and of the marriage settlement which I brought with me to the Plas. She also realized very quickly that although I have had a moderate education and have some talent in music and art, and know much about Welsh culture and natural history, I was not comfortable when talking about politics or the latest scandals involving local squires and their families. She saved me from demonstrating my ignorance on several occasions, and as the evening progressed, with the older ladies more interested in silly gossip than in sensible conversation, Mary Jane and I found ourselves together in a corner, chatting and laughing as if we had been lifelong friends.

By the time midnight had come and gone, I confess that I had drunk far too much wine, and as we took our farewells after a delightful evening David needed to guide me gently to my seat in the carriage. He assures me that I did not actually disgrace myself, and that I thanked our hosts most generously for their hospitality. Grandma said today, with a gleam in her eye, that I was the life and soul of the party, and I am not entirely sure whether her comment was intended as a compliment.

Apparently I slept like a baby all the way home, snuggled up at David's side as Grandpa Isaac drove the carriage along the rough Cwm Gwaun road, lit by the dim light of the stars and our candle lanterns.

ΩΩΩΩΩΩΩΩΩ

8. A Sowing of Seed

17th January 1797

Now to more sombre matters. Moses is causing me particular concern. He is recovering well from the beating he received in the Black Lion before New Year, and is up and about. His lacerations have healed well, and indeed Mrs Owen has been kindness itself in the treatment of her patient. But there has been no word of thanks from him, and indeed he is too morose to speak a generous word to anybody. He knows what happened to him in Newport, and he knows what a close shave he has had with the law, and he is probably ashamed of his actions. But there is a smouldering anger in him that makes me apprehensive and even anxious. Today, after breakfast in the kitchen, David insisted that he returned to work along with the other servants and labourers, for it is soon time for the spring planting, and there is much muck spreading, stone walling and ploughing to be done. The rest of the barley crop must also be threshed in the coming days -- hard, dusty work, but it must be done. I overheard Moses complaining bitterly about his aching limbs and bruised ribs, but David said that the exercise and comradeship would be good for him, and gave him no option but to obey. He also told the snivelling fellow that he was subtracting the cost of the rescue operation from his wages, and that he would get not a farthing in his pocket until the middle of March. "If you are not happy with this arrangement," he said, "you are at liberty to leave our service at once. Is that what you want to do?"

"Master," replied Moses, barely under control and with his countenance as black as a Castlemartin ox, "you will appreciate that I am not happy with the arrangement. You will also know that I have but a limited number of options at my disposal. I will stay. But I wish to place on record my discontent at the manner of your dealing in this matter." And with that, having done his best to provoke an ugly scene, he grabbed his hat and his heavy coat and stormed outside.

David barely managed to conceal his temper, and as far as I was concerned such insolence justified instant dismissal, but there is some strange tie that keeps this evil man under our roof, and David did no more than clench his fist and thump the table. Then the moment had passed, and it was too late to call Moses back. He is still a servant at the Plas, no matter how much I would wish it otherwise.

ΩΩΩΩΩΩΩΩΩ

3rd February 1797

I have obtained some enlightenment from a Saturday visit by Madam Bevan's circulating school. Grandpa Isaac says that the teachers have been holding lessons in these parts ever since he was a small child, using farmhouse kitchens, barns and chapel vestries offered by various supporters of education for the poor. He says that this is the first visit to the Plas since the fire. Posters were put up in Newport, Cilgwyn and Nevern a week ago, and the word has been passed round amongst the pupils regarding the date, the time and the place.

The weather this morning was unpleasant in the extreme, with a high wind and lashing rain. We thought that nobody would come, but shortly after dawn half a dozen urchins from the cottages near Gelli and Trefelin knocked on the kitchen door, and over the next hour or so thirty more pupils turned up. All of them carried the coppers that were needed to pay for their lessons, and all of them carried little bundles of food. Some of them were innocent wide-eyed children as young as seven or eight, and others were farm labourers and servants in their twenties or thirties who had been given special dispensations by their employers. I expressed my delight to David at this evidence of a deep thirst for knowledge, and he replied that if the weather had been kinder we would certainly have had sixty thirsty people at the door.

The school should have been held in the barn, but it was so cold and draughty in there that we decided to offer the kitchen instead. The teacher, an intense young man called John Jeremy, turned up at nine with a bag full of bibles and learning books, slates and chalks, and assorted educational aids including pebbles and blank sheets of paper. He was very grateful for our offer of warm premises, and accepted gladly. And so they all settled down on benches, stools and on the floor, for six hours of learning. Bessie,

A Sowing of Seed

Billy and Hettie joined in as pupils, as did two of Hettie's children. The only two who did not participate fully in the spirit of the occasion were Mrs Owen and Moses, the former because she was in effect denied access to her royal estate for the day, and the latter because he heartily disapproved of education for the lower classes. I thought it amusing that one who has moved down so speedily in the world should be so resentful of those who sought to move up.

During the morning David and I had to brave the elements since I had an appointment with Mary Shinkins Dressmaker in Newport. On the way to town the pony was very uncooperative because of the blustery wind and sheeting rain, and although we had our best oilskins over us on the trap we both got soaked. We dried out at Mistress Shinkins' house, and were warmed up with a nice cup of hot tea while she measured me up and talked of fabrics and ribbons and such like, and then we got soaking wet again on the way home. David promises me that we will get a new chaise or even a coach just as soon as the estate has cleared its debts.

When we arrived back at the Plas there was a refreshment break going on, and all the pupils were tucking into the contents of their food parcels. We changed our clothes and joined them round the kitchen fire with some bread and hot soup, and were soon swept up into the happy talk of reading and writing and counting. Some of the older pupils, including our own servants, were chatting enthusiastically about their progress in reading English, and I discovered that young Shemi Jenkins Blaenwaun, Sian Williams Gelli and various others from the neighbourhood were working their way through the Welsh version of St Matthew's Gospel. Presumably there was a good deal of mathematics going on in the kitchen as well. I asked John Jeremy Teacher how he managed to keep so many different lessons going at the same time, and he said "I just keep moving! I try to teach the little ones from the front, with a certain fierceness, for they need discipline and tend to fidget about a lot. Hettie's youngest boy is a proper handful, even with his mother in the room, and he would be better off in a fishing boat out in Newport Bay. But he already reads and writes better than his mother. The older ones are so keen that they would teach themselves if I was not here."

David and I offered to help out in the afternoon, since it was too miserable outside to do anything on the estate; and so we spent a happy couple of hours as teacher's assistants, helping little fingers to write letters and numbers on their slates, spelling simple words and going through the alphabet a hundred times.

We were exhaused when they had all gone, and wondered at Master Jeremys's stamina, for tomorrow he is in Nevern, and the day after in Maenclochog, and the day after that in Puncheston, and presumably this is how it goes on throughout the year. When we sat around the table for supper, later in the evening, we talked about the schools, and I discovered that Mrs Owen had learned to read and write under a teacher called William Jones who had travelled around the area some twenty years ago. She was still able to write more fluently than Bessie and Billy, but they reckoned they were catching up fast by taking advantage of the latest teaching methods. Those methods seem pretty crude to me, but maybe they were even cruder in the old days.

I was intrigued to learn that Grandpa has been a supporter of the circulating schools for many years, and that he is involved in some sort of a gentleman's meeting that makes plans for the future. He says there will be a proper school in Newport when some money from a grand lady called Madam Bevan becomes available. He puts a little money into the scheme whenever he can afford it, but claims that this gesture on his part has led him into conflict not only with certain of the gentry but also with the Rector of Newport. I could hardly believe this, but Grandma Jane and David confirmed what he said, and reminded me that there are many people in this community who -- for a number of reasons -- want the poor to remain in ignorance and fear, and who see education as a prelude to unrest and even revolution! What a strange little world we live in.

ΩΩΩΩΩΩΩΩΩ

10th February 1797

The miserable winter weather continues, and the rain has hardly let up since Thursday of last week. We are getting fed up with streaming water, ankle-deep mud, dejected animals and irritable servants. There is not even a view to enjoy, since we are some way above the cloud base. All I can see from my dressing-room window is a smudgy, turbulent mixture of grey and black mist which has swallowed up everything more than thirty yards distant.

A rider came galloping up the track this afternoon. He was in such a hurry that he might have been intent upon announcing the end of the world, and he was so wet that he might have been an ancient mariner recently struggled ashore from a shipwreck. He delivered a soggy letter from Squire Alban Watkins of Llannerch in the Gwaun Valley, declined our offer of a spell in the warm kitchen and a mug of hot buttermilk, and galloped homeward again through the deluge. I still do not know whether to laugh or cry at the contents of the letter. It was addressed to David, and this is what it said:

Llannerch, on the tenth day of February in the Year of our Lord 1797

My Dear Mr Morgan,
It has come to my attention, and to the attention of other gentlemen whom I greatly respect, including Rector Devonald, that a certain John Jeremy and his Circulating School paid a visit to Plas Ingli on Friday of last week. You should be aware that the said Master Jeremy is not universally welcomed in these parts, with good reason. He unashamedly promotes the preposterous idea that all people, no matter what their station in life, should have the ability to read, write and undertake mathematical calculations. Also, I have it on good authority that he uses seditious and subversive pamphlets and other literature in the course of his lessons. You will appreciate that the minds of young and innocent people are likely to be infected by such material, with grave consequences for those of us who strive for good order and stability in our community.

It would be a cause of much regret if your continued support for this gentleman and his ilk should damage the good relations that have hitherto existed between us. I trust you will be ever mindful of the responsibilities placed upon us for the continued protection and wellbeing of those less fortunate than ourselves.

Yours etc, Watkins, Llannerch

David read the letter out to Grandma, Grandpa and myself as we sat in the dining room, to an accompaniment of giggles, gasps, sighs, guffaws and foul words. Some of Grandfather's responses would turn my black ink red if I was to record them on the innocent pages of my little diary, so I will simply record that he was not amused. "That stuffed-up buffoon is still saying the same things that his father said forty years ago!" he spluttered. "He seems to think that the invention of writing as a means of communication was an aberration, and that if we all sit tight in our little holes it will simply go away." Then he got up and walked out to the kitchen, saying to David as he went, "You'd better reply to him, my boy. You know what to say, without any help from an old scoundrel like me." And so David penned the following reply, and will send it off with a messenger when the rain stops.

Plas Ingli, 10th day of February 1797

My Dear Squire Watkins,
I thank you for your communication on the matter of the Circulating School. I found your views very illuminating, and have given them careful consideration. You will be aware, no doubt, that my grandfather and my father have both supported the principle of universal education over the last fifty years or more, and I see no reason to change our family's attitude at this stage. I have enjoyed the benefits of a good education, and have no wish to deny these benefits to others who may be more intelligent than I. It is my view that those estates blessed with literate and numerate workers will be best able to cope with the changes that are being forced upon us; and I take some solace in the fact that many enlightened and progressive gentlemen of our mutual acquaintance share this view.

You may be interested to know that my wife and I assisted Master Jeremy in his worthy work at the Plas last Friday, and that this gave us much pleasure. You may also be interested to know that the only subversive and seditious piece of literature placed before the pupils was the Bible. You are welcome to pass this piece of intelligence on to the Rector.

Yours etc,
Morgan, Plas Ingli

ΩΩΩΩΩΩΩΩΩΩΩ

A Sowing of Seed

14th February 1797

Today is Ash Wednesday and the first day of Lent, and Grandma and Grandpa are all decked up in black on the grounds that this is the way it has always been. They say they will wear black till Easter Sunday. David and I will have nothing to do with this silly tradition, and neither will most people in the neighbourhood. We will go along with the fasting of Lent, to some degree, since hard rations are a necessity at this time of year in any case; but there is still work to be done, and in cold weather we all need good food in our stomachs to keep us going.

Yesterday was Shrove Tuesday, and Mrs Owen was hard at work with the pancake manufacture from dawn to dusk. Since it was a holiday many of the estate tenants and labourers called in for a pancake or two, and left full of praise for "the best pancakes in the world." They are indeed very good, and I sampled two, or three, or ten, myself. I sought to resolve some of the mysteries of the pancake business, but Mrs Owen is very secretive, and will not allow any prying eyes when she is making up a pancake mixture. I saw that she made three different types, using mostly oatmeal for the servants' pancakes which were served with treacle and butter, and wheat flour for the others. Some pancakes were made with yeast and were left to rise before baking on the bakestone, but others were made more quickly. All she would tell me was that the secret of pancake making lies in the proportions of milk and buttermilk used, and the use of vinegar and nutmeg as appropriate. "Just you be patient, Mistress Martha," she said. "In time I will share my secrets with you, but it would not yet be seemly since you have been married for barely six months." She was joking, of course, and we laughed together; but I understood that every expert woman in this world (and Mrs Owen is expert at any number of things) maintains her pride and her value by keeping certain things secret. What value would she be to us if Bessie or myself could do everything just as well as she?

Shrove Tuesday was a horrible day with flurries of snow and a bitter east wind, but it was not cold enough for the ground to freeze, and at breakfast David and Billy declared that conditions were perfect for the *cnapan* contest on Berry Sands. Almost every year they play in the game, which goes on for most of the day and in which the men of Newport pit

A Sowing of Seed

their wits and their strength against the men of Nevern. Last year they say that there were more than five hundred men on each side, and that by dark the game had to be abandoned without resolution. It seems to me the crudest of games since a greasy wooden ball has to be hurled about and carried by brute force to the opposition headquarters; but David says it is highly skilful, with three different sorts of players and with expert passing and running highly praised by players and spectators alike. In the game squires and gentlemen play on horseback, carrying clubs, and the common labourers and servants join the town boys in running about on the beach barefoot. Grandpa Isaac says that David and Billy are the secret weapons used by Newport since they play so well together, slipping the *cnapan* back and forth so quickly that opposing players know not where it is from one minute to the next. David has not played in the *cnapan* contest since the fire, but legend has it that in the contest of 1794 he and Billy, with the help of the Jenkins boys from Cilgwyn, showed such skill and endurance that the game went one mile, from one end of Berry Sands to the other, in less than six minutes, to defeat the enemy. This year, it has been put about that David and Billy, and the Jenkins boys, will be playing together again, and we heard yesterday that the gentlemen of Newport have put down large sums of money on a win for the town.

David was a little concerned this time that his little chestnut pony was not adequately prepared for the sport, but he thought she would make up in agility for her lack of size, and as we ate our breakfast pancakes there was much discussion of tactics. As an old hand at the *cnapan* game, Grandpa Isaac had much to say. The weather was so disgusting that the rest of us could not face the prospect of a day on the beach, shivering in the flurries of sleet and snow, watching half-naked men running about and riding their farm horses round in circles somewhere in the distance. Even Moses, who normally plays for Nevern, refused to turn out, claiming that his injuries were not yet adequately healed.

So off the warriors went, one behind the other on the back of the pony, to do battle. They did not return until it was dark, battered and bruised and caked in sand and salt crystals, and crestfallen since Nevern had won the contest. Having heard the news Moses, with a smirk on his face, was detailed to wash down the poor filthy pony, and to settle her in her stable with a warm coat on her back and fresh hay in her stomach. David complained bitterly that the squires from Nevern had laid on special carts and carriages to get the warriors down from the hills, and had promised them free ale in the event of a victory, and that the Newport side had been outnumbered almost two to one. Billy said that it was disgraceful the way that money was beginning to influence the true and honest traditions of sport, and David and he declared that they would never play the game again. We took no notice, for we all all know that they will be back on the beach again on Shrove Tuesday next year. As they spoke, it became obvious that they had enjoyed a few pints too many after the game, so we got them into a pair of bathtubs in the scullery, poured gallons of piping hot water all over them, and left them to thaw out in peace and quiet. The peace and quiet was soon disturbed by some extremely rude *cnapan* songs which Grandpa Isaac pretended not to know and which we ladies pretended not to hear, and in due time the warriors emerged to dress in clean clothes and to enjoy a large supper of Mrs Owen's pancakes.

Somewhat earlier than usual I felt it necessary to take David off to bed in order to soothe his injuries and give him the loving attention that a battered sportsman deserves after a hard day on the field of play. I am pleased to say that a little massage on appropriate parts of his body beneath the bedclothes had a wondrous effect, and that he had sufficient energy left, in spite of an empty head and a full stomach, for further sporting activity.

ΩΩΩΩΩΩΩΩΩ

20th February 1797

The little spell of snowy weather has passed over, and it is now more calm and sunny than we have a right to expect in the month of February. Clusters of snowdrops are peeping out like shy virgins from the shelter of old dry grasses and dead bracken in the hedgerows. There has been good progress with the threshing. A great deal is going on in the farmyard and on the land, with ploughing, ditch clearance and hedging in full swing. The building work is also proceeding apace.

The other evening Moses asked if he could go down to Newport to see some friends. We had no objection, and I saw him walking off down the track carrying a horn lantern and with his big cloak wrapped about him. He came in very late, when all except Mrs Owen were already in bed; and she confided in me next morning that he smelt of ale as he bid her good night and went to his room.

At breakfast I wondered to myself where Moses could have found money enough for a few mugs of ale, and concluded, without consulting him, that maybe he had generous friends. At about ten o'clock Billy came in and reported that two chickens had disappeared. He had noticed that they were missing when he let them out at dawn, and a search around the yard and in the orchard had proved fruitless. I mentioned this to Moses, and a shadow flickered across his face for an instant. "Ah yes," he said. "I have seen a big dog fox in the yard once or twice during this last week. Very hungry and daring he is, at this time of year. We must surely leave the dogs out at night in case the creature strikes again." Now I am not an expert in such matters, but I know that foxes and chickens do not go together very well, and that when a fox strikes there is pandemonium -- and a great deal of noise -- from the chickens that survive. A fox can only carry one chicken off at a time. Could even the craftiest of foxes have struck twice on the same day without any noise from the rest of the birds or any reaction from the farm dogs? I had my doubts.

Later, I mentioned my suspicions to David, and he said "I cannot believe that Moses would be fool enough to steal chickens from right under our noses. What possible motive could he have? Is he so desperate for a pint or two of ale? He must realise that if he was to be caught in the act he would suffer instant dismissal, and I could have him arrested by the constables for petty larceny. He would be humiliated, and publicly whipped or put in the stocks."

"You forget, David, that he has already been quite humiliated by the episode in the Black Lion. Maybe he does not have too much further to fall in the estimation of his family, his employers, or his cronies in Newport."

David agreed, but concluded "At the moment we have no evidence of a crime. But we will keep a careful eye on him. If he puts another foot wrong he will be out of here with a flea in his ear."

"I hope, *Cariad*, that he will not be out of here with part of our wealth in his pocket," I said as David went up to the office to work on his farm records.

A Sowing of Seed

That afternoon, when everybody was out of the house, I went through to the servants' quarters and looked for Moses' big cloak on the clothes hooks in the passage. I knew it would be there, for he did not wear it when working with the animals. Inside it, as I expected, there were a few of the downy feathers found on a chicken's neck, and traces of blood. Just then Mrs Owen came into the kitchen, having hung up her washing out in the yard. With my finger to my lips, I beckoned her to come into the passage. I showed her the feathers and the blood, and her eyes widened. She knew exactly what this meant, and she clucked like an old hen. "Mrs Owen," I said, "we will say nothing of this at the moment. But I may need your help on the matter in due course." She nodded her understanding, and we both went about our business.

I now thought Moses remarkably careless for an intelligent man. To tell the truth, my blood was up, and I was disappointed by his stupidity. The evidence we have is sufficient to dismiss him immediately, although a greater level of proof, involving some witnesses, might be required for a conviction at the Petty Sessions. I am now determined that this will be the end of Moses Lloyd, and I am beginning to formulate a plan in which he will bring about his own downfall. I will not speak to David about this, but I fancy that I know already how to precipitate him over a cliff.

ΩΩΩΩΩΩΩΩΩΩΩ

9. Invasion

22nd February 1797

The French have invaded Fishguard! I may not be able to write much, because the Plas has been in a state of pandemonium, and my mind is spinning like a top, and we are expecting the invading army to come marching into Newport tomorrow. Once they have taken over the town it will only be a matter of hours, so they say, before they move into all the surrounding farms and cottages, steal all their valuables, kill all the men and violate all the women.

It is now approaching midnight, and I am writing in my little dressing-room by the light of a candle. We first heard of the invasion at eight o'clock, just as we were settling down to a quiet evening in the kitchen. We had eaten our supper, and Hettie had gone home to her family. Someone came galloping up the track from Newport. He must have been risking life and limb, for it was very dark, and he had no lantern. He clattered into the yard, and when we opened the door to investigate the nature of this nocturnal visitation we saw that it was our neighbour Gethin Griffiths. He shouted from his horse, without dismounting "The French have landed on Pencaer! There is a general alert! There are three warships, and maybe more on the way. They have been frightened away from Fishguard by a shot from the fort, but they are now up against the cliffs at Carregwastad. On such a clear and calm night as this they will be putting thousands of men ashore, as well as arms and ammunition. Fishguard is in a panic, and people are fleeing inland for safety."

"God help us! But what about the defences?" shouted Grandpa Isaac.

"There is nothing to stop them on Pencaer. There are only a few Fishguard Fencibles in the town, and Colonel Knox is taking command. He has sent express messages to summon the militia from Haverfordwest and everywhere else, and I just saw a wild horseman galloping past the Black Lion, on the way to Llwyngwair Manor with a message for Major Bowen. They say the Newport Division will be wanted to march to Dinas to await instructions. Billy! You will be needed! Are you ready to go?"

"Of course I am," replied Billy without a moment of hesitation.

Invasion

"They say that if Colonel Knox has to retreat he will fall back on Dinas and then maybe on Newport if the French are too strong for him."

"That sounds sensible enough," said David. "Does the Colonel need more volunteers?"

"I should imagine so," replied Gethin, "especially if they know how to use firearms. But I must go and warn the Ifanses and the Tuckers and get my family away before it is too late! Can you warn the cottagers? God be with you!"

And with that he wheeled his horse and went off at the gallop up the track towards Dolrannog Isaf and Penrhiw. We were so amazed that at first we stood in the pool of light around the kitchen door in complete silence. Then David dragged us out of our lethargy. "We know not whether this is true or just idle rumour," he said. "But we will be fools if we do not take what Gethin says at face value. Billy, as a member of the Newport Division, you are summoned to duty and we must release you. I will go with you, and I will bring whatever firearms we have in the house. I know how to use them, and I have a good eye and a steady hand. I might come in useful. Grandpa, I ask for your blessing in this enterprise. You and the women should stay here and make ready to evacuate the house in the morning, if further messages should come up from Newport."

What David would have done had Grandpa withheld his blessing, I know not. He did not wait for it anyway. As he spoke he rushed about in the kitchen, grabbing a bag and stuffing into it some fresh bread, cheese, apples and other supplies. Billy ran down the passage to gather up warm clothes and a few essentials of his own. Then David ran into the dining room, and took the two sporting guns and two pistols, together with all the powder and shot available, from the gun cabinet. Then he sprinted upstairs, shouting over his shoulder "Billy! Saddle up the pony! Moses! You are also young and fit! Will you join us in the defence of our homeland?"

This took Moses by surprise, and for a moment there was silence. All eyes turned on him, and we all noticed the fear in his eyes. But he gathered his composure quickly, and said "I am still very stiff after my unfortunate accident in Newport, and I will probably be more hindrance than help. But I will go and tell the neighbours of the invasion immediately, and you may count on me, Master, to defend the household with life and limb if the French come marching over the mountain."

Invasion

"Huh! I'm pretty stiff myself after that *cnapan* game," shouted David, rummaging upstairs for his warmest and thickest clothes. "But you do as your conscience dictates. Go down to the Cilgwyn Road then, and knock on all the doors between here and the mill, and ask the Jenkins boys to tell everybody else in the cwm."

In just a few minutes of frantic activity the Plas Ingli military campaign was fully organized. Before rushing out, with his heaviest cloak wrapped around him and an old felt hat upon his head, David embraced me quickly and gave me a kiss on the lips. "Just you look after yourself, *Cariad*," he said. "Make for Cardigan if you have to evacuate the house. No doubt Grandpa will know what is best. And don't worry about me -- I have a duty to do, but I promise to be very careful." And after further embraces all round, he and Billy were off towards Newport, travelling as fast as the poor pony could carry them, lit only by the starlight of the February night. At the same time Moses ran and stumbled down towards the dimly-lit cottages on the Cilgwyn Road, looking for all the world like a swooping grey bat with bowed head, flailing arms, and cloak flying out behind him.

There was no time for tears, or arguments, or protestations, and indeed David had taken control of the situation so decisively that Grandpa had hardly managed to get a word in. To his credit, he was not at all offended, but said to me gently "Yes indeed! You have a good man there, Martha *bach*." This brought a lump to my throat and tears into my eyes, and I suddenly realized that I might never see him alive again. Images came flooding into my mind of poor dead soldiers, their bodies riddled with shot and their faces blackened with gun-powder, trampled underfoot by the advancing battalions of the French; and of David and Billy and their brave compatriots stuck through with bayonets and covered with blood; and of fearsome hand-to-hand fighting among the dark crags of Pencaer. I must have been frozen to the spot, for Grandma shook me by the shoulder, and said "Come now, Martha. Don't you get too caught up in wild imaginings. David and Billy will be all right. Now we have work to do."

So we have packed up baskets of food supplies and spare clothes ready for an instant flight by night or in the morning. We have hidden all our money and valuables in a canvas bag and have buried it in the manure heap in the yard. Grandma wanted to hide it in the hay loft, but I would not have that, as it seemed to me that the hayloft would be the first thing to go up in flames if the French invaders are intent upon destroying our farms and homes in the heat of battle. We have put all the shutters up and have piled up books and spare clothes behind all the windows and doors in case the house comes under enemy fire. We have brought all the axes, scythes, sickles, spades and other light implements into the house in the expectation that they may come in useful as weapons. Grandpa will be a good general, I am sure, if we are caught up in some dismal military episode. But we have no firearms, no carriage, and no proper means of defence. If we have to leave, we will take a pony and a farm cart, travel towards Nevern and then take the back road towards Cardigan.

There is nothing more we can do until dawn. I am on watch at the moment, and Grandma and Grandpa, Mrs Owen and Bessie are supposed to be asleep -- but I daresay they will be lying awake in their beds, eyes staring at the ceiling, ears alert for the slightest unusual sound. I have just been out into the yard, feeling for all the world like a military scout on some desperate mission. Luckily, the night sky over Fishguard is cloudless and starlit, with no sparks or flames from burning buildings; and the silence is broken only by the tawny owls down in Dolrannog Wood.

I too will find it impossible to sleep tonight, for the silence lies heavy as a shroud on the lifeless face of the land. Already I long for the dawn. I wonder where David is now, and I wonder what the morrow will bring.

ΩΩΩΩΩΩΩΩΩΩ

23rd February 1797

Today is Thursday. David and Billy are still on active service, and I have no news of them. Many of our neighbours think that we will all become the prisoners of some occupying force over a period of weeks or months, and that this area will become a battleground, fought over by the French and the militia which will arrive soon from England. However, during a day of high drama I have come to the view that the French will not succeed in their enterprise. I think we may be safe at the Plas, since it would surely take an army of twenty thousand men to take over every cranny of the countryside, and there is no sign that such an army exists.

Invasion

When we assembled at dawn in the kitchen, none of us had had any sleep. Moses had not returned from his mercy mission, but this did not surprise me. Hettie had not turned up for work, and this did not surprise me either, for with the town in a state of panic she would surely wish to stay with her husband and children. Grandpa, Grandma and Mrs Owen looked haggard, and they were all more worried than they cared to admit. The weather was still clear and still, and there were no sounds of gunfire or explosions, so we decided that we should stay put at the Plas, for the time being at least. There were cows to milk and muck out, chickens, ducks and geese to feed, and other morning duties to be fulfilled, and since we were now short of staff we all had to lend a hand.

Later, when we were at breakfast, several of our neighbours turned up at the kitchen door, anxious for news and desperate for advice. Moses had knocked on their doors last evening, they said, but had simply shouted "The French have invaded! Flee for your lives!" before running off into the darkness. Some families, including the Huws family of Plain Dealings, had taken their pathetic bundles of belongings and food, and had gone off to hide in the woods near Pantry. Other garbled messages had come up from relatives in town in the middle of the night, as if designed to cause maximum confusion; one was to the effect that the French were already on the outskirts of Newport, and another warned that the Fencibles had been routed and had fled to Haverfordwest. This latter rumour caused me great concern, for I knew that where the Fencibles were, David and Billy would be also, and that if they had really been routed these two dear brave men could be dead or injured. I knew not what to think or what to do; my mind told me that rumours are best disregarded, but my heart told me that I should go to Fishguard.

Grandpa urged the neighbours to keep calm and to stay at home for the time being, and assured them that if there should be any military action in the neighbourhood they should certainly hear the sounds of gunfire on such a calm day. In any case, he said, without horses and carriages what would be the chances of travelling faster than an advancing army? And what would be the merit of fleeing anyway? Where would they go, and what would they do when they got there? They saw the sense in what Grandpa was saying, and agreed not to do anything precipitate. Somebody went off to fetch the Huws family, and other refugees, back from the woods. Between us, we then set up a sort of Defence Committee with

Invasion

designated messengers and lines of communication, and Jenkins Brynaeron was dispatched to Newport in order to discover the latest news. I could not stand the prospect of sitting about the house all day, especially in view of my concerns about the fate of David and Billy and the Fishguard Fencibles, and I said that I would walk along the mountain ridge to Fishguard on a spying mission. The others, including Grandma and Grandpa, thought this would be foolhardy in the extreme, but I would not be deterred; and so I wrapped up in my warmest cloak, with an old bonnet on my head and my heaviest boots upon my feet, and took a basket of food with me, and off I marched. In the basket I also carried Grandpa's telescopic spyglass, which I knew would come in handy.

The walk took me almost three hours, since the mountain track towards Dinas and Fishguard is rough and winding. But as I walked I was heartened by the fact that there were no sounds of gunfire ahead. Also, as I walked parallel with the coast and looked down upon the turnpike road, I could see no troop movements of any kind. There were people on the road certainly, some walking, some on horseback and even some in carriages, but most of them were moving towards Fishguard. I reasoned that this was certainly a good sign; for if the French had taken over the town there would have been hundreds of refugees flooding eastwards. At last I reached the bluestone crags of Garn Fawr, and I climbed up onto the highest rocky summit. Below me I could see Fishguard in its hollow in the coastline, and beyond the town the bleak and rocky landscape of Pencaer. Out in the wide sweep of the bay there was not a single warship to be seen, and indeed the only vessels of any sort were half a dozen fishing boats and small merchant ships on the far horizon. There were a few billows of smoke towards Llanwnda which I thought could be coming from burning buildings; but in the town itself the chimneys were smoking just as they do on any frosty winter morning. I used my spyglass and could see a crowd of people milling about on one of the hillocks at the southern end of the town, but I could see no sign at all of military activity.

Thus encouraged, I picked up my skirts and trotted down the rough brambly slope towards Cwm Mawr and the western end of Dinas. Soon I was on the Fishguard road, striding along in the midst of a busy crowd of spies from far and wide, all determined to discover what was going on. Many of them were armed with sickles and axes, saying that they were intent on "going after the Frenchies". There did not seem to be very much fear in their eyes, and indeed it was heartening to see that the poor people who have lately been muttering of insurrection and revolution against the ruling classes were ablaze with anger at the thought of French feet on Welsh soil.

Before my accomplices and I dropped down into the cwm where the fisherfolk live, we passed Fishguard Fort, and were surprised to see that it was quite abandoned. One of the locals told us that the Newport Division had joined the rest of the Fishguard Fencibles there during the night, together with some motley volunteers, but that Colonel Knox (who was not much more than twenty years old) had ordered them to retreat at dawn when he heard that the town had come under French control. He had not checked the reliability of this report, which had proved in the event to be a false rumour. He had only three rounds with which to defend the fort, and had decided that it would certainly fall, with great loss of life, if the French had attacked. So off he and his men had marched, down the road to Haverfordwest, hoping to meet up with reinforcements. He had ordered the guns at the Fort to be spiked before leaving, but the artillery men had refused to obey; and indeed there was much discontent among the Fencibles, and the local people, over the poor leadership and apparent cowardice of the youthful and inexperienced colonel.

With the Fishguard Fencibles gone and no other militiamen or cavalry within ten miles, the town and its neighbourhood were totally undefended by the military throughout daylight hours. However, when I got to the town square there were hundreds of townspeople rushing about and organizing a military campaign of their own. I sat down outside the Royal Oak and ate my bread and cheese, for it was now past one o'clock, and took some note of the messages coming in from Goodwick and Pencaer. Some people who had fled from the farms and cottages on the peninsula said that there were certainly over 1,000 Frenchmen there, all dressed in black uniforms and well armed. But they had no food with them, and they were roaming all over the countryside stealing food wherever they could get it, and killing many farm animals. A few French soldiers had been captured in the night by some local scouting groups organized in haste by a certain Master Nesbitt, and they were now locked in the cellar beneath a house belonging to John Jenkins Tailor.

One gentleman, a Master Williams from near Pontiago, told me that the Frenchmen were an undisciplined rabble, and that the "Black

Invasion

Legionnaires" (as they called themselves) were mostly convicts and criminals who had no respect for their own officers. The commander and his senior officers had taken over Trehowel Farm as their headquarters, but there did not seem to be any proper military strategy, and little groups of Frenchmen were marching about hither and thither, and occupying prominent hilltops, more with a view to defending themselves than to attacking the locals. Indeed, he said that had met some drunken Frenchmen and Irish mercenaries himself on the road past Henner, and had been invited in a perfectly good-humoured fashion to join the revolution! Master Williams was an old soldier, and a well-read one at that, and he said he suspected that the French had come in order to provoke a revolt, assuming that the local peasants and poor farmers would take up arms and join them in overthrowing the hated gentry. Within the last hour, he said, their naval commanders had sailed off in their ships and left them to their fate, and with the locals not at all inclined to join their ranks, he suspected that their morale was entirely destroyed.

This story was confirmed by others who were coming into the square from the direction of Goodwick Sands, and the word spread that most of the French army was drunk and incapable, having consumed not only their own brandy but also copious quantities of Portuguese wine from a merchant ship which had run aground in a January storm. It so happened that barrels of this rough wine had found their way, by some strange circumstance, into almost every house and cottage on Pencaer; and I heard a reverend gentleman say, as he passed by, "We are saved, thanks to the Lord and the Portuguese wine trade!" I thought this to be a somewhat premature judgment, for we still knew not whether French reinforcements would be arriving before dark, and we knew that drunken Frenchmen in charge of loaded muskets could do much damage to the health of the local people. And I was aware that David and Billy were still missing, and were possibly confronting the French in some frosty field out on Pencaer at that very moment. I asked many people whether they had seen David and Billy, but they are not well known in Fishguard, and all I could discover was that various armed volunteers, some on horseback and others on foot, had been seen heading off towards the west with the intention of confronting the invaders.

After picking up whatever news I could on the square, I decided to climb up onto the hillock on the south side of the town, and set off along the street in that direction. The hillock was thronged with people looking out over Goodwick Sands and trying to make out what was happening in the distance. Many of those whom I met were keen to look through my spyglass, but none of us could make out any sort of military action on the horizon. There were many more women than men on the hillock, most of us dressed in our long red cloaks and many wearing the tall black beaver hats which have recently come into fashion in these parts. Somebody said "Why, we look just like a fierce army in our colourful uniforms! Since the brave men of the militia have left us all alone, we will have to fight the Battle of Fishguard for them!" There was more than a grain of truth in this, and I thought that from the heights above Goodwick, where the French scouts were certainly stationed, we must indeed have looked like a regiment of grenadiers preparing for battle.

Then, at about three o'clock in the afternoon, there was a great cheer from the town, and on closer investigation as to its cause I discovered that a number of local people had just returned from the fray with stories of hand-to-hand conflict and heroism in the face of inebriated Frenchmen. As I arrived on the square several other men arrived on horseback with booty including muskets, bayonets and sabres, and they told of ambushes and shots being fired. They said that at least two Frenchmen were dead, and that near Llanwnda two local farmers had been shot by soldiers who had been stealing their cows. Several local men walked into the square in an exhausted state, having been involved in skirmishes, and then two farmers from Llanychaer who had decided to take on the enemy shortly after dawn returned with three French prisoners in tow. They wore ill-fitting black uniforms, and they were dirty, drunk, and dispirited. They had their hands tied behind their backs, and they were roped together behind a horse. A spontaneous chant went up from the crowd, which soon turned to hissing and spitting, and I felt quite sorry for the miserable fellows in the midst of such hostility.

Then the hissing turned to cheering again, and striding onto the square came Jemima Nicholas, a cobbler woman of striking appearance, holding a leather-working knife in one hand, and in the other a long rope to which were tied no less than twelve Frenchmen in a row. Various other locals were marching alongside and in the rear of this strange procession, singing the verses of some stirring Welsh hymn. I never did get the full story from Jemima or anybody else in the midst of all the pandemonium, but when the invaders were safely locked up into the cellar beneath Master Vaughan's shop somebody asked her whether she had captured all these Frenchmen single-handed. "Why yes, *bach*," she replied, her ample bosom swelling so much with pride that I thought it would burst out into the light of day, "no problem at all for a tough old girl like me!"

"Too big a problem for the militia, it seems. How on earth did you manage it, Jemima?"

"Well, I caught up with them after they had fled from me, and then I just surrounded them!" she replied, with a laugh that would have struck terror into the devil himself.

It was now past four o'clock and I knew that I must set out for home. Even if I took the main road this time I knew that it would be pitch black by the time I got back to the Plas. There was still no sign of the militia, and I had no news of David and Billy, but as I walked out of the town I felt more confident with every minute that passed. There was a rumour that a large force of militia and cavalry under the command of Lord Cawdor was heading north from Haverfordwest. With Jemima and her friends in charge of the town square, and with the French soldiers apparently in disarray, it seemed to me that the worst of the crisis was past. No French reinforcements had been brought up, and the militia would certainly arrive during the night.

As I write, it is well past midnight. I have reported my findings to the family and to our nearest neighbours, and they are all greatly relieved by my news. I think I will sleep well tonight. I worry about David, but I feel in my heart that he is unharmed.

ΩΩΩΩΩΩΩΩΩΩ

25th February 1797

David has returned, and I thank God that he is safe and sound. Before now, we have not spent a night apart since our marriage, and these two nights of loneliness and fear have been almost unbearable. He came back late yesterday afternoon, trotting up the track on the back of his mud-covered pony and looking for all the world like a dastardly pirate, wearing a French officer's hat upon his head and carrying a sword and two muskets with fitted bayonets in addition to all his own firearms. His cloak was in tatters. He looked tired and yet elated, and it was the most wonderful thing in the world, having first cleared away all the weaponry, to hold him in my arms again and to feel his lips upon mine.

His story was in turns stirring, tragic and funny, and the telling of it took most of the evening. As he spoke, family and servants sat around the kitchen table, eyes wide and mouths agape. I will try to reproduce on the following pages the main episodes in the drama.

David said that when he and Billy rode down into Newport on the evening of the invasion, they found the town in a state of panic, with people rushing about in the streets seeking to sort out facts from rumours. Many of the men were packing their wives and children off in pony traps or carts, or on foot, towards Cardigan. Some refugees wealthy enough to own carriages were already coming in from Fishguard. Major Bowen and one or two junior officers belonging to the Newport Division of the Fishguard Fencibles were in town, knocking up the irregulars and getting them out onto the street. Once the men had reported for duty, lined up in their comical uniforms of striped flannel shirts, white breeches, buckled shoes and floppy felt hats, and carrying whatever weapons were to hand, they formed a column and marched off towards Dinas. The officers were on horseback, and they were the only ones to carry firearms. Billy took his place in the column, and David asked the Major's permission to take up the rear on his pony, alongside various other men who had turned up to help in the task of defeating the enemy.

Major Bowen had been asked to take the troop to Dinas, and to await further instructions, but when they got near the village they received a further message asking them to continue to Fishguard Fort. So they kept going, and reached the fort around midnight. There they found the youthful Col Knox in deep discussion with Col Colby, commander of the Pembroke Militia, who had ridden at the gallop all the way from Haverfordwest in order to obtain first-hand information. Most of the men belonging to the Fishguard Division of the Fencibles were out on scouting missions in the pitch blackness, under the command of a certain Thomas Nesbitt, a retired army officer who happened to be in the town when the alarm went up. Col Knox was worried that he had only 191 men at his disposal, instead of the full complement of around 300. Some had refused to turn out, but in the panic many of those living in remote cottages had not even been told of the emergency. While Billy and the other marchers settled into the fort, David and two other Newport farmers on horseback decided that they would join the scouts, so they rode on down to Goodwick Sands where they encountered Master Nesbitt at his makeshift command post. David and Tomos Gwyther were detailed to scout the area on top of Goodwick Hill, and that is when their adventures really began.

According to David, they started to climb up the steep slope towards Penrhiw at about two o'clock in the morning, both on horseback and each armed with one pistol and one sporting gun. They used footpaths rather than cart tracks so as to make maximum use of the shelter of the tall trees, and they suspected that the enemy troops were somewhere above them. They expected an ambush at any moment, but nothing happened, and they got to Penrhiw Farm, and the open ground around it, without mishap. They wondered where on earth the enemy might be, but then they saw sparks and smoke rising in the still night air from behind the rocks of Carnwnda, and they assumed that the French soldiers were camped around Llanwnda Church. They trotted forward gently towards the church, which was still not in view because of the high ground on its southern side. On reaching the rocks, they decided to climb to the summit, which was about sixty feet above them, in order to spy on the enemy. So they left their horses tied to a bush and scrambled up the slope through the bracken, crawling or grovelling along on their stomachs in the darkness.

At last they reached the summit and peeped over, and at exactly the same moment a group of Frenchmen who had been creeping up on the other side peeped over too. David says that he heard their heavy breathing, and swears that their noses were not more than six feet apart. All concerned let out mighty yells and scampered off downhill, reckoning that discretion was more appropriate than heroism in the circumstances. But David and Tomos saw enough camp fires and tents to be certain in their own minds that there were several hundred soldiers in possession of Llanwnda. They also knew that the French soldiers would come after them, since possession of this high ground must have been a prime military objective of their commanders. Sure enough, as they leapt onto their trusty steeds they were followed by a fusillade of shots, and the shooting continued until they were well clear, hidden by the trees and tall hedgerows towards Treseissyllt.

Invasion

David and Tomos now decided that they had had enough of lurking about in the pitch darkness on horseback, and they descended by the fastest possible route to report their findings to Master Nesbitt. He was well pleased with their discoveries, which he said tied in well with information brought back by other scouts. They had a good picture of the situation, and had even managed to take one or two prisoners. He said that all the other Fencibles had now returned to the fort, and he proposed to follow them there in order to get a few hours sleep before the battle that would certainly come on the morrow. David and Tomos were not inclined to retreat in this fashion, and on the basis that the French were hardly likely to mount a major offensive during the hours of darkness they found an abandoned cottage close to the beach in Goodwick and slept there instead.

David said that they were woken shortly after dawn by the sound of distant gunfire on the slopes above them, and assumed that there must be some skirmish in progress between the invaders and some local farmers. They ate a sparse breakfast of bread and cheese, confident that there was some resistance to the invader out on the peninsula. They then met a local man who came running along the beach from Fishguard with the news that the Fencibles had abandoned the fort and the town and were marching away from the enemy towards Haverfordwest. David and Tomos could hardly believe this; but they met up with about twenty other volunteers who came striding out from Fishguard, including the redoubtable Jemima Nicholas, and they held a council of war. They all agreed that there was no point in moving *en masse* against the enemy, since they would certainly be destroyed by cannon and musket fire. So they decided to spread out and harry the French in whatever ways they could, creating defensive positions where it was safe to do so, running away where it was prudent, and attacking if opportunities presented themselves. Most of the warriors were armed with axes, staves, pitch-forks and sickles, and only four men -- including David and Tomos -- had firearms. They decided to stay away from Llanwnda, since that was where the bulk of the French troops seemed to be stationed, and to concentrate their actions on the strip of land across the base of the Pencaer peninsula, between Goodwick and Pwllderi. They worked out approximate destinations among themselves, and then they set out, two by two and three by three, to defeat the French.

David and Tomos had the fleetest ponies, so they agreed to leave the Goodwick and Manorowen area to the footsoldiers and head for

Invasion

Penysgwarne, in the interior of the peninsula about two miles away. On another bright, clear morning with the sun already melting the frost off the grass, they climbed up the steep track to Trefwrgi and the more open ground above. They determined that they would keep well to the south of Llanwnda and the rocky ridge of Garn Gilfach and Garn Fawr, crossing fields and using rough cart tracks where possible. They passed a few cottages which were deserted, and a few more which were occupied by local farmers and their families who had barricaded themselves in and who were waiting for the end of the world. Through shouted conversations in Welsh through shuttered windows, David discovered that there had been no trace of the French in this area thus far. But then, on rounding a bend between two high hedges near Carngowil, David and Tomos were suddenly confronted by a small troop of half a dozen Frenchmen led by an officer on a stolen horse. Immediately David took a pot-shot at them with his sporting gun. He did not hit anything, but the French soldiers were so surprised that they took to their heels. The officer's horse shied and he fell off, losing his sword, musket and hat as a result. Then he scrambled to his feet and scampered off after his men, vainly trying to catch his runaway horse and leaving David and Tomos in control of the battlefield. "That was my shot," said David, "so I claim the spoils!"

The victors decided that pursuit was not a good idea, since two against seven did not represent very good odds, and so they turned back and took another route westwards, flanking round the southern end of the hills of Carngelli. David checked his new musket, and found that it was loaded and ready to fire. Now that they were armed to the teeth they felt more confident, and so they rode straight into an ambush. They passed beneath a little rocky outcrop and failed to notice that there was a French picket stationed on it. There was one shot from the enemy, and Tomos tumbled off his pony. Immediately David dismounted and managed to drag Tomos into the shelter of the hedge. He lay on his stomach in the grass, with Tomos moaning with pain beside him, and cocked his musket. He managed to get a sight of the ridge crest through the bushes, and after a few minutes of total silence a foolish Frenchman peered over the ridge in order to see what was happening. "I took careful aim," said David, "since I knew that I had only one shot. I pulled the trigger, and got him right between the eyes. He must have died instantly. As soon as they saw that their colleague was hit, the other Frenchmen turned and ran. I could not see them, but I knew from the commotion that they were fleeing. So I grabbed my pistol and ran up to the crest of the ridge, and fired after them. There were only three of them, and I let them go. Now I had a dead Frenchman face-down at my feet, and a wounded colleague at the trackside. I turned the Frenchman over and put him into a sitting position, since that seemed like the proper thing to do. He had a neat hole in his forehead and blood all over his face, so I couldn't really tell whether he was young or old. I felt a terrible remorse -- killing a man is a wicked thing -- and I still do, invasion or no invasion. The poor devil probably wanted no part of it anyway. But then I realized that I had better take care of Tomos."

That was the end of David's involvement in the Battle of Pencaer. I shall break my narrative at this sad point, for the hour is late and I hear my good man's weary footsteps upon the stairs. He has just returned from town, where he has no doubt told his story several times over in exchange for a dozen jars of ale. He probably has a very sore head, and as a good wife I must undress him and settle him down for the night. I promise that I will be very gentle with him.

ΩΩΩΩΩΩΩΩΩ

26th February 1797

This morning there are flurries of sleet in the air, and I am confined to my room with a slight chill. David and Grandpa have gone up onto the mountain with the neighbours to clear a new cart track through the bouldery slopes. The fire is burning merrily in the grate, and I have time to myself. I am minded to continue my recollection of David's narrative. If I leave it until the morrow it will surely go out of my head.

After the shooting of the French soldier, my brave husband discovered that Tomos had been shot in the left arm, and that he had broken his right shoulder when he fell to the ground. The ball was still embedded in his flesh, but David tried to stop the bleeding and strapped him up with strips of cloth torn from his cloak. After catching the two ponies, David managed to get his wounded colleague onto one of them. Then he ran back up to the dead Frenchman, took his musket, and said in French "May the Lord be

Invasion

with you, and may you rest in peace." He left him there, sitting against the rock, with his head slumped onto his chest, looking for all the world as if he was fast asleep. But as David looked north from his vantage point, he saw a large detachment of French soldiers marching in good order straight towards him and no more than a quarter of a mile away. Quickly he gathered up the weapons and other trophies, mounted his pony, and set off back along the way they had come with Tomos on his pony beside him. It was now mid-afternoon. Twice they had to take detours as they saw and heard rowdy groups of French and Irish soldiers ahead of them. David was intrigued that there were several nationalities involved in the invasion force, and he became convinced that they were all drunk, for there was no sign of military discipline.

Not far from Tynewydd, said David, they heard a great commotion on the road, and six local men came running towards them. They were very much out of breath, and they stopped for a moment to exchange intelligence. "Good day to you, gentlemen," wheezed their leader. "We are the Solva Irregulars. We came over this morning to fight the enemy, and we have just had a battle with them. We bumped into five soldiers near Carngowil. We advanced in good order, and managed to shoot three of them. One of them is dead. We chased after the survivors, but then another big group appeared, and we thought that a tactical retreat was called for. We were lucky not to be cut off. We are unsure how many there were, but the area around Carngowil and Carngelli is certainly now in their possession." David and Tomos related their story, and discovered that the leader of the Solva men was one Henry Whitesides, the builder of the famous Smalls Lighthouse. Apparently he had had a horse when they first encountered the French, but when they decided to retreat he had, like a true gentleman, released his horse so as not to have any advantage over his colleagues. And so off they went, trotting southwards while David and Tomos continued towards Manorowen.

Near Trellywelyn Wood the two men came across an Irish soldier slumped at the trackside after being violently sick. He was not drunk, but he presented no threat, and after drawing his pistol as a precaution, and holding it an inch from the end of the man's nose, David was able to pick up some useful intelligence from him. The poor man said that he was a mercenary, captured and then released from prison in France on condition that he joined the "black legionnaires" on their invasion. There were other

Invasion

Irishmen too, and the commander of the whole army was an American called Tate. Until he heard some people speaking Welsh at Trehowel Farm, he did not even know he was in Wales. He said that the expeditionary force had been told that the locals would welcome them with open arms, and would rise up with them in a great British Revolution to overthrow the king. They had all become somewhat demoralized, he said, when their ships had sailed off and when the locals spat at them, threw stones at them, and even shot at them with primitive sporting guns. To the best of his knowledge, at least two local people had been shot by the invaders, and three or four Frenchmen had been killed. Early in the morning they had been given brandy by the officers to help them keep warm, and since then they had found casks of Portuguese wine in many of the farms and cottages which they had looted. The Irishman thought that most of the army was probably drunk and incapable by now. They had no food, and scouting parties had been sent out to obtain supplies from the farms and cottages. Because most of the fires in the farms had been put out, they had no proper cooking facilities, and they had made fires out of furniture, doors and window frames so that they could cook the chickens and sheep they had killed. Some, including himself, had even eaten raw meat, and were now paying the price. He had seen a friend of his die in terrible convulsions. David asked him fiercely where the main force of soldiers was stationed, and he said after being sick again "Oh, please don't shoot me! I think there are some hundreds of them, lined up on the east side of the big rock where the church is, and another division is detailed to take up position on the hill they call Carngelli."

David said that he and his injured colleague could do little to help the Irishman, and as a prisoner he would have been more trouble than he was worth, so they bade him a cordial farewell and left him to recover on his own. Then they went down towards Manorowen, reckoning to continue into Goodwick by a safer route. Before dropping off the upland, they saw several groups of local people with French prisoners in tow; and they could also see, in the distance, a considerable black-coated force of French grenadiers moving south from Carnwnda. The two men came to a little cottage guarded by a fierce labourer wielding an axe, who became less fierce when they addressed him in Welsh. David convinced him to take them in since Tomos was in great pain. The man and his wife were kindness itself, and soon Tomos was being patched up. His open wound was cleaned with warm water and tidily bandaged, and his broken shoulder securely strapped. The warriors were given some hot buttermilk and barley bread while the two ponies munched at the hedge alongside the cottage. At dusk they continued their slow progress. They got to Manorowen just as it was getting dark, and just in time to see the militia arrive on the road from Scleddau. Lord Cawdor, the most powerful squire in Pembrokeshire, was in charge of a motley army of over six hundred men, mostly fencibles and cavalry, from as far afield as Haverfordwest and Pembroke, with many irregular volunteers in tow. They had been marching all day, with hardly a break, and they were very tired.

All were greatly surprised to find a small party of Frenchmen in the grounds of Manorowen Farmhouse. Lord Cawdor sent a troop of cavalry to intercept them, but after a brief exchange of shots they escaped into the gathering gloom. As commander, he was furious, for he knew now that the presence of the Welsh force would shortly be known to the enemy. He had already learned from Mr Nesbitt's scouts that there was a French position near Llanwnda. He held a hurried meeting with his officers, and decided to march immediately towards the enemy in the dark in the hope of pinning the French troops down and preventing a breakout from the peninsula. He gave the order to advance up the narrow track towards Trefwrgi and Carngelli, but when David saw this he dug his heels into his pony's flanks and rode up to him at full speed. "Sir!" he shouted. "I beg of you not to be hasty in this matter!"

"Who are you, sir, and what qualifies you to question my judgment as to the deployment of my forces?" hissed the commander in chief.

"My name is David Morgan," came the reply, "and I have been on the peninsula all day with my colleague who has been shot by the French. I know the situation exactly. To the west, and around the base of the peninsula, there are many scouting parties of French troops, but they are ill disciplined and many of them are drunk and sick. You have no reason to fear them, for they run rather than fight. I have killed one of them myself, and several others have been killed or wounded by local people. But I have spoken to an Irish soldier who is with the French, and I have no reason to doubt his word. He says that there are several hundred French soldiers with muskets well established on the east side of Garnwnda."

"Where is that?"

Invasion

"Close to the old church, and the highest point in the area. The Irishman also says a division is detailed to occupy Carngelli, a prominent hill much closer to here. I saw the troops approaching it two hours since, and they were in good order. As for the track you plan to use, I have been on it myself today, and it is deeply entrenched in the land and bordered by high hedges and woodland. You must ride in single file and your militiamen will be able to walk only two abreast. The way opens out only on the approach to Carngelli, and that is where the French black-coats will be lying in wait. Sir, I greatly fear for your safety and for the safety of your men. The Frenchmen will hear you coming, and if you are ambushed in the pitch darkness there will be a massacre. I beg you to reconsider, to use another more open route and preferably to delay your attack until dawn."

"Damned presumption, sir!" shouted Lord Cawdor. "What do you know, sir, about military strategy? Is it your business to conduct this campaign? We have wasted enough time. Advance!"

And with that, said David, he was brushed aside, and the whole army of six hundred men marched wearily off up the narrow road, with drums beating, and with a small troop of scouts and mounted officers in front and cavalry in the rear. They left only a small contingent at Manorowen, including various quartermasters, medical staff and irregular volunteers. David said he felt sick in his stomach as he watched the troops go, for he was quite convinced that there would be fearsome bloodshed, and that he would never see them again. More to the point, Billy was in the middle of the column somewhere, and he would be cut down with the rest of them. Tomos needed further treatment, and since there was now an army surgeon at Manorowen David was able to call on his skill to extract the musket ball from his friend's arm and to bind his broken shoulder-blade correctly. The two men, both dog tired, then settled down in a crowded billet in the manor house, forced down a rough meal of soup and oat bread at His Majesty's expense, and collapsed into an uneasy sleep. At about ten o'clock David woke suddenly, thinking that he could hear the sound of gunfire. He thought that the massacre had started, but then he realized that the sound was made by horses' hooves at the gallop. He staggered outside, and was greatly relieved when a messenger reported that Lord Cawdor had aborted his foolhardy advance before reaching Carngelli and had ordered a retreat before any shots were fired. His ragged army had turned in the lane and marched down to Goodwick Sands, and were now on the way to Fishguard town square, where they would spend the night.

David said that he and the other volunteers at Manorowen slept only fitfully, for there were frequent changes of watch and comings and goings involving messengers and scouts. Then, shortly after nine, a message arrived to the effect that the French had surrendered. The messenger said that a French delegation had arrived in the town centre on the previous evening, only an hour after Lord Cawdor had established his headquarters in the Royal Oak, with a letter from the French commander suing for peace. Lord Cawdor had demanded total surrender, and nothing else. This morning the surrender had been signed by the French officers, and the whole invasion force was expected to lay down its arms on Goodwick Sands at any moment. A great cheer went up, and after a hasty breakfast (again at His Majesty's expense) there was a general exodus from Manorowen and David, Tomos and everybody else headed for the beach.

When they got there it was mid-morning, and there was no sign of the French, but there was a great traffic of officers and messengers on the road that ran along the back of the beach between Fishguard and Goodwick. David and Tomos decided to continue to the town square, and as they trotted along they passed virtually the whole of the Welsh defence force moving out to supervise the surrender. They heard that the surrender document had already been signed in the Royal Oak inn. There were crowds of onlookers on Bigney Hill and Windy Hill, including many women dressed in their red shawls and tall hats. Some of the militias were to line the slopes overlooking the beach, looking as impressive and intimidating as possible, and the Fishguard Fencibles were to go down onto the beach to disarm the French and to take them prisoner. David spotted Billy in the column, and they exchanged greetings; it transpired that Billy had seen no action at all, and was thoroughly fed up with marching back and forth and sleeping rough.

On reaching the town square, David and Tomos tied their horses up at the side of the Red Dragon inn, enjoyed a pint of ale and entrusted their bundle of weapons (tied up in the remains of David's cloak) to the innkeeper. Then they went out to join the chattering throng as they waited for the moment when the French commander would appear and hand over his sword to Lord Cawdor. There was a carnival atmosphere, and much coming and going of officers dressed in a magnificent array of colourful uniforms. By one o'clock there was still no sign of the French commander on the square, or of surrendering troops on the sands, and an uneasy quiet spread over the crowd. Then an officer came out through the front door, held up his hand and shouted "Is there a gentleman by the name of David Morgan here?" David says he almost fell over with surprise, but he replied "Yes. Here I am", and found himself escorted into the presence of Lord Cawdor in one of the back rooms of the inn. The escort saluted and left the two men alone, closing the door behind him.

According to David's narrative, he bowed and Lord Cawdor saluted. Now that he could see him properly for the first time, David saw that he was a tall man, in his forties, with a slightly child-like face and a ruddy complexion. He was obviously used to being in charge of situations. The two men sat down and faced one another. "You are David Morgan, the gentleman with whom I spoke yesterday evening at Manorowen?"

"Yes sir, I am."

"Sir, I owe you the profoundest of apologies," said the commander. "Yesterday you provided me with some invaluable intelligence and offered me some soundly-based advice. My hasty rejection of your advice, and the haughty tone of my reply, is the cause of very great regret to me, and I apologize unreservedly. Will you forgive me?"

Somewhat taken aback by all this, David said "Sir, there is nothing to forgive. I know that you were under very great stress at the time, and that making quick decisions in such circumstances is not easy. I am sure that you acted in the manner which you thought most appropriate for the moment."

"I appreciate the graciousness of your reply. Between these four walls, I admit to you that as my militia passed up that narrow track towards Trefwrgi I became increasingly aware of the foolishness of my decision to advance in the darkness. We were vulnerable, to an unacceptable extent, to an ambush from the woodlands or from the hedges flanking the sunken track, and I admit to being greatly relieved when we reached the open ground without incident. At that point, much concerned by the intelligence you had given me, I sent scouts forward, and they almost stumbled into a large detachment of French grenadiers, dressed all in black and almost invisible, lying in the grass with their muskets and cannons trained on our army. They also spotted watchmen on the high ground of Carngelli. I know not how many of the enemy were stationed in these advanced positions, or how determined they were, or how well armed, but I immediately decided that we would press forward no further. I ordered my officers to supervise a retreat back down the track and thence to Fishguard. Luckily, the French let us go without firing a single shot."

Then he suddenly smiled and said "I hope you will hold it to my credit that I did at last take your advice!"

"Indeed sir, and it must be a great joy to all of us that this terrible episode has now been brought to a satisfactory conclusion," said David. "Also, we may all rejoice in the fact that fate has spared you and your colleagues of the militia, and that there appears to have been no great loss of life on either side."

"Quite so. But it could have been so much worse. If I had marched straight into that ambush in the dark, we would have had no defence and no effective retreat route. Unforgivable, in terms of military tactics. I shudder to think of it -- possibly hundreds dead, my own reputation in tatters, and the Trefwrgi Massacre handed down in British military history as the greatest ever fiasco on home soil. Tell me sir, how old are you?"

"Nineteen, sir,"

"And I perceive from your manner of speaking, and in spite of the fact that you were crawling about on Pencaer yesterday killing Frenchmen, that you are a gentleman. Where is your estate?"

"Plas Ingli, sir, close to Newport."

"Ah yes, I know of it. Small, but well run, so I gather. Did you not lose your family, and your house, in a terrible fire some years back?" David nodded and lowered his eyes. "Bad business indeed. I am very sorry. And you are now Master of the estate?" David nodded again. "Well, I have no doubt in my mind, sir, that the estate is in good hands."

Just then there was a knock on the door, and a youthful captain entered to announce that the French had started to lay down their arms on the beach. The interview was at an end. Lord Cawdor stood up and said "I must now attend to essential business." He held out his hand and shook David's hand firmly. "My dear Mr Morgan," he said, "it has been a pleasure to make your acquaintance. I suppose that in years to come I may be given the credit for defeating the French. But you know, and I know, that the total contribution of my army was to fire two musket shots, to march up to the top of the hill at Trefwrgi, and to march back down again. The French have in reality been defeated by the fighting spirit of you and your friends in the local community, and to a degree by their own incompetence. I consider myself to be considerably in your debt, for you have saved my reputation and possibly my life. Do not forget it. If, at any time in the future, you require my assistance, do not hesitate to contact me." And then he saluted and strode from the room.

David emerged into the afternoon sunlight, and he and Tomos followed the crowd along West Street to witness the French soldiers laying down their arms on the beach. Then, with Tomos still in great pain and keen to get home, they collected their ponies and their belongings from the Red Dragon and set out for home.

David has related his story to us around the kitchen table, and he is now in bed, washed and shaved, and fast asleep. I thank God for his courage, and for his sense of duty. We gather from people in town that the Newport Division of the Fencibles has been detailed to accompany a column of more than a thousand French prisoners to Haverfordwest. Billy is no doubt with them, and will probably not return home for several days, footsore and weary but probably some shillings better off following receipt of his military pay. Moses is still missing, but will no doubt return when he hears that the French have surrendered. And Lord Cawdor, the most powerful man in Pembrokeshire, is considerably in our debt.

ΩΩΩΩΩΩΩΩΩΩ

28th February 1797

Moses returned two days ago without saying too much about his movements during the invasion. He claimed that he was taking care of various relatives near Eglwyswrw, but we have heard that he was sighted in Newport on several occasions during the emergency.

Last night he went down to Newport in the evening, claiming that a good walk would do him good. No doubt he was intent upon scrounging a few jars of ale from his cronies in the Royal Oak. We did not expect him back until late, but we were still sitting round the fire in the kitchen at about nine o'clock when he came storming in with the blackest of scowls upon his face and dripping wet from head to toe. "Evening, Moses," said

Billy, all innocence. "Wet in town, was it? There's a funny thing for you, seeing as we've had a nice dry evening up here on the mountain."

Moses cast a furious glance in his direction, growled like a bulldog protecting a bone, and grabbed a flickering rushlight from the table. He said not a word to anybody, but stamped through to his room and slammed the door behind him. We all looked at each other quizzically, but it was clear that Billy knew something, and David asked him what was going on. Billy drew deeply on his clay pipe and simply said "I daresay, Master, that certain parties down in town were not too impressed by our friend's unwillingness to go off and fight the French, especially since he had some military training when he was at Eton. I do believe that he might have had a little visit from the *Ceffyl Pren*."

We all knew what that meant, and today Hettie brought further details with her when she turned up for work. Apparently Moses was expected at the Royal Oak, for as soon as he stepped inside the door he was surrounded by a gang of men from the Parrog who had been waiting inside. They were probably the same thugs who had beaten him up at the New Year. One of the men said "Moses Lloyd, you are summoned to appear before a special court to answer charges of desertion, treason and cowardice in the face of the enemy." His hands were tied with rope, and he was dragged outside onto the street. There he was confronted with a fearsome sight -- the *Ceffyl Pren* and his followers. According to Hettie, whose husband saw the whole thing, the *Ceffyl Pren* or wooden horse was a grotesque creature with a horse's skull crowned with straw and strips of rags, with a white sheet covering the body of the man who carried it. It pranced about making loud neighing noises. It was accompanied by six muscular "female" attendants with black faces and hair made of wisps of fleece, and all dressed in long woollen skirts, shawls and bonnets. One of them carried a drum and one a bugle.

On the street there was a "trial" in which Moses was charged and found guilty in less than a minute, and the spokesman for the *Ceffyl Pren* condemned the prisoner to be ducked six times in the old ducking stool down on the estuary. "Is that agreed by the jury?" he shouted, and "Yes! Yes! Yes!" shouted the crowd of onlookers. Moses had a rope tied around his neck, and with his hands still tied behind his back he was led like an African slave in the middle of a noisy procession through the town, with the drum beating, the bugle blaring, and the crowd dancing and singing.

Invasion

Somebody tied a sign around his neck which read "This man saved the King from the French." The *Ceffyl Pren* was at the head of the procession, skipping about insanely, and the six black-faced attendants took up the rear. What a sight they must have been! Down they went past the lock-up, observed by the mayor and the constable, who took no action at all when Moses pleaded with them to intervene.

At last, said Hettie, they reached the ducking stool, which looks like a big seesaw with a crude chair fixed to one end. It was high tide on the estuary, so the prisoner could be ducked into deep water rather than being dumped into black mud. Moses was tied into the chair and was apparently terrified that he might be drowned. But ridicule rather than revenge was the order of the day, and there was no point in struggling against such overwhelming odds. "Now we shall carry out sentence!" shouted the spokesman. "According to the ancient law of Hywel Dda, if he drowns he is innocent, but if he survives he is guilty as charged and convicted. What say you all?" "Agreed!" shouted the crowd, and then Moses was submerged six times in the icy water, yelling blue murder each time he went down and spluttering like a soggy dog each time he came up.

At last, with the punishment complete, the ducking stool was swung round and Moses was released, to a chant of "Guilty as charged! Guilty as charged!" He was then left standing on the shore, shivering, furious and humiliated, while the *Ceffyl Pren*, his beautiful assistants and the crowd all melted away in the darkness. So Moses made his miserable way home.

Later on David explained that the *Ceffyl Pren* is rarely used nowadays, and was last seen in Newport some years since, when a merchant had seduced a local girl, fathered twins and refused to admit paternity. He said that the rough justice meted out to the transgressor was normally justified, and hardly ever involved physical injury. It was, he said, a way for the community to enjoy some innocent fun and to show its disapproval for those involved in fornication, infidelity, informing on neighbours and so forth. Grandpa Isaac added that the antics of the *Ceffyl Pren* would not be needed if the law was administered effectively, and he said that he had himself been beneath the white sheet on a number of occasions as a young man. Be that as it may, and notwithstanding Moses' disinclination to fight the French, it sounds to me that the punishment he received at the hands of the mob was disproportionate to the crime, and I feel quite sorry for him.

10. Daffodil Time

3rd March 1797

Things are getting back to normal again. Grandma and Mrs Owen have been making malt, and tomorrow they will start brewing ale in readiness for the haymaking season. David is returning to the business of running the estate, after the broken work patterns of winter and the alarms and excursions connected with the invasion. Billy has just come back from Haverfordwest, with the Fishguard Fencibles now stood down and other militia taking over their duties in guarding the French prisoners. His side of the invasion story is very boring indeed, since he seems to have spent most of the time marching back and forth, first under the command of Colonel Knox and then under Lord Cawdor. He reckons that he marched well over a hundred miles over the course of three days, and he hopes that the King will give him some new boots. Moses is still in a very black mood after his undignified treatment at the hands of the *Ceffyl Pren,* but he is otherwise none the worse for his six duckings. Tomos is at home with his family, still in pain but mercifully free of infection.

The weather has continued cold, and last week there were three days of heavy snow when the mountain looked as beautiful as Heaven. In the snow flurries, I swear that I saw some white angels flitting about on the summit. When the thaw settled in, the trees shook off their heavy snowy burdens, and we had some glittering cascades sliding off the roofs of the farmhouse and the outbuildings. One of them landed on top of Hettie as she was walking in from the dairy, and left her feeling very undignified. Then we had two days of slush and mud and streaming water before the frost set in again.

I like this time of year, since it always engenders a warm and friendly spirit within the farmhouse, with everybody gathered after supper in the candle-lit kitchen, enjoying its warmth and savouring the exotic smells coming from Mrs Owen's cauldrons over the fire. Grandpa and Grandma enjoy the best positions -- as is right and proper -- in their high-back chairs on either side of the *simnai fawr,* and they sit there with their faces glowing like embers as they snooze the evening away. When he is awake, Grandpa

Daffodil Time

puffs away on his long-stemmed pipe. David, Billy and Moses usually sit around the kitchen table, playing cards or chess or reading cheap story books, and talking politics. I often sit and embroider cushion covers and bed covers in my favourite chair, and Bessie and Mrs Owen sit in the big settle with their knitting needles clattering, producing enough socks to replace those which the marching men of the Fencibles have recently worn out. Hettie sometimes stays overnight, and when she does the three of them hold knitting competitions. They take three lengths of yarn, each about ten yards long, from a ball of wool that sits in a basket on the floor. These lengths are knotted together, and once the knitting is under way the one who reaches the knot first is the winner. They chatter non-stop as they knit, and the movements of their hands and fingers are clearly controlled by some part of the brain that is inaccessible to normal human beings. Mrs Owen always wins these competitions by at least a yard, and never ceases to be delighted at the cheers which she receives as her only reward.

My favourite evenings are the story-telling evenings, which are usually triggered off by some piece of gossip. Last night Bessie said that there had been a report of a *canwyll gorff* or corpse candle down in the valley below Gelli, and Billy said "*Diawch*, that means somebody will be in a coffin before the week is out." Then the conversation got onto death, and death omens, and phantom funerals, and ghosts and such like. This was the first time we had talked of these things in the house since my arrival, for the deaths of David's parents and brothers and sisters are still too close to the surface for comfort, and maybe the loss of my baby just a few months ago has also caused a natural reserve to come to the fore. Now, however, it appears that we are all strong enough to get caught up in reminiscences and fifth-hand stories about spooky matters, and soon we were all involved in a good old-fashioned argument about superstition and fact, science and religion, imagination and reality. In turns we related our favourite tales of the supernatural, and Grandpa Isaac showed himself to be a master storyteller who could create terror in the hearts of his listeners more through his silences than his words.

David was very sceptical about all these ghostly things, saying that they are but the products of primitive minds; but I enjoyed taunting him about the narrowness of his education at Eton and about the inability of men of science to accept anything they don't personally understand. He got angry with me, which I found very amusing.

Daffodil Time

4th March 1797

Hettie brought up news from Newport today that there is a hunt going on in Fishguard for traitors who are supposed to have helped the French with their invasion plans. Apparently some people cannot believe that the landing at Carregwastad was something that happened purely by chance, and the authorities think that the French must have been guided ashore by some disaffected local people. Almost everybody known to have come in contact with the enemy is under suspicion; maybe some constable will come knocking on our door and will accuse David of being a collaborator because he has two French muskets in the gun cabinet and a French officer's hat hanging on the wall!

The witch hunt is apparently being conducted by a little group of gentlemen and merchants from Fishguard and Haverfordwest who are out to make mischief, and they are targeting all those who are known to read seditious literature or who are known to be Nonconformists. Some of the Baptists are even being accused of being Jacobite sympathizers, which seems to me just as ridiculous as accusing the Pope of being a secret disciple of Martin Luther. Hettie told us that two men named William Thomas and Thomas Williams were actually arrested but were then released as soon as it was discovered that they belonged to the Church of England! I must say that the more I hear of the behaviour of the magistrates and the upper orders of society, the more I come to the view that their brains have been addled by too much in-breeding. Grandpa, as a justice of the peace himself, tends to agree with me.

ΩΩΩΩΩΩΩΩΩΩ

5th March 1797

This afternoon we had a most interesting visit from three of the local squires and their wives. We were forewarned of it some days ago, when one of Squire Watkins' men rode up on a skinny pony. He delivered a note which said:

"Squire and Mrs Howell of Henllys, Squire and Mrs Watkins of Llannerch,

and Squire and Mrs Rice of Pentre Ifan wish to pay their respects to the Master and Mistress of Plas Ingli and their family on the afternoon of Friday 4th March. If convenient, they will attend at 3 o'clock in the afternoon for a short visit. The gentlemen will appreciate it if a time could be found for a private interview with Mr Isaac Morgan. They look forward with great pleasure to sharing a convivial hour in your company, and remain yours etc etc."

When this message arrived, David asked Grandpa what it was all about, and he swore violently, much to my amazement. It was clear to me that this was more than just a social visit, and that Grandpa was not at all looking forward to it. "The wolves are coming to snarl at me," was all that he would say. But Grandma added "Thank God we do not owe any of them any money. When we were rebuilding the Plas we were very careful whose kind offers of financial help we accepted. Some of them were not so kind as they appeared, and had we accepted their money and defaulted on our repayments the Plas would by now be in the possession of one or other of these vicious little men." I had met the Howell, Watkins and Rice families before, and had judged them to be petty and arrogant but not particularly evil or intelligent. I thought, therefore, that the afternoon might contribute to my education.

On the first stroke of the clock, at three this afternoon, three coaches came in a convoy into the yard, and the representatives of the local aristocracy climbed out to greet us. The three elderly gentlemen were carrying only their hats and sticks, having come on business. The three elderly ladies came carrying little bags of knitting and crochet work, having turned out either for the sake of appearances or -- more likely, I thought -- in order to assess the state of our family finances. They looked nervous, and I was struck especially by the darting eyes and tight thin lips of Mistress Rice. There was much bowing and curtseying, with expressions of artificial delight such as "My dear Master Morgan, what a pleasure to see you again!" and "Mistress Watkins, it is, as ever, such a joy to welcome you to the Plas, and such a pleasure to see you looking so well!" Many kind compliments were sent in my direction, and I must admit to having received them with a frisson of pleasure, but there was ice in the air, and I became more than a little inquisitive as to the reasons for Grandpa's apprehension. I knew that he did not respect our visitors, but I was unsure whether he feared them. I therefore observed quite closely what transpired when we all went into the house and sat in the parlour while Mrs Owen organized afternoon tea and cakes.

I was slightly irritated to find that our guests chose to speak English, even though they were all perfectly fluent in Welsh, presumably because English is now the preferred language of "polite" society. I thought I might use Welsh myself, just to make a point, but thought better of it. For this occasion at least, it was incumbent upon me to cooperate.

The three lady guests visited my dressing room in turn, in order to powder their noses and admire themselves in my full-length mirror. I observed them carefully -- Mistress Megan Howell well-bred, demure and dainty, Mistress Maria Rice nervous and as furtive as a ferret, and Mistress Myfanwy Watkins fat and arrogant. Then they settled with their handicrafts into one corner of the room, with the three squires in another, and it was clear that Grandma and I were required to join the ladies while David and Grandpa joined the men. The visitors knew, and we hosts knew, that they were our social superiors and that they would dictate the rules of engagement even though they were on our territory. For a few moments I scuttled about, pouring tea, being the good hostess and making small talk, and at the same time assessing the strengths, weaknesses and probable strategy of the enemy. Then, for better or for worse, and acting on impulse, I pulled up a chair and went and sat with the men, ignoring the ferocious glances thrown in my direction by Grandpa and David. One day I must try to control my impulses. "Well, this is very pleasant," I lied sweetly. "We are so sorry that your families were not able to accompany you today on your healthy trip into the countryside." I knew perfectly well that all the sons and daughters were in various town houses in Haverfordwest, enjoying the winter social season. "And may I enquire as to the health of the young Master Rice, and the Misses Watkins, and the young Master and Miss Howell?"

"Oh, Joseph is in excellent health thank you, Mistress Morgan," said Squire Rice.

"Yes indeed, the same can be said of my dear daughters also," said Squire Watkins.

"And I am pleased to report that John and Mary are both well, considering the cold and snowy weather we have been having," said Squire Howell.

"I am overjoyed to hear it, for we understand that many people have had a severe chill upon the chest in recent weeks," said I.

Then there was some talk about the farming crisis, and the high price of corn, and the subversive activities of the Nonconformists, with the three squires pointedly by-passing me with all their comments and addressing their remarks either to each other or to David and Grandpa. Grandfather and grandson tried to draw me into the conversation once or twice, but were headed off by the three of them, who were clearly used to working together. It was apparent to me that they were seeking to determine whether we, the Morganses of Plas Ingli, held any opinions and attitudes which might be construed as subtle but potentially dangerous departures from the "party line" laid down by those who saw themselves as the senior squires of the local area. This party line, without a shadow of a doubt, involved strict loyalty to the Church of England, profound mistrust of Methodists, Baptists and other Independents, and a rigid application of the law involving the use of the death penalty and transportation where permitted, to keep "paupers, vagabonds, and common people" in their rightful place at the bottom of the social order. At one stage David was invited to comment on the proposition that servant's wages must be held down at all costs, and caused eyebrows to be raised when he replied that wages and prices should always be considered together.

I was horrified at some of the attitudes betrayed by this trio of petty little men, and so I decided on a little innocent entertainment. I happened to know that Squire Rice's son Joseph had been in serious trouble with his father because he had accrued a debt of twenty pounds at the card tables in Haverfordwest some weeks ago. So I looked him in the eye and asked, with so much honey on my tongue that anybody blessed with a small brain would have been on his guard immediately, "And what, sir, would you consider, in this time of rising prices, to be a fair wage for a first ploughman working in your fields for a whole year?"

"Not a penny more than five pounds!" thundered the squire. "If we pay more, then it will be the end of financial probity. The flood-gates will be open and every servant and labourer for miles around would come pouring through!"

"But is it not the case that corn prices have doubled in the last three years while wages have stayed the same?" I asked innocently. "The labourers and their families have to buy corn to live. May I assume that this means more income for the landowners while the poor people are driven closer to starvation?"

The squire's eyes narrowed for a moment, and he exchanged obvious glances with his colleagues Watkins and Howell. Then, realizing that he had to release the tension, he gave a belly-laugh and said to Grandpa Isaac "My dear Isaac, you have a thoughtful young lady here, who will no doubt prove a blessing to you all as Mistress of the Plas! Her awareness of high economics and social issues does her credit, and I am sure that when she learns more about the manner in which our old estates are run, she will make gentlemen, lawyers and stewards entirely redundant!" At this, he and his cronies bellowed with delight, and slapped their knees, and wiped tears from their cheeks with their lace handkerchiefs, while Grandpa and David fidgeted nervously. I flushed a little at this deliberate slight; but then, a little surprised at my own strength, I decided to close in for the kill.

"Please forgive me for straying onto gentlemen's business," I said. "It is indeed much more appropriate, on a convivial occasion such as this, to talk of other matters such as music or literature. I trust that your son Joseph is enjoying the social season in Haverfordwest? I gather that the town is a veritable whirlwind of happy social events at this time of year."

"Oh yes indeed," replied the squire, still not quite recovered from his recent fit of good humour. "He is having an excellent time. You and your dear husband must, I venture to suggest, spend next season in town, if by then you have the estate back on a sound footing."

"That would be delightful. The balls, the races, the entertainments, the tea parties, the card tables. And thinking of which, I was so sorry to hear that your son has suffered from ill luck at the card tables of late. I trust that he has not been sucked too deeply into the whirlpool of debt as a result?"

"No, no, my dear lady, a trifling amount lost, a trifling amount."

"I am so pleased to hear it. And it is so good to know, sir, that your estate is in such good heart that you consider the annual cost of four honest farm servants to be but a trifle in the grand scheme of things. And now, gentlemen, please forgive me if I join the ladies. I must serve them some more tea and griddle cakes, and I have some important handicraft matters to discuss with them."

And having thus scattered my buckshot as widely as I dared, I curtseyed daintily, forcing all three gentlemen to stand and bow, and I left them, purple faced and lost for words, to nurse their wounds. I hoped that Grandpa and David had not picked up any incidental injuries, but I was reassured to note that they were both having difficulty in controlling the muscles at the edges of their mouths.

Having joined the three squire's wives and Grandma in the other corner of the room, I found that they were getting on well enough, drinking their tea and sharing items of intelligence about the minor adventures of local families. We talked of many things, including the price of tea and spices in Fishguard Market; the cloth bargains to be had just now from Master Shinkins the merchant down on the Parrog, who had just brought a ship in from Bristol; and the problems of getting decent serving maids now that they all wanted to work in the big towns. Then the three squires and Grandpa stood up as if at a pre-arranged signal, and Squire Watkins said "Pray forgive us, my dear David and my dear ladies, if we retire to the office with Isaac for just a few minutes. We have one or two small but important matters to discuss." And they bowed and waddled off along the passage, leaving David stranded like a beached sea creature and leaving us ladies to continue our discussions on small but not unimportant matters as we sipped our tea. David joined us with good grace, and enjoyed the griddle cakes more than the conversation. Luckily the three visiting ladies were in an amiable mood, for they clearly had considerable respect for Grandma Jane, and I did not have to deal with any darts fired in my direction. This meant that I could keep half an ear open for the sounds coming from the office, and more than once I heard raised voices and a desk being thumped.

At last the gentlemen emerged, all looking black as thunder, and Squire Rice announced that it really was time to be off before the darkness set in, what with so many dastardly rogues and vagabonds lurking in the hedgerows these days. I knew not what had been going on in the office, except to guess that it had not been pleasant; but I thought it was of some credit to civilized society that we all behaved with due courtesy towards each other in saying our goodbyes.

When the last of the three carriages had gone rolling off down the track towards Newport, Grandfather stormed back into the parlour and exploded. It was the first time I had ever seen him angry. "Aaargh! Those pathetic, self-obsessed, mealy-mouthed, pumped-up imbeciles!" he roared. "They think that they can dictate to me the way I behave, and the things I believe in, just because they own more acres than we do and because they think they have more sovereigns under the bed! Well, I happen to know that most of their acres are mortgaged, and that they are all on the run! They are scared to death, all three of them -- scared of change, scared of justice, scared of compassion, scared of anybody or anything that threatens the old order. They are thundering numbskulls, all three. They came here today simply to intimidate me, and I will not be intimidated! And one day, just you wait and see, I will repay this particular social visit!"

"There now, Isaac *bach*," said Grandma, as if she was consoling a crying baby. "Don't you worry about them. You just come into the kitchen, *bach*, and we will have another nice cup of tea, and then we will all feel better."

When Grandpa had calmed down a bit, he explained to us the purpose of the visit by the three squires. He was sure that they were acting as a deputation on behalf of a substantial group of local squires and gentlemen. They were clearly on the defensive, he thought, and they were frightened out of their useless little lives by any person of social standing who stepped out of line.

He said he had received an oblique hint that he was neglecting his duties as a Justice of the Peace, and that he should be prepared to appear more often at the Petty Sessions to deal with law-breakers. This had been followed by a suggestion from Squire Rice that the justices should work more closely together to swear in more special constables, to convict prisoners more quickly, to reduce the level of proof required for convictions, and to use the maximum sentences allowed by law. Squire Watkins had expressed his concern at the scale of food support that was going to the poor labourers in Plas Ingli cottages, since it reflected poorly on the support he was giving to his own labourers down the valley at Llannerch. Squire Rice enquired innocently as to the manner of our wedding, having heard, through the spy network, that it had been conducted some way away and had involved a marriage license. Squire Howell had hinted, ever so gently, that it was not a good idea to house our servants within the farmhouse while others, including himself, housed servants in hay-lofts or cowsheds. News of the jovial and generous nature of our Christmas and New Year celebrations had reached their ears, and they warned Grandpa that such fraternization with servants, tenant farmers and labourers could only lead to trouble in the long term. News of

Daffodil Time

David's adventures on Pencaer during the invasion had become common knowledge, said Squire Watkins, and while they applauded his courage and patriotism they questioned the wisdom of his actions in the company of peasants and labourers while other respectable gentlemen and squires were demonstrating their capacity for leadership as militia officers. And as for that dark-eyed and black-haired young lady named Martha Morgan -- well, the sooner she was brought under control the better, for no good ever comes of women poking their noses into gentlemen's business.

Finally, they had invited Grandpa to cease making contributions to the circulating schools in Newport, Nevern and Cilgwyn. Squire Watkins said that he had been "greatly saddened" by David's reply to his well-intentioned letter of last month. They said that an educated peasantry, capable of reading and writing, would pose an immediate threat to what they called "good order" since they would have access to the subversive pamphlets and books known to be circulating in the local area. And then, knowing that the Plas Ingli barn was still partly filled with barley while theirs were almost empty, they invited Grandpa -- not for the first time -- to join the ring of local landowners and yeoman farmers in holding the remainder of the barley crop until prices were forced above eight shillings a bushel. At this point, Grandpa said, he had called the interview to a halt by saying, between clenched teeth, "Gentlemen, I thank you for your concerns and your advice. I have heard enough to convince me that you and I are following different pathways. I had hoped that your style of thinking, and your style of behaving, had faded away a century since. I will report all you have said to my grandson, for he is Master of the Plas, and it is not in my power to take action on any of the matters on which you have seen fit to advise me, apart from those connected to my duties as a magistrate. Act as you will, but I warn you that your fear and loathing of change will serve you ill. I will act, and I trust my grandson and the rest of my family will act, according to the dictates of conscience and according to the guidance given to us in the Gospels. These are hard times for small estates such as ours. We may not survive any longer than you, but we will seek to go to our graves having made our peace with our God. And now, gentlemen, allow me to show you to the door and to wish you a safe journey home."

When we had absorbed all of this we did not know whether to laugh or cry. For myself, I found it quite an education, although I suspect that David and Grandma Jane were already aware of some of the attitudes and methods of the petty gentry. We decided that these men would henceforth be counted as our enemies, and that we could expect them to employ a variety of techniques in their future assaults upon our virtue. David is worried, and I am worried. But both Grandma and Grandpa assure us that not all of the local landowners share the views of Rice, Watkins and Howell. They say that there are many others, including Bowen of Llwyngwair, Laugharne of Pontfaen, and Prosser of Frongoch, who are more powerful than they, and a great deal more progressive in their estate management and their attitudes to education and provision for the poor. It seems to all of us that we need to work a little harder in forging alliances; and it seems that some interesting chess games, played for high stakes, may lie ahead of us.

ΩΩΩΩΩΩΩΩΩ

7th March 1797

The daffodils have come, and Moses has gone. We know not where he is, but tomorrow a warrant will be out for his arrest, and no doubt he will then be apprehended by the constables. It happened like this.

Two days ago, following our interesting afternoon in the company of the three squires and their wives, David and Grandpa decided that they would make some investigations concerning the price of barley. We have sold or used relatively little of the harvest thus far, and much of the crop is still unthreshed; but nobody can remember the barn so full at this time of year. There are several reasons for this. First, after the fire and the sales of livestock and the loss of farm servants that followed, much of the better land at the Plas was left fallow for two years. Grandpa and Billy agreed at the time that this would do no harm, for the land was in need of a rest. It was limed and grazed by the animals that remained on the farm, but that was all. Last year in the spring, Grandpa decided to plant up a larger acreage of barley than ever before, and because of the excellent summer weather the harvest provided eighty bushels to the acre. The crop has remained in exceptional condition because the Plas barn was re-roofed after the fire and modified to provide improved ventilation. We also think that many rats and mice were killed in the fire. So while other landowners have lost part of their crop through vermin, mould and fermentation, our crop has remained clean, dry and cool. Holding so much of the barley crop over the winter is a business fraught with danger, but Grandpa is teaching us that it is possible to "play the market" without exploiting the poor, since grain prices always rise in the early spring anyway, and those who take the biggest risks deserve to reap the biggest rewards.

Yesterday David rode into Fishguard in the early afternoon, and he galloped home again three hours later in a state of high excitement. "Barley prices are rising fast!" he exclaimed. "The invasion has caused a huge shortage in north Pembrokeshire generally, partly because of the damage done by the French troops on Pencaer, but also because of the need to feed the militias and the prisoners. Merchants have been buying up all the barley they can get, and most of the landowners have nothing left to sell. Prices are rising so fast that the poor people cannot afford to buy flour, and there are fears of more corn riots. Today the government has stepped in, and has banned all barley shipments for the time being. The grain that is still available has to be sold locally, and as a gesture of gratitude for the fortitude of the local populace while the French forces were roaming about on Pencaer, the government is buying at the market price and selling to the poor at five shillings per bushel. Now is the time to sell at maximum profit, without harming the interests of the poor!" Grandfather agreed, and we discussed our marketing strategy late into the evening. I also worked on a strategy of my own, without telling anybody else.

It so happened that Billy was out in Newport during the evening, visiting one of his lady friends. When he returned everybody was in bed. On the reasonable assumption that I was the only one awake, I quietly slipped out of bed, took a candle and went down to the kitchen. Billy was surprised to see me and started to apologize in whispers for the lateness of his return. But I whispered "You must not worry about that, Billy. But I have a small job for you to do before you go to bed. Take a lantern and go over to the barn. You know where everything is in there. You are good at counting. I want you to count the number of hessian sacks we have stored there. We may need to shift a lot of barley tomorrow, and if we do not have enough sacks we may have to get more from Shinkins Merchant in the morning."

Billy looked bemused at the apparent urgency of this matter in the middle of the night, but he whispered "Yes, Mistress Martha *bach*, I will go and do that straight away." And off he went, lantern in hand. Ten minutes later he was back, and reported that there were eighty-seven sacks in the pile by the door. "Thank you, Billy," I murmured. "That is all I needed to know. I think we had better hunt for some more first thing in the morning. Now I can go back to my bed and you can go to yours. A very good night to you."

When David and I woke this morning I told him of my little midnight mission, and of Billy's help, and while he was a little concerned about the underhand nature of my behaviour, he agreed that we had nothing to lose from setting a trap. When I opened the shutters and looked out on the world I saw that the weather was perfect for my purpose -- cloudy, with a stiff westerly wind and threatening rain. At breakfast, after the turnip cutting and milking, we all sat round the kitchen table, as usual, to plan the day's work. "Today, dear friends," said David, "we have an opportunity to solve some of the financial difficulties which beset us. The government is buying barley on a substantial scale to feed to the poor people in Fishguard and elsewhere. We have more left in our barn than anybody else, and we may choose to sell most of our harvest over the next few days. So we have several hard days ahead of us. All right?"

There was a murmur of excitement around the table. He continued, like a general deploying his troops, "Billy, as soon as you have finished breakfast I want you to go down and get six labourers to help us with threshing for however long it takes. Three of the Jenkins boys and three others from the bottom cottages. Bessie, I want you please to walk over to Griffiths Dolrannog Isaf, Ifans Dolrannog Uchaf, and Williams Gelli and ask each of them to give us at least one day's work to be credited on the lease. The work for them may go on through tomorrow, and possibly longer. We will need at least ten people in the barn, and I want three pairs of threshers working continuously. We will all have to help out with threshing, hummelling, winnowing, moving the chaff, bagging and stacking. Grandpa and I will help in the barn. Martha and Hettie can look after the dairy and the other tasks around the farm, and Grandma and Mrs Owen can look after the house. Moses, I want you to go into Fishguard with ten sacks of barley. Take the grey pony and gambo. There is already a pile of threshed barley in the storage bays. Load up the sacks yourself, but put the big oilskin over them when you travel, since there is rain in the air.

Daffodil Time

Try each of the Fishguard merchants, Williams, Probert and Milton, and when you are sure they are all working on the government intervention scheme, get the best price you can. I will give you a letter of introduction, and I want you to come back with the money and a signed bill of sale. Try to get back here by mid-afternoon if you can. If the price is good, I want time to organize half a dozen horses and carts for the next few days so that we can shift ninety per cent of what is in the barn. Are there any questions? No? So let's go to it!"

We gobbled up the rest of our porridge, downed the rest of our warm buttermilk, and went to it in a gale of coats and smocks, boots and gaiters, hats and shawls. David scribbled out a note of introduction for Moses, and gave it to him. Within ten minutes, everybody was out of the house except Grandma, Mrs Owen and myself. At this stage I brought them into my confidence, and asked them to take up station in the upstairs window at the north-eastern corner of the house, with the shutters open by only an inch or two, and to observe closely what happened at the barn door. In particular, I asked them to count the precise number of sacks of barley that Moses put onto the gambo. I had a premonition of what the total would be. Then I went down to help Hettie with chopping turnips, feeding all the animals, mucking out the cowshed, and setting things ready for the butter making in the dairy. As I worked I saw Moses fetch the pony and harness it between the shafts of the gambo. He took the big oilskin from one of the outbuildings, threw it onto the gambo, and went off round the corner towards the barn door. With David and Grandpa several fields away, moving the cattle to fresh pasture and checking the breeding ewes, he was all by himself. After that I did not see him for about half an hour, but then he emerged onto the farmyard, driving the pony and gambo, with his load of sacks all hidden beneath the oilskin. He opened the gate, passed through, and closed it behind him. Then off he went towards his doom, and as he went I gave him a cheerful wave, feeling like Jezebel.

As soon as he was out of sight I ran into the house and found Grandma and Mrs Owen mumbling and grumbling and clearly outraged at what they had seen from the upstairs window. "Well?" I asked. "What did you see?"

"Very furtive indeed, he was," replied Mrs Owen. "Looking around all the time. A good job we had only a little chink in the shutters, or he would have seen us. Tied up the pony by the door, he did, and after filling up the sacks inside the barn he took them out one by one and loaded them onto the gambo. Each one was put in turn under the oilskin, so you could not count how many was there. Then, when he was ready, he tied down the oilskin with a rope, and off he went."

"And how many sacks did he load?"

"Twelve," said Grandma.

"Twelve," said Mrs Owen.

Then I knew that the foolish, degenerate man had signed his own arrest warrant and, if we wished it, his own death warrant. I felt a sense of cold triumph in my stomach, but also a dread that we would now have to pursue this matter to its bitter end.

But none of us had time to mull over the consequences of our successful espionage operation, for there was too much to do. Mrs Owen was in a panic, for she was expecting ten extra mouths to feed once the threshing operation got under way in the barn. Grandma needed to be in the alehouse decanting ale from one of the big barrels. And I needed to be out cutting chaff and furze for the animals, and then in the dairy helping Hettie. Half an hour later Billy returned with his six extra helpers, and Bessie came back with our tenant farmers who had kindly consented to drop everything in order to help us. Some of the men carried flails with them, which was just as well since we had only two of our own. In no time at all the threshing operation was under way, with the steady rhythm of the flails on the threshing floor and the sounds of animated conversation and laughter among the men. Although it was cold and windy (and indeed they needed the wind for their winnowing operations) they all developed a healthy thirst, and there was a great demand for Plas Ingli special ale. "Tasty, but not too strong," said Grandma. "At the harvest we got it wrong this year, and the men got so drunk one hot day in the afternoon that they all went to sleep behind the hedge. This time we have to keep them at it."

At last it was time for a mid-day break for bread and cheese and pickled herrings, and while all the men were round the kitchen table I asked Billy to go out and count the hessian sacks again. "Again?" said Billy. "Again," said I. So off he went, to return with the message that there were seventy-five sacks on the pile. "So there we are," he said. "Moses has taken twelve sacks to Fishguard, filled with the barley, as the Master asked him to do." Then a frown came over his face. "Hold on a minute," he continued. "Did not the Master ask him first thing this morning to take just ten sacks to the corn merchants?" "Quite so, Billy, " I replied. "But let us be charitable, and assume that he made a little mistake with his counting."

As I spoke, the faces round the table were all ears and all eyes, for Moses had no friends in the local area, and nobody was particularly inclined to think well of him. There was a stony silence, brought to an end by David, who said "Bessie, we are going to be very short of sacks. Will you please walk down to Newport, call on Shoni Transportation and get him to turn out at once with his horse and heavy cart. Then go down to the Parrog with him and see if you can buy two hundred hessian sacks from Benji Walter at the corn warehouse. I happen to know that the warehouse has no corn in it just now, so he should have thousands of sacks lying around. Get back as soon as you can." Off Bessie went on her mercy mission, quite happily since Benji Walter is on her list of eligible bachelors, while the rest of us returned to our appointed tasks. I took David to one side for a moment and briefed him on the observations made by Mrs Owen and Grandma Jane early this morning.

Shortly before dusk, with some flurries of rain blowing in from the west, Moses returned with the pony and empty gambo. He seemed very cheerful, and went straight into the barn where all the men were still hard at work with their flails and shovels, covered with dust and chaff. He went straight up to David, smelling of cider, and said "Master, we are in luck! The price is ten shillings a bushel, and I have five pounds for you! Tomorrow the price may be even higher!" "Very good, Moses," replied David. "We will sort things out in a little while, when we have finished here. Go and put the gambo away, wipe down the pony and settle her into the stable with some hay. Then come into the kitchen in half an hour."

When it was too dark to see anything in the barn, the men abandoned work for the day. They had threshed a good part of the harvest, and six men should now be adequate to finish off the task over the next few days. There is a huge pile of golden barley in the middle of the floor, waiting to be bagged when Bessie and Shoni come up from town with a supply of sacks. Everybody came into the kitchen for supper, coughing and wheezing and beating their clothes to get rid of dust and chaff.

With everybody settled down around the table with their boiled potatoes and ham on their platters, David judged the moment to be right for a discussion with Moses. He told me afterwards that he had not wanted to make a public inquiry out of it, but it is not easy to obtain an arrest warrant for the son of a magistrate, even if he has been disinherited; and he wanted as many witnesses as possible. "Right, Moses," he said. "I am sorry that I was busy earlier on. Now tell us how you got on in Fishguard."

As proud as Punch, Moses said "I got to Fishguard and went to see each of the corn merchants and showed them your note. Master Milton was offering the best price, ten shillings a bushel, so I sold all ten sacks to him. Here is the five pounds, and here is the bill of sale." He handed over the money and the note, and added "Master Milton says he will take whatever barley you have tomorrow, even if the market price is higher."

"I am very pleased to hear it, and thank you for the money. Now then, how many sacks of barley did you take on the gambo?"

Moses was startled by this question, and cast a quick glance around the table. "Why, ten sacks, exactly as you asked me, Master," said he.

Then David turned to Grandma and Mrs Owen, who were standing next to the cauldron of boiling potatoes in front of the fireplace. "Now, Grandmother and Mrs Owen," he asked, "how many sacks of barley did you see Moses loading onto the gambo from the barn door?"

"Twelve," said Grandmother, and "Twelve, Master," said Mrs Owen, as the colour drained from Moses' face.

"I see. We appear to have some discrepancy here in our figures. Let us turn to Billy. Now then, Billy, I understand that you counted the sacks in the barn last night. How many were there?"

"Eighty-seven, Master."

"And how many were there when you counted them again when we stopped work for our midday meal?"

"Seventy-five, Master, and unless I am very much mistaken in the matter of mathematics, that is twelve less than there was before."

"Thank you, Billy," said David, sounding for all the world like Lewis Legal investigating some complicated matter to do with grazing rights or tenancy agreements. Then he turned to Moses and confronted him with the truth. "I trusted you to take ten sacks of barley to Fishguard, and we have solid evidence from three reliable people that you took twelve sacks with you under the oilskin. What did you do with the other two sacks? Did you sell them privately? If so, where is the money? If you cannot convince me otherwise, I will assume, Moses, that you have stolen barley worth one pound from me -- and that, as you know, is an offence that will lead you straight to the Quarter Sessions and possibly to the Grand Sessions. What have you to say?"

At this, Moses, as expected, launched into a counter-attack. "I am outraged, sir, that you should make such disgraceful accusations in the presence of all these people!" he shouted. "You have no evidence of any wrong-doing on my part, and these accomplices are all involved in some feeble plot to get me convicted for a crime I have not committed!" And he thumped the table with his fist and stood staring at David like a bull terrier in the last seconds before a dog-fight.

"Let me ask you, Moses," continued David, quite under control but with a tremble in his voice, "whether you have a further pound to give me following your transactions in Fishguard."

"No I do not!" thundered Moses, beginning now to get very agitated.

"When you came back this afternoon with the gambo, you smelt of cider. You have had no wages from me since Christmas, following your adventure in the Black Lion, and I am doubtful that you have any money to spend in the local inns. Where did you obtain the money needed to buy several pints of cider?"

"I have good friends in Newport, damn you! If they want to buy me a drink or two, that is no concern of yours!"

"Forgetting about your friends for a moment, shall we turn to the matter of the disappearing chickens? A little while ago two chickens disappeared from the hen house without any sound from the dogs. On the same evening you went down to Newport with your cloak wrapped tightly about you. May I please ask you, Mrs Owen, what you saw when you looked on the inside of Moses' cloak next day?"

"Blood, and the little downy feathers that come from a chicken's neck," replied the good woman.

"And I saw the same thing," I volunteered.

The consumption of ham and potatoes around the table had now completely stopped. All eyes were focussed on Moses, and he got up from the table and started to behave like a rat in a high-sided wooden box. "Damn you! Damn you all!" he screamed, with fire blazing in his brown eyes. "I can see that you want rid of me! You have hated me ever since I set foot inside this God-forsaken place! Well, let me tell you, I have hated every minute of every day since I came here! And I hate all of you, pathetic grubby peasants doomed to your short lives of toil and drudgery! Do you have any idea what it is like for a man like me, educated as a gentleman, to sweat and slave day after day in the mud of that wretched little garden and the slime of the farmyard? Do you know what it does to a man's brain to hear talk, day after day, of nothing but the weather, and animals, and lime spreading, and chaff cutting, and carting turf? I begin to feel more like an ape than a man, surrounded by idiots. And can you imagine what it is like to know that the idiots -- all of you sitting with your open mouths and your staring eyes around this table -- have roofs over your heads and wives and families, while I have a poky room in this miserable farmhouse and not a penny in my pocket? Do you know what it is like? Do you? Do you?"

After this outburst, he slumped into the settle, and buried his head in his hands, overcome with emotion. We all thought he was going to weep. Then Grandpa moved in, like a judge who had heard all he wanted to hear. "Moses Lloyd," he said, "I think it best that you say no more. I want to be fair to you, and there are so many witnesses here that you will certainly incriminate yourself if you continue in this vein. You may recall that I am a Justice of the Peace, and that I have the power to issue a warrant for your arrest here and now. I choose not to do that, for I am too close to your crimes. You should have been arrested following your disgraceful behaviour in the Black Lion inn. There were sufficient witnesses, and there was sufficient damage in the bar room, to have led to a conviction and to transportation to the colonies. One or two of the men in the inn, so I gather, were keen to press charges of attempted murder against you. David rescued you on that occasion, and we have nursed you back to health here at the Plas. Have you ever given anybody a word of thanks? I think not. You have thanked us now by stealing and selling two chickens, and stealing and selling two bushels of barley."

With all eyes on Moses, he continued: "Early tomorrow morning, David and I will travel down to Llwyngwair Manor and we will ask Squire Bowen to authorize a warrant for your arrest. Having obtained this from the clerk to the justices, we will give it to the constable, and he will come to arrest you immediately. A court will be summoned, and the magistrates will remand you in custody and commit you for trial at the Quarter Sessions. You will be taken to Haverfordwest Gaol to await your fate. When you are tried, transportation for fourteen years will be the least you can expect. You have until tomorrow morning to prepare yourself."

"Damn you, old man!" hissed Moses, his face twisted in a terrible contortion of hatred. "You are an evil, corrupt, scheming rogue, like your father and grandfather before you! You and your son were the ones who brought me here in the first place, and I see now that your only aim was to degrade me and humiliate me and destroy me! Your son is gone, thank God, and may his soul roast in the fires of hell! And a curse on you and your house -- you will never be rid of me, and I will see you all dragged down into the pit by the Devil and his demons!"

We did not know what to do or what to think, and I suppose most of us around the table became convinced that Moses was utterly mad, and therefore to be pitied. But his insults were not going down well with the Jenkins boys and the cottagers, and there were signs that they were beginning to think of laying hands on him, taking him outside and possibly beating him senseless. Grandfather put out a restraining hand and brought the proceedings to a close by saying "Moses, you have now insulted a Justice of the Peace in the gravest possible manner, in the presence of a room full of witnesses. I could ask my friends around this table to arrest you immediately. Your crimes are multiplying by the minute, and if you continue in this vein you will stray into a field of criminal activity for which the only penalty is death by hanging. I have told you what we will do in the morning. Until then, you are a free man. Use your freedom as you will."

Moses took the hint. He roared like a caged lion, rushed down the passage to his room, gathered up an armful of clothes, stuffed them into a soft bag, and ran back out again, muttering to himself in anguish. Some of the men looked at Grandpa, asking with their eyes whether they should stop the madman before he escaped, but he motioned them to sit still where they were. Moses stopped for a moment at the kitchen door, wrapped his cloak around himself, and managed to exert enough self-control for a final theatrical act of defiance. He let his eyes wander across all of our faces, and said in a voice that had me in mind of a hissing cat rather than a king of the jungle "If you miserable peasants think that you have seen the last of Moses Lloyd, think again. I swear by the Devil that I will return to haunt you and will see all of you to your graves!"

Then he swept off into the darkness, with that shambling run of his, with his arms flailing and his cloak flying in the wind, and disappeared like a wounded bat into the night.

Daffodil Time

11th March 1797

At last we can relax. We have been having a feast for the whole of the threshing and carting party this evening, and as I write I can still hear the boisterous celebrations going on down in the kitchen. The best ale is flowing freely. I decided to retreat to my room, for this is a man's feast and I did not wish to over-stay my welcome. Besides, after five days of hard labour I feel as if I could sleep for a week without waking.

It has taken us until now to thresh and move a thousand bushels of barley from the barn. And we have been blessed with a miracle -- six days of dry and windy Pembrokeshire weather at the beginning of March! We also had an abundant supply of sacks, delivered by Bessie and Shoni Transportation just before midnight the other evening. On the day after the confrontation with Moses, David rode back into Fishguard and agreed a deal with Milton Merchant to supply one thousand bushels of clean barley for six hundred pounds (or twelve shillings per bushel) within the week, under the government intervention scheme. Then he rushed around to all his friendly neighbours arranging for the loan of as many horses and carts, and men to drive them, as could be spared. He returned in a state of high euphoria, for he had never done such a deal before, and Grandpa slapped him on the back and said "Well done, my boy! You have the makings of an excellent farmer. Now let us deliver to Master Milton exactly what we have promised!"

The threshing floor was enlarged so that three pairs of men could work with their flails at the same time, and Hettie, Bessie and I were called in to help the men with beating off the sharp barley spikes, winnowing, clearing chaff and straw, and bagging. The dust was something terrible, and it will take weeks to get rid of it from our hair, our clothes and inside our lungs; for as we worked we must all have looked like snowmen. We worked with neckerchiefs tied round our faces, but they did not help a great deal. But we all enjoyed the gossip and the laughter and the shared mealtimes. There was a continuous procession of horses and carts coming to the barn door, being loaded with bushel sacks, and then heading off towards Fishguard. Grandpa, who is very fit for his age but who wheezes and sneezes if he works in all the dust in the barn, acted as the foreman and tally-man, and kept us constantly informed of our progress towards the thousand bushel target.

The frantic activity at the Plas has caused so much interest in the community that the labourers' wives and small children have all been coming up to watch, and many of them have offered to help without payment, but we have had to decline most of these kind offers because the workers were beginning to get in each other's way. We hear on the spider's web that some of the local squires (including our dearly beloved friends Watkins, Howell and Rice) are furious about the combination of good luck and good judgment that has led us into the deal with the corn merchant, but they are powerless to interfere, and even their veiled threats to some of the carters who are helping us have been disregarded.

Now it is all over. This afternoon David took the pony and trap and followed the last load to Fishguard. There, at the corn store, he met Mr Milton, and he was paid the six hundred pounds promised. Immediately, with the money in his pocket, he went to call on Lewis Legal, and together they travelled in the trap to see Gruffydd Tregroes, Rhys Cilshafe and Williams Langton to pay off the last of the Plas Ingli debts. They were each apparently surprised and disappointed to be paid the money and the interest owed, for they had expected nothing at all until Christmas and had no doubt prayed for a default on the debt which would have given them shares in the estate. Master Lewis completed all the paperwork, and got paid for it back in his office in the town, and then David cracked the whip and rode the trap homewards, feeling like a Roman emperor and singing Welsh hymns all the way. He still had one hundred and thirty-two pounds in his pocket. He would need only thirty-two to pay the labourers and the carters, and for the first time since the fire he could celebrate the fact that the Plas has no debts.

When David returned, tired and elated, there were embraces all round, and a few happy tears from Grandma Jane. We four Morganses had a short meeting in the office, and Grandpa reported that there was still enough barley in the barn for the animals, for the spring sowing and for our immediate bread needs, and enough turnips and hay to see us through till the summer. With so few animals now on the farm, the fodder supplies have lasted well. We decided that we could afford to give the servants a bonus and a modest wage increase now, with a view to bringing wages and daily rates for the labourers back up to the normal levels after the harvest. We will buy new breeding stock -- cattle, sheep and horses -- and new carts and farm equipment. David says we can buy a new chaise. We will also employ the oldest Jenkins boy from Blaenwaun to replace Moses. He will start next week, for we must now get straight into ploughing and planting, and continue with the building of the new cowshed and stable.

Moses has disappeared without trace. Early on the morning after the confrontation in the kitchen, Grandpa and David went to Llwyngwair Manor to see Squire Bowen, who is the senior justice in the area. They asked for an arrest warrant, and after explaining the charges and the extent of the witness evidence available, the squire had no alternative but to instruct the clerk to issue one. The fugitive is charged with insulting a magistrate, slander, petty larceny and grand larceny, and "Wanted" notices have been put up in town. The constables are searching for Moses, but my guess is that he is a hundred miles away and is unlikely ever to be seen again in this area. It will not be too difficult for him to melt into the background, since there are vagabonds and paupers on all the roads, and people do not pay much attention to men who sleep rough and keep moving on. He will probably have to survive as a highwayman or some such thing, since hard labour is not to his liking. I am still not happy with the manner in which David and Grandpa just let him go, but Grandpa says that as a justice he had to behave with complete propriety so as to avoid any accusations of prejudice or personal animosity. He says that he has to be exceptionally careful just now, with the three silly squires out to get him on any pretext whatsoever. I daresay that Grandpa knows what he is doing -- he has after all been learning, and practising, gentry tactics for a very long time.

I must stop. I hear David coming, somewhat unsteadily if I am not mistaken, up the stairs towards the bedroom. I am very tired. He is also tired, and he has had too much to drink. However, I quite enjoy loving him when he is drunk, and I am inclined to think that after today's good fortune a little celebration is in order. I have let down my hair, and I am already in my nightdress. Pretty as it is, I have it in mind, on a sudden and delightful impulse, to take it off and ambush him as he comes in through the door.

ΩΩΩΩΩΩΩΩ

11. Growth

12th March 1797

It is early morning, and a horrid one at that, with a westerly gale pummelling the gable end of the house and a torrent pouring out of the black sky. There is still not a glimmer of light in the east, and nobody else in the house is awake. I had to get up. Further sleep is impossible because I have a vivid dream still fixed in my memory. It was not a nightmare, and I did not awake in a cold sweat, but it was so strange that I must write it down before it slips away from me.

The dream was really about Moses and me. At first I was lying in his arms in the softest and most luxurious of beds, between purple silk sheets. (How can I have dreamt such a thing? The very thought of it appalls me.) He had no beard, and he had all his teeth, and he was a tender and passionate lover. But before we came to the peak of our loving he suddenly jumped out of bed and was transformed into a strange and manic figure which brings into mind the Pied Piper of Hamelin. He had a jester's hat on his head, and a red jacket, and breeches with one white leg and one black. He was dancing about and playing on a tin whistle, and I was so drawn by the tune that I jumped out of bed, naked as the day I was born, and followed him. He rushed out into the cobbled street of some magical city with magnificent palaces and buildings and gardens and fountains, and danced from one piazza to another, tootling something tuneless on his instrument. I followed, quite unashamed of my nakedness, but unable to resist the lure of the music. Moses knew that his playing was irresistible, and in the moments when he paused for breath he had a strange sneering smile on his face. As we went along we were joined by David and Grandma and Grandpa, and Bessie and Mrs Owen, and Billy and Shemi, and almost all of our neighbours and friends. Then David's dead brother Griffith appeared. Then a good-looking man and woman and three small children joined the mad dancing procession, and I knew that they were David's parents and little brothers Thomas and George and little sister Rose, who all died in the fire three years ago.

Soon a great multitude of people was following Moses and his magical tin whistle. But as they skipped and jumped and ducked and weaved I saw in my dream that not one of them was smiling. It was as if they were caught in some nightmarish trap from which there was no escape. Moses and the throng of dancers left the city and went out into a countryside of lush meadows and leafy copses, and then started to climb up into the foothills of a rocky mountain. Still he led, dancing and playing his strange tune with inexhaustible energy. I followed, still naked and shoeless, but strangely the rest of the throng appeared not to notice my shame.

We climbed ever higher, dancing through bogs and lakes, through narrow mountain passes and across barren rocky plateaux. There were terrible winds carrying sleet and snow from the fastnesses of the far north. I had no sensation of cold, for I was aglow with the effort of dancing. We danced across banks of snow and ice and mounds of broken rock. We danced along the edges of great ravines filled with boulders, and the sound of Moses' tuneless tune echoed back and forth and turned into a hellish cacophony. There were no signs of life in this desert country apart from the pied piper and his enchanted followers. Then I noticed that the dancers were falling to the ground one by one, until the great multitude was reduced to just a few hardy folk. Still Moses smiled and sneered, and still he led us upwards towards the mountain summit. I recall in my dream that I tried to resist the allure of the tune and the player, but I could not, and was drawn inexorably on.

At last, on the summit of the mountain, I was the only one left. Thick white clouds drifted past, and I could hear the wind thundering through the jagged rocks. On all sides there was a black void. I looked at my hands and feet, and after my mad scramble along gravel tracks and over broken boulders I saw that they were streaming with blood. Moses stopped his playing, turned and came towards me. Now the smile had gone, and there was menace in his brown eyes. I began to feel fear for the first time in the dream. I held out my blood-covered hands towards him, as if to fend him off. And suddenly he started to fight for breath, gasping and wheezing. He staggered towards me, clasping his breast and then his throat, and I could see that there was now panic in his eyes. As he grew weaker I felt a surge of energy, and I fixed my eyes upon his. I felt strong, and stood tall. Then he tried to grab hold of me, but I was protected by some strange force, and he could not touch me. He fell against a pinnacle of rock, spun around and was precipitated into the void. I saw his face. His eyes were wide with incomprehension and terror. As he fell to his doom there was a most horrible scream which echoed around me until it was at last consumed by the hungry wind.

And then I woke up with a start, disoriented and frightened by the frantic beating of my own heart. I lay for a long time with my eyes wide open, staring at the black ceiling and listening to the gentle rhythm of David's breathing beside me. Then I got up and wrapped myself in a woollen blanket before settling at my dressing table with quill in hand. Now I am waiting for the dawn, wondering what this strange dream can have meant. Is it a premonition or an omen, or simply some silly jumble of impressions, images, ideas, and instincts? I am certainly most confused, and need time to reflect.

ΩΩΩΩΩΩΩΩΩ

13th March 1797

After a day and a half of reflection, I am still not sure what to make of my peculiar dream. I have not shared it with David, since I have it on good authority that men do not like to hear of their wives' dreams when they involve other men, soft beds and silk sheets. However, I have decided that the dream was some sort of warning, and since I awoke this morning I have been obsessed with a single idea -- namely that Moses Lloyd is still a danger to us. I said as much at breakfast, and declared that in case anything should happen to any of us before Moses is brought to justice (as he surely must be) we should all write down witness statements that could be used at the Sessions.

Mrs Owen and Bessie and the rest of them were bemused, and possibly even amused, by my insistence on getting things down in writing. But I can be quite strong-willed when I want to be, and since nobody could come up with any convincing arguments to the effect that sworn statements would be a waste of time, I have devoted my day to the collection of literary masterpieces written onto scraps of paper. First of all I sat Mrs Owen, Hettie and Bessie down at the kitchen table, placed an inkpot and three quill pens before them, and set them to work.

Our faithful housekeeper writes well. She penned for me what she had personally witnessed with respect to the crimes of Moses Lloyd, and her statement said:

"I am the housekeeper of Plas Ingli, and have been in the employ of the Morgan family for twelve years. I do declare that in the month of February, round about the pancake time, I personally examined the cloak belonging to Moses Lloyd Cwmgloyn and saw blood and feathers from a chicken on the inside of it. This was the day after the chickens were stolen. I also do declare that in March I saw Moses Lloyd putting twelve sacks of barley on the gambo, and I heard him say to the master that he loaded only ten. I also saw him use great discourtesy towards the master and towards Master Isaac Morgan who is a magistrate, and I do believe that this was insulting and threatening behaviour on his part. He did also curse in a most unseemly fashion, and did blaspheme most horribly. Signed Blodwen Owen of Goat Street Newport, this thirteenth day of March in the year of our Lord 1797. Signed and witnessed by Bessie Gruffydd Eglwyswrw."

Bessie's handwriting was not very good, since she has only recently started with her school-work, but she has a quick brain and is getting the hang of fashioning letters and putting them together. Her spelling leaves something to be desired, but I will spare her blushes by making a few corrections. She took more than an hour to write as follows:

"My name is Bessie Gruffydd, and I have been a maid at the Plas for two years. I swear by Almighty God that in the month of December Moses Lloyd was in my bed without being invited, and was intent upon taking criminal advantage of me until he was evicted with the aid of a flagon of cold water. I did also see Moses Lloyd indeed very drunk and rude before the New Year after he had been in trouble in the town. I did also see and hear him abuse Master Isaac Morgan a Justice of the Peace after he had stolen two bags of barley. He did also utter blasphemous things and cursed the people of Plas Ingli in a most foul manner. Signed Bessie Gruffydd of Eglwyswrw, March the thirteenth 1797. Signed and witnessed by Hettie Jones Parrog."

And so it went on. Hettie and Billy also wrote down sworn statements of the criminal episodes involving Moses which they had personally witnessed, and I made quite sure that nobody wrote down anything which could be interpreted as hearsay. Sadly, the Jenkins brothers and others who witnessed the confrontation between Moses and Grandpa in the kitchen cannot write, although they may come in handy as witnesses in court. But Hettie went into town this afternoon, and she obtained for me two further written statements from regular drinkers in the Black Lion who had witnessed the mayhem caused by Moses in a drunken rage on the night when he was arrested.

Later on I will get David, Grandma and Grandpa to write down their recollections as well. However, for the time being I am satisfied. I will keep these statements safely in my wooden chest in case they should ever be needed. Having undertaken this strange exercise I must admit to a slight feeling of unease, and I have seen the rest of the family exchanging little glances as if to say "Oh dear! Martha is being silly again!". Maybe I have been melodramatic and mean-spirited, but following that strange dream I am determined that Moses Lloyd will never again lead the Morgan family in a merry dance, and that he will never lead me to the top of a mountain, dressed or undressed.

ΩΩΩΩΩΩΩΩΩ

14th March 1797

David is very amused by my literary efforts. I have never made any secret of my diary writing, and all the members of the family know that I regularly spend hours scribbling away at my dressing table, my hand illuminated by the spluttering flame of a candle, far into the night. David needs a deal more sleep than I do, since he spends his days in interminable toil on the farm, and he knows that I often get out of bed and write late at night or early in the morning. A couple of weeks ago he came in and disturbed me in full flow when I was writing something about the terrible squires and their appalling wives, and tried to read my Dimetian Welsh script. He is a good linguist, perfectly fluent in three languages, but he laughed and said *"Cariad*, I am quite defeated! I can understand words and phrases here and there, but the dialect is so peculiar, and your handwriting so disgraceful, that I cannot make head or tail of a single sentence, let alone a whole paragraph or a whole volume! It is certainly a very inscrutable diary."

"That, my dear husband, is as it should be," said I. "It is my own creation, and maybe this is all I will leave for posterity. It contains no startling insights into the human condition and none of my most secret thoughts. It certainly contains nothing unkind, *Cariad*, about you and your dear grandparents, for I love you all dearly. But I enjoy my writing, and the process of putting thoughts on paper brings me great consolation and keeps my mind in sharp focus. As a record of life on the side of Angel Mountain my diary may even have a little literary merit."

"I see, my dear Martha, that I am confronted by great determination. Do you plan to keep on writing for ever? If so, I shall have to build an annexe to the house, just to hold your volumes..."

"No, no, dearest. Maybe one day soon, if and when we are blessed with a child or two or three, I will put my quill pen and my book away and will never touch them again. Then, when I am old, maybe I will discover them in a dusty chest and entertain myself by reading of my youthful impressions and adventures! God willing, you will still be by my side, and I will read them for you and our children and grandchildren as we sit around our yuletide fire."

Then David laughed, tilted my head back and kissed me on the lips. "Martha Morgan!" he exclaimed. "You have more romance and sentiment in you than the rest of Wales put together. I trust that your prophecy of serene old age will be fulfilled. Now then, you carry on, for I have three letters to write before coming to bed."

In recalling this conversation I am struck yet again by my good fortune in having a man such as David by my side. It occurs to me that many a husband might be jealous of a diary written by a wife in an illegible hand and in an incomprehensible and archaic language. David, if he had any doubts about my love, might press me to translate what I have been writing day by day and night by night. He may even feel that I am giving time to my diary that I should be giving to him or to the upkeep of the house. But there appear to be no dark thoughts in his head. He seldom thinks ill of anybody, and he has an almost childlike faith in the love that binds us together. He gives me the space to do what I want to do and to be what I am. He exerts no pressure and has never asked me what I have written. So far as I am aware, he has never even looked at my diaries in my absence. When he says "Martha, how I love you!" he means it with every particle of his being, and I pray that I will never ever think ill of him or betray his love.

Growth

Now I have been day-dreaming and fantasizing, and I am aglow with passion. How wonderful are the mysterious links between mind and body, heart and soul! Is there anything in Paradise more perfect than goose down pillows and fresh linen sheets and the touch of David's rough hands and the gentle caress of his lips on my skin? Or the entwining of our bodies and the act of loving and the wonderful deep peace that follows? But now I hear his steady footsteps on the staircase! I can report that impure thoughts are flooding into my mind, although I declare myself uncertain whether I should be delighted or ashamed. The door of my dressing-room is opening. I can see in my mirror that he is standing behind me with a smile on his face. I keep on writing and pretend that I have not noticed him. The candle flame is flickering and the shadows are trembling. Now he has placed his hands upon my shoulders, and he is kissing the back of my neck. In the circumstances, with my hand shaking, and with a flush upon my cheek and a pounding in my heart, it is probably best that I abandon my literary efforts for this evening and devote my attention to other matters.......

ΩΩΩΩΩΩΩΩΩ

25th March 1797

I have a singular and frightening tale to relate. Three days ago we had the most peculiar weather conditions anybody could remember. After a bright day with towering clouds, it became very cold towards evening. As the sun went down the sky in the west burst into life, with yellow and gold shifting to red and orange and purple, and with colours that nobody could give names to. We could not see the sun, but shafts of sunlight penetrated seawards and over our heads. Some clouds were white and others were fringed with silver and gold, and with intense blackness at their hearts. If one turned around and looked eastwards the sky was the colour of lead and the lowering clouds were coloured like pitch. There was no other colour on the landscape, or in the sky, or on the sea. There was no wind, and there was a sort of empty echo in the air. Everything was bathed in such a strange grey luminescence that people came out onto the streets in

Growth

Newport, and stood in their farm and cottage doors, all gazing skywards with their mouths agape. The light was not coming from the sun, but it appeared to come from buildings and trees and from the ground itself. Then from the east there came rolls of thunder and flashes of lightning, and as people watched a white wall of hailstones marched towards them across the silent fields and then suddenly disappeared.

Some who watched this act of bravado from the forces of nature said that this was an omen of some terrible event to come, and others said that the end of the world was nigh. I was not convinced of this, but as darkness fell I noticed a continuous stream of seabirds flying inland from the coast. I began to feel that severe weather was on the way, and Grandpa confirmed this when he looked at his weather glass. "*Duw Duw*," he said, "I have never seen the glass so low. God help those poor devils who are out on the sea tonight. We had better shut every door tight and tie down everything that is loose."

There was just about enough light to see what we were doing, and all hands (including young Shemi Jenkins, who has just started with us) were summoned to get animals in under cover, all ricks roped over and tied down, barn and stable doors shut up with security battens, window shutters closed and fixed, and farm implements and other loose things weighted down with stones. Luckily most of the sheep were in the paddock next to the big barn, for the first lambs are due at any moment. The weather remained calm during the evening, and we all went to bed feeling that our suspicions were perhaps ill-founded. I snuggled up against David and drifted off to sleep, but in the middle of the night I awoke with a start, having had a dream so strong that it remained vividly in my head.

I could not get rid of the image of a raging flood down at the ford at Trefelin, sweeping trees, bushes, fences and animals in its path. I saw sheep and cattle swept along and drowned, and -- most terrible of all -- I saw Cilgwyn Mill, just a few feet above normal river level, collapse bit by bit into the torrent until it was utterly destroyed.

After this, I could not sleep again, for I knew that the little mill housed not only the waterwheel and the milling machinery but also Abraham y Felin and his wife and three children. After lying rigidly in the darkness for I know not how long, transfixed with the image of a disaster at Cilgwyn Mill, I woke David and told him of my fear. More asleep than awake, he held me in his arms and whispered "*Cariad*, don't you upset yourself about a silly dream. It was probably brought on by that strange weather we had in the evening, or by the salty bacon we had for supper. We all have nightmares sometimes. Now just you try to get off to sleep again. It will soon be time to get up, and once the lambing starts there will not be much sleep for any of us." And with that he drifted off into his slumbers again.

But still I could not sleep, and when the dawn came the image was as strong as ever in my head. I could not understand it, for as the first grey light stole up on us from the east there was still no wind and no rain. The sky was grey and heavy, but looking no more ominous than on any other morning in this strange half-season between winter and spring. I got up feeling uneasy, and when we all sat round the breakfast table with our buttermilk and oats before us Bessie noticed my nervousness. "Why, Mistress Martha," she said. "You do not look at all interested in your food. Are you not well?"

And so I poured out my heart to all of them, family and servants. They knew not what to make of my strange dream, and were at first inclined to dismiss my fears, but I added "We must get Abraham and his family out of the mill! They may not believe that something terrible is about to happen, but we must get them out! If nothing happens, then I will look foolish -- but that is a minor price to pay, compared with the price of five innocent lives. Please, please, all of you, you must believe me. You must believe me....." And at that, I am ashamed to report, I broke into tears and ran from the room and up to the bedroom, where I flung myself upon the bed, sobbing uncontrollably.

Bessie ran after me and tried to console me, and after some minutes Grandma Jane and Mrs Owen also came upstairs to pass on the latest intelligence. Apparently as soon as I had run out of the kitchen Grandpa had looked at his weather glass and cried "My God! I cannot believe this! The glass has gone even lower, and I can see it still moving downwards. Maybe Martha is right -- something terrible is going to befall us. I have heard of premonitions before, and this is surely one of them." Although it may have been against his better nature, as a firm believer in science as against intuition, David also decided that action was needed. "We must accept that Martha has seen something hidden from the rest of us," he said. "Abraham and his family may be in mortal danger. We must harness the grey pony to the trap and get down to the ford at once! Billy, hitch one of the other ponies to the gambo and follow as fast as you can. We will need it for their possessions. Shemi, go and warn your father and your uncles, and tell everybody who lives near the river to get out and onto higher ground. Grandma and Mrs Owen, can you check the sheep and deal with the other animals if we abandon you for a while? Then you'd better make some space somewhere in a corner of the barn -- we may have five extra people on the premises tonight."

And so, a few minutes later, the trap rattled away out of the yard with David and Grandpa on board, followed a few minutes later by Billy and Shemi on the gambo. They came back in the middle of the afternoon, having had no end of difficulty in getting Abraham and his family out of the mill. Apparently the building is actually owned by Squire Watkins Llannerch, and like a good tenant Abraham wanted to get his permission to evacuate the place and to leave it unprotected. But Grandpa insisted that there was no time for such niceties, and that protection was not an option. He said he would explain things later to the squire. He and David pleaded and even begged them to hurry. At last they got them out, together with their meagre possessions, and promised them that they would be cared for at the Plas. They squeezed everything onto the trap and the gambo. Then they crossed the gentle stream at the ford and struggled uphill all the way back to the Plas. As they arrived the sky darkened and a breeze from the west started to pick up. The message went up and down the river from Trefelin, and all the cottagers at Pantry, Allt Clydach, Parc-y-dyffryn and other low-lying places were warned to get out before the flood started. Some of them heeded the warning, and others did not.

We got the miller and his bemused family, and their possessions, into the barn just as the heavens opened. Never had such rain been seen before. There was a wind too, but the rain was so heavy and incessant that nobody noticed the storm that was blowing. It was as if sheets of water were poured over the lip of some mighty waterfall in the sky, so heavy that one could hardly walk through the deluge. The poor sheep huddled against the western wall of the paddock in a vain attempt to find some shelter. The sound of the downpour on the roofs of the house and outbuildings was deafening. Soon the whole land surface was streaming with water. It flowed off the mountain, round the house and across the yard, and when, in the midst of it all, Billy and David ventured out in their oilskins to inspect the animals they said that everything, including the steep mountainside, was covered in a torrent of water several inches deep.

Growth

It continued through the evening and for most of the night. None of us could sleep because of the noise, and indeed we were up for most of the hours of darkness trying to prevent the torrent from flowing in through the back door and out through the front. We used every brush and receptacle we could find, and old blankets and clothes were used as barriers. Grandpa said "Thank God for the new house. The old one was lower in the ground, without good steps before the doors, and it would certainly have filled with water." We all feared for those whose houses were less well built, and offered up prayers for those who lived near the river. In the pitch darkness, there was nothing we or anybody else could do for them.

Just before dawn the rain stopped just as suddenly as it had started. But the sound of running water continued, for all the gentle rivulets coming off the mountain, and all the pathways and sheep tracks, had been transformed into roaring mountain torrents. New gullies and crevices had appeared, and the floods had carried boulders, stones, earth and great rafts of turf down from the mountain and dumped them in the farmyard, behind walls and hedges, and on every piece of flattish land. Many of our walls had collapsed because of the pressure. Six sheep were dead, drowned in a paddock which we thought was the safest and driest place on the farm. With the rest of the flock heavily in lamb, God knows how many more we will lose as a result of the trauma they have suffered. We fear that our two fields of winter wheat are badly damaged, since the bare earth offered little resistance to the deluge. But we are all safe, as are Abraham and his family, and indeed we have much to be thankful for.

To give the end of the episode a cruel twist, the cloud cleared after breakfast, the wind dropped, and the sun came out. We all ventured out to inspect the damage. The old people at the two Dolrannogs have suffered greatly. They have lost animals too, and the ground floors of their houses are covered with thick brown mud. There is a high tide mark in Dolrannog Uchaf eight inches above the floor. Two of the hovels on the Cilgwyn road have collapsed, luckily without loss of life, and several of the others are very badly damaged. They were almost uninhabitable before, even in warm dry weather, and I dread to think what they are like now.

David and I walked down with Abraham y Felin to the ford at Trefelin. The river was flowing at a fearsome speed, and was at least eight feet above its normal level. As we watched the carcasses of three sheep and two cows were swept past us, bobbing grotesquely in the wild brown waves. Branches and even whole trees sailed past in the foaming, roaring maelstrom. It was out of the question to try and cross the ford, but from the north bank of the river we could see the site of Cilgwyn Mill. There was nothing left of it, save part of one gable end. As we watched, the torrent ate away at the soft grey mortar between the stones, and it tumbled down and disappeared without trace.

ΩΩΩΩΩΩΩΩΩ

28th March 1797

Our little world is returning to normal after the high drama of the flood. The weather these last three days has been glorious, with warm sunshine, a sky of the deepest blue, and a gentle breeze from the south-west. Two colours dominate the hedgerows -- primrose yellow and daffodil gold. There are still some snowdrops and little white anemones in the woods and on shady banks.   Even the blossoms flattened by the deluge and overwhelmed by streaming surface water have shaken themselves down and popped upright again, apparently none the worse for wear. And the little hedgerow and woodland birds whose half-completed nests have been destroyed have proved themselves to be quite indefatigable; they are immediately hard at work again on new nests, pausing every now and then to give short bursts of song from the treetops. The sheep which survived the disaster are now making up for lost time, and Billy is teaching young Shemi some of the secrets of the lambing business.

But the happy signs of spring cannot compensate for the great sadness which we all feel after the flood. No lives were lost, but there is debris everywhere -- broken branches, torn-up furze bushes and piles of dead bracken, smashed wooden gates, fenceposts, and pieces of buildings which collapsed under the onslaught. Many stone walls have collapsed, and God only knows how many tons of good earth have been swept from the bare fields. The Clydach river water level, which rose ten feet at the peak of the flood, is now almost back to normal again. Some of the drowned animals were swept out to sea. Others were caught up in the branches of trees, and many men are now involved in the grisly business of dragging them down and burying them. Most of the labourers and farmers of the area are still sweeping and shovelling earth and stones from their homes, and drying out clothes and bedding. Many people have had to move in with friends and relatives while their damaged buildings are repaired.

One consequence of the disaster which is causing great anger locally is the cruel and primitive response of Squire Watkins to the loss of his mill. This is not the first or the last time for a stone-built mill to be swept away in a flood; and indeed Grandpa tells me that two earlier mills by the Cilgwyn ford have been swept away in the past. He tells me that watermills have to be built very close to river level so as to extract as much power as possible from the water falling over the wheel. So I would have thought that building a mill is a risky business, but a business worth investing in because of the good profits to be made. But Squire Watkins is blaming poor Abraham for abandoning his mill and leaving it unprotected, in spite of Grandpa's assurances that nothing could have been done by any man, nor even by an army of men, to stop the force of water. The Squire is in a blind rage, so they say, and refuses to house the homeless family or even to help them to find accommodation in Newport. So they are still in the barn. Watkins is asking Abraham to rebuild the mill at his own expense, on pain of a prosecution in the Petty Sessions for neglect of duty. We all know that the threat of prosecution is an empty one. But the wretched miller is scared to death of his erstwhile landlord, who is after all a magistrate with a reputation for "fixing things" with his fellow magistrates. Abraham is now presented with an impossible task as well as being penniless and homeless, and is very melancholic.

I find myself very confused about my premonition and its miserable consequences. I cannot understand where my strange dream came from, or why I was chosen as the messenger of doom. I am more than a little frightened, and wonder if I have some sort of "second sight" which is denied to other people. Everybody says that Joseph Harries has the ability to see things in the future, which is why he is called *dyn hysbys* or "the knowing man". Am I also destined to be famous for knowing strange things, and does this make me into a wizard or a witch? As I write, I feel a flutter of panic in my stomach.

ΩΩΩΩΩΩΩΩΩΩ

Growth

31st March 1797

Today I have been greatly exercised by the strange behaviour of the servants. It started in the dairy early in the morning. When I arrived shortly after seven to perform my usual duty of washing out the milking things and salting the butter, I noticed that there was none of the usual light-hearted banter between Hettie and Mrs Owen. They were talking in whispers, and as I entered the whispers were replaced by an awkward silence. But they greeted me heartily enough, and the conversation was happy as we churned and splashed and tidied up. But there was a certain stiffness in our talk which made me feel uncomfortable, and I could not work out what was going on.

Later on I passed Billy and Shemi in the yard, and although they both said "Good Morning, Mistress Martha" and doffed their hats as usual, their voices were low, they averted their eyes, and were disinclined to talk about the weather in spite of the fact that it was a most beautiful spring morning. Even Bessie appeared stiff and embarrassed in my presence when I helped her to rearrange some things in the master bedroom.

When we all sat down to our midday meal of barley bread, butter and cheese I noticed that Grandma Jane, Grandpa Isaac and David were talking away thirteen to the dozen about the state of the lambing, the rebuilding of walls and so forth, and responded perfectly normally and naturally whenever I contributed to the conversation. But the servants appeared to be in another world, staring down at their plates, munching on their bread slices in silence, and looking desperate to get away from the table and back to their appointed tasks for the day. This was all most peculiar, for I have noticed a propensity among servants for making mealtimes last as long as the Master of the house will allow.

When we had all left the table I called David to one side and asked him if he had been aware of a strained atmosphere in the kitchen. He looked genuinely puzzled, and furrowed his brow in that strange way that men do. "Why no, *Cariad*," he said. "It all seemed normal enough to me. We talked of many things and ate well and drank well, and I was very pleased to see the way Billy and Shemi rushed off to continue with the lambing. Very commendable."

"But were you not aware of the silence among the servants," I persisted, "and their reluctance to look me, or you, in the eye?"

"No, I can't say I was."

I sometimes despair that men are so insensitive and so unobservant of human nature, and I said as much to my husband. I must have looked petulant and crestfallen all at the same time, so David took my hands in his and said "Look Martha, if you are worried that something is going on, it is not like you to simply brood about it. Why don't you look Bessie in the eye and demand to know what this is all about?"

Sometimes men can be quite sensible, so when David had gone out again to continue with his repairs of flood damage, I followed his advice. I found Bessie cleaning the shelves in the pantry, called her into the kitchen, and sat down with her at the table. "Now then, Bessie," I said. "There is something strange going on here today. You are all as black as the Devil's shadow, and I want to know why. Will you please tell me what I have done to deserve your displeasure?"

Bessie shuffled about, lowered her eyes and twisted her hands about on her lap. "It is a little difficult to explain, Mistress," was all she would say. So I lifted her chin with one hand and looked at her hard. Then I said "Bessie, I insist! I thought you were my friend, and you are causing me pain. Please, please, will you tell me what is on your mind?"

For a long time we looked at each other in silence, and then I noticed her lip tremble, and a tear came into her eye, and she threw her arms around my neck as she dissolved in a torrent of tears. "Oh, Mistress Martha! Mistress Martha!" she wailed. "We all love you so much, but they are saying terrible things about you, and we do not know what to say in your defence."

"Bessie, what do you mean?" I whispered into her hair as her tears soaked into my collar. "Who are they? And what are they saying?"

At last the poor dear thing composed herself somewhat, and was able to say in a trembling voice "They say, Mistress Martha, that you are a witch." She must have felt my body stiffen, and I daresay the colour drained from my cheeks, and Bessie regained her strength as I lost mine. Now she was holding me as I blurted out "But that is absurd. How could I possibly be a witch? I know nothing at all about spells and curses and potions and such like. In any case, I thought all this nonsense about witches was done away with two hundred years since! Sensible people know perfectly well that witches only exist in old stories!"

Growth

"We are sensible people, Mistress Martha, and we all know this to be true," said Bessie. "But the rumour is going around that only a person with supernatural powers could have predicted the flood that destroyed Cilgwyn Mill and made the miller and his family homeless. Many of the simple people from Cilgwyn and Newport hold you in awe and bless you in their prayers for saving Abraham and his family. But there are some who know that you are friendly with the wizard from Werndew. They also know that there is bad blood between your family and the Watkins family of Llannerch, and they are spreading rumours that to spite Squire Watkins you cursed the mill and called down demons to destroy it."

"But that is ridiculous!" I protested. "I don't even believe in little harmless demons, let alone horrid demons who can conjure up storms and floods! In any case, do you know where these rumours come from?"

"I have talked to Hettie about it, since she knows all the local gossip, and she says that Rose Watkins was overheard in town yesterday putting it about that you had placed a curse upon the squire's mill."

"The squire's daughter!" I exclaimed. "I should have known! I suppose we can take it for granted that the whole family will be involved in a whispering campaign. Is there no end to the malice and deviousness of those people?"

"I suspect not, Mistress. They are all cruel and heartless folk who have trampled many innocent people underfoot in their pursuit of riches. But they are not popular, and I would go so far as to say that many poor people hate them."

We fell silent for a while, and then I said "Bessie, there is one person who will know how to handle this, and he is my friend Joseph Harries. I have a mind to get the pony and gallop over to Werndew this minute, to seek his wise counsel."

A shadow came over Bessie's face, and she said firmly "Mistress, I would not advise it. People will get to know of it, and this will confirm their suspicions of a wicked pact between you and him. I think you should not involve the wizard in this matter at all."

Bessie was, of course, quite right. "So what should we do, Bessie?"

"I think, Mistress, that we should discuss things around the table at supper this evening," said she. "You have many more friends than enemies, and your family will know what is best."

Our interview was at an end. We had work to do, and I gave Bessie, dear kind friend that she is, a hug before we parted. I spent the rest of the day seeking consolation in hard work about the farm and in helping Abraham and his family in the barn. But my mind was full of dark thoughts and my heart full of mixed emotions, and when we sat down to supper my mood was bleak indeed. Bessie, to her eternal credit, asked David's permission to speak on a matter of some importance, and she told the assembled company everything she knew about the wicked rumours. The other servants backed her up, and told us what they knew about the gossip being passed about in the local taverns and over garden walls. David became increasingly agitated while the story came out, and then he reacted -- as I knew he would -- with absolute fury. He shouted, thumped the table with his fist, and let loose a tirade of abuse against the Watkins family. He stood up and looked as if he was about to set off on a vengeance mission. But Grandpa Isaac, who is a great deal wiser than David in the ways of the world, placed a restraining hand on his shoulder and pressed him back into his seat.

He was also very angry, but he said "Now then, my boy. We all know that this is malicious gossip, and we can be pretty sure where it has come from, but we will not get very far by over-reacting. Violence will not solve anything. All we need in this case is a little quiet diplomacy."

Everybody else agreed, and the talk went on far into the night. Gradually my black mood was replaced by one of gratitude, with family and friends around the table demonstrating a loving concern for my reputation and my wellbeing. We all decided that we would say nothing to the outside world of my premonition of the flood (for in truth none of us knows what to make of it). We further decided that we should put it about quietly that my warning was based on simple common sense. We will say that the strange weather on the night before the deluge, the seagulls flying inland, and the falling weather-glass were all signs of a coming catastrophe, especially to one such as I who had been educated to understand the ways of the weather. Further, since I had known that the mill had been destroyed at least twice before, prudence dictated that the mill should be evacuated before the river rose too high.

I pray that this approach will work. Our servants will talk to many people over the coming days, as will David and his grandparents. I doubt that Billy and Shemi will be able to resist saying a few rude things about the Watkins clan, but in my estimation a few rude words are in order.

Growth

7th April 1797

We have been in sombre mood at the Plas today, for it is the third anniversary of the fire in which five of David's family died. It also happens to be Easter Sunday, and this has caused us to feel very mixed emotions. My dear husband still bears the emotional scars of the fire, and these show on his face from time to time. I am aware that he still needs my support, and I give it to him with all my heart and soul, but he will still not speak about the fire or even put his feelings about it into words. Perhaps he still feels some deep guilt for what happened? I know not where the truth lies, nor how long it takes for an injured soul to mend itself.

It has been a bright day, but with a cold wind, and we wrapped up well for the journey in the chaise down to Cilgwyn Church for Easter morning communion. David drove, and Grandma Jane, Grandpa Isaac and I sat in the back, cuddled up together. The bright sunlight and the multitudes of daffodils in the hedgerows lifted our spirits somewhat, and we were pleased to see that there were good numbers of local people out on the road, some heading to church in Newport, others to Nevern and others to Cilgwyn. The Nonconformists were also out in force, intent upon celebrating Easter in their official and unofficial meeting houses. Before we went into the church we placed a beautiful bundle of daffodils and ferns on the Morgan family tomb inside its little enclosure, and we stood there in silence for a few minutes, arm in arm, lost in our own private thoughts and prayers.

Rector Devonald led the service, and while I do not count myself as one of his greatest supporters, I have to record that he had not forgotten the fire and that he gave us great comfort with well-chosen words from the pulpit and with a special prayer for the Morgan family. We have our differences over education and other matters, but it is heartening to experience the humanity and support which comes to the fore at times of crisis in our little community. And indeed we were all greatly touched by the kind words from many of our neighbours as we chatted outside the church following the conclusion of the service. With every day that passes I feel more and more privileged to be a part of the Morgan family, held as it is in such high esteem by so many good people.

Growth

21st April 1797

Today, a month after the flood, Abraham y Felin and his poor family moved out of the barn and have gone to stay with relatives in Brynberian. Squire Watkins is rebuilding Cilgwyn Mill and will probably invite Abraham to run it again when it is ready; there is, after all, no better miller within fifty miles, and the squire knows it. In thinking of such things I am moved to write of the whisperings about witchcraft which caused me so much anguish following the catastrophe. It is strange how such things can spring up like heather fires on the mountain and spread with terrifying speed across the face of the land, leaving devastation in their wake. And yet it is also strange how ephemeral they are, for a gentle shower or a change in the direction of the wind can simply snuff them out.

I thank the Lord that the wicked rumours about me have, so far as I can tell, been blown away by the quiet zephyrs of reason. Within a few days, at the beginning of the month, the tales put about concerning my skill in reading the weather signs were having an effect, and in the eyes of the superstitious poor people of the cwm and the town I was transformed from a black hag on a broomstick into a learned gentlewoman well versed in the ways of the weather. The daughters of the Watkins family, who had clearly started the rumours about the curse on the mill, are now themselves subject to ridicule, and they are not best pleased. I was reminded of my new status as a woman of science when Dai Darjeeling called on his monthly tea visit and sought my opinion, with a gleam in his eye, on the Indian Monsoon. As luck would have it, I recalled reading a book about General Clive a year or two ago. Thus I was able to tell Dai all about the Monsoon, and was able to inform him that I thought it a very good thing.

Now that the lambing, sowing and harrowing are all finished, I took the opportunity of spending an afternoon all by myself on the mountain. There was a stiff breeze which tumbled a never-ending succession of clouds in from the great ocean to the west. Some of them brought drenching showers, but the wind was warm and there were long spells of sunshine, and I saw no reason to sit at my embroidery or my reading on such a bracing day. I climbed up through the top fields, which are now populated by our breeding ewes and their little fluffy lambs. I tried to catch one or two of them, purely for the indulgence of holding them in my arms and giving them a cuddle, but they were too quick for me. Most of them stick close by their mothers, but they are remarkably fleet of foot even if they are only two days old, and the older lambs move a good deal faster than their mothers. Having failed in my kidnapping attempts, I spent a happy half hour watching the little creatures rushing hither and thither, hopping and skipping into the air, and demonstrating that it was good to be alive.

Then I climbed up onto the old blue mountain and scrambled through the jumble of broken slabs and boulders towards the entrance of my cave. The old raven was perched on the summit as usual, but to my surprise he did not launch himself into the wind and croak his disapproval, even though he must have had a mate nearby sitting on eggs or even feeding youngsters in the nest. I was flattered that he has now seen me so often amid the crags that he recognizes me and no longer feels threatened. I may be fantasizing, but I think he even looks on me as a friend.

Thus reassured by the youngest and the oldest inhabitants of the mountain, I spent a happy and serene hour in my cave, sitting on a dry bed of moss with my knees drawn up to my chin, dreaming of the future.

ΩΩΩΩΩΩΩΩΩΩ

26th April 1797

I have to record that I have had another strange and disturbing dream. In it, I found myself in an ancient and ruinous castle, not as a prisoner but as a chief executioner. I was doing duty in the execution of three men who were marched up from the dungeons in order to be hung on the gallows. They were blindfolded, and I knew not who they were, but each one in turn screamed and struggled as the noose was placed around his neck. I released the trapdoor for the first man to fall to his doom, and heard his neck crack. His blindfold fell off, and with horror I saw the face of Squire Rice. Then the second man was placed upon the trap, and the noose tightened around his neck. I pulled the lever. Again I heard the crack of the condemned man's breaking neck, and again the blindfold fell off. It was Squire Howell. The same thing happened with the third man, and he was revealed as Squire Watkins. Then the corpses, with their heads lolling about grotesquely, were dragged away, dumped onto an ox-cart, and driven off through the castle gate.

At this point I woke up in horror, and slept no more until the dawn chorus came to lighten my spirits. At breakfast this morning I endeavoured to behave as cordially as usual to servants and family, and during the day I believe that I betrayed nothing of my troubled spirit.

But there is a strange twist to the tale, for this evening, quite out of the blue, Grandpa Isaac knocked on my dressing room door when I was alone and said "Martha my dear, may I have a quiet word?"

"Of course, Grandpa."

He came inside, sat on the bed and said "Do you remember that strange social visit by the three squires and their wives?"

"Of course. How could I forget it?"

"I just want to give you a word of warning. During our conversation you raised the matter of Master Joseph Rice's gambling debts and put down his father in a fashion which, I have to say, caused David and me some considerable amusement."

"Yes, I remember," I said. "I was perhaps not very circumspect, and have subsequently regretted the fact that my tongue on that occasion moved more quickly than my brain."

"What is done is done," said Grandpa. "The pompous fellow deserved everything that he got. But you must be very careful, my dear. My spies tell me that the Squire is harbouring a very great degree of malice towards you. He is not used to being made to look foolish in the eyes of his peers. He thinks you acted arrogantly and insolently, and I have it on good authority that he felt insulted and belittled by your manner and your words."

Then he took both my hands in his and looked me straight in the eye. "Look out for Squire Rice and his cronies," he said. "He, and they, are out for revenge, and if they get half a chance to do you harm, they will surely take it."

ΩΩΩΩΩΩΩΩΩΩΩ

12. Speculations

5th May 1797

Today David and Grandpa set off early with the pony and trap to see some new ploughs and harrows being demonstrated near Haverfordwest. Grandma Jane and Mrs Owen went off to town to sell butters and cheeses and eggs, and the other servants were too busy with weeding and planting to pass the time of day in my company. The weather was warm and bright, and I was again drawn to walk on the mountain. So I wrapped up some wheat bread and salted ham, filled a bottle with fruit cordial, and set off with a spring in my step and a song in my heart.

As I walked past the rocks of Carn Edward I saw a white pony cantering along the mountain track in the distance, and as it drew closer I could see that the rider was none other than Joseph Harries. I waved and he waved back, and he trotted over to greet me. "Mistress Martha!" said he, as he dismounted. "How pleasant to see you on this fine spring day! I trust that you are well."

"Very well indeed, thank you," I replied. "And you?"

"Oh, fair to middling, as they say in the south of the county. Too much work and not enough money to live on, as usual. But I must not complain on such a day, with the sun high and all the creatures in creation celebrating the arrival of spring."

We exchanged pleasantries for a while and caught up on the latest news, and then Joseph said "I trust that you did not suffer too much at the Plas during the recent flood. I have seen some of the damage for myself along the river. Very bad business."

"Grandpa says there has not been such a flood in living memory," I replied. "We escaped lightly, but I suppose you have heard about the destruction of the mill?"

"Almost everything reaches my ears, Martha," said Joseph, with a gently amused expression upon his face, "including rumours and counter-rumours."

I saw that he knew all about the rumours of witchcraft, and that he knew exactly what the response of our family had been. I wondered for a moment whether Joseph could hear things from a distance of three miles, or whether he had an army of spies working for him, but I decided to speculate no further, for in truth I needed to talk to him about things I did not fully understand. So I said "Joseph, may I ask for your advice? I need to talk to you about premonitions and such things. I don't know if it is proper, but may I invite you to sit here with me on the rock and share both my simple lunch and my concerns?"

"My dear friend," said he, "you know that you can always turn to me for help, and indeed I am privileged to be asked."

So we sat together on the sunny rock, and while we tucked into our bread and ham I tried to express my fears about seeing things, dreaming things, and feeling things that appeared to be hidden from other people. And then I said "Joseph, do you think that I am a witch?"

At this Joseph almost choked on a large peice of ham, and had to clear his throat with a swig of fruit cordial. Then he bellowed with laughter so suddenly that his pony would certainly have taken off across the mountain had it not been tethered to a broken slab of rock. I flushed slightly, and when Joseph had regained his self-control he said "Forgive me, Martha. I see that you are embarrassed. I did not mean to make fun of you." Then he became serious, and took time to explain to me that there was still much to be learned about dreams, and premonitions, and instinct and intuition. He said that he too, like his father and grandfather, had premonitions, and was at a loss to explain them. But he said that although he knew many things which he would have preferred not to know, his guiding principle was that he should never use his knowledge to hurt or frighten any innocent person.

"But what if you happen to know something about a crime, or about some wickedness?" I asked. "Would you use your knowledge to right a wrong, or to prevent even greater wickedness?"

"Sometimes I would," he admitted. "But I would have to be sure about guilt or innocence, and sometimes I fear that I have made mistakes."

I understood what he was saying, and indeed I have often thought over recent weeks about justice and punishment, and about revenge and retribution. I tried to express what was in my mind, and Joseph stopped me by saying "These are deep waters indeed, Martha. I am still floundering in them myself, but if you are seeking a code to live by I suspect that your God has given you one that is not too wide of the mark.

Speculations

If I were you I would forget about punishment and leave that to others."

This made my temperature rise, and I said "Excuse me, sir, but do you not indulge in punishment yourself? Only last week I heard that you had placed a curse upon old Matthew Ifans in Nevern for stealing a chicken from his neighbour. Is that not punishment, and is that not witchcraft?"

Joseph shook his head and said "My dear Martha, you are very perceptive and very observant, but you still have much to learn. I do not indulge in witchcraft, and I never, never place curses. Curses are almost always self-inflicted, and almost always they arise from a sense of guilt. I admit that people are often in awe of me, and because they call me a wizard they expect me to place a curse upon anyone who crosses me. But I have no more special powers than you. That having been said, it helps me in my profession to maintain people's respect. A little apprehension on the part of one's clients is good for trade. It also helps to maintain law and order if those who are planning dastardly deeds know that Joseph Harries is watching them, and that his demons and goblins will bring retribution down on their heads." And he chuckled and looked me in the eye.

"Joseph, you make yourself sound like a trickster and a charlatan," I said. "But I feel it in my heart that you are neither. You are well educated, and kind, and gentle, and I know that you are a healer and a wise counsellor and a good friend to many people. I also know that you hardly ever take payment from the poor. But how is it that you so often seem to know the perpetrators of crime? It is said that you are in league with the Devil, and that he tells you things through the mouths of spirits summoned from the vasty deep...."

"Martha Morgan!" came the interjection. "Your fantasies are running away with you, and you have clearly been listening to more cock and bull stories than are good for you. Let me explain. I see myself as a doctor and as a student of the human mind and body. I know a great deal about herbs and medicines, and I have studied science for twenty years. My father was a wonderful teacher. I am blessed with a phenomenal memory, and when I see something or hear some snippet of conversation it becomes fixed in my brain. My father taught me that observation is the key to understanding." And to emphasise the point he said "Observation, Martha. Observation, not magic."

I could follow the drift of his discourse, but I was still puzzled, and I reminded him that I had not had an answer to my accusation about the curse placed upon Matthew Ifans.

Joseph shook his head in resignation, and said with a chuckle "You are very persistent, Martha Morgan. I will tell you the simple truth about that particular matter, but only because I recognise that you have very considerable powers yourself. I would tell nobody else. Now then. Are you listening carefully?"

"Yes. Pray contunue."

"Old Widow Shinkins from Ty Coch in Nevern has lost fifteen chickens over the last two years," said Joseph, "and she came to me in desperation some months back since she was convinced that there was no fox involved. She thought that young Simon Harry from the Trewern Arms was the guilty party, and caused a scene when she met him in the street by accusing him of theft. She was answered with vehement denials, and indeed his honour was vigorously defended by his family. So the old lady asked me to place a curse upon the lad. I said that I would do no such thing, but that I would try to resolve the matter for her. Next day I visited Nevern, made certain observations, and went home. I knew that the thief must have come from one of half a dozen neighbouring houses, and I knew all of the inhabitants and a fair amount about their family histories. Three days later I went to Newport market and made further observations which led me to identify the thief. It was a gentle old man called Matthew Ifans."

"How did you know that?"

"Wait a moment. I knew that Matthew was frail and poor, and that no purpose would be served by involving the constables. But he should not have stolen the chickens, and he would have to make recompense to his neighbour. So I went down to Nevern in the middle of the night and pinned a little note to his door. It said *Matthew Ifans, I know what you have done,* and I signed it *"Joseph Harries Werndew."* Next day the news was all around the village that he had been cursed by the wizard, but you will be pleased to know, my dear Martha, that no further action is now required since Matthew used part of his meagre savings last week to purchase fifteen chicks and two dozen eggs at Newport market. On Sunday he presented them in a little box of straw to Widow Shinkins, with his compliments, and now I hear that they are engaged to be married."

At this I could not resist the naive charm of the tale, and found myself laughing uncontrollably, in a most unladylike fashion. Joseph, who had not previously seen the funny side of the story, started laughing too, and at last we had to control ourselves for fear of frightening the pony. There was one last question, and as I wiped the tears from my eyes I asked it. "But how did you discover the guilty party?"

"Oh Martha," said Joseph. "You disappoint me. Think of the name of the old lady's house. Ty Coch -- red house. It is built on a most singular patch of red clay. Its like is found nowhere else in the district. The clay is covered in grass everywhere except around the chicken run, where it is exposed and muddy. When I was at Newport Market I looked very carefully at the boots and clogs of all Mistress Shinkins' neighbours. They all had black mud on them, but on the heels of Matthew Ifans' clogs, where he had omitted to wipe them properly, there were traces of red clay. I had my culprit." And he lifted his eyebrows and said "Now are you satisfied?"

"Yes, yes," I said, laughing. "But I am even more convinced that you are in league with the Devil. You see things that other people do not see."

"Only, my dear Martha, because they do not know where to look. I trust you never to reveal to anybody the things which I have told you today. But I must go -- I am treating a little girl who broke her leg down in the cwm last week. Her parents will be wondering why I am so late. Farewell." He took my hand and kissed it with a flourish, as if he were a fine gentleman taking leave of the queen. And then he untethered his pony, mounted it and trotted away towards Penrhiw without looking back.

What an extraordinary man! As I sit at my dressing table, scribbling by candlelight and looking back on another day of discoveries, I am more intrigued than ever by the talents of the wizard of Werndew.

ΩΩΩΩΩΩΩΩΩΩ

10th May 1797

This morning, when we were clearing up the kitchen table after breakfast, Bessie said nonchalantly "I was talking to Dai Darjeeling last night."

"I knew that already, Bessie," I replied. "I had noticed his little visit. Presumably to deliver another romantic poem, to give you a posy of bluebells and a quarter-pound of his best China tea, and to profess his undying love?"

Speculations

As Bessie poured out the hot water for the washing of dishes she grinned and said "Quite correct, Mistress. He seems to have taken a fancy to me, that one. But not even the world's finest tea will buy my favours."

"Never trust a tea merchant, Bessie. Too exotic by half. I assume that there was some hot news that you wished to pass on?"

A shadow flickered across her face and she said "Yes indeed. Dai travels about all over the place, and three days since he was down in the cwm. He says that a strange man has been sighted in the woods near Pandy. He is living rough, and Tom Flannel thinks he has been stealing chickens from Gelli Fawr. If Squire Owen catches him he will be strung up on the gallows tump within a fortnight."

"What is so strange about that?" I asked. "The woods are full of vagrants, and within the next month the Irish will start arriving for the hay harvest. Most of them live rough, and probably most of them steal chickens."

"The difference this time," replied Bessie, "is that the vagrant is a tall man with a bushy beard and a gap where his front teeth should be. He wears a big cloak. Not a lot of vagrants have cloaks. And one of the children from Pontfaen who saw him running through the wood says that he stumbled and waved his arms about like a mad thing. Does that remind you, Mistress, of anyone you might know?"

"Moses Lloyd? I cannot believe it!" I spluttered, greatly taken aback, in the middle of stacking the plates and platters. "Surely he cannot be so insane as to remain in this area when there is a price on his head? There must be some mistake. If I had been in his position I would have been east of the Forest of Dean by now, and would never again set foot within a hundred miles of this place."

"Well, Mistress, maybe he is even less popular east of the Forest of Dean than he is here. Maybe he is more insane than you thought. And remember that when he stormed out into the black night a couple of months back he cursed the Morgan family and swore vengeance. Perhaps he meant what he said."

At this I was gripped by a strange excitement, and this feeling intensified later in the morning as I realised the full import of what Bessie had said. Could this simply be a case of local people putting two and two together and making five? And could Moses really be so obsessed with his vendetta against our family that he would prowl about in the woods

Speculations

risking capture? Surely he must know that many of the local labourers would be only too pleased to grab him and turn him over to the constables in exchange for a golden sovereign or two? On balance I was still disinclined to believe that the mysterious vagrant in Coed Gellifawr could be Moses, but I determined to raise my concerns over supper. Tact would be needed, since I suspect that David and Grandpa Isaac still feel a degree of guilt over the manner in which they let the wretched fellow slip away from the tight grip of the law.

At dusk, as we tucked in to our *cawl* and crusty bread rolls, I asked the assembled company, innocently enough, whether anybody other than Bessie had heard the rumour about the man in the wood. David and his grandparents were blissfully ignorant on the matter, having heard no news from the cwm over the past few days. But the servants had all heard tales of one sort or another about a shadowy figure glimpsed fleetingly by a couple of labourers who had been poaching trout in the Pandy pools. Shemi said he thought it was most likely to be the ghost of one Elijah Tomos who had drowned in the river some years ago. Mrs Owen said it was most likely to be Squire Owen's gamekeeper out to frighten the poachers, and various other theories were also advanced. Only Bessie thought that the stranger might be Moses Lloyd, and indeed her theory was given short shrift by David and everybody else on the ground that he could not possibly be so stupid as to risk arrest by staying in the parish.

Then the conversation drifted on to other things, and I tried to convince myself that my sense of apprehension was irrational and even foolish. I have no recollection of any of the conversation, except for David saying "Martha! You look as if you are in another world this evening. Too much work and not enough play, if I am not mistaken. Have another glass of cider to help you relax, and we'd better get you packed off to bed nice and early for a change!" Everybody laughed, including myself, and the easy chatter rolled on into the evening.

Later on, with the servants in the kitchen and the Morgan family in the parlour, my mind was still fixed upon Moses. I tried to analyse my own emotions, and I convinced myself of my own loathing for the man. But in thinking of him I was interested to discover within myself a quickening of the pulse, a degree of foreboding, but no fear at all. Indeed I felt a most curious sentiment which is perhaps commonly felt by men but seldom by women -- a sort of excitement felt by a huntsman who has cornered his prey or a soldier in pursuit of the enemy, or a sportsman who has a great victory in his grasp. I could not understand my own heart.

Then I realised that I knew very little of the strange circumstances surrounding Moses' arrival at the Plas. As we all sat in mellow silence in the parlour, reading various books and newspapers, I addressed my query to Grandpa Isaac. "Since Bessie mentioned our friend Moses Lloyd this evening," I said, "I was wondering how it was that he came to the Plas in the first place. Is it true, Grandpa, that there was some deal with his father and that some money changed hands?"

He looked over the top of his newspaper with his spectacles on the end of his nose, and said, after a long pause "Now that is a very blunt question, my dear, and delivered like a thunderbolt from a blue sky. But you have been here for the best part of a year now, and as Mistress of the Plas you have every right to know. What I shall tell you is told in the strictest confidence, and must never be divulged to the servants or to anyone outside our family. Do you understand?"

"Of course, Grandpa."

And so, with his newspaper on his lap and the flickering firelight dancing upon his shiny forehead, he told me his little tale. "The beginnings of this affair go back a long way," he said. "For two hundred years or more there has been a feud between the Lloyds of Cwmgloyn and ourselves. I am not at all sure how it started, but feuds make people behave like idiots, and the enmity has gone on through the generations. I believe that in the past there have been at least two murders, four court cases and many disputes over land and grazing rights. I suppose you know all of this?"

"I have heard some rumours."

"Well, you also need to know that some fifty years ago this estate was in serious financial trouble. My father gambled away many of his assets and arranged some very foolish loans. When I inherited the Plas I worked like a demon to pay off the biggest debts, and the estate was almost paying its way, but then in 1788 I got wind of the fact that some of the local squires (all of whom were owed trifling sums of money) were going to call in their loans simultaneously and force me into insolvency. The estate would have become theirs. I took advice from Lewis Legal, and he immediately discerned that the loans were in my name personally. He drew up a document which passed ownership of the estate to my son, David's father.

Speculations

The estate was safe. This left William John Morgan as Master of Plas Ingli and it left me penniless. I was a pauper, thrown upon the mercy of my son. The squires were furious, but there was nothing they could do, especially when William did some astute buying and selling of stock and paid off my debts for me. Five years ago there were no debts and the estate was in good heart."

Grandpa turned to David and said "You knew all of this, David?"

"Only some of it," he replied. "But where do the Lloyds of Cwmgloyn come in?"

"This is where we move from high finance and law to matters of honour," explained the old man. "Much more difficult. Very difficult indeed." He paused for a long time, and puffed intently on his clay pipe as he gazed into the fire. He was choosing his words carefully. Then he resumed his story.

"Your father, David, was an honourable man, and it is a great sadness to me, Martha my dear, that you never met him. From the day that he became Master of the Plas he tried to resolve the festering dispute between the Lloyds and Morgans. To his credit, Squire Lloyd was similarly inclined, and relations improved. Then, about five years ago, there was a strange coincidence of events. William planted a very large winter wheat crop, and it was entirely destroyed by the weather. Suddenly he was deeply in debt. But then he heard that Squire Lloyd's disreputable son Moses had got into serious trouble in Oxford and that a severe family row had ensued. Such was the bad blood between father and son that Moses had been disinherited, and had been told to pack his bags and go."

"What had Moses done?" I asked.

"I am not at all sure myself," replied Grandfather. "But when William heard about this bad business he went to Squire Lloyd and proposed a deal. They had a very long discussion, and when he returned home the feud between the families was over. From what William told me afterwards, the Squire had made a cash gift sufficient to cover the estate's debts. In return, William had promised to take on Moses as a farm servant and to "make a man of him." They had shaken hands, but there were no documents or signatures, and on both sides the deal was a matter of honour. Moses was really given no option but to agree to the arrangement, for the alternative was vagrancy and the life of a pauper."

Speculations

"Now, Martha my dear," intervened Grandma Jane, speaking for the first time on this matter, "you may have some idea why Moses was a somewhat reluctant, and very inexpert, farm servant. If you thought him better suited to a life at the card tables of London than chopping turnips at Plas Ingli, you were quite right."

"But now he is gone," said Grandpa, "and I daresay we are greatly relieved. However, now that I have told you this history, you may understand a little better, Martha, why we were so tolerant with Moses. I have to say that you know only part of what has ensued. We have turned a blind eye so many times to his misdemeanours that an agreement between honourable men has been severely stretched. Following William's death in the fire I have done all I could to honour his name by looking after Moses and seeking to turn him from his wicked ways. And to his credit, David has done the same. We could, in all conscience, not have done more."

"But what of Squire Lloyd?" I asked. "Now that three generations of the Morgan family have failed to make an honest man of his prodigal son, what does he think about the deal made with David's father?"

"Huh! I think he has had good value for his money," said Grandma. "If he has any sense he will forget about Moses and get on with his life. But the Lloyds are strange people and there is no knowing how they will respond to this turn of events. I hear rumours that the Squire suffers from violent changes of mood and hears voices from Heaven. We will do well to keep an eye on him, for my female intuition tells me that the matter of Moses Lloyd is not yet over and done with."

And so we damped down the fire, took our candles and rushlights, and said our goodnights. Now that I have written of these things in my little book, I have to record for posterity that my female intuition is exactly in line with Grandma Jane's.

ΩΩΩΩΩΩΩΩΩΩΩ

13th May 1797

Can there be any month more serene than May, and anywhere on earth more beautiful than Plas Ingli in early summer? In truth, I know not

Speculations

whether it is spring or summer; perhaps the former, since the nights are still cold and the trees are still not fully clothed with greenery, but more likely the latter since there is fresh and extravagant colour washing across the landscape and since every corner and crevice resonates with birdsong.

We have had a windy and cold April this year, and then the first week of May was afflicted by still, misty weather with drizzly rain. Then, suddenly, the sun came out and the moisture was sucked out of the ground, and everything was transformed. Today, as on the past five days, I woke early to the sound of nature's choral symphony down in the Gelli and Dolrannog Woods. I rose quietly, leaving David fast asleep. There was not a breath of wind, and as I looked from my dressing-room window out over the cwm I felt as if I was on the high prow of a sailing ship, looking down on a soft white downy sea with bays and creeks and wispy waves washing up on distant wooded shores. There were even islands in the sea, where the tall yews of Cilgwyn Churchyard and the hillocks near Caersalem projected through its misty surface. Somewhere in the depths of the magic ocean of gentle mist a cuckoo was calling. Then, as I watched, the faintest of zephyrs caused the ocean to drift and tumble, and spill up across the hillsides, and break up into smaller pools, and finally to disappear completely. The sun having thus asserted itself, the cwm was transformed into a mosaic of greens, with the densest of shadows on the west-facing flanks of hills, copses and tall trees, and a golden yellow light flooding those features caught in the sunrise.

The birds on these last few mornings have been making up for lost time, singing like mad things, for the sheer joy of it now that there is food aplenty on the wing, on the soft ground and on bursting leaves and flowers. The early morning chorus washes up the slope towards the Plas, sometimes in waves and sometimes in a continuous surge of sound, echoed and amplified by the shape of the cwm. The sound is as blue as the ocean, for the breeze that carries it also brings the heady scent of bluebells from Gelli Wood.

Yesterday I celebrated my nineteenth birthday, and what a wonderful day it was! There was no large birthday party, and nor did I want one, but my time was spent in the most delightful of circumstances. My dear parents and sister Catrin travelled over from Brawdy for the afternoon, this being their first visit for several months. I was delighted by the warmth of their greetings, and by the natural and unaffected ease of the relationship that now exists between the members of my old family and my new one. Father and Mother looked very well, and Catrin has cut her hair to show off her elegant neck and fine features. She grows more beautiful with every year that passes.

There was so much to talk about -- Christmas, New Year, the French Invasion, the departure of Moses Lloyd, and the sale of the barley harvest -- that we hardly knew where to begin. In one of my brief pauses for breath Catrin reported that Morys had suddenly left the established church and joined the Nonconformists. I was greatly surprised by this news, but Father was perfectly nonchalant about it, and said that his change of allegiance had been inevitable since the day that David and I had been married. I raised my eyebrows at this, but Father would not elaborate. Instead, he declared that he was delighted to learn of the settling of all our debts, and fell into a deep conversation with David and Grandfather Isaac on farming and estate matters.

My mother Betsi and Grandma Jane wandered off to inspect the garden, chattering twenty to the dozen, leaving Catrin and myself to exchange sisterly confidences. There were a hundred secrets to share with her, and she had so much to share with me; and two hours flew by as we walked in the afternoon heat through the flowering lanes of Cilgwyn. We picked posies of bluebells, primroses, red campions, cowslips and buttercups, violets and daisies. For the first time I was able to share with her the anguish surrounding the loss of my baby; the joy of having as good a man as David at my side; the pleasures of my friendships with the good Doctor Harries, with Mary Jane from Pontfaen and with Sian from Gelli; the mixed emotions surrounding the dark presence and even darker departure of Moses; and the confusions in my mind on the matters of poverty and injustice.

Catrin listened and advised as an older sister should, and as we talked I realised how much I had missed her common sense and support over the past months. I said as much, but, as down-to-earth as ever, she replied: "What nonsense you speak, sister! Our days of childish confidences are over, and this is no cause for regret. You have a husband who is wise and strong beyond his years, and a new family with whom you must share new adventures."

"Indeed I do, but nobody knows my heart as you do."

Speculations

"Martha Morgan! I may have known the heart of my little sister back in Brawdy, but that Martha is now but a happy memory. The world has changed. Over the past year you have changed so much that I hardly recognise you. The same flashing eyes and black hair maybe, and the same tendency to arrogance and impulsiveness and cheeky good humour; but you are kinder and gentler than you were, and more considerate towards others. You hold your passions under greater control ...."

"Sister! Whatever do you mean?" I interjected, with a sudden flush upon my cheeks.

"Well, maybe not," laughed Catrin. "But I perceive that you are trying, and that represents progress. Take it from me, dearest Martha, that the only one who knows your heart nowadays is David, and that is as it should be, for I see that he is deeply in love with you and you with him. I envy you, for I have not known such love. Perhaps it will come. When it does, sister, I shall travel to the Plas and seek your advice, for while I have lived quietly in the shelter of our family home you have been battered by events of high drama and great emotion, and have come out of these storms slightly older but a great deal stronger. It would be presumptuous of me to offer advice to one so practised in the ways of the world, and foolish of you to seek it."

"Maybe not advice then," I said, "but a listening ear when needed, and a shoulder to cry on, and a strong back to share some of the burdens that life will surely heap upon us. We must write more often, sister to sister, and vow to help when help is needed. Agreed?"

And so we embraced and strengthened our sisterly bonds. I wanted to ask her about the circumstances leading to Morys' departure from his church near Carmarthen, but I realised that we were expecting other guests in time for afternoon tea, and decided that that would have to wait. We hurried back up the muddy path from Brynaeron just in time to see Mary Jane arriving at the Plas in her father's chaise. We shouted and waved and hurried on to meet her, and as we arrived panting at the front door Sian came striding up from Gelli. There was a pandemonium of greetings and introductions, in the midst of which I was presented with small birthday gifts from my friends. Then Joseph Harries arrived on his white pony, having trotted over from Werndew on the mountain track. There were more introductions and greetings, and as young Shemi Jenkins went off to the stable with Mary Jane's servant and the two ponies, we all went inside.

Speculations

The party was now complete, and we all settled down in the parlour for a wonderful spread of breads and cakes, tartlets and fruit marmalades, apple pies and whipped cream, all washed down with the best Ceylon tea which Gethin Griffiths had been able to obtain from his mysterious trading partners. Grandma, Mother and Mrs Owen rushed about with loaded plates and platters and hot tea urns, and insisted that I should not lift a finger since I was, for this afternoon at least, the guest of honour. Then David proposed a birthday toast for me, and everybody laughed and cheered and clinked their steaming tea-cups together and drank my health. A nice change, they all agreed, from the drinking of formal toasts in perry or porter!

As the babble of conversation resumed, I was struck for the first time by the strange assembly which I had convened. Billy, Bessie, Hettie and Mrs Owen were all present, on my insistence, as guests rather than servants, for I am already very fond of all of them and see them as friends. I did not presume to involve fifteen-year-old Shemi in the celebrations, since he has started with us only recently, and I knew that he would be happier in the kitchen with Mary Jane's servant, eating the same fare and drinking the same tea but spared from the trials of parlour etiquette. The three local ladies were perfectly at home, and although Billy looked at first distinctly uncomfortable in his Sunday best, he was soon swept along in the gaiety of the occasion and ended up looking for all the world like a ruddy-faced and contented squire. He spent most of the tea-party in animated conversation with David, my father and Joseph Harries; how often, I wondered, does a cow-man sip Ceylon tea out of a bone china cup in the presence of his master, a visiting squire and a local wizard? Joseph was a model guest, attentive to others when plates or cups needed to be filled, charming and jovial, cultured and even erudite. In another corner my mother was in deep conversation with Sian, the daughter of our tenant farmer Caradoc Williams, who would never normally mix socially with the gentry. Sian was a picture of blooming womanhood, rosy-cheeked, full-bosomed and simply attired in a grey woollen dress. Much to my delight, she soon abandoned the uncertainty and reserve which she had carried up the hill with her; in no time she was sparkling with effervescent good humour and causing mother to laugh so much that her stays were placed under great strain. Finally, David's grandparents struck up a warm relationship with Catrin and Mary Jane, both of them as elegant and calm

Speculations

as ever, and all four fascinated by the latest news of Parliament and of Revolutionary France.

I was pulled out of my reverie by David, who suddenly said: "My dear friends, I see that our party fare has gone down well and that appetites appear to be satisfied. I am aware that Martha's parents and sister Catrin wish to leave before the evening is too far advanced, since they have a long journey ahead of them. I am also aware that it is now almost five o'clock, with milking and other chores on the farm to be completed. But it is a wonderful evening; may I suggest that, for those who have the energy, a walk down to the cliffs would be appropriate, to see the sun setting over Pen Dinas? And would Dr Harries be so good as to lead us on our expedition?"

At this suggestion, a cheer went up around the room. Joseph agreed to be our leader, and after we had cleared away all the tea things Grandma and Mrs Owen volunteered to do the washing up. Billy and Hettie went off to get changed and to deal with the animals. Grandpa Isaac went off to sort out the Brawdy carriage and horses. We all said our farewells to Mother, Father and Catrin, and then the rest of us -- Mary Jane, Sian, Bessie, David and myself -- tramped off in the company of our expedition leader up onto the crest of the mountain, down the other side, and on to the wild cliffs between Aberfforest and Parrog. As we walked through thickets of heavy-scented and spiky furze bushes and unfurling bracken, Joseph showed us that he was no mean naturalist. He pointed out to us the locations of skylarks' nests in the heather and the nest site of the ancient raven of Carningli, and encouraged us to islolate the particular songs of warblers, finches and thrushes from the evensong now well under way in the copses of ash and oak on the north side of the mountain. He showed us small delicate flowers and herbs which we would otherwise have trampled underfoot, and explained their medicinal properties; he stopped to show us the footprints and resting places of badger, fox and hare; and he showed us the territories favoured by adders, grass snakes and slow-worms. He was bombarded with questions by his eager students, and almost always knew the answers; but every now and then he would say "I'm afraid that is something I do not know; I must remember to look up the answer in my book when I get home." David said afterwards that this was the sign of a good scientific mind -- a mind far sharper than one might expect of a quack doctor or a dabbler in magic.

Speculations

So the time passed in sheer enchantment, and when we came to the clifftops the enchantment was replaced by a sort of inebriation. We all professed that we could hardly believe the colours or profusion of the clifftop flowers, which were now at their best. We could not avoid walking on carpets of pink and red thrift, white sea campion, blue spring squill, yellow kidney vetch and clusters of ox-eye daisies. Here and there other flowers were in competition: viper's bugloss, sorrel and buttercups. Rich sweet scents drifted up from ground level and down from old furze-covered stone banks a few yards inland from the cliff edge. The clifftop flower border appeared to me to have been designed by an eccentric artist and executed by a mad gardener; for sane people could hardly have conceived such a palette of colours or such a mix of textures and heady fragrances. Joseph knew all the flowers, and the insects that sheltered beneath them or obtained nourishment from them.

Some of the flowers had tumbled in clusters over the cliff edge and now survived on little ledges and in crevices a hundred feet above the salt sea. But the crumbling rock faces were really the domain of sea birds rather than flowers -- and again we were amazed by the bounty of nature. Countless thousands of gulls, kittiwakes, razorbills and guillemots contributed to a cacophony of screeching, cackling and chattering which put the evensong of the woodland birds to shame, at least as far as the noise level was concerned. Beautiful it was not, but impressive it certainly was. There were birds everywhere, wheeling around the cliff faces like clouds of giant gnats on an August evening, diving deep for little eels and other small fish, resting in great rafts on the calm evening sea surface, and sitting on eggs on the minutest of rocky ledges, just out of the reach of storm waves. They were cackling, fighting, displaying and cooing like the black and white peoples of some strange and frenetic miniature city.

We walked for a while along the clifftop towards Aberfforest, the carpet of wild flowers still beneath our feet and the seabird multitudes still busy and noisy in their chosen domain. We passed a little beach occupied by oyster-catchers and some offshore rocks controlled by a group of stately cormorants. We passed one of the sea quarries used for the winning of slate slabs for roofing the cottages and building the quays of the Parrog. The working faces were now silent as sunset approached; ropes and chains hung limply from iron bolts in the rock face, and flimsy ladders cast long shadows across the most recent working ledges. Joseph told us that

Speculations

tomorrow, at dawn, there would be thirty men hammering, levering, blasting, cutting and carrying slate in this precarious and exposed place -- no doubt a pleasure in this sort of weather but a veritable hell in the winter with the wind in the north and a storm sea running.

Then we saw the sun go down over Dinas Island, a giant orange-red orb of fire against a dark purple background. There was not a cloud in the sky, not a wave upon the sleeping sea. As the sun sank out of sight the dark shadow of the headland lengthened and marched across Newport Bay towards us. Most of the seabirds fell silent, and we all stood speechless until the last glow of the sun had gone.

With a sudden chill in the air, and with darkness fast approaching, we retraced our steps up onto the mountain. It took us almost two hours to walk home, two by two and three by three, and I cherished my short and disjointed conversations with one friend and then another as we squeezed between trees and boulders, trudged up ancient green lanes bounded by hedges ten feet high, and finally came out onto the open mountain. By the time we got back to the Plas it was approaching midnight, and we were walking along the moorland path illuminated by the light of a thin moon and a million stars. Tawny owls were conversing down in Dolrannog Wood. On entering the warm and candlelit kitchen we decided that a hot punch would nicely round off a perfect day. At one o'clock in the morning Joseph took his leave, mounted his pony and set off along the dark dewy track towards Werndew. We told him to mind how he went, but he said his pony knew every inch of the mountain and would surely deliver him safely home even if he fell fast asleep in the saddle. We offered Mary Jane a bed for the night, and she gladly accepted, saying that she had warned her parents that she might not return until the morrow. Her servant slept on the floor in Billy's room. With everyone thus settled for the night, David and I trudged upstairs, almost too tired to wash, undress and climb into our bed.

Such was my nineteenth birthday -- an occasion filled with love, and laughter, and sound and colour, long to be remembered. I have, over the past month or two, been saddened to discover who my enemies are. Yesterday such sadness was banished, for it was a day anointed by friendship.

Speculations

25th May 1797

Something strange is going on. The night before last, we were awakened by a great commotion out in the yard. The geese were making the most noise, cackling and flapping their wings, but there was also pandemonium in the chicken house, and the dogs in their kennels were barking furiously. We immediately assumed that some intruder was prowling about, possibly with the intention of grabbing a chicken for his supper.

When he heard the symphony of animal noises Billy (who is a light sleeper) was out of bed in a flash. He lit his lantern from the kitchen fire and rushed out into the yard. There was heavy cloud and not much moonlight, so he saw nothing; but he says that he heard the footsteps of somebody running off down the track. He checked the animals and found that none was missing. Yesterday, over breakfast, we discussed the matter and came to the view that some poor starving vagrant passing through the locality had decided on an opportunist raid, and had caused more of a stir than he had bargained for. It occurred to me that the intruder might have been Moses Lloyd, but I could not believe that he could have been so clumsy as to disturb all the animals, and David agreed with me. And yet there was something about the incident that made me uneasy, and left me pondering about the sounds which had awoken me.

Last night I found it difficult to sleep, and I was lying next to David in our bed with my eyes wide open and my ears pricked, at around three of the clock. I knew that something was going to happen. It was a calm night, with only the slightest of breezes drifting across the hushed landscape. Suddenly I became aware of a change in the night-time sounds that find their way through the bedroom window. At first I could not work out what had happened, and then I realised that the sound of running water had stopped. The piped supply of water from Ffynnon Brynach, the faithful spring up on the mountain, had been blocked up or disturbed, so that water no longer splashed and gurgled into the big water trough at the side of the dairy. I got out of bed quietly, with the hairs rising on the back of my neck. Then, since our bedroom window looked the wrong way for any observance of the yard, I crept downstairs, crossed the kitchen, and opened the back door.

As I did so, pandemonium broke out. There was a great crash,

Speculations

followed by a rush of water. I knew that the water trough had been tipped over. In the same moment the dogs started barking and the geese started cackling, and I heard heavy running footsteps on the cobbled yard beyond the barn. I also smelt smoke. I screamed, rushed back into the house and shouted "Billy! Shemi! David! Everybody! There is a fire! Quickly -- we must get out of the house!" I threw a coat from the peg by the kitchen door over my shoulders and rushed outside, and realised straight away that it was not the house that was on fire, but the barn.

In my bare feet I stumbled in the darkness across to the barn door, and saw flames in the far corner where there was a pile of barley straw and chaff. I flung off my coat and beat away like a mad thing, and soon all of us were pitching in, beating at the flames with sacks and cloaks and coughing in the swirling, choking white smoke.

Soon the flames were put out. Then Mrs Owen and Bessie went back to the house to get lanterns. David and Billy took over, raking the hot ash and embers out into the middle of the threshing floor and making sure that the supporting timbers and walls of the barn were in no danger. In ten minutes it was all over, mercifully with no great damage done apart from some burns on assorted cloaks and coats.

We were all in a state of fevered emotion after what had happened, and became even more shocked when we realised that this had been no random attack by a chicken thief but something carefully planned. The arsonist had first been up on the mountainside to stop the water supply and had then tipped over the water trough before setting the barley straw on fire. He knew that with no water to throw on the flames, we would have had little or no chance of saving the barn had the fire taken hold. It was only by providence that I -- and the rest of the household -- had acted quickly enough to avert disaster.

Just in case the intruder was still prowling about in the vicinity of the house or outbuildings, we released the dogs to run free in the yard. They rushed about barking with excitement for five minutes, and then quietened down. There was little chance of either dogs or humans going back to sleep, since dawn was now not far away, and so we left the dogs in the yard, changed out of our smoky garments and settled into the kitchen for an official inquiry and a nice cup of tea. Grandpa poured a tot of brandy into his cup, claiming that a little hot tea-flavoured alcohol was good for the nerves. We could not -- and still cannot -- come to a consensus as to

Speculations

who the guilty party is likely to be. Mrs Owen, Grandma, Bessie and I all incline to the view that the intruder on both nights has been Moses Lloyd. But we have no proof at all, and the men all feel that the raids may have something to do with vagrants passing through the parish. They have an alternative theory that maybe Squire Watkins or Squire Rice is orchestrating some campaign designed to frighten us away from our nonconformist customs in the running of the estate. David says that there are plenty of poor starving labourers in Newport who will happily do us some damage or conduct a burglary for a fee of two silver shillings, especially if there is some guarantee of non-prosecution by the local justices if things go wrong.

There is some merit in this latter theory, since I cannot dispute that Squire Watkins has a reputation for evil and vindictive acts, but I was not convinced that the finger of guilt pointed in his direction. I turned to David and said "There is one feature of this business that I find difficult to link with Squire Watkins. Whoever did this knew the layout of the yard, knew how to get into the barn without disturbing the animals, and knew where the water trough and the water pipe were. He also knew how and where to break the water supply. Who would know such things? Only somebody who has worked at the Plas would have that sort of inside knowledge."

"Do you mean Moses Lloyd?"

"Of course I do."

"You may be right," replied David. "But we have not the tiniest scrap of evidence. And remember, Martha, that there must be twenty or thirty men in Newport and Cilgwyn who know exactly what the layout of this place is. Not long since the Plas was like a busy beehive when we were involved in the threshing and carting of the barley crop. How many men passed through this yard? Ten? Twenty? Every labourer who has helped with stone clearance, or with the hay harvest, or with the corn harvest, knows exactly how the barn is organized, exactly where the water trough is, and exactly where the pipe runs down the mountainside. The same can be said of those who are helping us nowadays with the building work on the cowshed and stable. I am afraid, *Cariad*, that there are many men other than Moses Lloyd who could have paid us nocturnal visits."

Grandpa and Billy agreed with David, and I had to agree myself that without more evidence I could not advance my case for the prosecution. So I let the matter rest. I am increasingly coming to the view that David and

Speculations

Grandpa do not actually wish to think any further evil of Moses. Maybe they hope that he has simply gone out of their lives, never to return. Maybe they are still bound by this strange code of honour subscribed to by David's father and by old Squire Lloyd. And maybe they still feel a sense of guilt at having let the wretched fellow run free after the theft of the barley when they should have clapped him in irons. There are male sensitivities here, of which I and the other women need to take due account.

I am tired, having not had much sleep over the past two nights. It is past ten of the clock, but before I climb into bed beside my slumbering husband I must record two further facts. First, the dogs are running free tonight, and we have decided to leave them out every night from now on just in case the intruder should be tempted to return. And second, an examination of the water pipe this morning revealed that it had been dragged away from its mountings right up at the spring of old St Brynach, high on the mountainside. To my mind that was not just an act of premeditated vandalism. It was an act of desecration by an evil man.

ΩΩΩΩΩΩΩΩΩΩ

26th May 1797

Last night there were no disturbances, and we all awoke refreshed and ressured that we have seen the last of the mysterious intruder. It was a beautiful morning, and the men left the house early to round up the sheep, for it is dipping time in the deep pool near Gelli. After finishing in the dairy and collecting the eggs I filled a couple of bottles with milk and went to the little pen at the back of the stable where I keep my five molly lambs. Their thirst satisfied, at least for an hour or two, I decided on a weeding session in my flower garden at the back of the stable. I worked hard for half an hour, and then sat on a log for a few minutes in the sun. As I sat there my eye was caught by a piece of paper pinned to the gatepost. Intrigued, I went over and looked at it more closely. On it were written, in large and confident letters, the words VENGEANCE IS MINE.

A wave of nausea came over me, and for a few moments I felt that I might faint. I tore the note off the gatepost and returned to my log. I sat there for I know not how long. But now I knew for certain that Moses was behind the arson attack and the damage to the water pipe. I have never seen his handwriting, and could not connect the paper with him in any way, but the message was clear, and there was only one man in the whole world, so far as I was aware, who might wish us serious misfortune and who might actually harm us by his own hand.

As I exercised my mind on this miserable business, I suddenly realised why I had been concerned by the sound made by the farmyard animals on the night of the first intrusion into our privacy. Only two of the dogs had been barking. We have six dogs. Four of them are sheepdogs, and they share a kennel near the farmyard entrance. We have had them for a long time, and they were always spoiled by Moses, for he appeared to enjoy the company of animals better than that of human beings. The other two dogs are terriers, purchased within the last month for helping with the cattle which we plan to buy. On the night that Billy rushed out and frightened the intruder they were barking and growling like mad things. I do not think that anybody else in the family noticed this anomaly, but I am now convinced that Moses crept up the farm lane, whispered to the sheepdogs and possibly gave them some sugar to keep them quiet, and was only diverted from his purpose when the geese sent up the alarm.

One further realisation causes me even now, as I write these words late at night, to feel a tightening in my breast. The flower garden is my territory. Nobody else goes inside the gate; it is my pleasure, and mine alone, to plant and weed and water, and it is I who will -- in due course -- pick my summer posies there. The note pinned on the gatepost was intended for me, and me alone.

Whether I like it or not, I am now being sucked into a personal conflict with Moses Lloyd. For better or for worse, I will confide in my diary but I will say nothing to David. Who knows where it will all end?

ΩΩΩΩΩΩΩΩΩΩ

13. Summer Days

3rd June 1797

Yesterday we had a most pleasant social engagement at Llwyngwair Mansion, the home of the Bowen family and the real centre of power and culture in these parts. David and I, together with Grandpa Isaac and Grandma Jane, were all invited to a "musical soiree" which commenced at six o'clock in the evening, and we took this as a sign of our enhanced status in the local community. Grandma and myself were delighted to have the opportunity to dress up in our summer finery, but both David and Grandpa huffed and puffed and complained heartily about the necessity of dressing up in tight waistcoats and heavy jackets and squeaking shoes. I sought to console them by saying that fine clothes, grand gestures and cultivated conversation were essential in the modern man, but they agreed that they would be far happier wearing old smocks and wooden clogs in a turnip field than wearing silks and satins in the lounge of a fine mansion.

At any rate, Grandma and I managed to get them out of the house and onto the chaise, and on a fine summer's afternoon we arrived on time at the elegant entrance of the mansion. We were greeted by Squire John Bowen and his wife Anne and daughter Ellie. I had heard much of them before, and of their absent children William and Thomas, but this was the first time I had met any of them face to face. All three struck me immediately as good and sincere people, and indeed this impression accorded with what I had heard about their support for the Methodists in Newport and Nevern and their generosity in matters relating to education for the poor. The Squire is held in the highest esteem by Grandpa Isaac, and indeed he thinks him the only honest justice of the peace in the whole region. He is a tall and elegant man with silver hair, a sunburned skin and deep blue eyes, and I was flattered to be given more than a moment's attention by him. But he did not, in his manner, stray beyond the bounds of etiquette, and he and his wife escorted Grandma and Grandpa into the house while leaving David and me to the sweet attention of Ellie.

Soon we were caught up in the grace of the occasion, with music performed by a string quartet in the lounge and with guests circulating through the well-appointed downstairs rooms of the mansion and through the french windows into the garden. I was delighted to find that Mary Jane and her parents from Pontfaen were among the guests, together with the Prossers of Frongoch and the Edwardses of Llwyngoras. Good wines flowed freely, and there were cold meats, sauces, excellent vegetables and delicate sweetmeats in abundance. Those of us who had some musical pretensions were prevailed upon to perform, and I played an old Welsh air on Ellie's harp which was well received. Grandma's harp playing is far superior to mine, and we were all delighted when she turned out to be the star performer of the evening. Indeed, after her performance of intricate *penillion* those who knew how to judge skill in this most difficult of musical disciplines freely admitted that they had had tears in their eyes. I observed for myself that as she played she seemed to drift into a sort of trance, with her mellow voice and delicate fingering producing sounds of extraordinary beauty with apparently no physical effort. With her straight back and fresh complexion and closed eyes, she was transformed for a few minutes from David's ancient grandmother into a woman in the bloom of youth; and I was forcefully reminded that she is still not sixty years old.

As the evening went on and the good wines and even better brandy loosened up both inhibitions and stiff collars, I noticed with some pleasure that both David and Grandpa Isaac were enjoying themselves a good deal more than they might have done in a muddy turnip field. I too enjoyed myself, and drank just a little more than was good for me. I spent much time in the company of Mary Jane and Ellie, whom I now count as a new friend. Like Mary Jane, she is both very good looking and very eligible, and the two of them attracted an endless stream of introductions and greetings from silly young men. As a respectable married woman I found myself, on several occasions, acting as a chaperone, which was highly amusing since they have both seen a great deal more of the world than I. Indeed Ellie has had a most refined education, and has spent much time in the company of her brother and other relatives on tour in Italy and Greece.

By ten of the clock both Mary Jane and Ellie were fed up of eligible bachelors, and the three of us decided to sit in the peace and quiet of the conservatory. We sat beneath a leafy palm in the warmth of a breathless June evening, with moths fluttering around the lanterns. We talked of this and that, and in due course the conversation turned to family alliances. I remarked that the three sturdy squires Rice, Howell and Watkins, and their delightful wives and offspring, were not present for the musical evening. Had they perhaps had some prior pressing engagement? "Oh no," said Ellie. "They very seldom have prior pressing engagements. There has been a falling out of our families, and they were not invited."

Mary Jane and I exchanged glances, and Ellie saw immediately that we shared a common view of the three families in question. "I perceive that you have had some dealings with them," she said.

"Indeed we have," I replied "We seek to maintain good relations with all the families in the neighbourhood, but these three do seem to have a somewhat conservative attitude to minor matters including religion, politics, commerce, education and justice."

At this, Mary Jane burst into giggles and said "Martha Morgan, you have not been here very long, but you clearly know what is going on. Maybe you know too much for your own good. Watch out, for if you are not careful you will join Ellie and myself on their blacklist."

"Oh? And what, may I ask, have you done to deserve their approbation?"

"Well, we are too sympathetic to the Methodists, for a start," said Ellie. "Then we give too much to the poor and too little to the rich. Then we have spurned the romantic advances of various of their male offspring. Added to which, we support the circulating schools. And as for our fathers, they are black scoundrels indeed, for they seek to administer justice in a manner which involves a degree of understanding and compassion."

"Outrageous!" said I. "Paupers and vagabonds, poachers and vagrants should all be transported to the colonies or strung up from the gallows, leaving the countryside clean and healthy for gentlemen of leisure to pursue their sporting activities without let or hindrance."

I told my friends of the encounters involving the alliance of the three squires, and of the exchange of letters concerning the circulating school. Neither Mary Jane nor Ellie was surprised, and it turned out that their families had been involved in similar difficulties. As we laughed and talked I was left with a clear impression that a gulf is opening up between the more enterprising and liberal landowners and those who are trapped by convention, debt or petty self-interest into a jaundiced and spiteful view of the world. "What a sad thing it must be," said Ellie, "to see your labourers, your tenants and even your fellow gentlemen as enemies or threats. I actually feel quite sorry for them, in the few moments when I am not feeling outraged by the injustices which they visit upon those who are weaker than themselves."

The talk then turned to the Lloyds of Cwmgloyn, and I expressed surprise at the fact that they were also absent from the musical gathering. "Oh, they were invited," said Ellie, "but declined as usual. Squire Lloyd is not well, and the other members of the family are seldom seen in good company nowadays. We think they they were all greatly affected by the bad business some years ago involving their son."

"You mean Moses?" I asked.

"Why yes. I had forgotten that you know him. I remember now that my father has been involved on more than one occasion in recent months in requests for warrants for his arrest. Is there not currently a warrant for him posted in Newport and Nevern? Something to do with petty larceny, and I daresay a good deal else?"

"Why do you make that assumption, Ellie?" I asked. "You sound as if you may know him a good deal better than I, even though he was our servant at the Plas for some years. Tell me more. I am very intrigued."

At this, Ellie turned to Mary Jane and sought her approval with the slightest of eye movements. Approval was given with an almost imperceptible nod of the head. So Ellie said "I was once very close to Moses. We almost grew up together, for our families were on the best of terms. It was assumed, when I was about thirteen, that we might even be married one day. He was a charming and lively boy, but there were two sides to his character. Sometimes he would be gentle and almost insecure, and on other occasions he would be so opinionated, arrogant and intolerant that I found him insufferable."

"I think I recognize the same person," I said.

Ellie continued. "There was also a very cruel side to his nature which I saw in his dealings with younger children. At last I became frightened of him, and I told him that I did not want to be his friend any longer. He flew into such a rage that I screamed and fled in tears, and my brother William had to pin him to the ground until he had calmed down. After that I had hardly any dealings with him, and he went off to Eton and Oxford and out of my life."

"He was a confused young man," said Mary Jane. "Indeed, my impression of him, at various balls and parties when I was young, was simply that he was a spoiled brat. More than once he tried to take advantage of me, and once I gave him a black eye for his pains."

Ellie then turned to me and exclaimed "Martha! Your big brown eyes are almost popping out of your head! Are you surprised that others should have had encounters with Moses Lloyd in the murky past? This is after all a small place. Those of us who belong to the ancient families have met socially at regular intervals, and we all know at least some of each other's secrets."

"So do you know why Moses behaved as he did?"

"Not really," replied Ellie. "He was certainly accustomed to getting his own way, and he appeared to be the apple of his father's eye. But his father expected far more of him than he was able to give. I know not what went on behind closed doors, but I am sure that he was beaten frequently as a child. Perhaps the beatings were justified, and perhaps not, but sometimes I saw the bruises and the swellings on his head and arms."

"Oh, how terrible!" I cried. "Was his father quite mad? And is he still mad?"

"Perhaps," said Mary Jane. "There are rumours to go on, but outside of the immediate family circle and the servants, nobody apart from Doctor Havard has seen him for four years or more."

"Now I feel quite confused myself," I said. "I am even inclined to feel sorry for the wretched fellow. Discipline is one thing but brutality is quite another. Why did he not flee from such an environment?"

"Well, in a sense he did," said Ellie, "for he went off to school, and college, and we all thought that this would bring him friendship, respect and security, and settle him down."

"And did it?"

"Apparently not. According to my brother, who was at college with him, his lifestyle left something to be desired, and he squandered much of his father's fortune."

I realized then that Ellie's brother, the same Major William Bowen who had led David and the Newport contingent against the French invader, was a direct contemporary of Moses. But I had not realized that they had been college friends. Now, with the matter of Moses Lloyd under detailed review, I could not resist raising a matter that has puzzled me since it was first mentioned by Grandpa Isaac last month -- namely the incident which led to the final split between Moses and his father.

"What actually happened in Oxford on that fateful day?" I asked Ellie.

"Was your brother there at the time?"

"No, he was not. But he heard about it afterwards, and was instrumental in getting Moses away from Oxford and back home in considerable haste."

I pressed Ellie again as to the details of the event. She looked around to ensure that there were no others in the vicinity, and asked us, in a very quiet voice, to swear that we would never repeat what we were about to hear. We both swore that we would never tell the secret to anybody, and then Ellie spoke again.

"William was in his rooms in Jesus College one afternoon when Moses came rushing in. He was in a state of great agitation. "I am accursed! I am accursed!" was all that he would say. He flung himself onto the bed and wept and moaned, drawing his knees up to his chin like a small baby. William could get no sense out of him, but at last discovered that something terrible had happened in a small village called Wolvercote, on the outskirts of Oxford. Moses pleaded for a bottle of whisky and gulped half of it down, straight from the bottle, but he would say no more. At last William decided to ride out to Wolvercote to find out for himself what had happened. When he got there he found that the whole community was in turmoil, and he discovered from various villagers that an hour earlier "a wild gentleman on a grey horse" had galloped through the village. It could only have been Moses. A small child had been playing in the street, and the poor mite had got under the horse's hooves and had been killed instantly. Children and adults screamed and wailed, and the child's mother rushed out of a cottage and picked up the corpse from the muddy roadway. She stood there with the child in her arms, not knowing what to say or do. Moses reined in his horse and returned to the scene of the accident. He realized what had happened, but in another moment of madness he shouted "Stupid child! Do you people not teach your children never to play in the king's highway?" Then he fished in his purse, took out a sovereign and tossed in onto the ground in front of the distraught mother. "There is something for your trouble," he said. "Give the child a decent burial. There are too many children in this village anyway." And he turned his horse's head back towards Oxford."

Both Mary Jane and I were speechless, and I realized that we both had tears rolling down our cheeks. But Ellie was far from finished. "According to the eyewitness accounts given to William, the mood of the villagers then turned angry. The menfolk crowded around Moses' horse, and he would certainly have been pulled to the ground and possibly lynched but for the intervention of an old woman who was reputed to be the local witch. She screamed above the commotion. "I have seen your evil deed," she screeched. "You have come in evil and you will go in evil. A curse upon you and yours. You will never find peace, and when your time comes an avenging angel will put her foot upon your breast and send you down to Hell." The crowd fell silent, and although Moses was terrified he seized the moment. He spurred his horse, shook off the angry menfolk, and galloped nonstop all the way back to Oxford."

There was a long silence, and then Mary Jane asked "Was that the end of the affair?"

"Almost," replied Ellie. "William obtained the name and address of the poor family who had lost their child, but did not admit that he knew the guilty horseman. He promised that he would return with help, and indeed he managed to raise twenty pounds from his college friends over the next few days. But he knew that he would have to get Moses out of Oxford and back to Pembrokeshire immediately. He packed his bags for him and put him on the Monday mail coach to Haverfordwest. Next day a warrant was put out by the Oxford magistrates for the arrest of an unknown horseman on suspicion of murder. And so Moses arrived home. God knows what version of the story he told to his father, but it was the last straw. There was a blazing row, and Squire Lloyd threw him out of the house and cut him out of his will. And I think you know what happened after that."

After another long silence, I said "Thank you, Ellie my dear, for entrusting us with this story. It is truly appalling, and I cannot begin to imagine the distress of the poor parents who lost their child. But what you have told us goes some way to explaining certain things which have happened in recent months."

"To tell you the truth," said Ellie, with a weak smile, "I am glad to get the whole story off my chest. William entrusted it to me shortly after he returned from college. But he and his close friends will not speak of this matter at all, and consider it a closed book. But a horrid crime has been committed, and justice has not been done. For some years I have felt that by keeping the story to myself I have somehow failed to alert others to the danger that might come from close contact with Moses Lloyd."

"But now he is gone," I lied. "And let us hope that he does not return to blight any more innocent lives."

The night was now far advanced, and the three of us decided that we had better resume contact with the rest of the human race. We did our best to lift our spirits, and indeed we were soon caught up again in the good humour of families and friends. At midnight we took our leave, and between Mary Jane, Ellie and myself there were especially warm embraces. Suddenly there is a broad band of intimacy around us, and it is a strange and fateful thing that the band should have the words "Moses Lloyd" writ large upon it.

ΩΩΩΩΩΩΩΩΩ

11th June 1797

We have had a busy month, blessed by excellent weather and a feeling that the Plas is at last recovering something of its former glory. The sheep are all sheared, and are much happier without their winter clothing. The crops are in and growing, and the lambs are doing well, and soon it will be time for the hay harvest. But there has been no time for playing with lambs and listening to the growing grass.

For a start, there has been building work under way, and the new cowshed is almost complete. We have given work to five labourers, and their wives and children, in quarrying stone from the mountain, carting and mixing lime mortar, and in fetching slate roofing slabs from the sea quarries at Aberrhigian. David and Billy have done most of the building work, helped occasionally by Gethin Griffiths and the Jenkins brothers. Grandpa Isaac has acted as architect and foreman, since he is now quite clever at calculating quantities and working out dimensions, having done it all before in the rebuilding work after the fire. The great beams that were seasoning in the barn have been heaved up into position to make a fine new pitched roof.

We have bought a new gambo and a new wagon from Lewis Carpenter in Newport, and four horses and a second-hand carriage from Heathfield near Letterston. I am delighted by the latter acquisition, since we can now undertake long journeys without being entirely at the mercy of the weather. Grandpa is teaching David about livestock. The two of them have bought a hundred yearling ewes from Maenclochog, on the other side of the mountain, and Billy and Shemi took the dogs and drove the flock back to the Plas two days ago. They are settling in well, but we will not let them out onto the common until the smell of their new territory has got into them. I asked Grandpa why he had not wanted to purchase sheep at Ffair Gurig in Newport, but he replied that he wanted to change the blood line and introduce some hardy mountain stock in the expectation of harder winters to come. When Ffair Gurig is held at the end of this month we will buy at least twenty calves, ten cattle and ten pigs, and we still need two draught horses and two riding ponies. With all this new livestock we will need to improve our field walls, hedges and gates, and young Shemi has been put in charge of six children from the cwm on repair work. It is the first time he has been in charge of anything, and he is as proud as a quivering peacock.

With all of these mouths to feed, mealtimes have been almost as frantic as they were during the threshing of the barley crop. But Mrs Owen has had everything under control, and she has conjured potatoes, chickens, salty bacon, cheese, leeks, potatoes, carrots and apples out of thin air and onto the table in spite of the fact that none of this year's crops are ready in the garden. When I asked her about this miracle, she replied, with a twinkle in her eye, "Rationing, Mistress, rationing."

Yesterday was David's 20th birthday, and when we woke in the morning to the lovely melodies of the dawn chorus I gave him a watercolour painting of the mountain, with the Plas in the foreground, on which I have been working secretly. When he saw it he was quite touched, since this was the first representation he had seen of the rebuilt house. "Thank you, thank you, *Cariad*, " he said, holding me tight in his arms. "It is quite beautiful. I will get a frame made for it, and I will put it on the wall in the drawing room in pride of place. Then we will all -- family and guests -- derive great pleasure from it in the years to come."

David asked for no great celebration of his birthday, for he knows that next year his coming-of-age will have to be celebrated in some style. But he did at least agree that we should enjoy a special family supper in the evening, having heard that Hettie had obtained a large salmon from the estuary under mysterious circumstances. During the morning, with the men all hard at work on the new cowshed, and with the sun sailing high in a cloudless sky, I formed the idea that I should take David off for a birthday picnic. I asked Grandma Jane if she thought he could be spared from the building work for a little while, and she said "Of course he can, my dear! He has been working non-stop on that cowshed and on the shearing for nigh on three weeks, and a break will do him good. You take him off for a couple of hours, and enjoy yourselves."

Thus encouraged, I took a wicker basket and lined it with a fresh linen cloth. I filled a flagon with our best perry and placed it into the basket, together with a couple of fine pewter mugs. I took half a loaf of fresh crusty wheat bread, a pat of salty butter, a lump of cheese, some slices of salted ham, a cupful of pickle, some handfuls of walnuts and hazelnuts, and a little bowl of wild strawberries from the hedge behind the house. Mrs Owen gave me some crystallized fruits and other sugary sweetmeats. Then I added two china plates and some silver cutlery, covered the picnic with a pretty embroidered napkin, and decorated the basket with daisy chains and posies of foxglove, red campion, purple vetch, dog roses and honeysuckle collected from the farm lane. I dressed in my prettiest summer dress, placed a white bonnet upon my head, and as the kitchen clock struck twelve I sallied forth to fetch my husband.

He was on the roof of the cowshed with Billy, putting slates into position. He had no shirt on, and the sweat was streaming off him as he worked under the relentless sun. For a few minutes I stood in the shadow of the stable and watched him, bronzed and fit, moving about easily on the slating battens and fixing the heavy slate slabs with wooden pins. How I loved him! Then he noticed me out of the corner of his eye, and shouted "Martha Morgan! What on earth are you doing there? You look as if you are setting out for a party or something!"

"You could say that," I replied. "But your assistance is required, and I will be grateful if you will descend that rickety ladder so that I can more fully put you in the picture." Then I turned to Billy, who had already guessed my intention, and said "Can you spare your Master for a couple of hours, Billy? It looks very crowded up on that roof, and too hot for slating. Anyway, it is not seemly for the gentleman Master of Plas Ingli to be working without his shirt on when there are so many strange women about the farm."

"I quite agree, Mistress," said Billy, with a big toothy grin. "There is no knowing where it will lead. He is a hopeless slater, and he just gets in my way. Too much talking and too many breakages. Grateful I will be, for sure, if you will just take him away for a while so that I can get on with some decent work."

David knew that something was afoot, but he played his part by mumbling and grumbling, and told Billy off with mock severity for his insolence. But he realized that he had no chance of staying on the roof in the face of such opposition, and he at last climbed down with good grace. I led him to the kitchen, and as soon as he saw the kitchen basket on the table the look of puzzlement disappeared from his face, and he said "Wife! I see that you have been making plans again."

"Indeed I have, husband," I replied. "There is a jug of cold water in the scullery. Wash yourself down if you please, for I cannot take a respectable birthday picnic with a man who is covered with slate dust and sweat and who is half undressed."

And so the charade continued, with David protesting and with everybody else trying to chase him out of the house, and at last I got him into the yard with clean breeches upon his legs, a clean shirt upon his back, and the picnic basket upon his arm. I carried a little rug to sit upon, and we walked off down the track, arm in arm, leaving the other inhabitants of the Plas to their appointed tasks. My husband has a very strongly developed sense of duty, and at times I find myself a little irritated by the stiffness of his demeanour, but I find that he loosens up with a little encouragement, and by the time we had reached the Cilgwyn road he had stopped feeling guilty about leaving Billy all alone on the roof. He looked at me, and I looked at him, and we realized that for once we were free to enjoy each other on a summer day while the rest of the world was hard at work.

There was no question as to where we would go. We did not even discuss it, and after walking through the leafy arches of the midsummer lanes for half an hour we came to the stile leading into Coed Tycanol. David helped me over, and then we were strolling in the deep shade of the wood, with gnarled tree trunks and twisted branches all around us, freshly unfurled oak leaves overhead, and soft moss underfoot. Everything was cool and clean, and the only sounds were the little warning cries of the woodland birds whose territory we had invaded and the busy whirring of a million insect wings.

Summer Days

We passed beneath the grey crags of ancient rock and the cave where the druids once lived, and smelt the juices of wild garlic leaves rising with each fresh footstep in an area where the ground was moist. Then we came to a little dry clearing, where the tree canopy was just open enough for shafts of sunlight to dapple the mosses and grasses of the forest floor. Without a word I spread our woollen rug on the ground. David put down the picnic and sat down. I sat beside him and snuggled up close, and for a while we were lost in memories, for this was the place where we had first loved one another on the 15th of June last year, and where we had loved on three other occasions on the days that followed. Then David sat upright and said, with a gleam in his eye and his best Oxford voice, "Wife! Here am I, an honest slater dressed to kill on a hot summer's day, exhausted after a morning's work beneath the cruel sun, and not a morsel in my stomach! I demand my dinner!"

So like a dutiful wife, and with a reciprocal gleam in my eye, I jumped up, curtseyed, and said in my most timid voice "Yes, Master! Yes indeed, Master! Whatever you say, Master!" With grandly exaggerated gestures interrupted by fits of giggles I laid out the picnic before him, and he tucked in as if he was Robinson Crusoe recently delivered from his desert island. I tucked in too, and the perry went down extremely well, and at last we lay on our backs, replete and contented beneath our oak leaf blanket in the humming and lazy warmth of a June afternoon. Time passed. There were little rustlings in the undergrowth where small animals scuttled about. We may have snoozed a while, and I am still not sure whether I travelled through the next few minutes in a dream or wide awake, but I have a recollection of David's lips upon mine and mine upon his, and laughter and tomfoolery, and garments shed, and his hands upon my body and my hands upon his, and squeals and sighs, as we loved again.

This time was unlike the others, for now there was no guilt and no furtiveness, no desperate longing and no learning of the ways of love. We laughed and we played, and in every move and every sound we melted together in joy. There was deep and lasting passion too, for when it was ended we were both exhausted, and fell asleep amid scattered garments and pewter mugs and china plates and breadcrumbs. From Heaven, the scene must have appeared to the Good Lord like the aftermath of some wild Roman orgy.

When we awoke the sun was dropping in the evening sky, and with a shock we remembered that we had promised to be away for no more than two hours. Hurriedly we gathered up our things, tidied ourselves up as best we could, and set off for the stile and the shadowy lanes leading to the Plas. We held hands as we walked, and there was beauty all around us. The sweet smell of wood smoke reached our nostrils from some cottager's hearth. A buzzard wheeled and called a thousand feet above our heads.

It was gone five when we reached home, and as we passed through the kitchen we became aware that we looked more dishevelled than was appropriate for the Master and Mistress of a fine country estate. Grandma and Mrs Owen were preparing a large salmon on the kitchen table, and they raised their eyes as we entered. "Hello my dears!" said Grandma. "I trust that you had a pleasant time?"

"Indeed we did," replied David, flushing slightly. "But we are sorry to say that we fell asleep after our little picnic."

"Don't you worry about that, Master David," said Mrs Owen. "We have managed perfectly well without you. Eating is a very tiring business when one is young." She winked at Grandma, and Grandma winked back. At this, both David and I blushed profusely, and rushed upstairs in a state of disarray.

By supper time we had regained our composure to some degree, and we enjoyed a wonderful evening of good food, good wine and good humour. But I am ashamed to say that, so far as David and myself were concerned, the flush remained upon our cheeks for the whole evening, and that every time my eyes met his my emotions were swirled about like flower petals in a whirlpool.

ΩΩΩΩΩΩΩΩΩΩ

18th June 1797

We are caught up in another troublesome episode, precipitated this time by the three Silly Squires. Again, I do not know whether to laugh or cry.

Some days ago, as usual on a Friday, Grandpa Isaac went into town on his favourite pony. His intentions were entirely honourable -- a little buying and selling, a little wheeling and dealing, and a few jars of ale with his cronies. He met up with Edwards Llwyngoras, Jenkins Brithdir, Prosser Frongoch and various others at the Castle Inn, and (according to his account) they were chatting quietly in an upstairs room when a deputation led by Rice Pentre Ifan and Watkins Llannerch strode in and confronted them in a most aggressive manner. The cause of the altercation is still not very clear to me, but Grandpa says that it was, superficially at least, to do with the administration of justice. Grandpa's friends have been increasingly active of late on the local bench, and at various petty sessions they have either acquitted poor people accused of assorted misdemeanours or handed out sentences which are perceived by some of the justices to be "soft". The justice's clerk, one Ifan Beynon of Berry Hill, is in the pocket of the "hard" squires, and indeed he makes his money out of convictions. Grandpa says that in recent weeks so many foolish and vindictive arrest warrants have been issued that law and order are in grave danger of breaking down.

Grandpa says that Squire Rice now accused him (not for the first time) of failing to take his responsibilities as a justice seriously, and became quite vitriolic with Squire Edwards and Squire Prosser on the basis that they have recently acquitted two poor starving women hauled before them for stealing three turnips. Both of these gentlemen are in their seventies, and neither is in the best of health, but they are very experienced justices, and they told Rice and his cronies that they were not prepared to consider cases brought before them "frivolously or maliciously", and they would certainly never commit anybody to the Quarter Sessions or Assizes unless reasonable evidence of guilt could be produced. "Look to it, sir," Squire Prosser said to the red-faced Rice, "or the Lord Lieutenant will be paying you a visit. You can not expect to throw people into the county gaol, or transport them, or string them up on the gallows tree, without evidence that will stand up under cross-examination by the likes of Lewis Legal or Will Final Testament. These men know their jobs and they know the law. The Lord Lieutenant is charged with keeping an eye on the Court Leet and the justices of this town, and I know for a fact that he will not have his jails filled up with so-called "felons" who have committed no felonies and so-called "vagrants" whose only crime is to sleep in a hedge."

Grandpa says that he and Squire Edwards also weighed in with harsh criticisms of the misuse of the judicial system by certain justices, and accused Rice, Watkins and the others of simply seeking to use the system as a tool for beating the labouring class into submission. "You will not succeed, sir," Grandpa shouted, "since respect for the law depends upon respect for the administration of justice. If you and your ilk go on giving out idiotic sentences, the people will see the law as an ass. And I will agree with them!"

"If you are so dissatisfied with our feeble attempts to keep law and order, my dear Master Morgan, why do you not do something about it?" hissed Squire Watkins. "Why do you not return to your duties instead of criticizing others?"

"Very well, sir, I shall do just that!" replied Grandpa, no doubt with steam coming out of his ears and his polished brow shining like the sun. "I shall, from this very day on, be available to do my duty. I will not be browbeaten by anyone who thinks he knows the law better than I, and I will endeavour, no doubt to your disgust, to treat all men and women as equal under the law. And now, gentlemen, I will ask you to be so kind as to leave us in peace. My friends and I are still intent upon enjoying a quiet jar of ale, and we have been considerably inconvenienced by your intervention. A very good day to you!"

Rice, Watkins and the rest of them were forced to retreat, leaving Grandpa to mull over the rashness of his decision. He says that his friends were overjoyed at the prospect of his return to the bench, and he now claims that he was forced back into the administration of justice against his will. But his protestations are not very loud, and when he recounted this episode to us on his return home I swear that there was a new gleam in his eye. Grandpa Isaac enjoys a fight, and he senses that a showdown between the two groups of squires is not far off. He is also very intelligent, and I am sure he would not be going into this contest without a strong conviction that victory is assured.

In my own small world, I too am in trouble, this time with Squire and Mistress Howell of Henllys. Three days ago Ellie and Mary Jane prevailed upon me to attend a meeting of the True Briton Society in Newport. I was happy to go along, for they told me that it was a sort of "friendly society" set up for the mutual benefit of poor people in the neighbourhood. When I arrived for the meeting, in the upstairs room of the Black Lion, I was greeted by my good friends and by more than thirty men and women from the town who were intent upon lifting themselves out of poverty and into something a little closer to comfort and security. Ellie, who took charge of the proceedings, collected and recorded the pennies contributed by those who had managed to save a little, and loaned out a few pennies here and there to those who were most in need. I know not whether these loans are ever repaid. She organized some medical help for three families down on the Parrog, and agreed to find legal help for a labourer from Aberfforest who has been arrested on the most dubious grounds for "loitering with intent to commit a felony". I do not fully understand the workings of the society, but it seems to me to be a most excellent thing which threatens nobody. When asked by four of the Cilgwyn women, I agreed very readily to become a patron of the Society, and contributed five shillings to the charitable fund.

When I left the meeting with my friends at half past seven o'clock I noticed that Squire and Mistress Howell were on the other side of the road, with little notebooks and charcoal sticks in hand. They made no attempt to hide themselves, and it was obvious that they were writing down the names of all those who had been present in the upstairs room. I gave them a cheerful greeting, for even the devil needs to be treated with courtesy if one is to keep the moral high ground, and said "I see that you are sketching this beautiful old inn! The light is just perfect this evening. As it happens, I too am interested in artistic pursuits, although I confess to a preference for water colour washes over charcoal drawing. Would you grant me the privilege of a preview?" And I started across the road towards them.

Not at all to my surprise, they both looked startled, slammed their notebooks closed, and then scuttled off without saying a word, with thunderous scowls upon their faces. The episode was observed by Mary Jane and Ellie, who both had fits of the giggles. I could not resist an attack of the giggles myself, and I fear that the Squire and his good lady heard us all too clearly as they retreated along East Street. When we had regained our composure poor Meg Ifans from Mountain West came up to me and said "Thank you for seeing them off, Mistress Martha. There is always somebody taking our names when we come out of our meetings, yes indeed, and we know not where it will end. Some of us are supposed to be at work, and even them as has the evening off will be in deep trouble if their masters are told -- as they surely will be -- that they are on Squire Howell's black list. I hear say that Squire Rice threw two men off his hay-making gang the other day for being True Britons, since his spies had told him they had saved five pennies each in the mutual fund. He said that if they had five pennies each to save, it was clear that they had no need of further pennies, and he gave their work to two other men instead."

I have no reason to doubt Meg's word on this matter, and I admit to a certain thrill of excitement now that I too am on Squire Howell's black list.

ΩΩΩΩΩΩΩΩΩΩ

29th June 1797

Grandpa Isaac has been involved in his first Petty Sessions since he came out of retirement. Ifan Beynon, the justice's clerk, has been working overtime in recent weeks taking complaints, recording witness statements, and issuing summonses, and he asked Grandpa to hold the Sessions in the kitchen at the Plas.

Grandpa agreed on the basis that it was easier than dragging himself off to some other venue, and he prevailed upon Squire Edwards of Llwyngoras to sit on the bench with him. They established themselves at the kitchen table and opened proceedings at nine of the clock. Having been evicted from her natural territory, Mrs Owen went off to Newport in a huff, to do some shopping. Various clerks, attorneys, witnesses, constables and prisoners appeared and disappeared. The clerk had ten cases down to be dealt with. In truth they were for the most part routine and very petty. Three of those charged with various offences failed to turn up, and warrants were issued for their arrest. There was one case of a disputed will which Grandpa and Squire Edwards managed to sort out to the satisfaction of both parties. A local shopkeeper was sued by one of his suppliers of paper bags and sacks for payment of a debt of twenty pounds plus ten pounds costs. The magistrates reduced the costs to two pounds and issued an order for payment of the debt. William James from Parrog was transported up from the town lockup on the back of a cart and hauled before the bench, charged with stealing a waistcoat and breeches worth 6d from a neighbour. The charge was proved, and the miserable fellow was released on bail of one shilling and committed for trial at the Quarter Sessions. Harry Evans of Cilgwyn (whom I knew to be one of the labourers living in the woods near Pantry) was charged with stealing a sheep from

Lewis Cilwen. He admitted his guilt and was remanded in custody also for trial at the Quarter Sessions.

Grandpa and Squire Edwards insisted on conducting the proceedings entirely in Welsh, on the basis that most of those charged could not understand English and would not have been able to defend themselves properly under any other circumstances. This ruling did not amuse a lawyer from Haverfordwest who had travelled up over the mountain for the Petty Sessions. The sole purpose of his expedition was to prove the guilt of a pedlar who had allegedly stolen some hay from the field of a client in order to feed his donkey. The pedlar spoke no English and the lawyer spoke no Welsh. Impasse. Grandpa dismissed the case (in Welsh) on the grounds that no evidence had been produced by the prosecution, and sent the pedlar on his way. The lawyer complained that in the past proceedings had always been conducted in English in Newport, and returned to Haverfordwest in a state of high dudgeon.

And so it went on. As I got on with my work and passed in and out of the kitchen I overheard parts of the proceedings. For the most part I thought this legal business very dry indeed. However, one case was very diverting. A lad of twelve was stood before the bench charged with poaching a rabbit from a field belonging to Squire Rice. Grandpa and Squire Edwards heard the charge and the case for the prosecution, presented by a pompous young lawyer from Fishguard. Rice's gamekeeper swore that he had apprehended the lad in the wood below the turnip field with the rabbit in his bag, and that since the rabbit was still warm his guilt was obvious. "His guilt may be obvious to you, my good man," said Grandpa, "but it not obvious to me. Any other witnesses?"

"No, sir."

Grandpa and Squire Edwards then consulted together, and the latter said "We do not find the case proved. The game laws are very complicated, but the rabbit in question might have been a far-travelled rabbit. You have not proved that it belonged to Squire Rice, or that it had been feeding on Squire Rice's turnips. Indeed, the fact that the rabbit was warm may have been the result of the fact that it was a warm day. It is not, in my book, an offence to carry a warm dead rabbit around in a bag. Case dismissed!"

When all the cases had been heard, the two magistrates agreed the payments which should go to the constable for transporting prisoners and so forth, but greatly offended Clerk Ifan Beynon by refusing to pay his outrageous charges for writing out summonses, taking witness statements, and attending the court. "Master Beynon," said Grandpa, "You have charged too much for your time. You must learn to listen more attentively and write more quickly." They awarded him half of what he asked for, warned him to apply more realistic charges in future, and sent him packing back to Berry Hill. Then they enjoyed a glass of midday port and shared a jovial luncheon in the cool shade of the dining room.

ΩΩΩΩΩΩΩΩΩΩ

14. Revelations

3rd July 1797

Things are settling into a happy routine again after the upheavals of the spring. In spite of the cold spring and unsettled weather of June, most of the hay is cut, dried, carted and ricked. The top fields are still to be done. The new cowshed is finished, and Billy and Shemi are delighted at the improved arrangements for milking and moving the milk to the dairy. At Ffair Gurig a few days ago we completed the purchases needed to bring our animal population up to what Grandpa refers to as a "proper" level. We all had to help out in getting our little drove of cattle, calves, pigs, horses and ponies up from the town to the Plas. The journey was accomplished without any major disasters, although we will probably have to pay out a couple of wheat loaves in compensation for the red roses eaten by the cattle in front of Tomos ap Ifans's cottage. The new animals are settling in well, and I have already started to train a pony with a reddish coat (whom I have named Rowan) so that I can ride her out myself.

Young Shemi Jenkins has been with us now for almost four months, and although he is only fifteen years old he is proving a great asset to the estate. He knows how to work, having been out on the land since he was nine. He has a strong back, an old pair of hands, and a good deal of intelligence inside his skull. He has a wonderful way with animals, and I do believe that he has a special language which he uses to communicate with them. The locals say that every now and then a member of the Jenkins family is given "special powers", and I begin to see what they mean. What is more, Shemi gets on well with Billy, and Mrs Owen treats him more or less as an adopted son. The lad is clearly delighted with his tuppence a day, his warm dry bed, and his filled stomach, and every time I see him at work I am reminded how little his illustrious predecessor Moses Lloyd ever did for the Morgan family.

Two days since, I travelled to Pontfaen with Grandpa Isaac, who had some business to discuss with Squire Laugharne. This gave me the opportunity to spend some time in the pleasant company of my friend Mary Jane, whom I discovered in her herb-garden. At her side I was able, at least for a while, to forget my recent obsession with the hardships suffered by the rural poor, and indeed it was too fine an afternoon to feel miserable about anything. So we talked of herbs, took a cup of China tea in the orchard in the shade of a famous old tree full of plumping apples, and talked further on anything and everything.

Afterwards I decided that I must spend more time in female company talking about anything and everything. Men have their uses, but I have observed that they are not very skilled in this particular art, and tend to talk of only one thing at a time. This must surely have the effect, over many years, of dulling the brain and hastening the onset of senility.

I have to record that my bleeding time is now very late. This may or may not be a matter of importance. I am in excellent health, and indeed David complains (mostly late at night or very early in the morning) that I have more energy than is good for him. I will approach the end of this month with more than a little interest.

ΩΩΩΩΩΩΩΩΩΩΩ

7th July 1797

News has reached us of another Petty Sessions, this time in Nevern Parish. The Sessions were held yesterday at Pentre Ifan, with Squires Rice and Howell presiding. Most of the cases dealt with were unexceptional, but there is outrage in the community over the case of an eleven-year-old girl from Brynberian who had been arrested and charged with stealing a spoon worth one penny. One William Williams (who is apparently a crony of Squire Howell) claimed that the spoon was his, although it was a perfectly ordinary spoon with no distinguishing marks. The girl claimed that she had found it in a hedge where a group of haymakers had recently been sitting in the shade and eating their midday meal. There was clearly enough doubt about the case for the magistrates to have dismissed the charge, but they heard the case entirely in English, leaving both the girl and her parents entirely ignorant of what was being said in court.

Since she was able to say nothing in her defence, and neither was anybody else, the case against her was found to be proved, and she was fined one shilling. Nine shillings were then added to this to cover the clerk's costs in bringing the case, leaving the distraught family with the almost impossible task of finding ten shillings. They broke down and caused quite a scene in the Pentre Ifan kitchen, and were on the point of being arrested for contempt of court when various friends succeeded in dragging them away. Squire Rice then made a "very magnanimous move" (his words) in agreeing to give the child a week to pay, and reminded her (in Welsh) that many have been sent to the gallows for less.

The poor labourers from the Brynberian area were in a state of near revolt yesterday afternoon, when word spread of this sentence. There was no opportunity for an appeal, for justice in these parts is normally summary and brutal. But when I heard about the behaviour of the Squires I went to see Ellie Bowen, and we decided that in order to calm things down we had better do something to help the family. Today we consulted with various colleagues within the True Briton Society, and we agreed to pay the ten shillings from the society's savings on the grounds that such an action would "alleviate distress among the poor people of the neighbourhood." We went this afternoon to the clerk's office at Berry Hill farm, and paid the money over in exchange for a receipt. We made it clear to Ifan Beynon that we were appalled at his greed and at the suffering he sought to inflict upon poor people. He replied, with a smile upon his face, that he was only doing his job and that he claimed no more than was allowed by law. Ellie and I were not amused by his flippancy, and left him with a flea in each ear.

ΩΩΩΩΩΩΩΩΩΩ

10th July 1797

Some days ago the weather broke, and brought strong winds from the west with torrential rain. The standing grass in the remaining hayfields has been flattened, and some of the cut hay which has not yet been turned is submerged in deep muddy puddles. Some of the wheat and barley crop is also beaten down, and we are all concerned that without a long dry spell in the coming fortnight our losses -- and those of our neighbours -- will be very great indeed.

Today the sun is shining again, thank God, but the air is too still. There is a clammy heat, and even those of us who are still healthy move about with heavy limbs and aching heads. The sodden landscape is silent, and even the hens and geese are quiet. The mountain is quiet too, but in the pit of my stomach I feel it sighing and exhaling, and shapeless clouds of white mist drift skywards like phantoms. We cannot see across the valley for more than a few moments at a time, and this airy open place is transformed into a little prison guarded by shapeless spirits and drained of colour.

Why am I writing of such trivial things? I have to admit that I am almost afraid to write what is really in my heart at this moment. My hand is trembling. But what follows must be recorded.

My sombre mood is not at all fashioned by the weather, but by a terrible menace which is prowling across this land. For a change, I suppose that the menace has nothing whatsoever to do with Moses Lloyd Cwmgloyn. Some strange ailment has swept through the community, and to the best of my knowledge more than twenty people are already dead. Nobody can remember anything like it, and there is puzzlement and even panic that this has happened in high summer rather than in the depths of winter. Some say that the disease is a sort of typhoid fever, and others say it is the plague returned. But the signs do not include fever, or sores and lacerations of the skin, or a swelling of the glands. Those affected have fearsome stomach pains; their limbs become heavy, and they suffer from the most terrible cramps. They vomit and retch even though their stomachs may be empty. They have a most extreme and uncontrollable sort of dysentery and some have a bleeding of the bowel. Their throats are swollen. They cannot eat, and they can hardly drink although they cry out for water. Even young people suffer appalling agonies, and those who have not the strength to fight die in the most degrading and filthy conditions.

Our sense of helplessness is increased because Havard Medical is himself close to death, having contracted the disease after ministering to poor people all over the parish. Old Jenkin Rhys on the Parrog was a medical man once, but they say that he too is ill. Grandpa Isaac has taken to his bed, but he is well nourished and tough as an old gander. He drinks clear, cool water from Ffynnon Brynach all the time, and he says he is not minded to die just yet. I believe him, but we are not untouched by tragedy, for Hettie's youngest child is dead, and poor Mrs Owen is beside herself, having lost two of her grandchildren. Both of them have gone home to their families. Young Shemi heard that his brother Joseph was ill, and arrived back home at Blaenwaun just in time to see him die. He had no time to mourn, for his grieving parents sent him straight back to the Plas for fear that he too might be afflicted if he remained beneath their roof. Billy is consoling him as best he can, but says he is in a very melancholic state. Bessie is still here, but her mind is elsewhere. Her mother has sent word that her little sister Mari is sick, but not sick enough to need extra nursing; and she has begged Bessie to stay away unless the child takes a turn for the worse.

Two days since, in the midst of the storm, after completing work in the dairy, I took our most placid pony and rode over the mountain to see if my friend Joseph Harries could advise me on the treatment of the dead and dying. The pony was terrified by the screaming wind and the sheeting rain, and it was as much as I could do to encourage her to press on. I arrived at Joseph's door shivering and soaking wet, to find that he was not at home. But the door was unlocked, so I tethered the pony where she could nibble at the hedge, and went inside. I stoked up the fire and sat in front of it on a three-legged stool; but the warmth did little to raise my spirits. I filled a black cooking pot with water, swung it over the fire and brought it to the boil. At about one o'clock in the afternoon Joseph returned, apparently quite unsurprised to find me sitting in a large puddle in front of his fire. He too was soaked to the skin. His eyes were sunken and his face was ashen, and he looked as if he had not slept for three days. "I saw your pony outside," he said. "It is a pleasure to see you, my dear Martha, but the circumstances of your visit are sad indeed. Four more dead in Pontfaen, and at least six in Dinas. But how are you? And your nearest and dearest?"

"We are well, thank you, Joseph. The only one of our family who is ill is Grandpa Isaac, and I believe he is already recovering. But we have death and illness on all sides, and I have come to seek your assistance and your advice. That is, if you are in a fit state yourself...."

"I am quite well. Mercifully free of the disease, but tired, very tired."

He could hardly keep his eyes open, and looked as if he might fall over. So I stood up, sat him down in front of the fire, and peeled his sodden cloak from his shoulders. I found some fruit jelly in his scullery and made a hot cordial, and we sat next to each other in the glow of the fire as we sipped from our pewter mugs. It soon became apparent to me that Joseph was both exhausted and angry, and at last he shouted "I cannot understand this! I cannot understand it at all!"

I did not reply, but left him to his thoughts. I perceived that we were both very hungry, so I found some black barley bread and a lump of stale cheese in the scullery and shared it between us. After some minutes he continued, in a voice now drained of emotion, as if addressing the flames of the fire. "I really have no idea what to do," he said. "All of my training, all of my books, all of the wisdom inherited from my teachers and my parents are quite useless in the face of this disease. I have remedies for fever, remedies for chest ailments and coughing fits, remedies for headaches and for cleansing the blood. But nothing works. The strongest herbs and the most potent essences are useless. Even in a deep trance I cannot see the enemy. I cannot even heal with my hands. I have watched three people die in the most horrid distress this very day."

There was nothing I could say, but I was moved to put my arm around his shoulder. I realized that for a man who has the gift and the destiny of a healer, it must be terrible beyond words to feel impotent at the bedsides of suffering patients, and to see death swaggering through the doors of his neighbours without bothering to knock.

At last I realized that my friend Joseph, our last hope in the face of this fearsome ailment, could do nothing more without sleep. So I said "Joseph, I see that you have given everything you have to give. You can surely achieve nothing more today either by going out again into the storm, or by consulting your healing spirits. It will not be seemly for me, a married woman in the house of a bachelor, to put you to bed and tuck you in like a small baby; but I will be obliged if you will use your last ounce or two of energy to remove yourself to your bedroom, take off those soggy clothes, and snuggle down beneath your nice warm blankets."

I was quite surprised to hear myself talking thus to a respectable gentleman old enough to be my father, but Joseph looked up, gave me a weak smile, and followed instructions by shuffling off to the little partitioned room where he had his box bed. "Huh!" he mumbled. "Thank you for reminding me, Mistress Morgan, of the joys of bachelor life!"

"My pleasure, dear Doctor," said I. "In five minutes time I will come in with a mug of hot milky cocoa for you, and I will take your wet clothes and put them to dry in front of the fire. When you have drained your bedtime drink, I suggest that you sleep for at least eighteen hours. After that, you will be in a better position to review the crisis that afflicts us all."

And so it came to pass. When I left a few minutes later, Joseph was fast asleep. I knew that as soon as he was able, he would ride over to the Plas. I cantered home along the mountain ridge past Bedd Morris and Carn Edward, with the wind and the rain now at my back. Unreasonable as it may appear, I felt a surge of confidence that Joseph Harries, wise man and soothsayer, might bring this dark episode to an end.

ΩΩΩΩΩΩΩΩΩΩ

11th July 1797

The funerals have started. Those taken to the bosom of the Lord have found their peace, but the poor people who have lost loved ones are in need of much support, for many are themselves ill. The normal traditions of the *gwylnos*, in which family and friends keep watch over the corpse during the night preceding the funeral, have largely gone by the board.

Today there have been eleven funerals, four in the parish church in Newport and seven in the nonconformist chapels including Caersalem, Jabes, Bethlehem and Ebeneser. The rector and the other pastors have been rushing hither and thither, making arrangements, conducting funeral services, ministering to the dying and seeking to calm the troubled breasts of those who have lost their nearest and dearest. There have been countless poignant moments and episodes of public and private grief. I have shed many tears myself. David and the other men have tried their best to remain strong. They have been running about from one funeral to another, sometimes acting as bearers, obeying the call of duty and also seeking to demonstrate the friendship and support which keeps a small community together. Grandma has stayed at home to keep an eye on Grandpa Isaac, but Bessie and myself have been out and about in cottages, farms and hovels all over the neighbourhood, doing what we can for the sick although we know little of medical matters. The stench of the dysentery is so terrible in most of the afflicted houses that we have had to work with kerchiefs soaked in lavender water over our noses and mouths. We have also been helping with food and drink for the mourners. Our own well-stocked larder has been a blessing in this respect, for wheat bread, cheese and smoked ham are in short supply in the average cottager's pantry. Our little trap, pulled by one of the new ponies, has been like a sort of military field kitchen, carrying supplies from one place to the next and enabling us to give rough and ready funeral transport to the elderly and infirm relatives of those who have died.

As is always the case in this unjust world, the under-nourished labourers and their families, in their draughty, leaky hovels, have suffered most. They seem to have neither the will nor the resources to fight the sickness. They seem to have little awareness of the need to keep clean, and it is a common thing to see piles of undergarments soaked in excrement next to pantry shelves where food supplies are kept. Dirt, damp, deprivation and death seem to go together. But small miracles have happened in support of the poor. Some wealthy merchants in Newport have organized a collection for those most in need, and thirty guineas have been raised for the purchase of food, blankets, clothes and medicines. Others who are free of the sickness have helped with nursing. Half a dozen casks of Spanish wine (undoubtedly smuggled) suddenly appeared in the church porch, and the rector has been decanting it into flagons and distributing it for use at the funeral feasts. Thomas Lloyd, the Lord of Cemais, who owns the ruined castle in Newport and lives somewhere in Cardiganshire, sent several cases of fresh oranges newly imported from Africa. Gethin Dolrannog has donated a tin of best Ceylon tea to every bereaved family, without divulging his sources. Shinkins Upper Crust has decided to use the whole of his stock of wheat flour to bake free bread for the suffering families, and his bakehouse is working round the clock.

But in the midst of all this kindness and good sense there is also lunacy. I heard today that a poor simple woman who lives down at Pantry Ford has been accused of witchcraft, and has been charged by her neighbours with working for the devil and placing a curse upon the neighbourhood. Stones have been thrown at her, and she has been warned not to set foot outside her door. To his credit, the constable in Newport will have none of it, and so far as I can gather her only crime is to have remained well while three of her immediate neighbours have suffered deaths from the sickness. Other poor people have resorted to the most irrational of remedies, including the use of poultices and plant extracts which even I know will kill rather than cure. Others have decided that they must smoke the affliction from their houses, since there is a folk memory that this was done last time the Black Death visited the area. Desperate ailments need desperate remedies, but people who are coughing and fighting for breath even when the air is fresh and clean are not really helped by clouds of choking black smoke, and I believe that two small children down in the cwm were inadvertently killed by their own family in this way. What a terrible, terrible thing.

Even more insane are the activities of some of the extreme Nonconformist sects in response to the tragedy. A group from Brynberian, led by one Tomos ap Tomos, has been holding impromptu meetings today all over the neighbourhood, preaching the message that the sickness is "the vengeance of Jehovah" upon a people led astray by wickedness and corruption. The leader himself, accompanied by half a dozen disciples, came and stationed himself in front of the Jenkins' cottage at Blaenwaun just before the funeral procession for Shemi's poor dead brother set out for Caersalem. There were maybe twenty people clustered around the cottage door. The self-appointed messenger from God, clutching Bible in one hand and cross in the other, roared out "My brothers and sisters! The hour is come! Vengeance is mine, saith the Lord! He hath seen wickedness, and greed, and debauchery, and he liketh it not!" At this, there was a chorus of Amens from the disciples, accompanied by wailing and beating of breasts. "And fury is upon his brow, and his right hand is raised in anger. And fire and brimstone shall fall upon the heads of those who fear not the Lord! Corruption and vanity shall be punished, saith the Lord, and the sins of the fathers shall be visited upon the innocent, and the plague shall strike at every door! And I say unto those who have ears to hear, repent, repent, REPENT!" Then, after a long and theatrical pause, he dropped his voice almost to a whisper, and continued: "And if thou dost confess thy sins, the Lord shall anoint thee and give thee peace, and salvation shall be thine, and Jehovah shall come and bless thy house and the houses of the meek, and thou and thy kind, who repent and are saved, shall dwell in the house of the Lord for ever...."

The *hwyl* was in him. I sensed that he was winding up for another crescendo, and I could sense that the poor people around me were terrified. Unable to contain myself any longer, I rushed up to him and shouted to his face: "Tomos ap Tomos! You should be ashamed of yourself! How dare you come here and intrude upon the grief of these poor people?" The Heavenly messenger was lost for words, and spluttered something incoherent. So I kept up my attack, in a state of high emotion. "These are good kind people who have done nothing wrong in the sight of the Lord! And you have the effrontery to pretend that the sickness and death they have suffered is a punishment from God? Punishment, from a God of Love? And how dare you presume to know the worth of other men! How dare you? How dare you?"

At this my emotions got the better of me, and I am ashamed to say that I dissolved in tears, but David, who had been inside the house to help with the coffin, came rushing to my side to support me. The mood of the crowd now changed, and the terror of the listeners was transformed into anger. David told me afterwards that Billy and the Jenkins boys might have grabbed the Brynberian evangelists and sent them off to Heaven with ropes around their necks or bootprints upon their skulls, but he managed to control the situation with the help of one or two older and wiser heads. He sent Tomos and his cronies packing with the threat that he would have them charged with holding an unauthorized religious meeting in the open air, and said that the constable would soon be knocking on their doors to present them with summonses. He will not carry out his threat, of course, but the zealots had the sense to realize that they had outstayed their welcomes.

At last things quietened down and the funeral was completed without further mishap. With the help of Bessie and the Jenkins women I regained my composure, and we spent the rest of the day helping with the food and drink at Blaenwaun and at four other bereaved households.

Now we are at home. It is late, and dark, and David and Billy are still out feeding the animals by the feeble light of their horn lanterns. I am exhausted after the intense emotions of the day. There are to be at least six more funerals tomorrow, and to my knowledge there have been another nine deaths today. Still more cases of the sickness are being reported. When will this all end? Joseph Harries has not appeared, and I wonder if he has caught the sickness. It would hardly be surprising if he has, for it is very catching, and he has been in close contact with many poor afflicted families. He does not have a very strong constitution himself, and exhaustion such as I observed in him the other day may weaken his resistance and his resolve. Ellie is away in Tenby for the summer season, but I have sent messages to Mary Jane at Pontfaen, my sister Catrin at Brawdy, and Sian from Gelli, and I have asked all three of them to help with the burdens of the morrow. I know that they will come if they can.

ΩΩΩΩΩΩΩΩΩ

12th July 1797

Today the hot, heavy weather has given way to fresher conditions, with a sea breeze blowing in over the mountain and into the cwm. This has given a lift to our spirits, and I have to record that I have seen the makings of a miracle. It happened like this.

The day started with great sadness, for David and I had to help with the funerals for Hettie's little boy Rhys, who was only seven, and Mrs Owen's grandchildren Owain, aged four, and Mabel, aged two. Luckily Shemi and Billy said they could deal with the animals between them, and Bessie stayed behind at the Plas to process the milk. The first funeral was in Newport and the other two in Dinas. As usual, the menfolk attended the funerals while we womenfolk dealt with the arrangements at the family homes. Then we had to get back to Newport to collect food, wine and clothing from the rector and from the parish clerk for distribution to the families most afflicted by the sickness. In the centre of town we bumped into Mary Jane and Sian, and as luck would have it Catrin appeared with a servant from Brawdy, having driven the chaise so fast on the rutted turnpike road that it was on the point of losing at least one wheel. We held a Council of War, and I realized that there was now a little group of ministering angels to carry on the work that Bessie and I had set in train.

Almost at the same moment a strong picture came into my mind of Joseph Harries on his sick bed. In my mind's eye he looked serene and in no danger, but I knew that I had to make the journey to Werndew immediately. I told David and the others of my premonition, and they all said I must go. "I will take you back to the Plas this minute," said David. "You will only be getting in our way if you stay here, and your mind will in any case be elsewhere. You can take the grey pony and go along the mountain ridge to Werndew."

Two hours later I knocked on the door of Joseph's cottage. "Martha? Is it you?" said a throaty voice from within. "Come inside if you please!" It was dark inside after the brightness of the July afternoon on the heather moorland, but once my eyes had grown accustomed to the light I saw, to my amazement, that Joseph was not in his bed but pottering about in his night-shirt, with a strange woollen night-cap upon his head. "Joseph! You should be in bed!" I said in my best motherly voice. "I had a premonition that you needed me, and so I had to come. And now I find you wandering about making up strange concoctions on your kitchen table. Are you determined to kill yourself when you should be resting?"

"Don't you worry about me, Mistress Morgan *bach*," said he, raising his head for just a moment. I could see that there was a gleam in his eye, and there was a sort of manic energy about him in spite of the fact that he was clearly not a healthy man. He spoke as he went on measuring out piles of some granular substance into brown paper bags. "The day after I saw you last I was indeed very ill, and I thought that I might die. But after my long sleep my mind was clear, and I tried to put together everything I had observed about this terrible illness. It affects the poor rather than the rich, as is usually the case with catching diseases. But why are all these poor people dying in the summer rather than the winter? Could it be that the disease itself thrives in hot conditions? Then I suddenly realized that the first person to die was a sailor from the Parrog, lately disembarked from a trading ship which has come in from the Barbary Coast. The Master of the vessel, Captain Abel Morgan, is also ill, for I tried to treat him myself the other day. There are far more cases of the sickness on the Parrog than anywhere else, and I then remembered several other distressed people telling me that the illness had struck their families on the day after visiting the Parrog in order to buy fruit, wine, silks and other goods. After that, one family has passed the ailment to another through normal day-to-day social intercourse. The connection, my dear Martha, is established!"

Joseph paused for theatrical effect, and the gleam in his eye became even brighter. "Joseph!" I exclaimed. "Are you quite sure of this?"

"Absolutely satisfied."

"So do you know what the sickness is?"

"No, I am afraid not. Maybe it is something unknown to medical science. It is certainly nothing to do with the Black Death, and it is not a sort of pox. It affects the stomach and the muscles, and the dysentery is so terrible that it takes all the water out of the body. Maybe it is a sort of typhoid or cholera, but I am quite sure it comes from Africa."

"Is there a cure?" I asked. "People are still dying, and those of us who are left are growing weary of funerals."

"I do not know of a cure," said Joseph. "But I have a treatment that works, and by means of it I think we can save all those who are not already at death's door. Martha, here we have it." And he scooped up one handful of white crystals and another of brown crystals from the heaps on the table. "Do you recognize these?"

I looked at them carefully and said "Why, they look just like ordinary salt and sugar crystals. Surely there is nothing magical about them?"

"No indeed there is not. They are simple and cheap, and even the poorest people have them in their pantries. The secret, my dear Martha, is in putting them together in a proportion which I have not yet perfected. But I am near enough."

"But how can salt and sugar make these poor people better? If you tell them to take a teaspoon of salt and sugar every now and then to ease their suffering they will simply look at you with pain in their eyes and think you mad or accuse you of witchcraft."

"They will probably do that anyway," said Joseph, "for doctors and apothecaries would not give a moment's thought to my hypothesis. What you have to do is melt the sugar and the salt in warm water and then make the patient drink as much of it as you can get down their throat. When I worked out the other day that this is a sickness from the tropics I knew that somewhere in my brain was a piece of information that would be useful. Then it came to me. I suddenly recalled a conversation I had about fifteen years ago with a sailor in the Black Lion in Newport. His name was Jethro. He was newly arrived on a sloop from the Indies, and he told me that on the voyage he had almost died from a terrible attack of fever and dysentery. He thinks that he might have been delirious, but he told me that he had a mad craving for water -- not fresh water but sea water. Now every sailor knows that if you drink sea water you die. He pleaded and pleaded, but his shipmates refused, as they saw it, to help him to commit suicide. His obsession with salt water continued, and in the night he crept up on deck, filled a bucket over the side of the ship, and decided to make his drink more palatable by adding a few spoonfuls of sugar. Then he drank it all down. And far from dying, he says that within a few hours his dysentery began to ease off and he felt the strength returning to his body. I recall that everybody in the inn -- including myself -- thought this was a splendid tall tale from a drunken sailor, and we laughed and slapped him on the back, and fetched him another quart of ale."

Joseph saw the expression of incredulity upon my face, and continued his animated account. "Once I recalled this, I set about some experiments upon myself," he said. "My own dysentery was very bad, but luckily I was not bleeding, and thought I had a fair chance of survival. So I made up a mixture of salt and water in equal proportions in a flagon of boiled water. I was violently sick. Too much salt, I thought. I made up another mixture, this time with less salt, and drank this down. Violently sick again. So I cut the salt down to about half a teaspoon in a quart of water, and increased the amount of sugar. It tasted terrible, but I drank it anyway. And, bless my soul, I kept it down. I drank another quart in the evening, and this morning yet another quart. And the dysentery has stopped! I can already feel the strength returning....."

"That may be so, Joseph," I said. "But you are still very sick, and you had better get back into that box bed of yours before you die from over-excitement." I put my arm around him and led him to his bed. The flesh had gone from his shoulders, and he seemed to have lost half his weight. He did not protest, but seemed relieved that he had now passed on his secret. He settled beneath his woollen blanket and closed his eyes.

"Now then," I said, deciding that it was time for me to take charge. "I will take all the salt and sugar you have, just in case there are any poor families who do not have enough in their pantries. I will replace it later. I will beg, borrow and steal supplies from anywhere and everywhere. I will ensure that packets go out to every single household afflicted by the sickness. God willing, and with the help of Joseph's Magic Mixture, we will bring this terrible episode to an end. But I must have an accurate recipe from you."

"So far as I can tell, Martha, the proportion of sugar to salt is about eight to one," replied the good doctor without opening his eyes. "Take some paper from my desk and write this down. One quart of clean spring water, properly boiled. Very important. When it is still warm, add half a teaspoon of salt and four teaspoons of sugar. Get it down the patient's throat by hook or by crook. Add some fruit cordial if you like, so that it tastes better. Repeat so that the patient drinks at least three quarts of the mixture every day. And fruit! The apple and pear crop is not ready yet. But oranges are very efficacious. If only we had oranges..."

"It so happens, Joseph, that the Lord Marcher has just given several cases of oranges to the poor people. They may even have come in on the same ship that brought the disease."

"A strange irony indeed. Never mind. Feed them to the sick. And that's it. All being well, the dysentery afflicting the patients will dry up, and with care and attention their headaches and coughs will also clear up. We must get these people fit and well in time for the corn harvest!"

Twenty minutes later I was cantering, as fast as was seemly for a lady, along the ridge to the Plas. Late in the afternoon David and sister Catrin arrived back in the trap, followed by Mary Jane and Mrs Owen, who felt that she could now do no more for her children and grandchildren in Dinas.

Immediately I relayed to the assembled company the strange story of Joseph's salt and sugar mixture. They were amazed, and although we were all very tired we set up a manufactory on the kitchen table. We summoned help from our neighbours, and more than a hundred little bags of salt and sugar were made up for distribution. I wrote out Joseph's recipe on innumerable scraps of paper, for those who could read, and we then sent messengers off in all directions on foot and on horseback with instructions to visit every household known to be affected by the sickness. Billy went off to Dinas and Shemi headed for Pontfaen and Llanychaer. David himself loaded up his saddlebags with salt and sugar packets and rode down to Newport, where he met up with the Rector and the parish clerk. They visited as many houses as they could, and put up notices in the church porch, on the town crossroads, down on the Parrog and on the front doors of all the inns, giving the magic recipe and urging people to use it with all haste for any who were suffering from dysentery. Although it was now nigh on ten o'clock, David got the town crier out of his bed and set him off around town with his bell, shouting the news to the suffering inhabitants.

It is now past midnight. We are all dead tired, and have eaten nothing more than a few scraps of bread and salt beef. Catrin and Mary Jane are asleep downstairs, and David is snoring next door. Soon I will go to bed too, but my mind is so active after the excitement of the day that I doubt whether I shall sleep.

13th July 1797

Thank God that the spread of the sickness is now under control. There are only a few new cases today, and the disease does not seem to have spread beyond the immediate area, maybe five miles west to east and three miles north to south. The death toll is about forty. A few more will die, but every afflicted family is now using the salt and sugar mixture and there are reports of instant relief from the distressing symptoms of dysentery on all sides.

Some still find it hard to believe that a flagon of salty sweet water can have such magical properties, but most have seen its effects for themselves, and Joseph has become a hero overnight. He has had a string of visitors at Werndew. Most of them have borne gifts which they could ill afford, and he professes himself very touched. This afternoon Catrin, Mary Jane and I took the chaise and went to Werndew ourselves. When we entered his humble cottage his face lit up and he said he had never before seen three such pretty pictures framed in his doorway. He declared himself instantly cured, but I fancy his recovery will take a little time yet.

Funerals will no doubt continue to occupy us for some days. David is very tired, having given his unstinting support to so many people, and he is beginning to fret over the delay to the hay harvest and the need to start on the cutting of winter wheat. I too am beginning to feel a great heaviness of heart as the crisis passes. I am weary after the constant hard physical work of the past days, elated at the healing achieved by Joseph in the neighbourhood and at my small part in it, and at the same time drained of emotion by close encounters with one family tragedy after another. Thank God that Grandpa is now almost well again, and that no other member of my dear family has been struck down.

Tomorrow Catrin will go home to Brawdy. We have had no time at all to talk of family matters. Mary Jane has already travelled home to Pontfaen. What good kind people they are! I should never have coped without their love and their selflessness. Now I cannot keep my eyes open for a moment longer. I must collapse onto my bed before I collapse onto my writing table.......

ΩΩΩΩΩΩΩΩΩ

15th July 1797

There is a strange and dreadful sequel to the story of the sickness which has afflicted our community, and in telling it I feel that there is an iron band clamped around my heart.

This morning, after doing my usual chores with the late molly lambs and in the dairy, I settled down in my flower garden to a spell of serious weeding. It was a glorious day, with bright sunlight and scudding clouds, and I was greatly relieved to be in the fresh air, with the scent of sweet flowers in my nostrils instead of the smells of sickness and death. I heard a little cough, and there was Hettie standing at the garden gate. "Good morning, Hettie!" said I. "What can I do for you?"

"Good Morning, Mistress Martha. May I have a quiet word or two with you?"

"Of course," I replied. "Just come in and sit next to me on this old log. This is the only really peaceful place on the farm, which is why I shut myself into it every now and then."

Hettie sat herself down and said that she had a message for my ears and nobody else's, and I had to promise that I would not even tell David about it. Suitably reassured, she said "Mistress, I have been asked to speak to you by a sailor called Eli Davids, who is suffering terribly from the sickness in a lodging-house down on the Parrog. He thinks he is going to die, and I think so too, for he was too far gone when the wizard's magic drink first passed his lips. He is actually from Fishguard, but he has sailed often out of Newport on vessels owned by the local merchants. He says he will surely go to Hell if he does not speak to you before he dies, and he pleaded with me, with tears in his eyes, to prevail on you to visit him this very day."

"Good gracious!" I exclaimed. "What a strange business. What on earth could I have to do with a dying sailor-man from Fishguard? I should have thought that if he needs help he should get it from a doctor or a priest. Why is he here rather than at home?"

"He became ill as soon as he landed from his ship about a week since. He was taken in by Widow Daisy Jones, and has been too sick to move. Daisy thinks he will not see today's sunset."

So it was that I took a bundle of bread and cheese and set off for

Newport, having told David and the others that I was intent upon seeing Will Clog about some new shoes and Master Price Very Nice about some new cotton fabrics recently arrived from America. Half an hour later I was knocking on the door of Daisy Jones' cottage on the Parrog sea-front. The good lady invited me in and took me to her back room. Then she retired discreetly and shut the door. Once my eyes had become accustomed to the gloom, I approached the bedside of the poor dying sailor. His skin was sallow, and his sunken eyes were dark and filled with fear. The stench of dysentery filled the room. He lifted a bony hand towards me and motioned me not to come too close. "Stay where you are, Mistress," he whispered. "I know that the sickness is very catching, and God knows I have have done you enough harm already."

I thought that this comment was more than a little puzzling, but also very touching. The poor man could not have known that I have been nursing more than a hundred of the sick and the dying over recent days, and that I have washed and cleaned the dead and seen them to their graves. After a long pause he found the strength to continue. "Are you Mistress Martha Morgan of Plas Ingli?"

"Yes, I am."

"Are you the wife of Master Morgan, who lost his brother at sea?"

"That is correct."

Then he uttered a long sigh, and I saw that tears were rolling down his cheeks. "At last, at last I meet my judge," he said feebly. "I cannot ask you, Mistress, for forgiveness, but may God grant me peace, for I have lived these last two years in torment."

I could not for the life of me discern his meaning, so I said "You have surely done me no harm, Eli, for I have never met you before, and it seems to me that I have nothing to forgive."

"Is there anybody else in the room?"

"No, we are quite alone."

There was another prolonged pause. Then he fixed his grey eyes upon me and told me his story. It took more than an hour, for he was very close to death and the emotion of the moment was almost too much for him to bear. This is what he said.

"I was signed up for Captain William Watkins' ship called the "Sara Jane", working between Bristol and Parrog. A couple of years ago -- I think it was in April -- we took on three extra crew. One of them was a young man called Griffith Morgan. He was the happiest lad you ever did see, Mistress, set from the moment he stepped on board to be a master mariner and in charge, one day, of his own ship. The night before we sailed I was in the Ship and Anchor, with some of my old shipmates, and a bit the worse for wear, as one tends to be, if you get my meaning, on the night before a voyage. A tall fellow came in and motioned for me to come outside. I was a bit puzzled, Mistress, but I went out with him. He had a sort of olive complexion, brown piercing eyes and dark hair, and he spoke like a gentleman. He had a big cloak wrapped about him. "Eli Davids?" says he. "Yes indeed," says I. "Sailing tomorrow for Bristol?" says he. "Quite correct," says I. Then he says "I have a task for you, Eli. There will be a young man on board with you by the name of Griffith Morgan. You will no doubt be working with him on the deck when the tempests rage about you. It is easy, at such times, for new and foolish deck-hands to lose their footing and to be swept away by the merciless sea. I have five silver sovereigns in my hand. They are yours for the asking. There will be fifteen more when you return from Bristol without Griffith Morgan. Do you get my meaning?" Then he opened his hand and showed me the five silver sovereigns. I was well past sensible thinking by this time in the evening, and I daresay, Mistress, that my eyes opened wide in amazement, for I had never seen such money before. Accursed fool that I was, I took the coins from his hand."

Thus far into the story my emotions must have been writ large in my face, for the poor fellow stopped and buried his face in his hands and sobbed uncontrollably. At last he looked up and said plaintively "You knew Griffith Morgan?"

"I knew him well."

"And you know the tall man with the cloak?"

I swallowed hard, and said "Yes, I know him."

"I still do not know his name, for I never dared ask. As soon as I had taken the money, he grabbed hold of me by the collar and pulled me close so that he looked me straight in the eye. "Eli Davids," says he, "if you do not deliver I will kill you." And he threw me onto the ground and went striding off up the Parrog Road towards Newport. Oh my God, what was I to do? Now I was stone cold sober, and shaking like a leaf. I left my mates in the inn and went back to the ship. I tried to sleep but could not. Next morning young Griffith and the others came aboard and we sailed on the morning tide. We took a week to Bristol, with gentle breezes and a flat sea. The money from the stranger was in my purse, but it felt to me as if it was in my stomach, growing like a monster and consuming me from inside. In Bristol, and on the first day out of port I hardly ate, and felt weak at the knees. Young Griffith and the others asked if I was ill, and told me to go to my bunk. But I would not. Looking back, I think I was out of my mind."

I saw that he was desperate for a drink of water, and I held a mug to his lips as he took a few weak sips. Then he continued. "We hit a squall near Lundy. There was pandemonium on the ship. The Captain was at the wheel, looking for'ard and trying to read the sea. He sent Griffith and me aft to stow ropes and other loose things, and the others for'ard to trim the sails. The ship shuddered as it hit a big wave, and I saw that Griffith and I were alone. He had his back towards me. I hit him hard with my full weight and he flew over the side. I waited for half a minute, and then shouted "Man overboard! Man overboard! Captain, come about! Come about!" He heard me, but of course he could do nothing. We had too much sail anyway, and if he had tried to bring the ship about we would have been lost."

At this point the poor man stopped for several minutes, his breathing more shallow than it had been, and his strength ebbing away before my tear-filled eyes. What was I to do? What was I to say? I gave him a few more sips of water.

Then, with his voice barely audible, he completed his appalling tale. "We survived the storm," he said, "but I was almost mad with the thought of what I had done. They say, Mistress, that we stopped at Tenby and Dale to unload cargo, but I have hardly any recollection of the rest of the voyage. When we got back to Newport Captain Watkins rode up to Plas Ingli to tell the family that Griffith was lost at sea. Two nights after that I was in the Ship and Anchor when the tall man with the cloak appeared at the door. He caught my eye and motioned me outside. He said not a word, but gave me a purse with fifteen silver sovereigns in it. Then he turned and disappeared into the darkness."

"And where have you been since then, Eli?"

"Everywhere but Newport," he replied. "Mostly working out of Fishguard or Cardigan for other captains. I wanted never to come to this place again, for there has not been a single night over the past two years when I have slept soundly in my bunk, and I knew that if I returned the

Devil would take me to Hell. And look at me now, face to face with my Maker, and face to face with my judge."

"Eli, I am not your judge. God does not give it to any man or woman to be the judge of another between one world and the next."

"You are my judge, Mistress Morgan. It is your fate and mine. I dared not tell my tale to your husband, for I hear that he is a good and gentle man who has already suffered much. As the brother of poor Griffith Morgan he would surely have been destroyed by the truth. Better that he should not be reminded of his grief. Better that he should continue to believe that a tragic accident took his brother away from him. Now I have told you my tale and I confess my guilt in this terrible affair. Do you find it in your heart to forgive me?"

He looked at me with pain-filled eyes, and his look contained fear and guilt and sorrow and relief and hope all at the same time. What could I do? What could I do? Here was the man who had killed my husband's dearly-beloved brother, asking me to give him comfort and compassion in his dying moments. What could I do?

For better or for worse, I took his hands in mine, and whispered "Eli Davids, with all my heart I forgive you for what you have done. Now sleep, and may God give you peace." And his eyes closed, and his hands went limp, and Eli Davids went to his Maker.

As I write I find myself shaking with emotion, and I can contain my tears no longer. I must stop. Perhaps, if I have the strength, I will write more tomorrow.

$$\Omega\Omega\Omega\Omega\Omega\Omega\Omega\Omega\Omega$$

17th July 1797

Two days have passed, and at last I feel able to write again. It is early evening. David and the other men are helping with the winter wheat harvest at Trewern, and they will probably not return until the dew starts to fall.

Following the death of poor Eli Davids I sat at his bedside for a long time. Then I pulled his sheet up and covered his face, and went out to find

Widow Daisy Jones in her back scullery. "Eli is dead," I said.

"I thought he was not long for this world," said she. "The poor tortured soul should have died three days since, but somehow he kept himself alive until he had met you. Has he found peace, do you think?"

"I believe so."

Then I offered Daisy a pound so that she could arrange a decent burial for the sailor-man. "No, no," she said. "He knew he was going to die today. This morning he gave me a purse with twenty silver sovereigns in it. Where on earth did he get such money? That is quite enough, indeed, to pay for a burial and for me to take something for his lodgings. The rest I will send to his sister in Fishguard."

So I took my leave and walked back up to the town in a daze. Eli had carried his twenty sovereigns -- his blood money from Moses Lloyd -- around with him for two years, probably afraid to touch it, let alone spend it. I could not get over this poignant twist in the tail of his personal tragedy, and it convinced me that he had not been a bad man but a good man led astray by one with a strange talent for doing evil.

I had enough presence of mind, when passing through the town, to call in and look at some shoes at Will Clog's workshop, and then I bought a small piece of fabric from Mistress Price Very Nice. This would at least prevent me from telling lies about my visit to the town. But my heart was not in the business of shopping, and I must have looked pale, for the traders both looked at me with concern and enquired after my health. I walked up Greystones Hill and realized that I was very hungry, and so I sat at the roadside and ate my bread and cheese. Then I went home, feeling with every step along the way that my legs would collapse beneath me. Grandma and the servants were in the kitchen, and they all looked alarmed when they saw the pallor on my cheeks. "Martha *bach*," said Grandma, "are you all right?"

"Yes thank you," I lied. "I have had a long walk, which was perhaps unwise. I think that the exertions of recent days are at last catching up with me. I think I need to sleep for a week."

And so I went to bed, even though it was still not six of the clock. Bessie was particularly concerned about me. She reads me a good deal better than she reads a book, and she knew that something had happened to me in Newport that had brought me to the edge of despair. But I was determined to tell her nothing, and I maintained the pretence that it was simply my body that needed rest. I slept uneasily for a couple of hours, and managed to eat a little supper which Bessie brought up to me on a tray.

When David returned from the harvest field with the other men Grandma immediately told him that I was in bed, and he rushed upstairs in a panic. I was awake, and he cried "Martha, what is wrong? You look as if you have seen a ghost! Do you think you have caught the sickness? Shall I ride over the mountain and fetch Joseph?"

"No, no, dearest," I said, managing a weak smile. "Calm yourself, if you please. I am sure I have not got the sickness. I am simply tired -- very, very tired. A good rest will put me right, just you see. Now you go downstairs again and get your supper, and stop worrying." Reluctantly he agreed to go and eat his meal, but I knew that he would not stop worrying about me, and I knew that he half expected me to descend again into a deep trough of melancholy like that which had afflicted me following the loss of our baby. Then I slept for a very long time, and I have no recollection of David either coming to bed or getting up in the morning.

Yesterday I stayed in my bedchamber all day. I could see through the window that a sea mist was rolling up from Newport into the cwm, and it thickened so much that it enveloped the Plas. The flat greyness and the thin light matched my mood. David and his grand-parents, and dearest Bessie and Mrs Owen, popped in and out of the room at frequent intervals, inquiring after my health and ministering to my every need. As the mist drifted back and forth on the flank of the mountain, so I drifted in and out of sleep.

In my waking hours my mind was in a turmoil, and I felt crushed by all the burdens of mankind. Why, I asked myself, did I have to carry the full weight of Moses Lloyd's wickedness? Within our family, we were all aware of his sly tricks, his petty crimes and his vindictive nature. But only I knew that he had killed a small child in his wild student days in Oxford. Only I knew that he had damaged the pipe at Ffynnon Brynach and tried to burn down our barn. And now it was only I who knew that he had paid a poor weak-willed sailor-man to kill David's beloved brother. In bearing these burdens I knew that I could not divulge any of this to anybody. I could not confide in Bessie, or Mary Jane, or any of my other friends for fear that a word or a gesture here or there might cause the whole story to tumble out.

Revelations

And it was quite unthinkable that I could say anything at all to David, for he must now be protected at all costs. He talks like a tough old taskmaster, but in truth he is weaker than I. He is gradually recovering from the traumas of the past, and it is my duty in life to make him happy. If he was to be given the slightest hint of the extent of Moses' evil he would be destroyed. He would never, never be able to come to terms with the fact that he had befriended, trusted and even protected, at considerable cost to himself, a man who had in effect killed his own brother. He would never forgive himself for failing to dig into Moses' past and for assuming that the wicked creature had learned from past misdemeanours. And how would he look back, in years to come, at the moment when he let him run off into the night after the theft of the barley? Or at his reluctance to think ill of the man when it was patently obvious to the rest of us that the fire in the barn was not the work of some passing vagrant? I could see no way out, and as the complexities of the situation whirled about in my mind I came inexorably to the conclusion that it was my destiny to carry this knowledge of Moses Lloyd to my grave. I also knew that it was my destiny to confront the man again, and I became utterly secure in the conviction that his fate and mine were locked together.

After another night of deep sleep I awoke this morning feeling a little stronger. There was a hazy sun lighting the valley as the last of the sea mist melted away. I got up and joined the others for breakfast, and they were delighted to see me up and about. I did not feel very communicative, for if truth be told my head was still full of dark thoughts and my shoulders were still bent beneath my secret burden. But my dear David, and the others, were very felicitous, and they were delighted when I said that I had it in mind to take a walk on the mountain in order to clear my head. "Take care, Martha," said David, "for the rocks are still wet after the sea mist. But the skylarks are singing, and by noon it will be very hot. A walk will do you good. Be back by one, or we will worry about you."

I gave a weak smile and assured them that I would not be away for more than two hours. Then, with my stout boots upon my feet and a sun-shade in my hand, I set off up the slope towards Ffynnon Brynach. There I stopped and anointed myself, and as I looked down towards the Plas a wave of emotion came over me. The attentiveness and the love of David and his grandparents, and the servants, touched me in a way that was raw and angry, and I could not understand my own reactions. I felt that I could no longer control my own heart. Instead of lightening my burden, the thought of these gentle, lovely people and their concerns made me feel more miserable than ever. I climbed towards my cave, and I swear that I remember not a moment of the climb, for my thoughts were a thousand miles away. Suddenly I was at the entrance, with the little rowan tree on my left and the two massive boulders on my right. I noticed that the resident pair of old ravens were perched quietly on the crag above. They were watching me, with their five offspring perched quietly beside them.

I contained my emotions until I was inside the cave. Then I fell onto my bed of moss and wept.

I held nothing back, for I knew that nobody could hear me. I wept for a long time, and fear and frustration, anger and grief were carried away in the soft echoes of the cave. At last I became calm again, and I realized that apart from a few tears here and there I had not wept properly for a very long time -- in fact, not once since the realization of Moses Lloyd's misdemeanours had started to enter my mind and my heart. Now I sat at the mouth of the cave and looked out at the bright and busy world. A wonderful serenity came over me, and also a sense of iron resolve. I knew then that I would not be defeated by Moses Lloyd, nor by my own foolish emotions. I knew that I would give David all of my love and that nothing would deter me from my course. My instinct told me that I would be afflicted by terrors more fearsome than those within my own head over the coming weeks, but my instinct also told me that I would have the strength to survive.

I am not very practised in mystical matters, and I have to admit to a somewhat shaky faith, but as I left the cave and headed back down the mountainside towards the Plas I said "Thank you, Brynach and your guardian angels. You have been good to me today."

ΩΩΩΩΩΩΩΩΩ

20th July 1797

What a fickle creature I am! Some days since, following my sad encounter with Eli Davids, my spirit was all but crushed. But now I feel that I have rediscovered myself, and new blood is coursing through my veins.

Yesterday I was surprised, and very touched, to receive a deputation of about twenty poor people from Parrog and Newport who arrived at the Plas bearing gifts. They came marching up the track, accompanied by a donkey pulling a little cart, just as I was in the middle of washing my hair. I assumed that they had come to see somebody else, and I was greatly embarrassed when Bessie called me out into the yard to meet them. I stood with my hair wrapped up in a towel while they went through a little ceremony. Four small girls curtseyed and presented me with posies of flowers from the summer hedgerows, and then the leader of the delegation, one William Reynish from Parrog, made a little speech thanking me for my "selfless devotion and gentle ministrations" to the poor people of the district during the time of the dysentery sickness. He then presented me with three barrels of mackerel freshly caught in the bay, a new bonnet and a pretty lace shawl. The latter items must have cost them a good deal, and I was quite overcome with emotion when they all clapped and cheered before going on their way. According to Hettie, I have become a local heroine! In truth I have never felt very brave, let alone heroic. Nonetheless, while the Grim Reaper was stalking through the district it did not occur to me for a moment that I might do anything other than fight him with every fibre of my being.

Now I have so much energy, and so much to do, that Bessie and Mrs Owen say that they cannot keep up with me. They grumble cheerfully that if I am not careful I will do both of them out of their jobs. David is of course delighted, and says that it is a constant source of mystery to him that women should swing so violently between the depths of despair and the heights of elation. In truth it is a source of mystery to me too, but my new-found vigour and the deepening of my love for my beloved husband have brought a ready response beneath the sheets, and we have enjoyed two breathless and wonderful nights of passion.

With the fine weather continuing, and the wheat harvest now moving from the dry lowland farms to those on the south-facing mountain slopes, our services are constantly required by our neighbours, as we will need theirs in a week's time. But today we have taken a break, and we have all been to Haverfordwest on our new carriage for the wedding of my dear brother Morys. David and I have seen him only twice, very briefly, since the day that he married us near Carmarthen last year. Some weeks ago, having left the established church and joined the Baptists, he accepted a call to Bethesda in Haverfordwest. He declared in a letter to Catrin that the loss of a comfortable living was a small price to pay for his freedom. He was happy to be entrusted with the pastoral care of a growing flock of non-conforming Baptists, and even happier to move closer to his intended, one Nansi Mathias from Roch. When we heard about his move we knew that wedding bells could not be far off, and indeed we were overjoyed when the invitation to the wedding arrived two weeks ago.

So off we went first thing this morning in all our finery, rolling down the lane to Cilgwyn, splashing across the ford at Trefelin, and pulling away up and over the mountain to the county town. What scenes there were when we all met at the Bethesda manse! For the first time in three years the members of my family were all together -- Mother and Father, brother Morys and sisters Elen, Catrin and me. Elen looked very beautiful indeed, and Bristol society obviously suits her. She wore an expensive white silk gown which was apparently at the very height of London fashion, and her hair was taken up cleverly to show off her elegant neck. My own poplin dress looked distinctly agricultural by comparison, but I have long since stopped worrying about city trends; and since I received many kind compliments as to my appearance I think I stood up well under close scrutiny. The belle of the occasion was of course Catrin, with her petite figure, her fair hair and blue-grey eyes, her happy laughter and her easy way with both friends and strangers.

Elen is now twenty-four and Catrin is twenty-one, and they are both still unmarried! Seldom can an old married lady like me have had two such eligible sisters. I asked them if they needed any assistance in the matter of matrimony, to which Elen replied that she is married to her music and Catrin replied not at all. Later, outside the church as we waited for the bridal pair, she confided to me that she did have a certain interest in one James Bowen of Castlebythe, and that she would be moving shortly to the big house to take up a position as tutor to his little sister Mary. I squealed with delight, and said "Catrin! How wonderful! Castlebythe is only six miles from the Plas. When you take up residence, send me a message immediately, and I will walk over to see you. You could do worse -- I do not know your James, but the Bowens are very well respected locally. And of course you will be living just up the road from Mary Jane! You two can meet and extend the lovely friendship which you developed during the time of the sickness."

The wedding was a strange affair in two parts. First there was the formal business, conducted strictly according to the law in the echoing spaces of St Martin's Church since nonconformists are not allowed to conduct their own marriage ceremonies. The service was pruned down to its bare essentials. It was led, by leave of the vicar, by Jonas Jones, an old college friend who met Morys at Oxford and who now looks after three parishes near Llangwm. My dear brother was very nervous, but stood tall and proud. Nansi, now Mistress Reverend Morys Howell, was, in contrast, a picture of serenity. After the exchange of vows, the blessing and the signing of the register we all walked up the road to the little chapel of Bethesda where a much more convincing celebration took place, with much loud praying, a deal of lusty hymn singing, and a beautiful wedding oration from Jonas. The couple made their vows again, and said that as far as they were concerned this was the real moment at which they became man and wife.

I know not what to make of Nansi. She is a plain girl with a formidable intellect and a somewhat forbidding countenance. I gather that she likes nothing more than to read a good Greek tragedy (in the original Greek) of an evening, and that she is much given to good works. But she is pleasant enough for all her erudition and holiness, and I daresay she will make Morys a very loving wife and give him a comfortable home. Mother says that the poor fellow has lived in bachelor squalor for far too long, and that it is high time somebody took him in hand.

We had a convivial time at the wedding breakfast, although I suffered from having to sit next to one of Nansi's ancient uncles. I would have liked a little more to eat and a good deal more to drink. But Nansi's family is not a wealthy one, and expenditure was held closely in check. I gather that her father is a local merchant renowned for making unprofitable deals. Moderation was the order of the day, for the Nonconformists do nothing to excess, even on those rare occasions when the father of the bride is a powerful squire with a family fortune behind him. And when a cleric gets married I daresay that constraints become even more severe, with fierce deacons detailed to watch out for any signs of debauchery among the guests.

Revelations

Oh dear, the foregoing reads as if it had been written by some old flea-bitten she-cat. I must learn to be more charitable, and now that I come to think of it I am really in no position to criticize, since David and I had a wedding of doubtful validity with no guests and nothing at all to eat or drink afterwards......

At the end of the formal proceedings we all circulated on the lawn of the manse in the afternoon sunshine. This gave me the opportunity -- at last -- of meeting some of my cousins, uncles and aunts, and also my old friends from Solva and St David's. They all wanted to meet David, and the poor thing was all but overwhelmed with their attentions. As I had expected, he was hugely popular with all my old girl-friends. He is naturally shy, but he is broad-chested, fair haired and blue-eyed, and there is no man on earth who is more handsome. He is not the best-dressed of gentlemen, as Master Price Very Nice keeps on reminding him, but he is tidy enough to be shown in public, and since he spends almost all of his time in the open air he has a fresh and healthy complexion. He has no pretensions. He has a very easy way with people, and because of his lack of guile he is, I am afraid, all too easily influenced and led astray. Indeed, with half a dozen excited young ladies clustered about him like bees around a tasty blossom I felt it necessary, at one stage, to give him a little gentle protection. I had to remind my friends, with a twinkle in my eye, that David Morgan was a respectable married country gentleman and that I was keeping a careful eye on proceedings. Then I moved off to talk to Nansi's father.

But I could not keep my eyes off David, and I must have appeared a very distracted conversationalist. My attentions were ten percent with Master Mathias and ninety percent with my husband. How I loved him! It is a salutary thing to see one's man in other company sometimes, just to keep one's love refreshed and renewed. In the end I could resist it no longer. As soon as the opportunity presented itself I walked across the lawn, extracted David from his little circle on the pretext that he was needed in the house, and led him into the lounge. Then, when I thought that nobody was looking, I took him in my arms, and gave him a long kiss on the lips. The occasion was less private than I had anticipated, for three deacons were sitting silently in a dark corner eating cucumber sandwiches. One of them coughed politely, and I was greatly embarrassed when I saw them. Not for the first time, the thought occurred to me that one day I must try to control my impulses. I think I must have blushed, and so did David. But the deacons clearly did not mind my outrageous behaviour in the least, and all three of them broke into broad toothy grins. They stood up and bowed in perfect harmony, and in response I curtseyed prettily and David bowed very theatrically. Then we all roared with laughter, and spent a few hilarious minutes in each others' company.

Thus reassured that even chapel deacons are human, David and I returned to socialize on the lawn. I still had some work to do. When I left home in a hurry almost a year ago, the story was put about in the community that I was taking up a tutor's position that had suddenly become vacant in Llandovery. Those closer to the family must have suspected that I was rushing off to get married to David, for our youthful love for one another had been obvious to all who knew us. Many must have suspected that I was with child. More recently the news that I was now Mistress Morgan of Plas Ingli must have become known to everybody in the Solva and Brawdy district. At any rate, this afternoon, when the opportunities arose, I was able to tell my old confederates what had really happened, only omitting the bits about my pregnancy and the loss of my baby. In these explanations David and the other members of the family were a great help to me, and I think we were able to convince all those who had ears to hear that we had married secretly, for love and in a hurry all because of the impoverishment of the Plas Ingli estate and the need to secure the family succession as quickly as possible.

"And have you started a family yet, Martha my dear?" asked Great Aunt Lizzie, in a very loud voice.

"Not yet," said I. "But we are working on it."

Everybody laughed, and David changed the subject, but as the talk turned to the latest scandal involving the town mayor, I had to turn away for a moment with a sudden recollection of the poor little mite I had lost last autumn on the kitchen floor of the Plas. But the moment passed, and the rest of the afternoon swept by in a warm breeze of reminiscences and news gathering.

Late in the day I fulfilled one small ambition. I have had a gnawing concern that in conducting my marriage ceremony my brother Morys had somehow destroyed his career in the church and lost most of his income. Now I managed to corner him and to press him on the manner of his departure from the established church. "Was it something to do with our wedding?" I asked, looking him straight in the eye. "I sense that you may have bent church rules a little too far." Morys winked and said "You are quite correct, Martha. The Bishop was not amused. But don't you worry about it. No laws were broken, and you may rest assured that David and you are indeed man and wife. I was looking for a way out of the church, and a little more excitement in life, and your hurried marriage gave me both!" He roared with laughter, and embraced me, and would say no more.

As the red orb of the sun sank behind St Martin's church steeple we, the Morganses of Plas Ingli, had to say our fond farewells and take our leave. The ponies pulled us up Prendergast Hill and out of town towards the mountains, and I had a lump in my throat. I cuddled up against David, and offered up a silent prayer of thanks for the two generous and stable families which had brought us together and which now gave us strength.

ΩΩΩΩΩΩΩΩΩ

26th July 1797

Today, as I worked in the Dolrannog Isaf cornfield with the other women under a scorching sun, Mair Griffiths and I got to talking about the fire at the Plas in which five members of David's family and one of the servants died. With so many recent demands upon my time, I have not given the matter any thought since the anniversary of the fire back in April. But now some little mouse of a memory started to nibble away at the back of my mind, and ran around inside my head for the rest of the day. Certain recollections of the things I had been told about the fire began to make me uncomfortable, and when I got back to the Plas this evening I began to thumb back through some of the earliest entries in my diary.

In the entry dated 8th September last year, I found what I had been looking for. The entry confirmed my recollection that David and Griffith used to sleep in a downstairs room. I read that before the fire started Mrs Owen had heard footsteps on the stairs, and that she had assumed that either David or Griffith had been upstairs to fetch a book to read in bed.

She had further assumed that the nocturnal reader had left a lighted candle at the top of the stairs, and that this is what had caused the fire.

These assumptions have, so far as I can gather, never been properly examined, since it is an unwritten law in the new Plas Ingli that the fire is never talked about. I had no wish to dig into the open wounds which still disfigure the souls of David and his grandparents, but the more thought I gave to the matter, the more troubled I became. Then I realized that David never, never reads books at night before going to sleep. I had to investigate further. I decided on an oblique approach, and at the supper table steered the conversation onto literacy, books and pamphlets. We all volunteered information on the literature which we had most recently enjoyed, and Grandpa told us how delighted he had been to rediscover John Bunyan's "Pilgrim's Progress", which he had first read as a young man under the guidance of his tutor. The summer nights, he declared, were made for devouring good books, for with his declining eyesight he found candle-lit winter reading increasingly uncomfortable. Then I said to David "See what you are missing, husband! I do declare that since we were married I have not once seen you sit up in bed at night and read a good book."

"Martha my dear," replied David with a laugh, "you know perfectly well that when I am tired I am fast asleep before my head hits the pillow, and when I am not tired reading is not an option!" We all laughed heartily, and he continued "I do not think I have read a book at bedtime since I was ten years old. Come to think of it, neither did Griffith, for Father encouraged us to sleep early and rise early, and to read by the light of the morning when eyes are sharp and minds are clear." I did not pursue the matter further, and the conversation rolled on to other things, but my worries intensified as the evening wore on.

Now it is almost midnight. The house is quiet and David is fast asleep. I have been looking again at my old diary entries, and drawing together titbits of information gathered since I arrived at the Plas. Everything is now clear to me. Moses Lloyd started the fire at the Plas which killed six people. It was he who raised the alarm, but Mrs Owen told me that when she rushed out of her room to find smoke swirling about, he was fully dressed and had boots upon his feet. What sort of a man, on waking up to find his house on fire, would get up, dress and put his boots on before raising the alarm? Further, in the stories I have heard about the fire-fighting, Moses figures hardly at all. I gather that he rushed off to fetch help when water was being carried from the pond to fight the flames; it did not strike me at the time, but what sort of a man would rush off to fetch help when the neighbours were already there, with an inferno consuming the house, and with five people trapped upstairs?

In the cold horror of this realization on the cause of the fire, two further images flashed into my mind -- that of a small child trampled to death beneath the hooves of a galloping horse, and that of a poor young man sinking in terror beneath the storm-tossed waves of the Bristol Channel. The first killing may have been an accident; the second certainly was not. Now confirmed in my belief that Moses was a murderer as well as a petty thief, I thought back to further incidents at the Plas, and realized that the falling beam that might have killed Grandpa Isaac must also have been the work of Moses Lloyd. Had he not known every detail of Grandpa's Friday routine? Had he not been close at hand to affect an heroic rescue? And had he not milked his moment of glory for every last drip and dribble?

In recording all of this, I also have to record that my determination to protect David from the truth is now absolute. Any hint of the extent of Moses' evil, let alone a full explanation of it, will tear open his ancient wounds and cause a gangrene of remorse and guilt. So I will be quiet. But I hereby record, for whomsoever may read these words in centuries to come, that my feelings for Moses Lloyd have changed again, for the last time. In turn I have found him intriguing, fascinating, and even charming. I have found him to be petty, devious, dishonest, intimidating and cruel. He is a coward who refused to fight the French. I know him to be a thief and a thug with an unusually malicious and vindictive side to his nature. I have been frightened by him, disgusted by him and perhaps even obsessed by him. But now fear and loathing have been replaced by a cold anger. I know that when I meet him again, as I surely will, I will have to confront him with his part in no less than eight deaths, for I need to have his guilt confirmed from his own lips.

Forgiving poor Eli Davids was one thing; forgiving Moses Lloyd is not an option. If it is my destiny to meet him alone, may God help me, for I fear that only one of us will walk away from the encounter.

ΩΩΩΩΩΩΩΩΩ

30th July 1797

There have been no sightings of Moses, and indeed no rumours of strange men in the woods, for nigh on two months, and I pray that the wretched fellow has finally decided to bless some other part of the country with his presence. I feel a little more at ease, and with the harvest at its peak there is much to do in the kitchen. Mrs Owen is preparing mountains of loaves, lumps of cheese and butter, slices of salt beef, pickled herrings and so forth, since we are expecting the harvesters at the Plas tomorrow. A barrel of beer has been brought in ready for uncorking. There will be at least twenty appetites to satisfy. But yesterday and today it has been raining, and we have been involved in a most peculiar social occasion.

It is not considered polite to issue social invitations at times of peak activity on the local estates (lambing time, the hay and corn harvests, sheep dipping time, and so forth), but sometimes invitations are issued at short notice if the weather is bad. Last evening a messenger came up from Squire Rice of Pentre Ifan inviting David and myself, as Master and Mistress of the Plas, to an afternoon tea party "at which we would be afforded the opportunity of meeting certain elegant visitors to the neighbourhood." Grandma and Grandpa were delighted not to have been invited, and David and I were very tempted to reply that we were too busy with other matters to attend. However, we thought better of it, and decided that perhaps the Rice family was seeking to thaw the somewhat frosty relations which have developed between us over past months. So we gave a note to the messenger expressing our great delight at the honour of being invited, and confirming that we would arrive at three of the clock.

We took the pony and trap and covered ourselves with oilskins, and quite enjoyed the trip through the warm summer rain to the farmhouse of the Rice family. I had not been there before, and was surprised to find that it was much smaller than the Plas, and that it was not in the best state of repair. One of the servants took the pony and trap, and we entered the house to find that there were only a few people present. Joseph, the wayward son of the family, was being wayward somewhere else, and the "elegant visitors" were two scatterbrained nieces from Mistress Rice's side of the family who had come down from Aberystwyth for a few days. Also present were three elderly spinsters from Newport and two cattle merchants and their wives from Eglwyswrw. A most peculiar gathering!

There is really not a lot to write about. We were greeted civilly enough, and since I looked somewhat bedraggled after our journey through the rain Mistress Rice insisted that I should pop up to her dressing room in order to powder my nose and fix my hair. This I was happy to do, since it gave me the chance to discover that the house and its furnishings were a good deal less elegant than I had anticipated. Both Squire and Mistress Rice made a great show of fussing around us and enquiring as to the health of the rest of the family, and trusting that Grandpa had recovered from the effects of the sickness, and so forth. We ate a pleasant enough tea, listened to one or two pianoforte pieces performed by the girls from Aberystwyth, and talked of the weather, the harvest, the poor state of the local shipbuilding industry, cattle prices, and the building works currently going on up the road at Trewern.

In short, we talked of nothing remotely interesting or controversial, and I found it very difficult to discern what was going on in the minds of our hosts. Squire Rice, who can be over-bearing, brutal and tactless, was jovial and polite, and indeed the degree of attention he paid to the replenishment of our cups and plates was quite extraordinary. Mistress Rice, with her hard lips and furtive eyes, does not find it easy to relax, and although she was obviously trying to be the good hostess, there was an edginess about her behaviour which I found quite disconcerting.

David chatted to the cattle merchants for a while, but we both found the atmosphere so stiff and strange that after two hours we exchanged eye signals, explained that we had many preparations to complete for tomorrow's harvest, and took our leave. What an extraordinary occasion!

ΩΩΩΩΩΩΩΩΩ

15. Descent into Hell

1st August 1797

The sun is shining again today, and after a breezy night the cornfields are
drying out nicely. The men think that by noon conditions will be dry
enough to start on the harvest. After that -- if the weather holds -- we will
have ten days of frantic activity at the Plas, first in three fields of wheat and
then in three fields of barley. The work will involve most of our neighbours
and a few itinerant labourers as well. The labourers are from Wexford in
Ireland; David says that they are good workers, and that they have been
coming to this area for years at the end of July.

It is the first of the month, and after assessing the estate finances,
David informed the servants this morning at breakfast that he was
increasing their wages with immediate effect. They have all been very
loyal, having suffered a wage reduction after the fire and having strained
every sinew to help us get the estate back on its feet. So as from today Billy
and Mrs Owen will be earning eight sovereigns a year, Hettie six, Bessie
five and young Shemi three. In addition, David conjured five silver
sovereigns out of a hat, with a degree of theatricality that I thought
unnecessary, and presented one to each of the servants. These, he said,
were in the nature of extra payments, as a reward for the financial
hardships that all had endured over the past two years. In the midst of
cheers and laughter, he said "Thank you, dear friends, for your hard work
and support. I now judge that the time is right for a little loosening of the
purse strings. But please don't spend your new-found wealth too quickly.
If the harvest does not go well, I may need to borrow some money off you
in order to pay your weekly wages!"

The sense of euphoria was enhanced when David announced, proud
as a peacock, that we were expecting our first child. I have suspected as
much for some time, but now I am certain, having missed two bleeding
times and having become aware of my recent peculiar swings of mood. For
the last few days I have been suffering from waves of nausea, and
yesterday I was feeling so giddy that I had to lie down for a while. I
thought at first that I was suffering from the after-effects of eating Mistress

Descent into Hell

Rice's salmon paste, and I toyed briefly with the idea that I might be going down with the sickness which has so sorely afflicted our neighbourhood, but then I decided that I was pregnant. Come to think of it, it was only a year since that I was experiencing very similar symptoms, although then my morning sickness in the third month was most distressing. I trust that this time around my discomfort will be less.

But following David's announcement there was no time for thoughts of morning sickness or for apprehension about the future, for celebration was the order of the day. Grandpa and Grandma were overjoyed, and both had tears in their eyes when they gave us warm embraces. There were more hugs and kisses from Mrs Owen, Hettie and Bessie, and David and I were greatly touched when Billy said "Master and Mistress, as for Shemi and me, very moved and delighted we are by your good news. We knows that there are rules and regulations about such things, but please can we each give you a hug?" We gladly consented, and the corporate hugging session was greatly enjoyed by all.

Then, although it was still not seven and thirty in the morning, Grandpa insisted that we should all drink a toast to the new baby. He fetched a good bottle of Portuguese wine from the cellar, and the best crystal glasses, and we all said "To the next Master or Mistress of the Plas!" and drank down the ruby liquid. That having been done, the women of the household immediately started to behave like mother hens, clucking around me, sitting me down, and bombarding me with good advice. That was my last glass of wine until the baby arrives, said Grandma. No hard labour in the harvest fields from now on, said Mrs Owen. And forget about the milk churning, said Hettie, since the violent exercise involved was certainly not suitable for a fine lady with a child in her womb. And Bessie, who has not yet had children of her own, decided that I was to have a nice rest every afternoon between the hours of two and four.

Bless them all. I am touched by their concern. Of course they all know that I lost a child last autumn under the most traumatic of circumstances, and they are determined that nothing will go wrong this time. They need not worry. I am feeling strong and healthy, and secure in the love of my husband and my family and friends. This time I will keep my baby, and nothing, but nothing, will be allowed to disturb the course of my pregnancy. Before the end of March next year the Plas will again echo with the innocent and lovely cry of a baby.

Descent into Hell

3rd August 1797

Yesterday I received a message from sister Catrin to say that she has moved to Castlebythe and is now employed as tutor to young Mary Bowen. I therefore determined that I would immediately pay her a visit. This morning the weather was still fine and dry, and since David refuses to allow me to be involved in the cutting, raking, gathering or stacking of the harvest for fear of over-exerting myself, I asked if he would mind me taking a walk to the mansion of the Bowen family. "How can I mind, *Cariad*?" said he. "You must go and see your sister and welcome her to the district. It is a wonderful day for a walk. Off you go, but try not to be too late back."

So I took some refreshments in a basket, and off I went on my six-mile march. The day was warm, but I was in excellent spirits and the miles flew by. I strode down into the deep woodlands of Cwm Gwaun at Llannerch, up the other side of the valley to Tregynon, then on to Morvil. Being new to the area, I had to ask the way once or twice, but the natives were friendly and well-informed, and not once did I go astray. Soon I was traversing the heathery flank of Mynydd Castlebythe, less than a mile from the little village which was now to be my sister's home. I sat on a high hill in the sunshine and ate my lunch, and at about two of the clock I knocked on the front door of the big house. Mistress Bowen gave me the warmest of welcomes, and did not mind in the least that I disrupted a French lesson upon which tutor and pupil had recently embarked. I was overjoyed to see Catrin, and soon we were settled on a bench in the Castlebythe herb garden exchanging confidences. The first item on my list of happy matters for discussion was of course my pregnancy; and having celebrated that we moved on to talk of Master James Bowen, and the Bowen family generally, and the wedding of Morys and Nansi, and everything else under the sun.

Time flew by, and we were invited into the shady lounge for afternoon tea by Mistress Bowen. The men were away helping with the harvest on one of the Puncheston farms, and so I have yet to have the pleasure of meeting James, but we three women sorted out the problems of the world without male assistance. Suddenly I realized that the sun was low and that I had a walk of three hours ahead of me. Mistress Bowen offered me a bed for the night or a carriage home, but I felt full of energy and independence.

Descent into Hell

I insisted that I would walk home, and said that I would surely be back at the Plas by ten of the clock. By then I assumed that David would be worried, but not worried enough to send out a search party. I did accept the offer of a candle lantern and a tinder box to help me through the dark woods of Llannerch, and having extracted a promise from Catrin that she would come and see us soon, off I went.

The evening was quite magical -- still and warm, with the air full of fat moths and skinny bats, and with crickets chirping madly in the long grass alongside the footpath. I dropped down into the gloomy valley of Vaynor and climbed up onto the airy flank of Mynydd Morvil. And then the most dreadful and inexplicable thing happened.

As I walked I became aware that the stillness of the dusky evening was being disturbed by strange sounds -- drumbeats, distant cries of distress, blood-curdling shouts, the neighing of horses, the clashing of metal upon metal, the thunder of hooves upon turf. The sounds came closer and closer, and I felt the hairs rise on the back of my neck. I looked up into the darkening sky, and out of the purple sunset glow of the western horizon moving shapes began to materialize. They came closer and closer, as the sounds became louder and louder, and within a few minutes there was a phantom pitched battle being enacted directly overhead. Troops of mounted cavalry from the east rode madly into other troops coming from the west. Their battle-cries sent a chill into the depth of my soul. There was an incessant drumbeat, and an overlay of raw trumpet blasts.

Swords and spears and battle-axes struck helmets and shields and armour and naked flesh. Horses fell with terrible injuries and writhed and struggled on the ground. Men fell with screams of agony and lay groaning until they were dispatched by the weapons of their adversaries. Hails of arrows streaked across the firmament, many of them thudding into the bodies of unarmed retainers. Armoured foot soldiers rushed across the battlefield and became locked in mortal combat with their enemies; I saw heads cleaved and bodies run through and limbs hacked off. The cries of battle, and the carnage of man and beast, at last became so horrendous that I could stand it no more, and I fell to the ground and covered my head with my cloak in a vain attempt to escape from the phantom battle.

I know not how long it lasted. It seemed like an age, but it was probably no more than fifteen minutes. Then I was aware that the sounds were fading. Cautiously I uncovered my head and looked up into the sky, and I saw the aftermath of the battle -- dead and dying horses and men, discarded shields and weapons, arrows and spears sticking out of the ground, and trees and bushes painted red with blood and scraps of flesh. I heard the groans and sighs and the last vain cries for help of those abandoned on the battlefield. And as the light, and the images, faded, I heard the baying of wolves and saw their red eyes glowing in the darkness.

Then it was all over. An eerie silence descended on the landscape, and above me was a velvet sky crackling with stars. I was shaking all over, and indeed I was so terrified that I had no idea whether I should walk to left or right, uphill or downhill, in a landscape that now filled me with dread. My terror was compounded by confusion, for I knew not what to make of the sights and sounds that had assaulted my senses. Had I been dreaming, or was the battle in the sky real? What, in any case, is reality? Had I been chosen as an observer of something happening this very night, but over some distant horizon? Had I observed some fearsome episode from the past, now repeated as a grotesque theatrical performance in the great arch of the night sky? I inclined to this latter view, since the warriors and their weapons seemed to me to be very old.

As I sought to calm my troubled nerves and tried to decide what to do next, a miracle happened. The sky was flooded with a white light, and I saw the dim outline of a cottage not a hundred yards before me. I hurried towards it, and saw a light in the window. I knocked on the door, and as I did so the bright light faded away. The door was opened by an elderly gentleman, who immediately invited me inside when he saw that I was shaking like a leaf. "Come inside, come inside," he said. "Let me introduce myself. Morris Higgon, Trepant. A young and beautiful lady like you should not be out alone on the mountain at this time of night. I perceive that you have seen the battle."

I was astonished by this remark, but also relieved, for I had begun to doubt my own sanity. "Why yes," I spluttered. "It was horrible, quite horrible. Have you seen it too?"

"Oh no. But many others have seen it over the years. You have just observed the Battle of Mynydd Carn, which occurred hereabouts in the year 1081. The army of Trehaearn and Caradog came from the east and the army of Gruffydd and Rhys came from the west. A very bad business indeed, which left thousands dead on the field of battle. And your name?"

"Martha Morgan of Plas Ingli."

Descent into Hell

"I am very pleased to meet you, my dear. I have heard a great deal about you, and I am pleased to say that it is all good. Now then, I will give you a nice hot cup of cocoa, and while you drink it I will organize my pony and trap and take you home. You are in no fit state to walk home through the haunted shadows of Cwm Gwaun."

So I settled by the peat fire and drank my cocoa while he harnessed up his pony, and within twenty minutes we were trotting home via Gelli Fawr and Cilgwyn. The peat fire, the hot cocoa and the warmth and civility of Master Higgon all helped to calm me down, and by the time I disembarked in the dark yard of the Plas my equanimity was quite restored. It was ten minutes before ten o'clock. David and the others were still up, and were just starting to get worried about me. The good kind gentleman would not come inside, but I promised that I would call in to see him again very soon to thank him properly for his chivalry. We all said "Goodnight!" and he flicked his reins and was gone.

I have said nothing of the battle in the sky to David, and as I write these words he is fast asleep next door without a care in the world. But I have in my mind some little snippets of my conversation with Master Higgon during our half-hour journey home. Two things which he said have made a profound impression upon me. First, he insisted that I must interpret the sights and sounds of the battle as a premonition of some fearsome event to come in my own life. "This is always the case," he said. "Five times over the last sixty years I have had travellers knocking on my door in a state of panic after seeing the battle, and five times disasters have befallen them within a few days. So beware, my dear young lady, beware. Watch everything and everybody, and be prepared to defend yourself and those whom you love."

This was not exactly a message that I wanted to hear, but then came the second thing that sticks in my memory. "I daresay you saw a bright light after the battle had faded away from the sky?" he asked.

"Why yes. It was the light which enabled me to find your cottage."

"And what colour was the light?"

"White."

"Well, that's all right then," said Master Higgon, and would say not a word more.

ΩΩΩΩΩΩΩΩΩ

Descent into Hell

5th August 1797

The nightmare has started. This morning I was on the point of setting out for Werndew, in order to have a chat with Joseph about my strange premonition, when a horseman galloped into the yard. He carried a package with an elaborate seal upon it. He assumed that there might be a reply, and so we asked him to wait a while. As he went with Shemi to wipe down his horse and to have a bite to eat in the kitchen, David and I took the package into the parlour and sat down at the window table with Grandma and Grandpa in order to examine its contents.

Strangely it was not addressed to "David Morgan, Gent", as might have been expected, but to "The Occupier, Plas Ingli, Newport." It proved to contain several documents written in the florid hand of one Elijah Willaby, Clerk of the Court of Chancery in London. One was a summons, demanding that "the occupier" should attend in person at a hearing at 10 o'clock on 12th August to answer a charge of illegal occupation of the Plas. A second was a copy of a sworn affidavit by Squire Watkins of Llannerch stating, in dense and convoluted legal language, that he was in possession of a 1792 document signed by William Morgan (David's father) and witnessed by Benjamin Rice of Pentre Ifan which recognized his entitlement to the Plas Ingli estate in the event that a loan of five hundred pounds was not repaid within five years -- namely by the 22nd day of July 1797. A third document was a copy of a legal opinion from a London attorney called Thomas Elias which stated that in his view the claim on the estate was well founded in law. And the fourth was an eviction notice from Alban Watkins, Squire, of Llannerch and Plas Ingli, demanding "that the family of Isaac Morgan should cease its illegal occupation of the house and estate known as Plas Ingli, and should remove themselves, together with all servants, animals, goods and chattels within one week of the case being proved in the London Court of Chancery."

When David had finished reading out the documents the four of us sat in total silence around the table. To be frank, none of us could believe what we had heard. Then we all started to speak at the same time. Expletives and explosions and expressions of incredulity echoed around the room.

At last we calmed down enough to examine the situation with a degree of reason. Grandpa has an unpredictable temper and a picturesque turn of phrase when he is in the mood, but he knows about the law and he knows far more about the history of the estate than the rest of us. Now he took control of the situation. "I know that Watkins went to London about three weeks ago. My spies tell me it was in a last desperate attempt to borrow money to cover his debts, thereby replacing one set of debts with another. He is in deep, deep trouble. But I am absolutely sure that William never took a loan from him in 1792. In fact, Watkins' reputation as a blood-sucking villain goes back much further than that, and only a fool would ever have borrowed money from him. William was not always prudent in his use of money, but he was not a fool......"

"Might he have done a deal while in a state of inebriation?" asked David. "One hears of people signing their lives away when affected by the demon drink."

"Impossible!" interjected Grandma Jane. "William could take his drink remarkably well. In fact, I never saw him drunk. Besides which, he would never, in a year of Sundays, have dropped his guard in the presence of Watkins Llannerch."

"No, I am utterly convinced that these documents are fakes and forgeries," said Grandpa. "In my experience disputes over debts, estates and mortgages are always dealt with by the judge at the Great Sessions in Haverfordwest. I have never heard of a matter such as this being dealt with in London. So do we simply throw the documents in the fire? I fear that such an action may rebound on us. Our problem is that we have before us a sworn affidavit, a legal opinion, a court summons, and an eviction order to deal with. We had better assume that the clerk of the Chancery Court, and the man he has hired as his attorney, are corrupt. But proving corruption is quite another matter. If we do not handle things very carefully, we may well have an unpleasant visit from the Sheriff in a fortnight's time and end up living with the paupers in Pengelli Wood."

Then he placed his forehead upon his fists and thought for a long time, while the rest of us contemplated the dreadful prospect which he had now opened up before us. Then there was a knock upon the lounge door, and Mrs Owen poked her head into the room. "Master Isaac," she said, "the messenger has had some bread and cheese and a flagon of ale, and he wonders whether it is your wish to deliver a message back to London."

"It is not my decision, Mrs Owen. Ask the Master of the Plas. The future of this estate is in his hands."

Immediately David said "Thank you, Grandpa. I will do what you would do, and what my father would have done had he been with us still." Then he turned to Mrs Owen and said "Tell the messenger to wait fifteen minutes. I will shortly have a letter for him to transmit to the Court of Chancery." He took a sheet of paper and a quill from the writing desk, thought for a few minutes, and then wrote the following words:

To the Clerk, Court of Chancery, London.

Sir,

I have the honour to be in receipt of your communication dated 23rd July in the year of our Lord 1797. I also have the honour to remind you that I am not only the "occupier" of the house and estate of Plas Ingli, but am indeed the lawful Owner and Master of said house and estate. I will be grateful if you will address me as such in any further communications on this or any other matter.

As a law-abiding citizen I will obey the summons on the assumption that it is properly issued, and I will attend at the Court of Chancery at 10 o'clock on the 12th day of August. I will also dispute and disprove the legality of any document supposedly signed by my father and now in the possession of Alban Watkins of Llannerch. I will dispute the legal opinion of one Thomas Elias, attorney, and will further contest the legality of the eviction notice which I received today through your office. I do not intend to move from this place until I am carried away from it in a box.

You may inform Master Elias, if he is acting for Squire Alban Watkins, that I will seek full recompense through the law for the damage inflicted upon my family and myself as a consequence of this malicious litigation.

I will also seek full recompense for the placing of this matter in the hands of His Majesty's Chancery Court in London rather than in the hands of the Court Leet of this Ancient Borough of Newport, or of the Great Sessions in Haverfordwest. It will not have escaped your notice that the timing and the location set for the hearing of this matter are extremely prejudicial to my case since witness evidence will be well nigh impossible for me to obtain.

I am, Sir, Yours faithfully,

David Morgan

Master, Plas Ingli, Newport

Dated the fifth day of August 1797

When he had finished the letter, David read it out and Grandpa said "Bravo, my boy! You are getting the hang of this legal language. And you also appear to know much more of the law than I had imagined. When the

Descent into Hell

Clerk of the Court transmits the contents of the letter to Thomas Elias and thence to Alban Watkins, he will begin to shake in his boots. God damn him! I will see him yet on a ship to the penal colonies, and I will stand on the quayside at Plymouth and wave him a cheery farewell."

So David's letter was signed and sealed, and dispatched with the messenger. It will probably take four days to get to London, and it will pass through the hands of maybe six different riders. Pray God that it arrives safely.

Having thus signalled that it was the intention of the Morgan clan to fight Alban Watkins in court, we had to turn our attention to strategic matters. For maybe an hour we discussed the best course of action. There was still an estate to run, so Billy was told to carry on with the harvest and to organize the labourers as he saw fit. Then, shortly after nine of the clock, David and Grandpa took the trap and rode off to see Squire Bowen of Llwyngwair. They assumed that he would know what to do, and they also assumed that on the forthcoming trip to London they would need allies. They were away for six hours, during which time we women were left in control of the house. And a very miserable house it was too. Bessie and Hettie were out in the harvest field with the men, and Mrs Owen, Grandma and I went through the motions of preparing the midday meal for the harvesters, cleaning the dairy and tidying the house. We had to tell Mrs Owen what was going on, and her swearing was even more colourful than Grandpa's. It did little to cheer us up, and for long periods we three worked in silence, hardly daring to contemplate the implications of Watkins' treachery.

The tension in the house became almost unbearable, and my own black mood was not at all lightened by a strong attack of the morning sickness which caused me to lose my breakfast and lie down for an hour. At about three o'clock the men returned, and there was an injection of raw energy. We were surprised to find that Lewis Legal accompanied them, armed (as is the way with lawyers) with piles of dusty documents. The house was transformed into a military headquarters. David rushed about packing clothes into a bag. I followed him from one room to another, and during our peregrinations he told me what they had been doing.

He said that they drove the pony hard all the way to Llwyngwair. As luck would have it, the squire was at home, although the rest of the family was in Tenby for the summer social season. David showed him the documents newly arrived from London, and apparently he almost had an attack of the apoplexy. "Poppycock! Stuff and nonsense!" he shouted. "I have never seen such rubbish in all my life! These documents cannot possibly stand up in a court of law. This is a matter for the Great Sessions here in Pembrokeshire, and London attorneys involve themselves at their peril! I will not have it! What on earth is the Court of Chancery coming to? There must be charlatans in charge, no doubt bribed with money stolen from the poor, and fools and idiots working as clerks and attorneys! Probably Watkins has bought the judge as well. We must not allow this pestilence of corruption to spread for one moment longer. I will come to London with you, and we will take my coach."

David and Grandpa were flabbergasted at this turn of events, but they were in no position to refuse. The squire then told them that he personally was owed five hundred pounds by Watkins, and that the Llannerch estate was on the verge of ruin. The big landowners, he said, always know in intimate detail the financial affairs of the lesser landowners. He said that he doubted the authenticity of the 1792 document which would now be the central exhibit in the court case, but that it could not be entirely ruled out. "If there is a piece of paper with a signature witnessed by Rice Pentre Ifan," he said, "then it is probably not worth the price of the ink. The man will put his signature to anything, so long as he is well paid."

The Squire then said " We will set off for London this very day, not later than four of the clock. Who is your solicitor?"

"Lewis Legal of Fishguard."

"A most excellent fellow! We must bring him with us. He has a brain as sharp as any London judge, and he knew William well. Lewis can attest to his good character, and he will know that there was no family debt and no other reason for William to borrow money from Watkins in July of 1792. Kidnap him from his office if necessary, and tell him to bring with him any documents which have William's handwriting and signature upon them. He will be well paid for his services if he wishes, but I suspect that as an old friend of Plas Ingli he will come to London just for the excitement. There are not enough ladies of pleasure in Fishguard for a man such as he, and we may be away long enough for him to have a very pleasant time indeed after working hours."

David says that his jaw dropped. The Methodist squire's eyes twinkled for a moment, and then he continued with his high-speed planning. "We will stop in Narberth for the night and then continue with all haste to London on the morrow. If we complete the journey in five days we will be lucky. But once there we should have one clear day to organize our defence. I have several old friends who owe me favours, and they will look after our case. There will be no fees. They will also assist me in digging up the dirt which will undoubtedly be connected with the names of Thomas Elias and Elijah Willaby, and in finding out interesting things about the judge."

At this point, David said that he and Grandpa could hardly believe what they were hearing, and that the squire paused in response to the wide eyes and open mouths of his listeners. "My dear kind gentlemen!" he exclaimed. "I see that you are appalled by the methods which I propose to use when this matter is decided in London. You may think that it is corrupt for a local magistrate like Howell to send an innocent pauper to Haverfordwest workhouse. You have lived too long in the country. London is a dirty and degrading place. Corruption swirls like tobacco smoke through every grand house, every street, and every court of law. When I was a young man I worked in chambers there for ten years, and I lost my innocence on the first day. Let me assure you that when there is a case to be won you leave no stone unturned. And this case is not a frivolous matter. You stand to lose everything that you and your family have worked for, over many generations. You have already suffered far too much. I have the greatest respect for the Morgans of Plas Ingli, and I will simply not allow a pair of vicious petty criminals called Rice and Watkins to take your birthright away from you. Good Christian gentleman I may be, but my goodness stretches only so far."

"Thank you sir," said Grandpa Isaac. "I am sure that we would have been quite lost in this miserable business without your help. My gloom has been lifted at least a little by your words and your confidence, and I think I can say the same for my grandson. Now then, what else should we do? Would it be prudent to collect signed and witnessed statements from other gentlemen of this neighbourhood, both attesting to the good character of William and to the past misdemeanours and unsavoury character of our friends Rice and Watkins?"

"You prove, my old friend, that it is never too late to learn! Go to it. Master David, take the pony and trap to Fishguard, and don't come back without Lewis Legal. Master Isaac, borrow my chestnut hunter and ride to all those of your confederates whom you can reach by three o'clock, and get witnessed statements from them. I will call at the Plas with the coach at four o'clock, and we will leave for London immediately."

Squire Bowen was as good as his word. And now they are gone, four good men on a mission to save the virtue of our family and to save us from destitution. The squire seems supremely confident, but I cannot tell whether his confidence is well founded, for legal matters such as this are complex indeed. Perhaps he is just spoiling for a courtroom battle in which he personally has nothing to lose. Perhaps he sees this as his opportunity to squash Squire Watkins and Squire Rice underfoot as a cart-horse might squash a mouse. But whatever his motive may be, he is certainly an effective and clear-headed leader, and there is nobody else in the neighbourhood to whom we can turn.

Grandma Jane is probably lying awake in the room next door, and I fear that I will not sleep much tonight. My bed is cold without David, and I have not the faintest idea when he will return. Two weeks? Three weeks? I know that my heart will break if he is away for longer. Bessie has been doing her best this evening over supper to cheer me up, but I fear that I may be on the edge of another descent into deep, deep melancholia.

ΩΩΩΩΩΩΩΩΩ

8th August 1797

I have just had to endure the two most miserable, shameful and degrading days of my life. I have been humiliated and dishonoured, and I am now incarcerated in a filthy dungeon in Haverfordwest Gaol as I await my fate. I have a searing pain on my back, and my injuries are still bleeding. My dress is crusted with blood. I can hardly bear to lie down, and I feel only slightly more comfortable when I am sitting or standing. I am falsely charged with grand larceny, and I will have to languish in this foul place until the middle of September when I will be judged at the Quarter Sessions. The evidence against me appears to be conclusive, and in the absence of a miracle I fear that my fate will be either transportation to the colonies or death on the gallows.

Descent into Hell

The dungeon which will be my home for the next six weeks is in the basement of the old ruined castle, perched on a rock high above the town. Outside the barred and glassless window there is a sheer drop of a hundred feet down onto the roofs of shops and houses. Escape is impossible, and the only way in and out of my cell is through a hinged grille in the roof secured by a heavy lock. The grille has to be lifted aside before a flimsy ladder can be slid down to allow entry or exit. It is searingly hot, for the summer heatwave continues unabated. I am in solitary confinement, presumably because I am classified as a dangerous criminal who might infect other prisoners with indescribable wickedness if I was to come into contact with them. The only items of furniture are a wooden bed against the wall and a bucket in the corner. Three times a day I am given black bread and thin soup to eat, and I can slake my thirst from a flagon of water which sits upon the window sill. This morning (as, I assume, will be the case on all mornings) I was allowed a small bowl of water for washing and cleansing my wounds.

As I confront the prospect that my short life may soon come to an end, and as I seek to come to terms with my predicament, I am sitting with my little book and pen beside the window, making use of the last light of the evening. Today I was allowed one visitor, and my beloved Bessie brought a small bundle of my possessions. I had not had a chance to communicate with her, but she knew what to bring -- a small mirror and comb, a little bottle of lavender water, talcum powder and dressings for my wounds, a clean shawl and petticoat, two oranges, and my diary, a pot of ink and some sharpened quills. She had to part with a silver shilling in order to see me, and another one in order to leave her small bundle; but my jailer, a tough old woman called Mistress Griffin, does appear to have some humanity, and we must be grateful that she is open to bribery. Bessie was only allowed to spend five minutes with me, but that was enough for us to determine the actions which she urgently needed to take. By now she will have sent a message to my parents in Brawdy, been to see brother Morys at the Bethesda manse, and will be on her way back to Newport to alert Joseph Harries, Mary Jane, Ellie and my other friends as to my plight. In fact, I am certain that they will already have been made aware, through the local news network, of the appalling events of yesterday.

Before the light fades completely, I will try to describe what happened. Quite early in the morning, at about eight of the clock, there was a great commotion in the yard. We were all at the breakfast table, and when we went outside to investigate we were confronted by a posse of about a dozen ruffians armed with bludgeons and staves. They had a horse and cart with them, and riding in the cart were Ifan Beynon, the clerk to the justices, and John Wilson who has recently been sworn in as town constable. Master Beynon hopped off the cart and marched up to the kitchen door. He then waved a piece of paper in my face and said "Are you Martha Morgan, Mistress of Plas Ingli?" I thought this a ridiculous question, and said "You know perfectly well who I am, Master Beynon, since we have already met on a number of occasions in the recent past."

Then, to my horror and to the complete astonishment of Grandma and the servants, he explained that the piece of paper in his hand was a search warrant, and that he had come to investigate a crime "of the utmost magnitude and seriousness." He said that the gentlemen with him were all special constables sworn in that very morning to ensure the apprehension of any criminals who might be at large in the neighbourhood. He then summoned John Wilson and six of the thugs to join him, and made to push past us into the house. Billy and Shemi blocked the door, and Grandma insisted that she should be shown the search warrant. Reluctantly Master Beynon showed it to her, and after reading it carefully she confirmed that it was in order. She said "Huh! Signed by Justices Rice and Howell. I thought as much." Then she motioned to Billy and Shemi to stand aside.

The happy clerk, accompanied by a very embarrassed constable and six of his accomplices, strode into the kitchen. Master Beynon asked Grandma, Bessie and me to follow, and strode across the room, along the passage and up the stairs. He appeared to know exactly where he was going. He marched into my dressing room, where his men made a great show of turning things over, pulling out drawers and throwing garments and ornaments about. But he made a beeline for the old-fashioned tapestry hanging on the wall. He pulled it out so that he could see the back of it, and then shouted "Aha! What have we here?" And there, pinned to the back of the tapestry, was a grotesque ruby brooch which I had never seen before. I felt the blood draining from my face, and I thought I might faint. "I ask you all to observe this!" said the clerk to all those present in the room. "You should each make a careful note in your mind as to the details of this discovery, and as to the reactions of this woman, for your recollections may well be required in court."

Descent into Hell

Master Beynon then triumphantly unpinned the brooch, wrapped it up in a piece of cloth, and put it in his pocket. Then he nodded to the constable. In a state of high embarrassment, the poor man took out a piece of paper from a little bag and proceeded -- with some difficulty, for he was not a very good reader -- to read from it. "Mistress Martha Morgan of Plas Ingli," he intoned, "you are hereby charged with grand larceny, for the theft of a ruby brooch valued at twenty pounds, being the property of Mistress Maria Rice of Pentre Ifan, on the thirtieth day of July in the year of our Lord 1797. Master Ifan Beynon is authorized, on behalf of His Majesty the King, to take you into custody and to bring you before the court of Petty Sessions at Pentre Ifan in Nevern Parish this very morning at eleven of the clock. You will be given every opportunity to present your defence in advance of judgment. Signed Benjamin Rice and George Howell, Justices of the Peace, this 7th day of August 1797."

My recollections of what happened next are hazy, but the scene must have resembled that which occurred long ago at Bedlam. I think that I might have lost control, for in truth the possibility of finding myself in a predicament such as this had never, never occurred to me before. I wept and protested my innocence over and again. Grandma and Bessie wept too, and said that there must have been some terrible mistake, and some other explanation for the presence of the brooch behind the tapestry. Mrs Owen and the other servants came rushing up the stairs when they heard the outcry, and were intent upon protecting me with their lives. Indeed they would have assaulted the constables had not Grandma realized that such action might have resulted in injury to themselves and brought the law down upon all of their heads. So under her calming influence they stood aside as the armed thugs led me out of the room. All of them, including Billy and Shemi, were in tears. Bessie hurriedly threw a cloak over my shoulders. I was led out into the yard. One of the men then tied my wrists with a thin rope. I was put into the cart, and hauled off like a common felon or murderer to face the full weight of the law at Pentre Ifan.

As the cart creaked down to the ford at Pantry and then along the Pentre Ifan road people came out of their cottages and stood white-faced and uncomprehending as the posse went past. I was so ashamed that I pulled my cloak over my head in order to hide my identity. Then the movement of the cart, and the turmoil in my head and heart, brought on a violent attack of the morning sickness, and I had to ask Ifan Beynon three times to stop the convoy so that I could be sick at the side of the road. On one occasion, when I raised my head, I noticed that Billy, Bessie and Grandma were following, on foot, a short distance behind the convoy. They were not allowed to come too close, since Constable Wilson thought that they might attempt "a dastardly rescue", but Grandma shouted that Shemi had gone to Newport to fetch Will Final Testament and to bring him directly to Pentre Ifan. This gave me some encouragement, and I knew that my friends would not abandon me, but in truth I have never felt more desolate, for I knew that the four men who might have offered me salvation were at that very moment bumping along in their own uncomfortable horse-drawn conveyance on the road to London.

I fear that I am now very distressed, and the light has faded so much that I cannot write more. Mistress Griffin will allow me neither candle nor rush-light. I will try to sleep, and will continue in the morning.

ΩΩΩΩΩΩΩΩΩ

9th August 1797

I have slept hardly at all, and I am in excruciating pain because my open wounds have been bleeding and sticking to the back of my filthy dress. Every time I move some encrustation is pulled off and the bleeding starts again. Because all the injuries are on my back I cannot help myself, and I pray that Mistress Griffin will come before too long and dress my wounds for me. The bells of St Martin's have just chimed six of the clock, and there is just enough light in this dim place to continue with my woeful narrative.

When my captors and I arrived at Pentre Ifan we found that the Petty Sessions were already under way, with Squires Rice and Howell seated behind the kitchen table. I was hustled in and forced to stand before them, with waves of nausea passing over me. I was confused and dejected, but determined that I would not tell them that I was with child. Grandma, Billy and Bessie came in and stood in a corner, followed by several other people from the neighbourhood, and they were guarded by two men with bludgeons. The constable wanted to untie my wrists, but Squire Rice refused to give his consent, saying that dangerous prisoners should be accorded no comfort and no respect.

Without further ado, Squire Howell announced that he would be chairman of the bench in view of Squire Rice's personal interest in the matter to be judged, and said "The court is now in session! I will tolerate no disorder from the public gallery, and matters will be dealt with expeditiously since we all have the harvest to attend to before the weather breaks."

He then summoned the Clerk to announce the cases to be heard, and was informed by Master Beynon that there was but one case, in which one Martha Morgan was charged with grand larceny. At that moment young Shemi came rushing in, and I could tell from the look on his face that he had been unsuccessful in obtaining the services of Will Final Testament. "Are there any attorneys for the prosecution or the defence?" asked the Squire. "None for the prosecution, my Lord," said Ifan Beynon, "since cross-examination and such things will hardly be required. For the defence, I am informed that an attempt was made to obtain the services of Will Final Testament in Newport, but I happen to know that he is otherwise engaged at the Petty Sessions in Eglwyswrw this very morning."

"Oh dear, what a sad coincidence!" said Squire Howell, with a radiant smile on his face. "No matter. The course of justice cannot be delayed. Let matters proceed!"

At this, Grandma shouted from the back of the court "George Howell, this is a disgrace! The case should be adjourned and heard on another day! Martha will have no opportunity to defend herself, and no opportunity to demonstrate that the charge against her is based upon a malicious falsehood"

"Jane Morgan!" yelled Squire Howell, banging his fist on the kitchen table. "If you are not careful I will have you locked away for contempt of court! Constable, take that woman out into the yard, and keep her there until this case is finished." And Grandma was led away, leaving me feeling even more isolated in a hostile and fearsome environment.

After that I felt so ill with the morning sickness that I have only the haziest of recollections of what transpired. I remember the clerk reading out the charge. I remember being asked whether I pleaded guilty or not guilty, and replying in a weak voice "Not guilty." I remember pleading to go outside in order to be sick. I was refused permission and was sick all over the kitchen floor. The court was adjourned for five minutes while the mess was cleared up. Then Mistress Maria Rice was called. She looked even more nervous than I, but she read out the oath in a shaky voice and then gave her evidence. It was perfectly short and simple.

She said that on the thirtieth day of July she had held a social gathering at Pentre Ifan for a few friends, including Master David Morgan and Mistress Martha Morgan. Before the guests arrived, she said, she had been in her dressing room choosing jewellery suitable for the occasion, and had chosen a pearl necklace and emerald brooch. She had left other jewellery out on her dressing table. Later on, she said, the Morganses of Plas Ingli had arrived, wet from the heavy rain, and Mistress Morgan, the defendant, had accepted the invitation to pop up to the dressing room to tidy herself up. She had been the only guest to visit the dressing room, and she had been upstairs for some minutes. Later on, after a pleasant social occasion, and when all the guests had gone, the hostess had gone back upstairs to change into less formal clothes, and she had discovered that a ruby brooch worth twenty pounds was missing. She was absolutely distraught, she said, because this was her most expensive and sentimental item of jewellery which had been passed down in the family for several generations. She said that she had searched everywhere, over several days, and had been extremely reluctant to think ill of Mistress Morgan. But at last, she said, she recalled that the Morgan family was in severe financial crisis, and she concluded that Mistress Morgan had succumbed to temptation and stolen the brooch in the hope of selling it in order to repay some debts. She had accordingly gone to the constable in Newport to report the crime and to indicate where her suspicions lay, and he had taken the matter forward from there.

I was stunned into silence by this story, and would have denied it vehemently there and then, but I was given no chance, and Ifan Beynon and Constable Wilson then gave their evidence in turn and described the happenings at Plas Ingli including the finding of the brooch. All three key witnesses then placed sworn, signed and witnessed affidavits before the court, and Squire Howell took these into his possession.

I was then called to swear the oath and give evidence, but in truth I became very confused, and still felt very ill. With no legal gentleman to guide me I blurted out a succession of denials, repeated myself on several occasions, and must have appeared the very personification of a petty criminal with no effective alibi or other defence. I said that the estate was not in financial difficulty; that I had no reason to want to steal any jewellery since I preferred to dress plainly rather than ostentatiously; and that in any case I had not seen any jewellery at all on Mistress Rice's dressing table when I sat in front of it to brush my hair and tidy myself up.

"This is outrageous, Madam!" shouted Squire Rice, unable to contain himself any longer. "Are you saying that my wife is a liar?"

"I am telling you, sir, that I saw no jewellery upon the dressing table, and that I did not steal a ruby brooch."

Then Squire Howell asked if I wanted to call any witnesses. He refused to allow Grandma back into the kitchen on the basis that she had already misbehaved herself quite enough, but the bench heard Billy, Bessie and Shemi. They all said that they had recently received wage rises and that in their view the estate was not in financial difficulty; but all three of them were attacked without mercy by the two justices on the grounds that they were speculating about matters beyond their ken. When they stated their new wage rates I saw that the two squires bristled; and on other matters of fact all the servants could do was to confirm what they had seen of the events at the Plas, which helped my case not at all.

Finally Squire Howell asked for the ruby brooch to be exhibited. The clerk took it out of his pocket and unwrapped the piece of cloth which surrounded it. "Is this your missing brooch, Madam?" he enquired of Mistress Rice. "Indeed it is, Sir," she replied. The brooch was then shown to Constable Wilson and the other constables who had been present in my dressing room this morning, and they all confirmed that it was the brooch unpinned from behind my tapestry. It was then given to Constable Wilson for safe keeping.

The die was cast. There was nothing more that I could do to disprove the charge which was before the court. The two squires went into a brief consultation, and then Squire Howell said "Silence in court!", which I though quite unnecessary since all those present in the kitchen were holding their breath. "Martha Morgan of Plas Ingli, we have heard the case against you and we have heard your defence. All proper procedures have been followed. We find you guilty as charged. Only the other day one of our fellow justices, one Isaac Morgan, said that justice must be administered equally, without fear or favour, to both the rich and the poor. We agree absolutely. We therefore sentence you to be stripped to the waist and to be taken behind a cart from the Gallows Tump in Newport to the

Descent into Hell

Black Lion Inn. You will be publicly whipped until the blood flows upon your back...."

At this I almost fainted, and had to be supported by two of the special constables. There was pandemonium at the far end of the room, and I heard Bessie screaming and Billy and Shemi shouting. They were dragged outside, and the Squire continued "We further commit you for trial at the autumn Quarter Sessions in Haverfordwest, and you are hereby remanded in custody until your case is heard. You will be transported this afternoon to Haverfordwest Gaol. The court is dismissed!"

What followed was like a descent into hell. I was not allowed to speak to Grandma or the servants, and I was thrust roughly into the cart which had been waiting throughout the proceedings in the yard. The guard of special constables was augmented by a dozen or so ruffians from the hovels around Pentre Ifan, all no doubt having been offered a few pence for their work as upholders of the law. Then the procession set off for Newport, with the horse and cart flanked by the peacekeeping force. The men were all armed with bludgeons, pitchforks and axes, as if they expected trouble. My cloak was taken away from me and was retrieved by Bessie. It took us about an hour to reach Newport from the east, and we had to march right out to the west end of town where the gallows tree is located. One of Squire Rice's henchmen found a drum from somewhere, and beat it at the head of the procession in order to attract attention. People started to poke their heads out of doors and windows, and soon a sizable crowd was trailing along the street. Grandma and the servants were still present, and I saw them explaining to many friends and acquaintances what had happened.

At the far end of town the cart was turned round and my humiliation began. I was forced to get off the cart, and two of the men tore at my dress until I was stripped to the waist. Another man untied my stays and threw them into the ditch. I was so terrified that I could not cry or even speak. I was then tied by my wrists to the back of the cart and pulled along behind it. A horsewhip was produced, and the constables and hired hands took it in turns to scourge me as we moved slowly along the main street to the crossroads and on to the Black Lion inn. Some of my tormentors were so horrified by what they were being paid to do that they refused absolutely to cooperate. Others "whipped" me so gently that I could hardly feel the strokes. But about half a dozen of the real ruffians appeared actually to enjoy their work, and they lashed me across my back again and again without any hint of compassion. I cannot begin to describe the pain and the shame that I felt, and I became aware eventually that my wounds were bleeding. I could feel the blood running, and I could see out of the corner of my eye that the tip of the horsewhip was stained red. Although the journey through the town took no more than twenty minutes it seemed to me that I was caught in eternity and would never, never escape.

But somewhere in the depths of my soul I found a crumb of courage, and I determined that I would not weep. I also thought of my dear husband, and of the child in my womb, and I realized that I had no reason at all to feel guilt or to be intimidated by the cruelty of my tormentors. I knew that I was the victim of a monstrous injustice, and I decided that I would walk erect and hold my head high. A cold fury burned in the pit of my stomach. As I passed people on the roadside I looked them in the eye, and I also sought the gaze of the men who wielded the whip. According to convention they should have stopped as soon as blood was drawn; but these men were clearly under instructions to beat me to the point where I collapsed. They continued to lash at me, but they would not look me in the face; and this gave me a power over them and a new strength in the midst of my searing pain.

By the time we reached the Newport cross-roads my legs were beginning to give way beneath me and I started to stumble. But I became aware of a change in the mood of the crowd. First they had come out for the sport and the spectacle, expecting to see the routine whipping of some poor vagrant or drunkard. But when they saw that it was Mistress Martha Morgan of Plas Ingli being pulled behind the whipping cart their mood changed to wonderment, for they had never before seen a member of the gentry treated in this way. Then, as the story of the morning Petty Sessions passed through the onlookers, and as they saw the blood flowing freely upon my back, the mood changed again, and I was aware that rotten vegetables, eggs and other food scraps were being flung towards me and that a great growl of anger was beginning to roll around the streets. I briefly thought that my humiliation was now complete, and I felt that my composure was on the point of collapse; but then I realized that neither the anger nor the food scraps were being directed at me. They were directed at my tormentors, and soon they were cowering beneath a veritable barrage of rubbish and abuse. People ran alongside the procession, throwing punches at the constables, spitting at them and kicking out at them. I recognized some of the good people who had, less than three weeks ago, visited me at the Plas bearing posies and gifts following the outbreak of the dysentery sickness. Now, in self-defence, the constables lashed out with their bludgeons and other weapons, and I fear that some of the townspeople were injured as a result. Then two chants started up in the crowd and grew to a crescendo. One of them said "Let her go! Let her go!" and the other said "Rice and Howell -- give us their heads! Rice and Howell -- give us their heads!"

Then the whipping stopped. Indeed, it had become impossible. Constable John Wilson, who had been given the task of meting out my punishment, did his best to keep his forces tight around the horse and the cart. I was bundled back on board and one constable did me the small kindness of untying my wrists and helping me to cover my bleeding upper body with my torn dress. He also took off his waistcoat and put it across my shoulders. But then he became more concerned about his own safety than mine, for the crowd was now almost out of control. He and his colleagues managed to rush the horse and cart over the remaining two hundred yards to the Black Lion inn, and having thus discharged their duty and earned their pennies they scattered.

The crowd gradually calmed down, and I saw Grandma pleading with some of them not to interfere any further since this was likely to do more harm than good to my cause. Constable Wilson was now, much to his chagrin, left in sole charge of proceedings, and had to bind my wrists again and tie me to the handrail of the cart in case I should be snatched away by angry townspeople. Ifan Beynon, the clerk to the justices, had been inside the Black Lion enjoying a few mugs of ale while my scourging had been going on, and he now emerged to issue further orders. He dragged two rough fellows from the dark recesses of the inn and commissioned them to accompany the constable and the prisoner to Haverfordwest forthwith. He told them they would have very little to do and that they would be well paid, so with a shrug they climbed on board the cart and sat on either side of me. The constable was given some sort of official document (no doubt recording my sentence from the Petty Sessions). He then climbed up on the front of the cart, cracked the whip, and away we went.

The journey from Newport to Haverfordwest Gaol took more than two hours, and I have few recollections of it. My wounds were giving me the most terrible pain, and the high sun beat down without mercy. But in spite of my extreme discomfort I think I must have settled into some sort of fitful sleep, for in truth every last ounce of physical and nervous energy had been drained out of me.

And so I was delivered into the tender mercies of Mistress Griffin, who gave me a sip to drink and a bite to eat. Then she did her best to cleanse my wounds before helping me down the ladder into my dungeon and shutting me in for the night.

ΩΩΩΩΩΩΩΩΩ

10th August 1797

Time hangs very heavy in this place. My conditions have not improved, but I feel that the cross which I bear has lightened just a little. I am very lonely, but being incarcerated in my own private dungeon does have its compensations. I gather that conditions in the other cells are far worse than in mine, with up to six miserable prisoners crowded together, some of them ill, some of them mad, and others intent upon suicide. I can hear their cries and their moans of despair echoing around the castle walls at all the hours of day and night. I wonder what dreadful things they have done, and what dreadful things are being done to them? I now believe that I am in solitary confinement simply because I am a lady, and because the jailer feels that I need some protection from the criminal classes.

Yesterday Morys and Nansi came to see me. They were not allowed to come down into my cell, so we had to communicate through the grill in the ceiling. We spoke in Welsh, since Mistress Griffin and the other jailers, like most natives of the county town, understand only English. They said that I was allowed only one visit per day for five minutes, so we had to speak quickly. How I wished that I could have embraced them! But I told them all about the appalling things that had happened to me three days since, and promised them that I was quite innocent of the charge upon which I had been convicted. They believed me of course, and swore that they would now institute a campaign in the town and beyond to secure, at the very least, my release on bail. However, they did admit that as new arrivals in town their network of contacts was not very great, and that Morys was viewed with some suspicion by the mayor and the burgesses in view of his recent defection from the established church. I was personally not convinced that their campaigning would have any effect. They said that Mother and Father were in town; they were distraught at what had happened to me, and had promised to come and see me on the morrow. Then a brutish jailer shouted to Morys and Nansi that their time was up, and they were hustled off, leaving me behind with tears in my eyes.

My injuries have started to heal, and Mistress Griffin has come down the ladder on several occasions, yesterday and today, to change my dressings and to apply a healing ointment given to her by three mysterious kind gentlemen. I suspect that she is being paid to help me. She will not tell me who the kind gentlemen are, but I think that they might be the deacons from Bethesda. She tells me that they call at the gaol every day in order to bring succour to the needy, and that they have been doing this for as long as she has been working here. They are not allowed to see me, but they must know that I am here, since Morys will have told them. This realization has made me feel very humble and very foolish, for it is not long since I wrote some arrogant and flippant words about them in my diary following the wedding of Morys and Nansi. If I ever get the chance to meet them again I will kiss each of them in turn and ask for their forgiveness.

This morning Mother and Father were allowed into the prison and were permitted five minutes of communication through the grille. It was a dismal experience, for dear Mother could not contain her tears, and that set me off weeping as well. The result of all this emotion was that we communicated hardly at all, and they were hurried away after their allotted five minutes complaining about heartless jailers, inhuman rules and regulations, and the need for complete reform of the prison system. However, Father did manage to drop down to me a little bag of freshly picked blackberries and an orange which he had secreted away in his pocket, and I gobbled them down ravenously. As they departed they shouted that I should keep my spirits up, and that they would have me out of my dark dungeon in no time at all. I wish that I could share their optimism.

This afternoon I was hungry and very miserable, feeling sorry for myself above all else because I felt that my friends and family from

Descent into Hell

Newport had abandoned me. Only Bessie had been to see me two days ago, and I wondered what had happened to Grandma Jane and the servants, and to my good friends like Mary Jane, Ellie and Joseph Harries. How I longed for their love and support! But then there was a hubbub in the prison yard over my head, and I heard a very familiar voice calling my name. It was Joseph! Soon I saw his sharp features and gleaming eyes through the grille. He had a big grin upon his face, and I too grinned when I heard the rattle of keys and realized that Mistress Griffin was going to give him access to my cell. She opened up the grill and let down the ladder. Joseph climbed down, carrying a bag in his hand, and then she followed, locking the grill after her and putting the key into her pocket. This I thought remarkably stupid, since Joseph and I could have knocked her on the head, taken the key, let ourselves out and affected a spectacular escape. But I was not up to strenuous heroics, and thought better of spending the rest of my life as a fugitive.

Mistress Griffin settled herself down on the floor in the corner and said "Mistress Martha, I am here as a chaperone, for there is no knowing what a gentleman visitor might get up to. This gentleman is an official gentleman. He says he is a doctor come from the Lord Lieutenant of the County to check your wounds and your general state of health. He says that it would not do me nor the head jailer any good if you was to go and die on us."

"It wouldn't do me much good either," I replied. "But thank you very much for your concern, Mistress Griffin. I appreciate your kindness in permitting Doctor Harries to visit me. May I embrace him? I always embrace my doctors."

She shrugged her shoulders, and I gave Joseph an embrace which was longer and more intense than etiquette permitted. But in truth I needed it, for I have felt more vulnerable and lonely over these past few days than at any time in my life. Then it was down to work. Joseph asked to see my wounds, and looked away as I opened the top of my filthy dress and lay on my front on the hard bed. He said in Welsh "Oh, dear God, this is terrible! My poor, poor Martha! Those thugs who brandished the horse-whip certainly earned their few pence."

He started to clean my wounds and complemented Mistress Griffin on the work she had already done. He took out various ointments and dressings from his bag, and worked systematically, bringing immediate balm to both body and soul. As he worked I asked "Have you heard about the incident at the house, and the case at the Petty sessions, and the public whipping through the main street?"

"Yes yes. I have heard it all, from a number of different sources. Grandma Jane is wonderful, and she gave me a meticulous account which could not have been bettered. She is doing her best to run the estate at the moment, and is trying to get the harvest finished."

"Alone? But she needs help!"

"Don't you worry, Martha. Billy is proving to be a good organizer of men, and all the neighbours are helping. Grandma has also formed a fearsome female war council with Ellie and Mary Jane. These two good ladies moved into the Plas yesterday, and your sister Catrin joined them this morning. She asked for a few days of leave as soon as she heard of your misfortune, and Master Bowen readily gave his consent. Although the Plas is missing its brightest star, the house is now packed with beautiful unmarried women, and Billy and Shemi think that they are in heaven! Nobody, but nobody believes that you committed this crime, and there is a deep fury in the town and country at the brutality which you have had to endure. The Rice and Howell families have been virtually cut off from contact with the rest of the community, and many of the shopkeepers in town are refusing to serve them."

"Oh, thank you, Joseph, for your reassurance. I am very touched."

At last he finished working on my back and turned away while I adjusted my torn dress as best I could. Then he came and sat next to me on the bed. He gave me several spoonfuls of foul-tasting liquids, which I swallowed obediently. He took out of his bag two freshly baked wheat loaves and some butter and cheese, and gave half to me and half to Mistress Griffin. She did not complain, and neither did I. Then, as we women ate, he took my hand and looked into my troubled eyes. "Now then Martha," he said, "we have to get to the bottom of this affair. I am utterly convinced that we are in the middle of a huge conspiracy to pervert the course of justice, and I already have several matters under investigation. I want you to think very carefully and answer my questions as accurately as you can."

"I will try."

"First there is the matter of the brooch behind the tapestry. You are quite sure that Bessie could not have put it there?"

Descent into Hell

"Absolutely not! She is completely trustworthy, and when Ifan Beynon discovered it she was more shocked than anybody."

"As I suspected. This is what she told me herself. She also told me, when pressed, and with a red face, that she never cleaned behind the tapestry because it was too heavy and dusty."

"Where is this leading us, Joseph? Are you suggesting that the brooch might have been there for some time?"

"Indeed I am. However, in order to confirm this I went yesterday to examine the brooch. It is now held, as it should be, by Constable Wilson in the Newport lockup. He will bring it into Haverfordwest as a key exhibit when your case is heard at the Quarter Sessions. I insisted on examining it, and he was very cooperative."

"How on earth did you manage that?"

"You must remember, Martha, that doors always open for a wizard," he replied, with a mysterious glint in his eye. Then he said "The brooch was still enclosed in its piece of cloth just as Ifan Beynon had left it. I examined it minutely. The surface and outermost pieces of metal were slightly tarnished but shiny where the brooch had been handled, but when I looked through my magnifying glass I saw that the back of the brooch, and the spaces between the woven strips of metal, were caked with dust. My dear Martha, that brooch has been collecting dust for months. If it had been in a jewellery box, or if it had been cleaned recently, or indeed if it had recently been placed behind your tapestry, it would have been quite clean."

"Joseph, you should be a special constable!"

"No thank you, my dear. That would be an insult to my intelligence. Now think. Is there any occasion on which Mistress Rice, or any one of her friends, could have placed that brooch behind your tapestry?"

I thought for some time and said "I do not think so. I am not in the habit of giving Mistress Rice the run of my house." Then I suddenly recalled the strange visit which we had had from the three squires and their wives in the spring. "Oh my goodness," I exclaimed. "There was indeed one occasion, when the Rices, Howells and Watkinses invited themselves to the Plas. I think it may have been in March. The men were very aggressive, and were angry with Grandpa Isaac. Now that I come to think of it, each of the ladies used my dressing room in turn, in order to powder their noses or do whatever was needed. They seemed to be working hard at being sociable, and I recall that Mistress Rice was nervous and furtive."

Joseph breathed a sigh of relief. "That is all the information I need," he said. "Guilt is established. I take it as read that you noticed a similarly nervous pattern of behaviour in Mistress Rice when you were recently invited to Pentre Ifan?"

"Why yes. Now that you mention it, I was quite disconcerted by her shifty eyes, perspiring hands, and staccato style of speaking. And she was very insistent that I should use her dressing room when really I was quite unconcerned about my damp hair. I went upstairs just to please her and, I am ashamed to say, to have a look at the rest of the house."

"Perfectly normal female behaviour, Martha. One last question. When Ifan Beynon went into your dressing room with the search warrant, what did he do?"

"I think he went straight to the tapestry and looked behind it," I replied.

"Did that not strike you as strange? If you had entered the room with a search warrant and had been searching for a brooch, where would you have looked?"

"I suppose I would have looked in the jewellery box or in my dress wardrobe, or maybe, if I thought it might be hidden, in the depths of my bedside chest."

"Precisely. Ifan Beynon is a stupid man, and he had clearly been told where to look. The rest of the conspiracy is all too obvious. It has probably been planned in meticulous detail for at least six months. I suspect that the dramatic message which has pulled David, Squire Bowen, Lewis Legal and Master Isaac to London is a part of the same conspiracy. The timing of this episode was designed to catch you at your most vulnerable, my dear, when the men in your family were away and when both Lewis Legal and Will Final Testament were engaged on other business. These three squires are intent -- for some reason -- on destroying your family and destroying the Plas. And the extent of the conspiracy is quite frightening, involving the clerk to the justices and the justices themselves, as well as their wives."

"Joseph, I can hardly believe all of this!"

"You are too young, too good and too innocent, my dear friend. But you have been gravely hurt. There is now a fire within me, for you have confirmed all of my hypotheses."

Then he suddenly stood up, nodded to Mistress Griffin, and indicated that he wished to leave. She stirred herself off the floor, shook the crumbs off her lap, climbed up the ladder and unlocked the grille. Joseph said "Farewell, Martha. I will now go and set about the business of getting you out of here. I will also take my revenge upon these evil people."

His jaw was set, and there was a ferocity in his demeanour that I found quite frightening. "Oh my God," I said. "Please be careful, Joseph. I am terribly afraid that you are going to do something stupid."

"No, no. Don't you worry about me. Doing stupid things is not my style. I have my own quiet methods of bringing retribution down upon the heads of those who hurt my friends and offend justice. Now then, I have much to do, and you may not see me for several days. Keep faith, and keep smiling. Your wounds will soon be better. Tomorrow Grandma and Bessie will come to see you in the afternoon."

And he gave me a quick embrace, climbed the ladder, and was gone.

Now I am alone again, and all I can hear are the late afternoon sounds of the busy town drifting through the bars of my window. Joseph Harries has the extraordinary habit of making my mind buzz like a swarm of bees, and with so many thoughts rushing about inside my skull I fear that, once again, the night to come will be spent wide awake.

ΩΩΩΩΩΩΩΩΩ

13th August 1797

Now I have been here for almost a week. What a dismal place this is! I have heard about prisons before, but I could never have imagined the misery of being cooped up in a small space about ten feet by ten feet in extent, with a stone floor, a constant wind blowing in through the barred window and out through the grille in the ceiling, and nothing but a hard wooden bed to sit upon. It has been raining off and on for the last two days, and this has caused the walls to run with water. My clothes are damp and the blanket upon my bed is damp, and there is nothing I can do to dry things out. Yesterday I asked Mistress Griffin for a replacement blanket, but she said it was not allowed. But today two dry blankets miraculously appeared, and this lifted my spirits greatly. It seems that the three mysterious gentlemen may have been at work again, and I am now more than ever convinced that they are the three deacons from Bethesda.

I have told Mistress Griffin that I am with child; in fact, she had already guessed it since I have been sick every morning into my personal bucket. I am pleased to say that her fierceness has reduced a little. I have been pleading with her for several days to be let out for some exercise in the yard, and today she acceded to my request. She put some heavy iron manacles on my wrists and then led me up the ladder and out into the yard. There I was able to walk round in circles for fifteen minutes. I enjoyed the relative freedom, although in truth it was not quite up to the standard of a walk in the country, for I was entirely contained within a circle of walls about thirty feet high. But at least I saw the sun and the sky, and a little flock of pigeons flew down and perched on one of the battlemented towers. My jailer tells me that perhaps she will let me out again tomorrow for a walk if I behave myself.

I have had a number of brief visits (if communications through a ceiling grille can be called visits), and I am happy that the "five minutes a day" rule is not now so strictly applied. I suspect that this is because those who wish to visit me are all prepared to pass a few pence to Mistress Griffin for the privilege. It seems that she is perfectly happy with this arrangement. She prefers female visitors, presumably because this falls within prison rules; and I have had the pleasure of entertaining Grandma and Bessie, Catrin, Mary Jane and Ellie, and today Mrs Owen and Hettie. Yesterday I even had a visit from Sian Williams Gelli and three of the tenants' wives, and I was very touched that they should have given up a whole day to journey to Haverfordwest to see me.

At long last I have been allowed to receive some clean clothes; consent was given by my jailer on condition that I donated my old and filthy ones to her. She says that they will scrub up nice and clean, and that after repairing the torn fabric she will pass them on to her daughter who is about my size. I have also been allowed some food parcels to supplement my miserable prison diet; again Mistress Griffin is happy so long as the supplies are split fifty-fifty with her.

Morys has been allowed to visit me once or twice, on the grounds that he is a minister of religion, but my real guardian angel is his wife Nansi, who now calls in at the prison several times a day to cheer me up and to smuggle in small luxuries like bottles of perfume, fruit cordial drinks, quill pens and ink, and books. Her actions, and her loving and cheerful disposition make me thoroughly ashamed when I remember my reactions on first meeting her at her wedding. I thought her plain and dull; may God forgive me, for she has a quiet radiance and a great inner strength to which I can only aspire.

There is no news about any bail arrangement or of any attempts to overturn my cruel conviction at the hands of Squires Rice and Howell. I hear that Joseph is working hard on his investigations in the Newport area, and is questioning the validity of the court procedures on the day I was convicted, but he is not an attorney and his influence is limited. Grandma and Ellie are seeking the support of other justices known to be friendly with our family. But these men, upright and honest as they are, are very reluctant to interfere in Petty Session affairs outside of their own neighbourhoods and involving other magistrates. There may well be public approbation of my persecutors, but the network of influence and debt and family ties within the gentry is so complex that a sort of paralysis seems to be setting in. Nobody seems to be prepared to threaten the power base of these evil men. All the local squires, so far as I can gather, say "Bad business about Mistress Morgan" and roll their eyes and tap their fingers on their desks, and then get on with the harvest.

The more I think about it, the more impotent I feel and the more angry I become. If only David, Squire Bowen, Lewis Legal and Grandpa Isaac were here! They are real men, and they get things done. But they are stuck two hundred and fifty miles away in London, possibly at this very moment embroiled in their wretched court case. Apart from them and my dear friend Joseph, who is doing what he can, there does not seem to be a single man left in Pembrokeshire who has the spine to tackle the villains who seek to destroy me.

ΩΩΩΩΩΩΩΩΩ

14th August 1797

Last night I was in a very melancholic mood, and the stripes on my back were still very painful, so I slept only in snatches. But then, just as it was getting light, I had a disjointed dream about an elegant military gentleman wielding a sword and driving crowds of French soldiers into the sea. I sat up with a start and knew that the man in the dream was Lord Cawdor. I took this as an omen and an inspiration, and cursed myself that his name had not come into my mind at an earlier stage of my imprisonment. At once I tore two pages out of my diary and penned the following letter:

Haverfordwest Gaol, 14th day of August 1797

To the Hon Lord Cawdor of Stackpole

Sir,

We have not met, and I trust that you will forgive my impertinence in writing to you. My name is Martha Morgan, and I am Mistress of Plas Ingli near Newport. As I write, I am incarcerated in a foul cell in the bowels of Haverfordwest Castle, having been cruelly misused.

I have been falsely and maliciously convicted for grand larceny by Squires Rice and Howell sitting at the Petty Sessions in Pentre Ifan House. This happened on the 6th day of August. I have been publicly whipped and humiliated through the streets of Newport, and I am now remanded in custody to await my fate at the Quarter Sessions in Haverfordwest in the middle of September. The stripes on my back are beginning to heal, but I am with child, and the morning sickness which afflicts me compounds the misery which I feel about my prospects.

I swear before you and before God that I am innocent of the charge on which I have been convicted; and I further declare that in my belief Squires Rice and Howell, and their families, and Master Ifan Beynon, clerk to the justices, are involved in a conspiracy to pervert the course of justice. I believe that Mistress Rice has lied under oath in order to secure my conviction.

These are serious allegations, and I make them with a heavy heart, but I know them to be true and will maintain them until my dying day.

Attempts by my family to secure my release on bail have fallen on deaf ears. Also, I fear that my dear husband David and his friends (Squire Bowen of Llwyngwair, Master Lewis the lawyer from Fishguard, and Isaac Morgan of Plas Ingli) are in London to deal with some litigation about ownership of the Plas, and they are all quite ignorant of my plight.

I am at my wit's end, and know not what more I can do from my prison cell in order to secure justice. But I recall that my husband once did you a small service on the occasion of the French Invasion at Pencaer, and that you encouraged him to turn to you for assistance in the event of a pressing need.

Sir, I feel that our family is currently in desperate need of assistance, and I beg of you to show us the hand of friendship. If you cannot help, I fear that I will personally go to the gallows and that our family will be destroyed by the evil that has been done.

Your obedient servant
Martha Morgan

I knew that Billy and Shemi were due to bring me some fresh food supplies during the course of the day, and I determined that Billy should be sent on an errand of mercy with the letter in his bag. By midday they had still not arrived, and when Mistress Griffin brought me my gruel and black bread I pleaded with her not to turn them away if they arrived at the prison entrance during the afternoon. The promise of half of the food parcel was sufficient to secure her cooperation, and I was overjoyed when, at about three of the clock, I saw Billy and Shemi grinning down through my ceiling grille after handing the food parcel over to my jailer as a deposit. We exchanged pleasantries for a while, and in truth I was very pleased to see them, for they occupy a special place in my affections.

But then we got down to business. I pulled my heavy bed into the middle of the room. I stood on it and reached upwards at my full height, and Billy lay on his stomach on the grille and stretched his arm downwards. Thus I just managed to pass my letter to him. "Now then, Billy, forget about returning to the Plas tonight. I want you to take this letter and place it personally in the hands of Lord Cawdor of Stackpole. Don't let anybody else touch it."

"Very good, Mistress Martha," replied Billy, plunging the letter deep into a pocket on the inside of his jacket. "But what does his lordship look like?"

"I daresay you will know him when you find him."

"And I fear, Mistress, that I don't have even the faintest idea where Stackpole is."

"Don't you worry too much about that. I am afraid I am as ignorant as you as to the whereabouts of his estate, but it is somewhere in the south of the county. Lord Cawdor may be at home, or he may be in Tenby for the social season, or he may be out yachting. God help us if you can't find him. Take Shemi with you. Go to my brother Morys at the Bethesda manse and borrow his two horses. You may also need to borrow some money in case you are away for several days. Can you do it?"

"Of course, Mistress!" said Billy.

"No problem, Mistress Martha," said young Shemi. "Just you count on us. We will move heaven and earth to get you out of there."

Then Mistress Griffin appeared and chased them away. By now my two knights in shining armour have gone riding southwards in a cloud of dust on their mercy mission. I have enjoyed my half of the food parcel which they delivered, but I have to say that my one real desire at the moment is the taste of freedom.

ΩΩΩΩΩΩΩΩΩ

18th August 1797

The miracle for which I have so fervently prayed has happened. I am at home at the Plas, luxuriating in clean clothes scented with lavender, fresh cotton sheets upon my bed, and vases of late summer flowers placed upon every shelf, chest and window sill. My dressing-room window is wide open, and I can smell the strange dusty fragrance of August and hear the hum of pollen-gathering insects. Perhaps I am in heaven.

Bessie is singing downstairs as she cleans the dining room. She is clearly not too upset with me, for the first thing I did when I came in through the door yesterday was to scold her for not beating the dust out of my tapestry more frequently, front and back.

Where do I start? I will pass over my last two days in prison, for they were days marked by brief visits from friends and family and long periods of gloom. I became increasingly depressed as news arrived of my father's failed representations to the Lord Lieutenant for my release on bail, and my brother's failure to secure a writ against Squires Rice and Howell for false imprisonment. Yesterday I became convinced that nothing could now save me from the gallows, and I was contemplating my fate while gazing into a bowl of pea soup at lunchtime when I heard a jangling of metal up above me in the prison yard. I recognized the sound of Mistress Griffin's keys, and sure enough her ruddy face appeared above my grille. "Mistress Martha!" she grinned. "Gather up your things! Time to go home!"

I could hardly believe it. She unlocked the grille and threw it aside, let down the ladder and came down to help me. Then she gave me a great bear-hug of an embrace, which greatly surprised me, for she had thus far kept her distance and kept her emotions in check. I was so touched that I burst into tears, and she had to console me as a mother would a small child. "Sorry to see you go, I am," she said, wiping away her own tears, "for in me own way I've grown quite attached to you. I was greatly afeared, Mistress, that it was your fate to be strung up on them old gallows. But God bless you, for now you are free."

So with my pathetic bundle of possessions I scrambled up the ladder and out into the yard. I could hardly believe that I had no iron manacles on my wrists or ankles. I daresay I looked like a scarecrow, with matted hair, wild eyes and bare feet. Mistress Griffin led me through a heavy door and across another yard, and then showed me into the jailer's office. There I was met by Lord Cawdor. He motioned that the head jailer and Mistress Griffin should leave us alone, and they left obediently. He was just as David had described him, with a boyish face and upright posture. He was immaculately dressed in a maroon frock coat, and he smelt of camphor. He bowed deeply, held out his hand for mine, and on receiving it kissed it with a flourish! I was covered in confusion, and did not know whether to curtsey or cry.

"My dear Mistress Morgan!" he said. "What a pleasure to meet you! You have been most cruelly used. Most cruelly used indeed. Are you well?"

I could see that his question was an honest one and not simply a formality. So I said "I thank you, sir, for your concern. I have to admit to feeling weak, and filthy, and miserable, and hungry, and lonely, and occasionally sick, but otherwise I am quite well."

He laughed and said "I hear what you say. But I also see a vital spark in your eye, and I perceive that it will take more than a draughty dungeon and a spell in solitary confinement to get the better of the young Mistress of Plas Ingli!"

Then he pulled up a chair for me to sit on, and sat down on another chair, facing me. "I am sorry I took so long to rescue you," he said. "But certain formalities are required. Let me start at the beginning. Your excellent servants found me three days since. I was out in the middle of the Pembroke River enjoying luncheon on the yacht of an old friend when two young fellows came rowing up, shouting in Welsh at the tops of their voices. My servants tried to shoo them away, but they would have none of it, and they said they were on a mission of life and death, and that somebody very dear to them would certainly die if Lord Cawdor did not receive, hand to hand, a certain message which they were carrying. I overheard all of this and agreed to take the message, although in truth people send me life and death messages every day of the week. I invited the fellows on board and took the message. What were their names again?"

"Billy and Shemi."

"Ah yes. Billy and Shemi. Excellent fellows. Do you know that they had been to Stackpole and Tenby and Freshwater East before tracking me down to Pembroke? I like to see men with initiative. When I read your letter, my dear Mistress Morgan, I was dumbfounded. I recalled the strength and determination of your young husband when he saved me from disaster near Goodwick last winter, and I recalled my offer of help should it be needed. A gentleman never forgets his debts. And when I read of the deep pit of humiliation into which you had been cast by those evil squires Rice and Howell I went right off my honeyed ham and new potatoes. I recalled a whole range of other humiliations which they and their colleague Alban Watkins have heaped upon other innocent folk in the north of the county. Such men bring both the gentry and the law into ridicule and disrepute."

"I thought, sir, that your estates were in the south of the county?"

"Oh no, my dear Mistress Morgan. Through marriage and inheritance I actually own several farms north of the mountains, and I visit them frequently. I suspect that very shortly I will own at least three more. To get back to the business in hand, I was greatly struck by the passion and pathos of your letter, and immediately decided to act upon it. You will understand that I could not immediately accept that everything in your letter was true. It was, and is, almost inconceivable that a woman of your station should be incarcerated in this foul place, let alone horse-whipped through the streets. First, I questioned your servants in great detail as to what had happened on the day you were apprehended, scourged and thrown into gaol. Satisfied that something was gravely amiss, I returned to the shore with your men Billy and Shemi, thanked them for their perseverance and told them to return the horses to Haverfordwest and get back to Plas Ingli. Then I went straight to my lawyer in Pembroke and looked into the affairs of the Pentre Ifan, Llannerch and Henllys estates. As I suspected, deeply, deeply in debt, all three, and indeed on the verge of bankruptcy. I found out who the main creditors were. Some of them owed me substantial sums of money, and I prepared letters to them in which I gently encouraged them to call in their debts from these three estates in view of the fact that I might shortly be calling in mine. Perfectly legal and gentlemanly, Mistress Morgan. I refer to it as the "domino effect" for the calling in of one big debt instantly triggers off a whole host of other little demands for money owed."

"You seem to know much about the affairs of other estates, sir," said I.

"Indeed I do," replied Lord Cawdor. "I know all about Plas Ingli too, and I am very impressed. At any rate, armed with this essential knowledge I went to Haverfordwest this morning in my coach to investigate the records of the Petty Sessions from the Newport area in the Lord Lieutenant's office. I have to say, my dear lady, that I was appalled by what I saw. I saw case after case where vicious punishments had been visited upon the innocent or meted out for the perpetration of the most minor of crimes, and there were at least six cases where the word "corruption" was writ large in invisible ink across the court records. The names of Rice, Howell and Beynon figured prominently. With the approval of the Lord Lieutenant himself, I then took the coach across the mountain to Newport and paid a social visit upon the Rice family. I will not divulge the essence of my conversation with the squire and his wife, but when I left I had these two pieces of paper in my hand."

He waved two densely handwritten pages before me. "Are they confessions?" I asked in my innocence.

"No, no. They will perhaps come later. One of them is a signed and witnessed affidavit from Mistress Maria Rice dropping her charge against you and then stating that the whole matter of the ruby brooch was an unfortunate mistake..."

I gave a hollow laugh and intervened "Some mistake, sir, as I think you might agree?"

"Quite so. A feeble document, but sufficient for my purpose. The other one is an order from a sitting of the Petty Sessions this very morning at Pentre Ifan, with Justice Rice presiding and clerk Ifan Beynon in attendance, countermanding the order which remanded you in custody in Haverfordwest Gaol. This piece of paper is needed by the head jailer before he will let you go."

"What a coincidence! I had not realized that a sitting was due today."

Descent into Hell

"My dear lady, the Petty Sessions are convened as and when they are required. I gently suggested to Squire Rice that it might be a good idea to fetch the clerk and convene a court this very morning, and of course he agreed with me. Now I see you are very tired, and I have gabbled along like an old turkey for far too long. I will give this order to the jailer. Off you go. I suggest that you go down to see your brother. He lives, I believe, not a stone's throw from here?"

"Yes sir. In the Bethesda chapel manse."

"Good, good. Get a warm bath and a change of clothes. If you need a doctor for your injuries, call Doctor Wilkinson from High Street and tell him to send me the bill. In two hours' time my coach will call for you and will convey you back to Plas Ingli. As for myself, I have other legal matters to pursue arising from my investigations in Pembroke, Haverfordwest and Newport. I will come and visit you and your husband next time I am north of the mountains. But rest assured, Mistress Morgan, that you will not be troubled again by Squires Rice, Watkins and Howell. I bid you good day!"

And before I could say anything at all in the way of thanks, he bowed deeply and swept out of the office. Mistress Griffin returned and found me shaking like a leaf. She wrapped a thick cloak around me and offered her arm, and found me some slippers for my feet. Then she led me gently down Castle Hill, past St Martin's Church, and to the sanctuary of the Bethesda Manse. There I met Morys and Nansi and my dear parents, who first of all thought that they were looking at a ghost. They found it hard to believe that I had suddenly been released on the flimsy evidence of one piece of paper; but I explained that the paper was far less flimsy than that which had put me into prison in the first place, and that the jailer might have been impressed, to some degree, by the hand which carried it.

Our reunion was as emotional as one might expect within any tight-knit family. I was given a steaming and frothy bath, a stomach full of manna from heaven (it is very useful to have a cleric as a brother), and more loving care and attention then was good for me. I borrowed some clothes from Nansi. Then I asked Morys to call in the three chapel deacons. They arrived and admitted, somewhat bashfully, that they were indeed the three gentlemen who quietly ministered, day after day and week after week, to the needs of those who were incarcerated in the Gaol. They were overjoyed at my release, and they did not complain when I fulfilled my vow and gave each of them a big kiss on the cheek.

Descent into Hell

20th August 1797

Tomorrow is my first wedding anniversary, but there is no great feeling of celebration in my heart, for my beloved David is still in London. There has been no word from him, and the threat of eviction and penury still hangs over us like a thunder cloud. But I have gained some comfort from the words of Lord Cawdor, and dare to hope that Squire Watkins will get his just deserts when confronted in court by David and Grandpa and their expert colleagues. For the sake of my family and my friends and my unborn child I must be of good cheer.

In truth there is much to be cheerful about. The memory of my homecoming, after ten days in prison, still gladdens my heart and brings a smile to my lips. As I rode over the mountain in Lord Cawdor's private coach I felt like Cinderella going to the ball. It was evening, and a golden sun was settling into the sea off the tip of Pencaer. We rattled down the track towards Newport and Cilgwyn, scattering sheep and lambs in all directions. I was dreadfully tired, and the stripes on my back were still giving me pain, but every sight, every sound, every ephemeral scent brought me the greatest of pleasure. After only ten days of deprivation! Dear God, I thought, what must the small pleasures of freedom mean to those who are incarcerated for months or even years?

I became so lost in my reverie that the Plas crept up on me. Suddenly the coach stopped. One of Lord Cawdor's coachmen opened the door, and I stepped out, feeling as stiff as an ancient matron, onto the familiar dusty slate slabs of the yard. Mrs Owen poked her head out of the kitchen door to see whose conveyance had just arrived, and when she saw me she simply stared. She literally could not believe her own eyes. And then she screamed "Oh! Oh! Mistress Martha! It is you! It is you!" And then she dithered on the doorstep, not sure whether to go back inside to tell everybody else about my arrival or to rush out and embrace me. Then they all abandoned their supper and came tumbling out -- Grandma Jane, Bessie, Hettie, Billy and Shemi -- and there was a pandemonium of tears, laughter, embraces, and everybody talking at once.

We insisted that the coachmen should stop the night at the Plas, for it was now getting dark and the road to Haverfordwest is not at all suitable for nocturnal expeditions involving heavy coaches. They were quite happy at the prospect of a night away from home, and Billy and Shemi took them round to the stable where they unhitched the four horses, wiped them down and stabled them for the night. Soon we were all settled into the kitchen exchanging news of the past extraordinary ten days. Mrs Owen conjured up cold meats and good cheeses and wheat bread and cider and ale from the pantry, followed by crystallized fruits and blackberry custard. The others drank and ate heartily, and indeed became somewhat inebriated. But the mad chatter became too much for me. I had little appetite for food or drink, and I appeared so weary that Bessie at last packed me off to bed.

My last memory of the evening is one of sheer bliss, as I sank into my old familiar feather mattress with a silk nightgown around my body and a fresh cotton sheet tucked under my chin. The sounds of animated conversation and happy laughter rolled up the stairs. Outside my window a garrulous tawny owl told the world that he too belonged on the stony slopes of Angel Mountain.

ΩΩΩΩΩΩΩΩ

21st August 1797

I am feeling much better. Since last Saturday I have slept a great deal, and I am gradually regaining my appetite. The red weals across my back are healing. I am endlessly pampered by Bessie, and I have told her everything about my experiences in prison and about the circumstances surrounding my release. In turn she has confided to me that she is in love, not with her long-standing admirer Dai Darjeeling but with Benji Walter, the corn merchant from Parrog. Apparently, following my humiliation behind the whipping cart and my incarceration in Haverfordwest Gaol, an endless stream of people came up to the Plas from Newport and Parrog to offer help with the harvest or whatever else needed to be done. Most of their kind offers had to be declined with thanks, but Benji insisted on helping with the carting of the harvest, and it appears that a slight attraction between him and Bessie turned, over the sheaves and the stubble of the barley field, into something much more beautiful. I am delighted for her, and told her so. She is a dear, dear friend, and she deserves all the happiness in the world.

One other wonderful thing has happened today. A horseman galloped up the driveway shortly after breakfast and delivered a letter from David, miraculously in time for our wedding anniversary. I took the letter inside and sat down at the kitchen table, with Grandma and the servants around me. We all knew that it contained news of the court case in London. I hardly dared open it. My fingers trembled and I could feel my heart racing. But at last I broke the seal and unfolded the paper. Much to my embarrassment, I had to read the letter out aloud. This is what it said:

Boar's Head Inn, Bow Street, London
14th August 1797
My Dearest Martha,

I love you so much that I can hardly bear to be away from you. I hope that you receive this on our wedding anniversary. If you do, remember me every minute of the day. My heart is filled with your beauty and your grace, and I shall rush home to taste your lips and fold you into my arms just as soon as I can.

I trust that you are well and that life goes on at home quietly and without incident. I envy you the gentle routines of the Plas, for London is a dirty, smelly, violent place, and I cannot wait to get out of it.

At this point I am afraid to say that I broke down and wept, quite overcome by his expression of love and by the sudden realization that he knew nothing of the appalling things which have happened here since he and Grandpa left. Bessie held me in her arms, and Grandma had to take over the reading of the letter. It continued thus:

The Plas is safe and Watkins is defeated!

Then Grandma, who has been like a rock in the midst of a maelstrom, broke down and wept as well, and I realized what a knife edge she had been living on for the past three weeks. I embraced her, and our tears melted together. And then they turned into tears of joy, for the servants were dancing around the table and shouting and laughing. At last we all calmed down, and I was able to resume my reading of the letter, as follows:

We have had a great victory in the court, thanks, it must be said, to the wonderful skills of Lewis Legal and the quite extraordinary network of contacts maintained by Squire Bowen. On our arrival in town on the night of 10th August we found an inn and immediately started our investigations. We called first on two of John Bowen's old legal friends, and within two hours they had discovered the name of the judge for the hearing, the whereabouts of Squire Watkins, the name of the clerk of the Chancery Court and the address of the attorney named Thomas Elias.

Next day we set to work on the case. We put a spy onto Alban Watkins and told him to follow him through the day. He earned his shilling very easily, for Watkins was clearly not expecting us to turn up, and spent the whole day in various coffee houses and establishments of ill repute! Lewis Legal and Grandpa went to the Chancery Court and met the clerk, and asked for prior sight of the documents which would be used at the hearing. He refused, so Master Lewis had to get an injunction forcing him to release them. When they saw the document said to have been written by my father it was immediately obvious that it was a forgery; the handwriting was quite unlike that on the old documents which Master Lewis had with him, and the signature was a wild fabrication.

Squire Bowen and I went to the Law Courts and discovered that the so-called attorney called Thomas Elias was not a qualified attorney at all, but an insignificant legal clerk with a reputation for forging documents and defrauding innocent litigants who have come into London from the countryside. We then discovered that the trial judge was a cousin of Squire Watkins who had himself narrowly escaped removal from the bench on a number of occasions and who had a very colourful private life. And as for the clerk to the Chancery Court, one Julius Smyllie, we found three ex-attorneys who had nothing to lose by giving us sworn affidavits to the effect that he had accepted bribes for "fixing" claims over disputed property. Squire Bowen made copious notes about the careers of all three gentlemen. Then, when I returned to the inn to catch up with the news from Grandpa and Lewis Legal, Squire Bowen disappeared into the back streets of London with the intention of conducting further business.

I fear that the hearing in the Chancery Court was a sad disappointment to us. We arrived early and met four other gentlemen whom Squire Bowen had asked to appear as witnesses. When Alban Watkins arrived he almost fainted when he saw us. He looked round like a cornered rat, but he received no assistance from anybody. Indeed, he found that his cousin had been replaced by another judge, that clerk Julius Smyllie had gone missing and had been replaced by his assistant, and that there was no sign at all of Thomas Elias. The hearing lasted for only a few minutes. At the outset our attorney entered a strong protest that the case had not gone straight to the Great Sessions in Haverfordwest, and argued that the matter in dispute did not fall under the jurisdiction of the Court of Chancery. The judge nodded, but said nothing. Then Squire Watkins gave his evidence in a state of high

Descent into Hell

nervousness and was torn to shreds by Lewis Legal. The so-called "1792 document" supposedly signed by my father was produced for the court and was shown immediately to be a fake. Lewis proved that the only genuine thing upon it was Squire Rice's signature. The "legal opinion" signed by Thomas Elias was then interpreted by the judge as a fraudulent attempt by a clerk to portray himself as a qualified attorney. And the summons and eviction order (copies of which we received in the post) were immediately impounded by the judge as documents issued in the perpetration of a crime.

Much to the disappointment of Squire Bowen and Lewis Legal, we were not even asked by the judge to present our case. Instead he banged his desk and thundered "Case dismissed!" Then he pointed to Alban Watkins and said "And you, sir, are under arrest. I have seldom, if ever, seen such a crude attempt to pursue a fraudulent claim on another man's property. Charges will be prepared by the acting clerk to this court, who has heard today's proceedings. You will be remanded in custody, and your case will be heard not in this court but in the criminal court at the Old Bailey. I will now also issue warrants for the arrest of Benjamin Rice of Pentre Ifan and Thomas Elias and Julius Smyllie of this town. All three are parties to this crime, and you will be tried in the same court and on the same day for criminal conspiracy."

And that was that. Squire Watkins is in prison awaiting trial. The constables are scouring London for his accomplices. The judge who had been lined up by our dearly beloved neighbour has taken early retirement. And two special constables have been dispatched to effect the arrest of Benjamin Rice. They may well arrive at Pentre Ifan and take him away on the very day that you receive this letter, for they will probably travel in the mail coach.

Sadly, our business here is not complete. The date for the trial of Alban Watkins and his accomplices has been set for Monday 30th August, and the judge has formally requested that we should all appear as witnesses. He does not expect that the case against the conspirators will last more than one day. My dearest Martha, I long to be with you to celebrate our great victory, but if we travel home now we will simply have to turn around and return to London straight away. This would not be sensible. Instead we will go and stay with Squire Bowen's sister in Hampstead, and perhaps do some exploring of the city. I can hardly afford it, but I am minded to do a little shopping of gowns and bonnets if I can obtain some sound advice as to the latest fashions.

We will celebrate together when we return. Every ounce of love in my body is yours, and yours alone. Look after yourself and our little baby, and try to avoid excessive excitement. Tell Ellie that her father will write. Grandpa sends his love and kisses to Grandma, and says he will write tomorrow. Affectionate greetings to everybody else at the Plas.

Your ever loving husband
David.

After the high emotion of the morning connected to the reading of David's letter, our pattern of work on the estate has been somewhat disorganized. I have been resting, but the others have been going about their tasks in a state of high euphoria. No matter -- the harvest is done and the gleaners are making the most of what is left. This evening we have been celebrating, and I have to admit to taking a glass of wine or two. In the circumstances, my husband and my baby will probably forgive me.

ΩΩΩΩΩΩΩΩΩΩΩ

22nd August 1797

Today has been another warm, bright day, and I have been out picking blackberries in the hedgerows. My back still pains me, but I hope that within the next three days I will be well enough for some weeding and harvesting in my little garden, which has been sorely neglected.

It has been another day of turbulent emotions. News came this morning that the world has started to fall in on the Watkins, Howell and Rice families. As expected, Squire Rice was apprehended yesterday afternoon by the special constables from London, and was taken away only half an hour before two more special constables arrived at Pentre Ifan with arrest warrants signed by Lord Cawdor. One of them was for the Squire himself, based on a charge of conspiracy to pervert the course of justice and another charge of false imprisonment. The constables were greatly upset when they found that the Squire had been hauled off to London, for this deprived them of their fee of five shillings. The other warrant was for the arrest of Mistress Rice, on a charge of perjury or lying under oath. She was taken away in a state of collapse, and Hettie arrived with the news that she had apparently gone quite out of her mind even before the constables arrived.

Descent into Hell

Thomas Tucker Penrhiw came up to the Plas after breakfast to tell us that news of Squire Watkins' imprisonment in London has reached the big house at Llannerch. He says that Mistress Watkins and daughters Rose and Daisy were writing out invitations to a celebration party (presumably to celebrate the acquisition of Plas Ingli) when the news reached them, and he says that the house has now descended into utter panic. The three of them are packing their bags for a rapid departure for London, and Master Tucker thinks that we will never see them again. I do not know whether I should laugh or cry.

Mrs Owen went shopping in Newport early this morning, and came back with news that Constable John Wilson has been "requested" by Lord Cawdor to serve arrest warrants on clerk Ifan Beynon and Squire George Howell of Henllys. Both are charged with conspiracy to pervert the course of justice, with the false imprisonment of "a lady, viz Mistress Martha Morgan of Plas Ingli", and with maliciously wounding and causing great distress to the same lady. Master Beynon is already in custody in Newport, and will be taken to Haverfordwest following a Petty Sessions to be held tomorrow. Squire Howell has gone missing, and the same gang of special constables who took me by force from the Plas a fortnight ago are now scouring the countryside around Henllys and Velindre Farchog in the hope of apprehending him. Mistress Howell and her son and daughter have gone rushing off to Carmarthen in the family coach and are apparently greatly afraid that the law will catch up with them there. I know not what misdemeanours they may have committed, but you do not flee unless there is something to flee from.

I was trying to come to terms with this deluge of hot news when Catrin, Mary Jane and Ellie arrived simultaneously, having previously agreed with each other to turn up at the Plas at eleven of the clock. What a reunion we enjoyed! Of course there were tears and embraces, and we four had so much to talk about that we almost missed lunch. We sat in the orchard and chatted beneath my favourite pear tree. They already knew most of what had happened to me, for indeed the three of them had kindly moved in to the Plas and had helped out in the first difficult days following my arrest. But there were many details to be filled in, and all had different perspectives on my story. I found, much to my surprise, that I have developed something of a reputation in the community, and that there has been a great upwelling of affection for the Morgan family, for the Plas and for me personally. I gather that my humiliation and imprisonment are being used by the poor people in a campaign highlighting the virtues of the old and gentle manner of running estates as against the vicious and petty methods employed by Rice, Watkins, Howell and others. I am not at all sure that I want to be a symbol or an icon for anything, and said as much to my friends, but Catrin said "Don't you worry, Martha *bach*. They will soon realize that you are as human as the rest of us! In a few days' time this business will be over and done with, and the gossip in the town will be about the size of Mistress Jones' cabbages and the outrageous colour of Mistress Ifans' bonnet!" And we roared with laughter and carried on with our chatting.

They left at two of the clock, having observed that I was very tired. They promised to call again in three days' time. I slept for a couple of hours, and then was awakened by the sound of a pony trotting into the yard. I knew at once that it was Joseph coming to pay his respects and to rejoice in my freedom, so I dressed quickly and rushed downstairs. I gave him a warm embrace. "Oh Joseph!" I cried. "How wonderful to see you!"

"My dear Martha," said he. "You are looking much, much better already. Well done. Well done. Are you getting enough rest? And how are your wounds coming along? Healing nicely, I hope? And the baby? Everything all right? Morning sickness not troubling you too much, I hope? And as for....."

"Calm down, Joseph," I laughed. "One thing at a time! Come and sit with me in my garden, and I will tell you everything."

So we went and sat on the bench next to my little clusters of lavender and thyme, and talked and talked. With Catrin, Mary Jane and Ellie, before and during lunch, there had been four people all speaking at the same time; but now my dear wise friend and I talked one to one, calmly and with a sort of serene discipline which Joseph seems to carry around with him.

He apologized for his failure to get me out of prison, but explained that none of the justices he approached would listen to the strong evidence of conspiracy and false imprisonment which he presented to them, and none of them would sign a bill of complaint. He became convinced that justices are very reluctant to involve themselves in the affairs of other justices. He said he was at his wit's end when news reached him that I had been released. "I see my failure in this regard as a blot on my copybook," he said, "although I gain some consolation from the fact that neither your father or your brother could obtain your release in spite of valiant efforts and contacts in high places." But then he brightened and said "I do, however, take the greatest delight in the fact that you got yourself out of prison, by your own initiative and by using your own wits, regardless of the appalling circumstances in which you found yourself. Lord Cawdor helped, of course, but if you had not written to him he would be in ignorance of the affair to this day, and you would still be in your filthy dungeon. Well done, Martha. Well done." And he looked me in the eyes as a proud father would a child, and held my hand.

Then the conversation turned to the three squires who had jointly been responsible for the visitation of a host of ills upon me and my family. "When you left me in prison," I said, "you looked so fierce that I feared for their safety. What did you do to them?"

"Don't you worry, Martha," he chuckled. "I did nothing cruel or illegal. I simply visited Squire Rice and Squire Howell in turn and insisted on handing each of them an envelope in person. I said to each of them "Sir, I have a very personal message for you. I will be grateful if you will read it carefully and take full account of what it says." And then I looked each of them in the eye, and bowed, and took my leave. Perfectly simple and gentlemanly. Squire Watkins was in London, but I surmised that his wife was intimately involved in his nefarious activities, and so I went to Llannerch and saw her instead."

"And what did the messages say?"

"Each one said *"I am watching you, for I know what you have done. Signed, Joseph Harries Werndew."* That's all! Now who could possibly take offence at that?" And he slapped his knees and bellowed with delight.

"Joseph! You are very cruel."

"Not at all, my dear Martha. The cruelty is all theirs. It is not mine to condone or to condemn. But I have found in the past that my reputation is quite sufficient to expose guilt where it exists. By sowing a small seed in the mind of a guilty person it can grow and grow until it can no longer be contained. If Squire Howell, and Squire Rice, and Mistress Watkins, choose to believe that I have placed curses upon them, that is a matter for them."

"Oh dear," I said. "Such terrible things are happening all around me! Did you hear that Mistress Rice has gone out of her mind?"

"That does not surprise me. I understand that there is some very erratic behaviour going on just now in the Watkins and Howell families also. Guilt is writ large on the faces of all those involved."

Joseph tried to cheer me up, but in truth my emotions were, and still are, very disturbed. Now he has gone home, and I am sitting in my dressing room. After the happy laughter of today, I am now overwhelmed with tiredness, and I feel thoroughly miserable. News came this evening that all those owed money by the Llannerch, Pentre Ifan and Henllys estates have called in their debts. Lord Cawdor has obviously been at work. The three families are destroyed, and their estates are insolvent. No doubt all three will be acquired by Lord Cawdor himself or by some other powerful squire. Another message came with Billy when he returned from the Castle Inn. The body of Squire Howell has been found hanging from a tree in Pengelli Woods. There is no doubt that he has taken his own life. Am I supposed to remain cheerful in such circumstances?

ΩΩΩΩΩΩΩΩΩΩΩ

16. Desecration

24th August 1797

This is the most difficult thing that I have ever had to write since the day that I started my diary just over one year ago. But I have to do it for the sake of my own sanity.

Yesterday morning I awoke and immediately felt very distressed. I realized that Squire Howell's death was likely to be followed by several others. Such is the severity of the charges against Squire Rice, Mistress Rice, and Squire Watkins, and so strong is the evidence against them, that they will all surely hang. I suppose I may be required to give evidence against them. Ifan Beynon, Thomas Elias and Julius Smyllie may also hang, or at the very least be transported to the colonies.

When I thought of all this I was desperate for some help in unravelling the strange and cruel ways of the world. I knew that I would get sympathy and a degree of understanding from Grandma and the servants if I had chosen to talk things over with them, but I knew that they all had jobs to do and that they would not help me to clear my head. Then I wondered whether I should go over the mountain and talk to Joseph; but I concluded that he has a simple and almost amoral view of the world which differs in some respects from my own. I wished that I had paid more attention to Rector Devonald's droning sermons or tried to understand the ancient prayers repeated endlessly in Cilgwyn Church. Thoughts about salvation and redemption, sacrifice and reward, violence and peace, justice and retribution, wickedness and virtue chased about inside my head, and at last I sought solace in a little hymn book which Ellie gave me some time ago. I found it in the library and read some hymns by Master Charles Wesley, and this gave me a degree of comfort. I copied two of them down and promised myself that I would give more thought to the words on another occasion.

Then, feeling somewhat more composed, I settled down after breakfast and wrote a long and loving letter to David. I told him all about my adventures, and sought, over and again, to reassure him that I am well and that our baby is safe. As I wrote, how I longed for his return! I addressed

Desecration

and sealed the letter and gave it to Shemi, and asked him to get it onto the next mail coach to Cardigan and thence to London. Then I took a light lunch, and since I was feeling stronger and since the day was warm and dry with a southerly breeze, I decided on the spur of the moment that I would climb up the mountain.

Bessie helped me to dress, and raised her eyebrows when I said that I would not wear my stays. In truth I could not bear them digging into my lacerated back. I told her that today I had no intention of spending time in civilized company, and surmised that the ravens on the mountain would not be too concerned with etiquette. Then I said that I would not be long. I climbed slowly up through the thick summer bracken to Ffynnon Brynach, anointed myself with the cool fresh water, and scrambled on among the bluestone boulders which might have led me to the summit. But then I was overcome with a sense of great weariness which afflicted my soul as much as my body, and I realized that I needed a period of quiet contemplation in my cave. I turned left, passed between the high pillars of rock and saw the slit of the cave entrance near the little rowan tree. The pair of old ravens wheeled overhead with their five offspring, all croaking their alarm signal. By the time I had realized that they were worried not about me, but about someone else, it was too late.

As I stepped into the dark entrance of the cave I was grabbed by a pair of strong hands. I knew immediately that they were the hands of Moses Lloyd of Cwmgloyn. I was outraged that this man, of all men, should have defiled this most secret and sacred of places. I screamed and fought like a cat, but there was not much strength in me, and at last he threw his whole weight on top of me and forced me to the ground. I have never been so terrified in my life -- not even during my whipping in Newport, not even when I saw the battle in the sky. Then I thought of the child in my womb and recognized that I must not fight, but think. I closed my eyes and let my body go limp, and this probably saved both me and my baby.

My assailant was breathing hard, taking in great gulps of air. He rolled off me and took a minute or two to regain his composure. Then he seized me under my armpits and dragged me deeper into the cave. He laid me out on something soft, which I thought might be a cloak or a blanket. I kept my eyes closed. He tied a rope around my right wrist and attached it to some fixed point in the cave. Then I felt that he was doing the same to my left wrist. He pulled the rope tight, and too late I realized that he was stretching me out in some grotesque imitation of a crucifixion. I opened my eyes and kicked out with my feet and tried to free myself from the ropes, but he was too strong for me, and the more I struggled the more intense the pain became as the ropes bit into my skin. I also felt a searing pain on my back, as the whipping wounds, so near to healing, opened up again and soaked my dress with blood.

I realized now what his real intention was, and I thought that so long as my legs were free he would find it difficult if not impossible to use me. So I kept on kicking out, and indeed made contact with the side of his head on one occasion. He shouted "Damn you, Martha Morgan! Lie still, damn you!" He became more and more furious, and at last he hit me with his fist across my right cheek. I was momentarily stunned, but he did what I wanted by taking another rope and binding my ankles together. Then I thought of my baby again, and stopped struggling.

Several minutes passed as we both regained our breath. I looked at him, and saw that he was leaning back against the wall of the cave with his eyes closed. He looked wild and unkempt, with a long stringy beard. Because of his missing front teeth, he looked old rather than young. His clothes were dirty, but they were not the clothes he had worn when he left the Plas. They were more like the clothes of a gentleman, with woollen breeches and stockings, a loose-fitting cotton shirt, and an embroidered waistcoat. I wondered where he had got them from. I looked round the cave, and realized that he had been in residence for some time. There were traces of a fire in the far corner, and some pots and pans. There was a leather bucket containing cold water, and a sack containing vegetables. On a slab of rock there was a half-eaten loaf of black bread and a dead rabbit. The floor of the cave was well-trodden, and my little bed of moss had been heaped up into a corner where it had presumably been used as a pillow. Again I experienced a sense of revulsion and desolation at the thought of this man living and sleeping in my private sanctuary in the heart of the mountain, where once Saint Brynach had prayed to his God.

I saw that Moses had opened his eyes and was looking at me. "So, Mistress Morgan of Plas Ingli, we meet again. What a pleasure, to be sure, although the circumstances leave much to be desired."

I did not reply. "So. Not even a formal greeting," he sneered. "I had heard that the Mistress of the Plas, the greatest beauty in West Wales, was always ready with a flashing smile and a cheerful word."

Desecration

There was a long silence. Still I said nothing. "I have been waiting for you here, off and on, for most of this month," he said nonchalantly, cleaning the dirt out of his finger nails. "My plans were disrupted when you were whipped through the street and hauled off to prison. That was a bad business, and I had no part in it. I told Squire Howell that I did not want you injured. When I realized you had been released I came back here again. I knew that you would come up here sooner or later, to commune with the saints and the angels."

Now I could restrain myself no longer. "You knew about this cave?" I asked.

"Now that's more like it. A conversation at last. Of course I knew about the cave. Every time you walked from the Plas up onto the mountain I followed your movements carefully. I have sharp eyes, and time and again I saw you disappear behind the two tall pinnacles of rock close to the rowan tree. I knew that there was something here, and suspected that it might be a cave. I came up here very early in the morning, one day in July, when everybody was preoccupied with the dysentery sickness. I found it very quickly, but left no trace of my visit for fear of frightening you off. As it happens, things have worked out excellently, as I am sure you will agree."

I realized then that Moses Lloyd had anticipated this confrontation for a long time, and I thought that great care was needed if I was to get out of the cave alive. I had nothing to lose, I thought, by trying to find out what was in his mind. "You mentioned Squire Howell," I said. "You have been talking to him?"

"Oh, frequently. He has been a good friend to me. When you and your accursed family hounded me out of Plas Ingli I spent several weeks on the run. But I could not stay away from you, and I returned to live in the woods, moving only at night and sleeping by day. I found a good cave in Tycanol Wood, and spent some time there. Then I went to speak to Squire Howell, who was in my debt. He left food for me at a certain spot in the woods, and gave me clean clothes on two occasions. He agreed to let me use a ruined cottage in Pentre Ifan wood which was reputed to be haunted. None of the locals dare to go near it, and I had complete privacy. Not very comfortable, but adequate for my purpose."

"Adequate for your purpose? What do you mean?"

At this Moses knelt beside me and pushed his face to within a few inches of mine. He whispered in a way that made my blood run cold. "My purpose, Martha Morgan, since the day that I met you, has been to possess you. Do you not realize that I loved you from the moment that I first set eyes on you? I have wanted you every minute of every day since your arrival at the Plas. I sought your favour and your kindness. And what did you do? You played with me as a child plays with a toy. And then you tossed me aside, and engineered that business with the barley so that I would be vilified by the miserable, grubby family that occupies the Plas. Do you know what rejection means, Martha Morgan? Do you know?"

Now he was shouting, and his hands were at my throat. I could do nothing but close my eyes and hold my breath. At last he calmed down, and sat on the earthy floor of the cave a few feet away from me. "I am sorry if I hurt you, Moses," I said. "You did not exactly help your own cause, what with one thing and another. But surely you must have seen that David and I were happily married, and that we would never allow anybody to drive a wedge between us?"

"Oh, I realized it all right. And I was reminded of it when I watched you and your beloved David at play in Tycanol Wood."

I was dumbstruck by the appreciation that Moses must have observed us when we loved, time and again, on a bed of moss beneath the oak trees on the occasion of David's birthday. Then I remembered certain small sounds when we had been in the wood, and the smell of wood smoke. Now I must have looked as pale as a ghost, for Moses burst out into laughter. "You look surprised, Mistress Morgan. In truth I was surprised myself when the two of you walked into my domain in the wood, cooing like turtle doves. I had to douse the fire in my cave and was quite convinced that you would stumble across traces of my little encampment. But you had other things on your minds. Very entertaining it was too. When you were relaxing afterwards I thought I might dispatch the pair of you there and then. But then I realized that I was not in the mood."

I remained silent, and tried not to react inappropriately. There had, after all, been no shame in what David and I had done. But it was not easy to come to terms with the fact that Moses Lloyd had observed that most intimate of moments when I had conceived the small child which was now in my womb. I breathed deeply and determined to do nothing which might inflame his passions again. More to the point, I now had to face up to the fact that Moses Lloyd was quite insane.

Desecration

"I think that today I am in the mood," said Moses at last, in a voice that crackled like ice. "This business has gone on for long enough. Today I shall take my pleasure with you, as I have wanted to do for the last twelve months. I am not easily deflected. Then I will cut your face." At this, he pulled out a knife and touched my throat with its tip, so that a little trickle of blood ran down towards my bosom. I was so petrified that I could not move a single muscle. "Shall I cut you before or after? What do you recommend, Martha Morgan? No, if I do it before, there will be blood everywhere, and that will make the occasion a very messy one. I will do it afterwards."

Then he put the knife onto the ground and sat back on his haunches. He was enjoying the fact that I was in a state of abject terror, and wished to prolong his pleasure. "I have wanted to cut your face for a long time," he said. "Since you rejected me and betrayed me I have, in a strange sort of way, come to resent your beauty. Some time ago, as I lay in that miserable shack in Pentre Ifan Wood in the pouring rain, I came to the view that since your beauty is the source of your power over David and your power over me, it would have to be destroyed to set me free." Then he laughed in a way that I felt to be almost inhuman. "What a strange fantasy!" he said. "My goodness -- what peculiar creatures we human beings are!"

His laughter faded away and there was another silence. It was broken when he took a deep breath and said "Then, when I have finished with you, I shall kill you. You realize, of course, that only one of us will walk out of this cave this afternoon? It will be me, because I am stronger than you, because I have planned everything in meticulous detail, and because I have other things to do before I leave this place for the last time for a new life in London. Tomorrow I have a meeting with my friends Rice, Howell and Watkins so that we can refine our plans."

I knew that I had to keep Moses talking, and so I seized the opportunity. "You know, I suppose, that Squire Howell is dead?"

"What do you mean, dead?" hissed Moses through his teeth.

"They found him yesterday, hanging from a tree in Pengelli Woods. They say he took his own life."

"Impossible! I saw him just the other day. He was not a happy man, but he seemed to be coping. You are lying!"

"I promise you that I am not. And since you have been up here in my cave you may not have caught up with the news that Squire Rice has been taken to London by two special constables and that Squire Watkins is already in prison. It seems that they will both hang. I am afraid that your friends.........."

Now I had foolishly pushed him across the boundary between rational behaviour and insane behaviour. He roared as he had roared back in the spring in the kitchen of the Plas, and grabbed his knife from the floor. He thrust it within an inch of my face, and shouted "Damn you, Martha Morgan! Tell me that this is a lie, or by God I will cut your throat right now and dispense with the preliminaries!"

If cowering had been possible in the circumstances I would have cowered, but in my terror all I could do was to whisper "I swear by Almighty God that this is true, Moses. I swear that it is true."

Once again Moses slumped back onto his haunches, and then sat back against the rocky wall of the cave. He moaned and then said "Idiots! Stupid, impetuous, incompetent fools! I told them not to rush things. And what do they do? I try to work with people who are the scum of the earth and they end up bungling everything! I told them to keep it tight! And now I will have to do everything myself. Every single thing!"

Then he went to the entrance of the cave and sat there for several minutes, blocking out all the light from the interior. While he sat there I sought to compose myself, and I tried to make out, in the gloom, where the ropes binding my wrists were fixed and where the knife now lay on the floor. I decided that although I was still in mortal danger, and would probably have to die, I might be able to create a small opportunity for escape. I thought that if I wanted to seize the initiative, it was now or never. I devised a strategy that involved a very high degree of risk, but I could think of nothing else. So I said "Moses, can I ask you something?"

"What is it? Damn you, can't you see that I am thinking?"

"Did you really kill that small child in Wolvercote when you were a student?"

He rushed back into the interior of the cave and grabbed me by the throat until I started choking. "How did you know about that?" he raged. He took his hands away and at last I was able to reply. "There are some people who know about it. Some of your old friends at college, so I believe."

"That was an accident! It should never have happened! Stupid child, playing in the street where horses go back and forth. It should never, never have happened......."

There was a pause as he seemed to recoil from the recollection of the incident. Then I swallowed hard and said "And did you pay twenty silver sovereigns for the murder of Griffith Morgan when he was at sea?"

Then he lost control completely, and hit me in the face, over and again, with his fists until I thought I should pass out with the pain. My cheeks were blackened and my lips were split. I feared that my nose had been broken, and I feared that I had now precipitated my own demise. But suddenly he stopped and tried to regain control of himself. "How did you know that? Damn you, Mistress Martha Morgan, for you ask too many questions and you know far too much. How did you know?"

A long time passed before I could reply. "I did not know everything. A sailor called Eli Davids told me, before he died of the sickness, that a man had paid him to kill Griffith. I guessed that it was you."

"Correct. You are too intelligent for that David Morgan. A pleasant fellow, but not too bright. You and I would have made a very good team."

I saw that he was a little calmer. I had no wish to argue about David, so I continued along my dangerous path. "And did you cause the beam to fall and almost kill Grandpa Isaac?"

"Why do you want to know that? And what is that old man to you anyway?"

"I am very fond of him. And if I am to die today I want to know the truth or falsehood of certain things that are fixed in my head."

Then he laughed a hollow laugh. "The condemned prisoner in search of the truth! I like it! Very well. I have nothing to lose. What I say to you today will sink into the walls of this cave and into the heart of this old mountain, and my words will go with you to your grave. Yes, I arranged it carefully. An amusing little episode. Victory for Moses if he had been killed and victory for Moses the hero in the event that he survived. Sadly, I placed the beam six inches too far to the left."

"And did you steal money from the old women in Newport at Christmas?"

"Of course. I am not surprised that you guessed it was me. I needed some sovereigns to pay off a couple of gambling debts. Besides, a man needs a drink or two at Christmas, and before the *Plygain* I had not a penny in my pocket."

Desecration

"Was it you who disconnected the water pipe and started the fire in the barn back in May? I found your little note."

"Yes. I assumed that I would be suspected. That was a risk worth taking. I daresay I gave you all a good fright. I could not resist leaving the note in your garden, and thought that you would probably understand who had written it. Very entertaining. But in truth the whole episode was not very cleverly handled. I had the dogs organized, but the geese rather let me down. I thought that the removal of your barn might lead to some financial difficulty for the Plas and might smooth my path on future enterprises."

"And did you start the fire at the Plas which killed David's family?"

He looked me straight in the eye for an eternity, and I could feel my heart beating wildly. Then he said, perfectly coolly "Of course I did. I am surprised that nobody else has ever come to that conclusion. Mind you, I have had to work hard to perpetrate the myth that David went upstairs to fetch a book and left a lighted candle on the landing."

"Did you really mean to kill all those innocent people?"

"Not at first. But everything went wrong, and I had to make adjustments. I went upstairs first of all, when I was sure everybody was asleep, with the intention of stealing the chest of family savings from under the bed in the master bedroom. Everybody in the house knew that it was there. There was enough moonlight for me to see what I was doing. I was pulling it out when Mistress Morgan began to stir, and I had to smother her with a cushion. Then I thought I had better do the same to her husband in case he woke up too. He kicked a lot before he died, and I was sure that the whole house would have woken up. But I finished him off with my knife. I waited, perfectly still, for about fifteen minutes, and nothing stirred in the house. I pulled out the chest and opened it, and saw that it contained at least two thousand pounds. Did you know, Martha Morgan, that the estate was so wealthy?"

I was so horrified at what I was hearing that I could not reply.

"No? Well, neither did anybody else. I thought that there might be a couple of hundred pounds at the most. Now I had a dilemma. How could I get all of those gold and silver coins out of the house without waking everybody up? I put about forty sovereigns into my pockets but I could not carry more. In the end I took the sheets off the bed and wrapped the rest of the coins in small bundles, very painstakingly, so that they could be moved without any sound. I could not risk taking them down the main staircase or the back staircase, so I put all the bundles of coins in a pillow case and decided to take a chance by throwing it out of the window. The master bedroom overlooked the yard, and the pillowcase might have burst if I had thrown it there. But the children's bedroom overlooked the grassy bank by the orchard, and that appeared a better bet. I went into the children's bedroom with the loaded pillow-case, and started to open the window. Then.... do you really want to hear this?"

I looked at him in wide-eyed horror, for I knew what was to come.

"I will tell you anyway. Thomas woke up and looked at me. There was only one thing to do. I put a pillow over his face and held it there until he stopped breathing. Then I did the same thing to the other two, George and Rose. Very easy, very clean. After that, it was quite straightforward. I opened the window as quietly as I could. It squeaked on its hinges. I waited again for several minutes, but still nobody woke up. I threw the pillow case down onto the grass. There was a soft thud. Still nothing stirred...."

By this time I was again paralyzed by fear, not because of the details of the narrative, horrifying as they were, but because Moses was talking to himself. There was not a sign of remorse. He was talking about a game or about a little episode which had no more than a passing significance. He talked about human lives as if they had no meaning and no value. He clearly had no conception of what it is to love, or to belong. He clearly was not in the least concerned about the destruction of an honourable family and about the blighting of a multitude of other innocent lives. In his madness, he appeared to live in some sort of fantasy world, and I was very afraid. I had started off in the belief that I might be able to postpone my fate and possibly even out-think him, but now I understood that with this man nothing -- but nothing -- was predictable.

He continued to the gruesome end of his story, looking not at me but at the open door of the cave. I surmised that he had never articulated any of this before. "It was only then that I conceived the idea of the fire. Five deaths in a fire instead of five murders -- an excellent alternative scenario. And a burnt-out chest, leading everybody to assume that the family treasure had melted away and gone up in the flames. And I could arrange it so that nobody would suspect me of the theft, and nobody would suspect me of killing the Morgan family. I quietly took about twenty small candles from the candle box in the master bedroom. I lit one of them with the tinder box and then I lit all the others, placed strategically on the beds and carpets and on piles of clothes. Some of them I put at the tops of the two staircases. I calculated that it would take about ten minutes for all of them to burn down and ignite the fabrics, after which an inferno would very rapidly develop. Then I crept downstairs, went into my room and waited. You know the rest."

There was another very long silence. I sensed that I had very little time left to me, so in a desperate attempt to postpone the inevitable I whispered "I think I know the rest. And the Plas Ingli treasure?"

"Ah yes, the treasure. That was really the start of my problems. When the fire was raging and everybody was rushing about trying to get the flames under control, I was able, unnoticed, to go round to the bank beneath the children's window and recover the pillow-case. I dragged it and hid it behind some bushes, and went back to help with the water carrying. Then I shouted that I would go off to get more help. I went down the lane, and doubled back around the orchard. I recovered the pillow-case and spent about half an hour, while the fire was at its height, digging a deep hole and burying it. Then the heat became so intense that I had to retreat, and the bushes and the trees around the orchard caught fire. But my job was done. I could return at some time in the future and recover the money at my leisure."

"And did you?"

"Damn it, no. I never thought that the Plas would be rebuilt. After the fire I went away for several weeks and spent some of my money. Then I returned expecting to dig up my treasure on a derelict site. I was greatly surprised to find building work under way. Not only that, but the new house was a different shape from the old one. The bushes on the bank had all been burnt off, and everything was so changed that I could not work out precisely where I had buried the money. There was nothing for it but to offer my services again, to a family that I despised and who gave me no respect. By every demon in Hell, how I hated the prospect of spending more years in their company! But I could not go digging around without attracting attention, and so I bided my time. I decided that it would be best to destroy the estate bit by bit, and if that meant removing the members of the family one by one, then so it would have to be. Even without the treasure I think I would have sought the destruction of the Morgans of Plas

Ingli, for the members of my family have long memories."

"You had dealings with the three squires. What did all this have to do with them?"

"When I saw that there was a certain animosity between you and them I went to see them. They wanted the destruction of the Morgan family and the Plas Ingli estate, for their own reasons. I knew that their estates were all in financial trouble, so I told them about the Plas Ingli fortune without telling them where it was. They wanted a part of it, and they wanted the Plas Ingli land to split between themselves. We determined, quite simply, to get rid of you. I would conduct small campaigns upon the ground, and they would orchestrate a more complicated strategy from a distance. The problem was that our liaison was not as good as it might have been. It was not easy, with me having a price on my head and with those three idiots proving not to have the brain-power of a rabbit between them!"

Suddenly his dream-like reverie ended and he turned to me with fury in his face. "Why am I telling you all of this? Damn you, Martha Morgan, for you have rejected me and delighted in my misery. You are the cause of all my troubles and the troubles of Rice, Howell and Watkins. You have thwarted me at every step of the way and you have sent all three of them to their deaths." He took a deep breath, and then said "Now I have talked enough, and I will extract my revenge!"

Without saying a further word he flung himself upon me. He tried to kiss me, but I spat at him and started to scream. I struggled with every ounce of energy left in my body, but with hands and legs tied there was little I could do to resist. I continued to scream, and he said "Scream all you like, Martha. Nobody will hear you, for the wind is in the south." But he got more and more angry with me, and slapped me across the face several times, and eventually tore a piece of my skirt off and gagged me with it. At last I had no energy left, and I lay at his mercy, quite exhausted. He was, I think, almost exhausted himself, but then he tore away the front of my dress, exposing my breasts. He looked surprised, and then he threw his head back and roared with laughter. "No stays, Mistress Martha?" he shouted into my face. "What a pleasure it is to discover that beneath that elegant exterior you are no better than a common whore!" Then a sense of utter loathing and desolation came over me as I felt his hands upon me.

I knew that I was to be defiled and dishonoured, and that this would be worse, far worse, than the humiliation I had felt at the hands of my tormentors behind the whipping cart. I closed my eyes in the realization that there was now nothing more I could do. Then he lifted my skirt and my underskirts. He lay on top of me. He was in a highly agitated state, and sought to force my legs apart. Then he realized that my ankles were tied, and he fetched the knife and cut the rope. He forced my legs wide apart and lay on top of me again. He started to press himself against me so hard that I gasped for breath. Then he started to do something with his hand near his private parts. I prepared myself for every woman's worst nightmare. But suddenly he started swearing to himself, and I realized that he was having difficulty with the flap on the front of his breeches. He went back onto his haunches and started to undo the flap.

In that instant, there came into my mind a curse that said "an avenging angel will place her foot upon your breast and send you down to Hell." A thousand images flashed before my eyes, and a cacophony of sounds thundered in my ears. A dead child beneath a horse's hooves. A young man sinking in terror beneath the waves. The last gasps of three children and their parents suffocated by an inhuman monster with not a shred of humanity in him, and all for a few silver coins. The frantic efforts of David and his brother to fight their way into an inferno, not knowing that those they loved and tried to save were already dead. I felt again, in an instant, the whiplashes of my tormentors in the main street of Newport, and smelt the filth of my prison cell and the black smoke of burning barley. I saw David's face, and the faces of my family and friends, and I saw the faces of my children as yet unborn. I recalled my dream in which I had conquered Moses on the mountain top and cast him down to oblivion.

A white rage permeated my whole body, and for a fraction of a second the strength of every poor soul who had been persecuted by this monster flowed through me. Without opening my eyes I pulled my knees up to my chin like a coiled spring, and then I shot my feet forward. More by luck than judgment I connected with Moses' chest and he was flung backward with a force that I cannot begin to understand. There was a sickening thud as his head hit the wall of the cave. Then he fell on top of me. I think I must have fainted.

When I recovered my senses Moses was still on top of me, and I could feel the rough pressure of his bearded face on mine. The weight of his body was insufferable, and at first I could not understand what had happened. Then I opened my eyes and saw his brown eyes staring into mine. But they were lifeless eyes. Moses Lloyd was dead. Blood was dripping from his mouth onto my neck, and I realized that the back of his skull had been smashed.

A strange calm now came over me, and as I look back I cannot understand why I was not sent quite out of my mind by the horror of the predicament in which I found myself. I was gagged and bound, with my arms still stretched out like those of Christ on the cross, and I had the lifeless corpse of a big man lying on top of me and almost suffocating me. But gradually I composed myself and decided that I must extricate myself bit by bit without causing myself any further damage. I tried to remember where Moses had left the knife, and thought it might be somewhere near my right leg. So I moved my feeble body as best I could in order to tip him over to my left. It took a long time, but at last I managed it, and he slid off me, trapping my left leg. I struggled more, and in due course released that leg too. Then I tried to find the knife, and at last felt the metal touching my right knee. With infinite patience I moved it up towards my right hand. I had to stop many times and fight for breath, for the gag was still tied across my mouth and breathing was not easy.

At last I got the blade into my hand. I cut my fingers as I tried to manipulate it, but soon I got hold of the handle, and with infinite care I managed to saw my way through the rope. There was blood everywhere, but now my escape was almost complete. I turned and cut the rope holding my left hand. I tore away the gag from my face and untied the knots around my wrists. Then I collapsed as I was hit by a wall of pain and exhaustion, and I wept uncontrollably for a long time.

In due course I recovered my composure. I started to assess my situation. My back was bleeding profusely from the opening up of my old wounds. I had my own blood on my right hand and Moses' blood on my neck and breasts. My dress and my petticoats were in shreds. My head ached and felt that it might explode. I had two black eyes. My lips were bleeding and swollen, and my cheeks were swelling up from the beating I had received. I had cut the back of my head against the cave wall, and my hair was matted with blood. I had cuts and grazes on my legs and on my elbows from the times when I had been struggling. My whole body ached and my limbs felt so heavy that I feared I would never again be able to stand, let alone find my way back down to the Plas. Apart from these few problems I was in excellent condition. And I was convinced that my baby was still safe in my womb in spite of the exertions and traumas of the last two hours.

I swore to myself that I would never say a word of this episode to any living person until the day I died. On my return to the Plas I would seek to explain away my appalling injuries and my tattered clothes as the result of a fall into a deep crevasse and my gargantuan efforts to climb out of it. But before I could return to civilization I had to get rid of the body. I crawled gingerly to the entrance of the cave and was hugely relieved to discover that there was still a world outside. Grey clouds were scudding up from the south and the sun was sliding down towards the sea. The ravens were sitting silently on their crag and watching me. I found a very deep cleft in the rocks not far from the cave entrance, and I decided that this would be Moses' grave.

For the next hour or so I heaved and rolled his heavy body, inch by inch, towards this cleft, having first trussed it up with the ropes which not long ago had held my own arms. At last I reached the burial site, and without any ceremony or regret I tipped the corpse in. It thudded to a halt about twenty feet below me. Then I threw in every trace of Moses' occupation of the cave, including the ashes of his fire. And finally I threw in as many rocks and stones as I could carry, so that no trace of the burial could be seen from above.

The cave was cleansed, and the purity of Angel Mountain restored. As the light faded, I crawled and staggered my way down the boulder-strewn slopes. I drank for a long time at the old healing spring of Ffynnon Brynach, and anointed myself. I washed off as much blood as possible. I tried to cover my body with the shredded remnants of my clothes. Then I completed my journey through the head-high bracken and the rough upper fields, at the point of utter exhaustion. Somehow, on hands and knees, I dragged myself into the yard, and collapsed as I reached the haven of the open kitchen door.

Grandma found me there some minutes later, and says that she screamed in horror and at first failed to recognize me. She called for Bessie and the other servants, and they carried me in and placed me on the kitchen table. They were all quite appalled when they saw the state I was in, and they took a very long time to strip off my bloody rags, clean me up, dress my wounds and get me into bed. I have told them my cock and bull story, of which they will certainly not believe a word. You do not get rope burns, black eyes and knife cuts by ambling about on heather moors and climbing out of rocky chasms. But I care not a jot what they think. At last the nightmare is over.

ΩΩΩΩΩΩΩΩΩ

28th August 1797

The nights are colder now, but the late summer heat-wave continues. Five days after my ordeal it is still difficult to sleep, but I have obtained some solace from watching the brightest and whitest of full moons drifting across the firmament. There appears to be no part of my body which is free of aches and pains. From Heaven, I probably look like the Baby Jesus wrapped in swaddling bands, but the Lord has at least spared my virtue, my unborn child and my writing arm.

It is before six in the morning. I am sitting at my familiar desk in my dressing room, looking out over the cwm. The morning chorus of little birds is at its climax, and Cilgwyn is submerged beneath its sea of mist. Soon the sun will melt it away and warm the cottagers who are stirring their peat fires, or feeding their Christmas pigs, or rubbing their sleepy eyes, or gulping down their breakfast buttermilk.

Downstairs, in the kitchen, there are familiar sounds. Billy is dragging on his boots and clearing his throat. Bessie is humming a little tune, which confirms that she is still in love. Mrs Owen is clattering about in her clogs, being busy. Now she is pouring spring water into the black pot which hangs over the fire. Soon she will start malting the barley, in readiness for making the Christmas ale. Grandma Jane is still asleep.

Soon David and Grandpa Isaac will return, having defeated their enemies with the help of their friends. God knows what they will think of my battered state, but I will stick to my story and the truth will never, never pass my lips. It shall remain a secret that I have defeated my own greatest enemy, and at the same time have acted as an avenging angel. The punishment meted out to Moses Lloyd was no less than he deserved after the endless persecution which he has visited upon the Morgan family.

I feel a lump in my throat, and a tear in my eye, and a sermon coming on. But I am too confused for sermonizing, and have too little strength to write at length. But suddenly I am overcome with a great passion for life. I have a baby in my womb and this time I will not lose it. If God wills it there will be more to follow. In the years to come I will give them my protection and my love until they are old enough to fly from the nest. I have a wonderful husband, two good old people who will be wise counsellors, and a circle of faithful friends who have shown their worth in the most trying of circumstances.

I am now resolved to write no more. My blessed and ever-patient Diary, I shall miss you. I am an inveterate scribbler, and indeed I have gained much solace from the hundreds of hours spent with blank pages before me, my inkpot beside me, and my quill pen in my hand. The last year has been turbulent indeed. I feel that I have aged ten years, but with my worst enemies defeated and the most evil man on this earth rotting in a stony grave. I shall forget the shadows of history and face the sun.

Tomorrow I will set Billy and Shemi to digging on the bank near the orchard. I will pretend that I have had guidance from a ghost that there is a treasure there. A pillow case containing two thousand pounds or more will come in very handy for the estate, since I daresay that none of us will get a penny back in costs from the forthcoming court cases.

Tonight I will write my confession. I will seal it and slip it between the pages of this, my last diary entry. Then I will place my volumes and my other secret things into my tin box. I will lock it and throw away the key. Then, when I am well enough, I will climb up through the trapdoor into the attic and I will hide it in a dark corner. Some day, when I am dead and forgotten, somebody will chance upon my box. It will be a man, for women do not grovel about in dusty attics. He will force the lid open and (if he can read my special language) he will have access to the secrets of my heart. I pray to God that he will have the grace to forgive me my indiscretions, my selfish ways and the wicked things that I have done.

Bessie has just come in to dress my wounds. She may or may not understand why I have tears in my eyes. I trust that the good Lord will bless my life, and the lives of all whom I love, to the extent that nothing else will happen that will be worth writing about.

ΩΩΩΩΩΩΩΩΩ

17. CONFESSION

I confess before God and before my children, as yet unborn, to the murder of Moses Lloyd Cwmgloyn on the 23rd day of August 1797. I will not confess before my husband David. What I did was quite deliberate. I have no regrets, and I ask for no forgiveness, for the dead man was the incarnation of the Devil himself, having set himself the task, for reasons beyond my understanding, of destroying the sweet, kind Morgan family of Plas Ingli.

To the best of my knowledge, he caused the deaths of at least eight innocent people during his evil life, and tried to kill at least three others. In his passion for destruction, he is now himself destroyed. I will never reveal the whereabouts of his remains, for he deserves no Christian burial.

I write this on Angel Mountain, 28th August 1797

Martha Morgan

Model: Rhiannon James   Photographer: Steve Mallett

The Angel Mountain Saga

Eight volumes are now available in Brian John's best-selling series -- now with about 82,000 copies sold. The saga was referred to by *The Bookseller* as "a self-publishing phenomenon." Please buy through your local bookshop if possible; alternatively all of the titles can be ordered from the publishers, Greencroft Books, by visiting our web-based bookshop:
http://www.brianjohn.co.uk/bookshop.html

The eight books

On Angel Mountain (Part One), Greencroft Books, 2001.
ISBN 9780905559803. A5 paperback, 328 pp, £6.99.

House of Angels (Part Two), Greencroft Books, 2002.
ISBN 9780905559810. A5 paperback, 432 pp, £7.99.

Dark Angel (Part Three), Greencroft Books, 2003.
ISBN 9780905559827. A5 paperback, 432 pp, £8.50.

Rebecca and the Angels (Part Four), Greencroft Books, 2004.
ISBN 9780905559834. A5 paperback, 432 pp, £8.50.

Flying with Angels (Part Five), Greencroft Books, 2005.
ISBN 9780905559841. A5 paperback, 400 pp, £7.99.

Guardian Angel (Part Six), Greencroft Books, 2008.
 ISBN 9780905559865. A5 paperback, 256 pp, £6.99.

Sacrifice (Part Seven), Greencroft Books, 2009.
ISBN 9780905559902. A5 paperback, 352 pp, £7.99.

Conspiracy of Angels (Part Eight), Greencroft Books, 2012.
ISBN 9780905559933. A5 paperback, 352 pp, £7.99.

Note: Parts Seven and Eight fill in gaps in the novel "Dark Angel".